EVERSTAR

CANDACE J. THOMAS

SHADESILK
PRESS

Paperback Edition 2020
Shadesilk Press, LLC

Edited by Penny Freeman, MeriLyn Oblad,
and Elizabeth Gilliland
2nd Edition Shadesilk Press, LLC
Published in the United States of America
Cover Design/Inside Graphics
by Monika MacFarland
Ampersand Book Covers
BISAC:
Fantasy; High Fantasy; Magical: Adventure; Coming-of-age
ISBN: 978-1-7335011-6-3
Library of Congress
2 0 1 9 9 1 9 1 0 4

TO MIA, MY MIRACLE

AND

JULIA, MY GIFT

THE EVERSTAR SERIES

Vivatera

Conjectrix

Everstar

EVERSTAR

IGNIS MOUNTAINS
LUX LUCIS
THE NORTH
NETHERFIELDS
TRISTUS RIVER
WIL
BLACK
WOO
SHARLOT
MUSUNGU MARSHES
SOUTHWIC
UNDE
PARBRAVEN

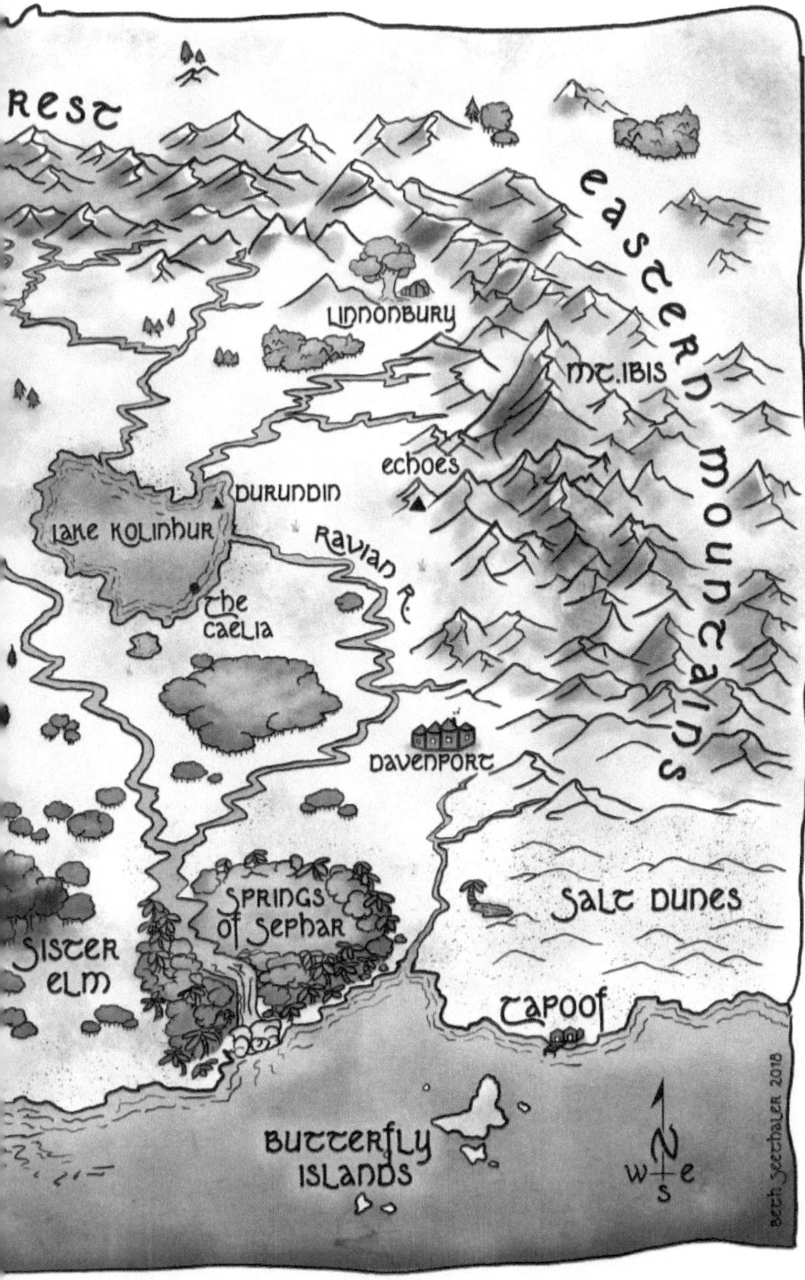

REST
eastern mountains
LINNONBURY
MT. IBIS
echoes
DURUNDIN
LAKE KOLINHUR
Ravian R.
The
CAELIA
DAVENPORT
SALT DUNES
SPRINGS
of Sephar
SISTER
ELM
TAPOOF
BUTTERFLY
ISLANDS
W N E S
Beth Seethaler 2018

PROLOGUE

The cold iron bars felt soothing on Reynolds' open sores, stinging hot from the whip. He could feel the blood from the swells, the welts close to bursting. He closed his eyes again, feeling every throbbing inch. The pain stayed with him, his own punishment for leaving Naomi. Nothing would ever be so painful.

He took in a deep breath, alone now in his dank dungeon cell. Each intake sent shocks through his body.

Reynolds closed his eyes against the flickering torches. He relived the most recent events in his head, identifying each detail: the small jingle from the keys the large guard wore, the direction of the air, the specific time when the doors opened, the smell of rainwater, the loose bolt near the third rung by the door that with the right pressure would snap.

Snap.

> *Naomi stood on a tall hill dressed in white, the fringe of her garment singed by fire. Her penetrating stare seared through him, her distant green eyes pleading and helpless. The souls of hell surrounded her, sucking what spirit she had from her body. She screamed and reached forward.*
>
> *She jumped. The earth moved and the wide abyss opened, swallowing her.*
>
> *Fire gathered around, faces appearing and disappearing within the smoke, extinguishing her light.*
>
> *No!*

Reynolds opened his eyes, sucking in the putrid air around him, remembering once more how he lived while the others did not. Sweat built on his forehead until it poured down in a steady stream.

The hope of Naomi surviving hurt more than the guilt of her being dead—so he locked down his anguish and clung to it.

"She is dead, and I am lost."

He sank down again into despair.

A soft voice carried through the stone cell. "You do not understand lost."

Reynolds turned, surprised. No one was ever thrown in that corner of the darkest dungeon, he was certain of it. He squinted through the darkness. In the distant, flickering torches he could not see a face but sensed a presence.

Aware of his vulnerability, Reynolds straightened. "How long have you been there?"

The cell held its eerie stillness until a rough laugh echoed. "Long enough."

"I thought I was alone down here."

"You are."

Reynolds looked closer. He couldn't imagine someone in the small cell across from him, which was more like a cage. "Who are you?"

"I am a prisoner, much like you." The man's quiet calm was unnatural and unsettling. "And what should I care about masquerading nobility pretending to be wounded by an inevitability?"

"Are you talking about Sharrod?"

"I talk of many things."

Reynolds focused on the black mound he only assumed was the prisoner. It shifted soundlessly against the stone. "I'm not interested in your riddles. I preferred the silence, old man."

"What I am in need of is a messenger."

Reynolds rested back again. "I'm no messenger."

"Oh, but you are, Reynolds Fairborne."

The hairs stood up on the back of his head. He searched the voices in his memory for a match but came up empty. Even his magic couldn't help him here. "How do you know me?"

"I know you can escape, but you do not."

Reynolds stared out into the darkness, seeing only shadows dancing around the walls. A panic fell over him, an unsettling urgency beyond the cell which held him. "Tell me who you are."

The man's dark eyes slid to the light. ". . . An enemy."

"An enemy who would see me succeed."

The old man shifted, a glint of light crossing his crooked nose, but still Reynolds could not see his face. "I have many enemies, much like you. You are a rogue of your own making."

"How do you mean?"

"I'm very aware of the alchemist's hand in your life. As well as what you did with the magic that created the Vivatera."

Reynolds' hands pushed the sweat from his face, physically feeling the anxiety flood throughout his body. His sleepless mind ran through every person who knew these facts; very few remained. "How do you know Lytte?"

"Lytte was in my confidences before he fled." The man flicked a bit of stone as he talked. "You were his apprentice. You are the forbearer of magic and the corrupter of nature. You worry you have failed, but you have already succeeded."

Reynolds gripped the iron bars. "Then why am I still alive?"

"The same reason I am still alive." The old man turned to the light, and his bulbous eyes pierced into Reynolds' doubts of the man's identity. "Just in case."

Reynolds took in the man he knew as an enemy, someone who had ordered his men to hunt him down like a criminal. During the last ten years of this king's reign, Reynolds had not rested. He studied the face of the man he remembered as King Reinoh, dead to the city but alive in the small prison cell.

"We have knowledge Sharrod may need," the old king's harsh voice slithered out like a snake. "It is his mistake."

Reynolds crept closer to the man. The withered skin hung around his bones like draped linen, weathered and wrinkled. Lesions pocked what flesh had not been marred with whips. "What do you know?"

"Sharrod will soon gather the six stones together. But the seventh will undo the rest."

"Yes, I know this—"

"Shh!" the man silenced him. "I do not talk of the girl." The king's head rested near the bar, and Reynolds could see the matted hair of the once regal leader. "I talk of the Everstone."

Part One

Two brothers were given a challenge and a gift.

Work together to build a world, and together they shall
inherit.

Each labored with their own hands to till the ground and
bring life to the world.

Each gift brought complemented the other.

But then one brother gave the gift of time and fortified the
ground to enrich the soil naturally.

The other brother gave the gift of gain and infused an angel
oak seed with magic.

His brother found the corrupted seed infecting the growth
of the world.

He brought it before his brother, furious at his action.

In anger each fought for control of the earth.

They drew weapons of destruction, ready to slay the other.

Among the lilies stood a sister who loved them both.

She knew not of the corruption but ran to save.

Unseen to one, she stood before his blade and received a

blow of everlasting death.

Their father, in his anger, banished both of his sons.

The quarrelling son he sent to the heavens to forever look at

the world he could not touch.

The slaying son he banished to the underground, forbidden

to see the world he had built.

And the father planted the seed and watered it with his

tears near the body of his fallen child.

And there grew a tree.

— The Histories

CHAPTER ONE

The cold air felt crisp against Naomi's skin. Wind whipped around her delicate frame. Blond curls untangled from her braid and allowed the wild strands to dance across her face and neck. She climbed higher in the tree that day than she had before. The twisted knots and spiraling branches brought her a peaceful serenity. There, she could find answers.

On the farthest edge of the mountain village, the tree stood tall, overlooking Linnonbury. Naomi sought out the solitude it could give, desperately needing a quiet place away from the pressures bearing down upon her shoulders. The hike up the steep cliffs proved tricky, though Naomi graced the climb like a dancing bird among the rocks and crags.

The people of the village named the tree the Guardian, watcher over the village, protecting it from afar. Over the years, some of the villagers had tied charms to its long branches for safety and protection. In the wind, the tiny trinkets tinkled like fairy bells, enchanting the hilltop as its over-reaching arms stretched out toward the heavens.

Naomi sought out the tree's memories and communicated through her touch. From its smooth bark, she learned of its history and the life it looked over, longer than recorded time. It spoke to her in images, loving her for the magic she had and the person she was. Every time she came to the tree, it revealed something new. Then, one night she fell asleep cradled in the crook of its limbs. That night, as she dreamed, the Guardian told her of the great myths and the beginning of everything. She awoke under a gentle protection of frost with a new appreciation for the magical world of Parbraven and the name of an ethereal goddess on the tip of her tongue. The threads of magic pulled her closer to a place she didn't know but would decide her fate.

Naomi thought about telling the others—her sister Sera, the mystic Jeanus, or even her mother, Andriana—but something told her to keep it secret until the information would be useful.

She had returned to the Guardian a few times after that, never learning as much as she had the night she slept there. That particular day, Naomi returned for a different purpose. She needed to say goodbye to the great tree, knowing she would never return.

From the tallest branch she could reach, Naomi watched the rolling world of Parbraven stretch out before her eyes. Her heart constricted heavily, filled with unexplained emotion. She felt that if she had to make one more decision, no matter how little, she would sob uncontrollably. However, looking over the beauty before her eyes, feeling the wind sweep around her cheeks, she couldn't cry, only smile. She felt more alive than ever.

A soft cry came to her ears, like a scared bird. Looking down, she could hardly make out a small figure near the footholds of the tree. She heard it again: it was a name. Her name.

"Naomi!" The voice carried away with the wind.

How did he get up here? Taren shouldn't be climbing this height with his body still healing. *Why would he come here?*

The peace she felt a moment before disappeared and was replaced with a worry that lingered within her limbs. A turn of season had come since they first came to Linnonbury, since her magic had crumbled the darkness within him—the day he told her why.

Naomi nimbly descended as fast as she could through the tangled limbs and tinkling charms. She saw Taren as she neared the lower trunk. "Why are you here? You shouldn't be on your leg."

Taren stood near a large protruding root at the base of the tree. He didn't look at her. Instead, he gazed toward the inescapable view of the horizon. He silently stood there, watching the shadows fall around them.

Naomi scaled down the long root until she stood behind him. She could feel the heat streaming from his body. The marks of sweat around his neck and arms told her how hard he had tried to find her—a need she did not understand.

"Taren?" She whispered his name, afraid to disrupt the harmony he might feel.

He didn't turn toward her. "I wanted to know where you escaped to."

"Escaped?"

He sighed. She couldn't see his expression but saw the tightness in his jaw. "Yes. I think *escape* is the perfect word."

The sky began to change from a bright sunset orange to a strange pink and then purple. Naomi sat at the base of the tree and watched in silence. How she would miss these evenings alone with only her tree and the wind—two of her favorite friends.

She glanced again toward Taren, analyzing the calm storm that he was. The dark magic which had plagued him no longer existed, erased from his body. It had become such a part of him that Naomi felt it had prevented her from knowing Taren—the real person he was inside. What magic that remained with him didn't communicate, like a wounded dog refusing to yield to its master. The enigma which shadowed his thoughts and feelings frightened her more than before.

Taren obeyed the magic. He had trusted everything it commanded of him, and in everything, the magic had been right. With its silence, he had no compass to direct him, no hungry urge for control.

But that wasn't why she feared him.

Taren had acted with obedience in the Echoes. Stabbing her gave the Vivatera the choice to save her life. He did it with a conscious thought, combining the magic she possessed with the Vivatera brought the two together. But he now knew that he was being controlled. And yet, she still did not know how to trust him. For days he sought her out, and she evaded him. She had been successful until now, and Naomi felt shame upon seeing the evidence of his arduous effort to find her.

"You're right," Naomi admitted. "This is my escape. I won't get another chance to experience this solitude again. We both know I won't be returning."

At this, Taren turned to face her. Naomi saw for the first time that the coal black coloring in his eyes had disappeared. He looked gentler, kinder. The poisonous magic had vanished, leaving what once was there: earthy green eyes the color of the forest.

His gaze held her trapped in wordless communication. She could feel he knew the truth without speaking. So many times he had told her the magic would end her life, that she had to die to save the world.

"Naomi," he started but then stopped. He eventually turned away again.

After a moment passed in silence, Naomi walked to the cliff edge and stood behind him. "How did you get up here?"

"I'm not as crippled as everyone believes." He moved his arm reflexively. The bandage no longer held it in place. "That's why I came up here. I had to test my strength and—" he paused, drawing in air before continuing, ". . . and I had to find you."

Sharp pain stabbed at her ribs. Naomi swallowed air, quickly filling her lungs. She couldn't avoid him here. "Why?" her voice sounded so far away, like a whisper in the wind.

She feared what he would say, what he would ask. She remembered the words he'd said to her: *"With every stolen glance, you will know that I love you."* The world didn't make sense to her. He couldn't love her—he hated her. He only wanted the magic.

But she knew it wasn't true. As much as she wished to believe he hated her, he did not. The way he looked at her, talked with her… She'd seen a different side to him, a caring side that had never before had the chance to appear.

"I want to know something." His voice traveled away from him. "I want to know how you did it."

Naomi looked at him. "How I did what?"

Taren's jawbone stood out sharp on his face, his dark hair whipping down in his eyes. "How did you remove the dark magic?"

Naomi stared in astonishment. This was what he wanted to talk to her about? "Really?" she blurted.

He faced her, his green eyes apologizing. "I want you to know the truth. After . . ." He struggled to find his words. "I went to Southwick looking for my father. I met Sharrod there. He wanted me to lure you to Ignis." He stopped again to organize his thoughts. "I did it because . . . Sharrod promised me he could take away the dark magic. He would set me free. But you did it. Not him. I want to know how."

"Oh, Taren." Compassion overwhelmed her, and she couldn't help but reach for his forearm, then hesitated. It was in her nature to care for others, but it scared her to show it to him. "I don't have the answer—"

"You do," Taren interrupted. "You have to."

"I don't know how important it is to know."

Taren turned away from the falling sunset and sat near the base of the tree. He sank his head in his hands.

Naomi followed cautiously, sitting on the grass before him. She thought back on the battle for his soul, the magical wall built around him, the shards of magic crashing around him, the image of a cowering, frightened Taren rocking back and forth.

"Taren. I'll help you however I can, but I need to know why."

He lifted his head, looking away again, distant. "I need your help. I'm no longer whole. When I'd get angry, my magic was always ready. But I can't be angry any longer. Every time I think of you taking the dark magic away, I feel guilt and agony. I feel sorrow for everything I had to put you through. I don't know how to recover."

Naomi felt the tremor inside her and, in the quiet, pondered what she should say. "I couldn't see you trapped any longer," she finally stated. "I had to release you."

He shook his head. "No, you didn't. I didn't deserve it."

Naomi softened. "No one should feel so much pain. I don't like seeing pain. I did it for the right reasons."

Taren only sat in silence, not responding.

"And, I don't think it's gone. Your magic. I think it's scared." Naomi almost laughed. "You are the last person I would imagine explaining magic to. You know magic more than anyone. But I don't think magic is the same for you as it is for me. I was poisoned, the same as you. The same elements created the magic. But all around me, I had people who cared what happened, who cared for me and I for them. I think that's the difference. Living without caring what happened to you or caring about anyone, and now you . . ." Her words quieted, realizing where she was going.

Taren looked up, setting his eyes on her. The green still felt so unfamiliar, but she knew the feeling he hid beneath. A silent moment passed between them before he broke it. "Tell me about this tree?"

"The tree?" Naomi felt startled by this sudden change in direction.

Taren rubbed the smooth root trunk with the back of his hand. "Why do trees obey you? I remember a sharp blow to the head caused by a tree."

Naomi had forgotten it was Taren from whom she ran near the Echoes. He had kissed her, his poisonous magic persuading him to take the opportunity and find out what he could about her and the magic she possessed. A large oak had protected her, bashing him upside the head and bending enough to make a bridge to safety. Naomi found herself blushing at the memory. She quickly stood up, shaking it away.

"Come." She held out her hand to help him stand.

Taren took it, though he didn't immediately stand, looking at her slender fingers. His eyes lifted to hers. "Promise to tell me someday, when you know what she is telling you."

He knew more about the tree than she had figured. "I will."

Naomi braced her feet, preparing to power all her energy into helping Taren stand, though he didn't need her help and stood with ease. "It's getting dark. We need to get ready."

The sun had nearly gone, showing the first stars of night. After talking with the tree, Naomi had more respect for them—the stars, the trees, and the ground.

"Let me say goodbye." She walked to the trunk. Her small hands pressed down, her thumbs circling around.

"Thank you," she said out loud, as if it had ears. "Thank you, my dear Guardian." She leaned in and gently kissed it. "You bring me hope. Pera will find you, and she will thank you." With this she stood, her hand brushing against the trunk and gently slipped away.

"Pera?" Taren asked.

"Later, I promise." Naomi took one last look and turned down the darkening path, afraid she'd never experience the solitude again.

A screech echoed around the valley. Naomi nearly lost her footing as the cry created a tremor within her body. It was sundown when she reached the valley floor with Taren following. The stars shone brightly above her head now, only the dome-shaped lights of the Linnonbury houses reflecting the patterns above. In the distant shadow of the mountain, she saw a large form move closer to the ground.

"A dragon," she whispered. "They're back."

Naomi took off running. Taren yelled after her. Her heart pounded as her bare feet lightly padded across the snow-dusted ground. The sight of a fire-eater meant Sera and Arie had returned. A council had commissioned Arie and Sera to track two specific people who Jeanus suggested should advise her in what should happen—Spotswood Shadower and Lytte.

Naomi feared for all of them. She didn't dare drive her dreams to search for them. Her dreams were too vulnerable to magic, and if Sharrod was indeed looking for her, then she had to keep them away as much as possible.

Closer and closer she drew to the dragons, and the warmth in their bellies glowed distinctly blue and red, like lightning bugs trapped in colored jars. The fiery red hair of her sister stood out in the dark.

"Sera!" she yelled, waving her hands.

Sera turned and gave a sad smile.

Naomi ran into her older sister's arms. "You were gone so long. I worried you might not return." When she drew away, Naomi saw the concern in her eyes. "What happened?"

"Oh, Naomi," she said, rubbing her shoulder with reassurance. "So much to tell."

"There you are," a voice came from behind Sera. Arie looked casual as always, his long hair disheveled from the ride. He grabbed her in a bear hug and lifted her from the ground. "You okay?" he asked as he set her down. "You're distant."

Naomi stared at the same gray eyes as Reynolds, his brother, and the anguish lit inside her soul again. She took a deep breath and pushed it back. "You're very perceptive, Arie," she commented. "Don't worry about me."

Arie patted her head like a little girl. "That's my job now."

"Did you have any luck? Is Spotswood with you?" Naomi thought of the last time she had seen Spotswood, in his underground dwelling, the Durundin, before the rumbling started and the trolls attacked.

"The Durundin all caved in. I couldn't find anyone around. Just lots of horse dung and tent poles."

Sera directed her toward the house. "Naomi. Let's go inside. We have lots to discuss with everyone."

Naomi hadn't seen it before, but a figure stood behind Arie, nearly in a shadow, a slight frame she couldn't immediately recognize. He reminded her of Zander, the same lanky build and sickly posture. His mousy brown hair stuck up around the back, fanning like a peacock. He stood tall, though the freckles on his nose betrayed his youth.

"Jack?" someone called his name. Taren emerged from the darkness and headed straight for the boy. "What are you doing here?"

"Jack, is it?" Arie turned toward the stranger. "He wouldn't tell us his name. We followed your directions to the camp in the Willows. He was the only one there. The only way we knew he could talk was his constant wailing. He hasn't said a word the entire trip back. I think he's a little traumatized."

Sera elbowed him. "Taren? Would you help Jack inside? He's pretty weak. Naomi, could you get him some food?"

CHAPTER TWO

Jack later provided more details about how the Willows was compromised and the intense nature of the invasion. Many died, as Naomi feared; the few boys left alive were captured and taken to Southwick. Among the casualties were the defenders: Aristotlis, who stood valiant among the others and Lytte, who was found dead from what looked like suicide. The boys gave in at the loss of the alchemist and were slaughtered. Jack survived only because he watched from the trees, afraid to make any sound.

Listening to the details made Naomi sick, and she left for her room. It felt as if something invisible squeezed her on both sides, and she fought for breath. She stumbled to the window. The cool night air rushed in, filling her emptiness as she sucked in the crisp smell of snow on evergreens.

Her Lytte was gone. It hurt—a powerful, gnawing ache which twisted her insides. Her mentor while in the camp with his comforting wisdom and genuine kindness, Lytte helped her understand how important she was. He was the first she learned to trust, the first to teach her about the magic, the one who revealed the secrets of the stones, the stories, everything . . . And he meant everything in the world to Reynolds. It hit her all over again. She felt the helplessness gnaw her bones raw, the desperate need to find Reynolds and share the hurt that his mentor had vanished from this earth.

But had he?

The question popped into Naomi's mind so suddenly she had to cling to the railing at her window for support. Lytte's stain would be here, floating like a ghost among the magic, his spirit stuck between worlds like all the others.

After everything she'd experienced, being face to face with the souls of hell, she'd forgotten how personal the connection was for her, the enormity of saving the dead as well as the living.

Once she could breathe, her mind raced a mile a minute. She no longer wanted to be there in the safety of Linnonbury. She had to get to the camp. She had to find Lytte.

Stains were pulled to the place where they first experienced the magic. But it didn't happen for everyone like that. The lost stains in the River of Souls were trapped there by the Fire Mistress Alene. Maybe the magic pulled one where the memory was strongest. If that were true, then

Lytte could still be lingering at the Willows or, nearby, the Blackwoods. It was the best chance she had.

The night felt invigorated now. She looked out and saw the soft glow of the dragon's belly full of fire.

Without a second thought, Naomi looked around her room, grabbed her shadesilk cloak, along with a few other random items, and threw them into a sack. She glanced at the pair of boots graciously bestowed upon her by Reynolds, the leather torn and scuffed, the lacing badly needing repair. She felt a tight connection to them, and yet, she lost her freedom wearing them. She blew a kiss in their direction, then stood on the ledge in her bare feet and leapt into the evergreen forest and away from the people she loved.

Taren watched Naomi leave the room. He clenched his fist, feeling apprehensive, like he should follow, but he had asked a lot of her that night. She needed space away from this. Away from him.

He turned toward Jack, watching his expressions closely, the sweat on his face, his watery eyes. As long as Taren had been in the camp, he had known Jack. He had grown up in the camp, had learned his craft of magic— animal charmer, if Taren remembered right. He wouldn't have expected this blubbering survivor.

But it was the way he turned his head or covered his eyes with his hands. The movement looked fluid, unearthly, and peculiar. He wished he could push his magic as he had before to touch the aura and communicate.

Taren concentrated and tried to reach it, push down . . . snatch the threads.

But it kept quiet. The calm storm would not come when called.

But the girl would know. The little girl who read the secrets of others—she could find what Jack was hiding.

"Excuse me." Taren stood up.

Voices called after him, but he had already found himself sliding down the icy steps toward the village.

A small lamp burned in the front window of the yurt not far from the village center. Elian would be awake, Taren thought. He spent most nights reading histories and life sketches of Parbraven, pouring over the ancient pages and scrolls. Over the past few weeks, Taren had spent time with the philosopher in his attempts to resolve his own frustrations with magic. Elian would understand.

The cold air bit his knuckles as he gently rapped on the door.

Elian answered, looking ruffled from his studies. "Taren?"

"I need to see Lottie." The words rushed out.

"Lottie is in bed—"

"I'm sorry, but I need her to come with me."

Elian evaluated the look on his face. "Come in, come in."

Taren entered, feeling the warmth on his face from the quiet fire in the center. The sight of the stacks of books and scrolls reminded him of Lytte's tent in the Willows. He felt urgency course through him.

"Taren?" Elian turned to face him. "Is something wrong?"

"I need Lottie's magic. My magic won't work. I need her to confirm my suspicions."

"Of what?"

Taren's patience grew thin, his anxiety worsening as if he knew he was right. "Please. Can I talk to her?"

He watched Elian's expression furrow with concern. He looked back at Taren with understanding in his eyes. Elian nodded before exiting without a word. Moments later he returned with the little girl holding his hand. She wore only a nightshirt and long socks.

"I wasn't asleep," Lottie said almost defensively. "I pretended, but I like looking at the stars through my window."

Taren watched the innocence in her smile. He forgot how young she was, not yet eight years old, but had witnessed so much. He sat on the edge of an armchair. "Lottie. I need your help."

The young girl smiled. "I would do anything for Naomi. What do you want me to do?"

"All I need is for you to touch someone." Taren's mind wandered, thinking of what to say to a child. "You know the woman who gave you that scar?" He pointed at the long, thin line that ran down the length of her neck where the Louving had tried to kill her and steal her blood. "I think there is one here."

"Really?" Lottie sounded excited.

"She is not going." Geneive, Elian's wife, came from another room behind them. "I do not want her around another one of those creatures."

Taren stood. "She will be safe with me, I promise you. If I don't find this out, then the whole village may be in danger. She has the chance to save us all."

Elian sighed. "Go get dressed, little one," he whispered to Lottie.

Without a second thought, the girl ran back to her room. She returned in her leather-hide pants and woolen boots. A knitted woolen hat adorned her head, betraying her age.

"Let's go. Don't worry about me." She kissed her new mama and papa goodbye and took Taren's hand.

Though Taren tried to hustle, the little girl sauntered after him as if she didn't feel the same urgency.

On the way, she asked questions, innocent questions like the position of the stars or how leaves know to change colors. Taren, who had never contemplated such things, had no answer. He felt robbed of a childhood, having been exposed to magic when he was younger.

"What if it is a shape-shifter?" Lottie asked. "What will you do? Will you hurt him?"

Taren didn't know the answer. "I don't want to hurt him. I don't want to hurt anyone any more. But I guess I'll do what I need to, to keep Naomi safe."

"She's special."

Taren's lips curved into a thin smile. "She's priceless."

They had reached the house again, but from the corner of his eye, Taren saw a shadow move in the dark. His guard went up. *There are more of them.*

"Stay here."

Lottie looked at him, defiant. "No. You promised Elian you would keep me safe."

Taren clenched his fist but gave up the fight. "Come on, then."

He backed away from the house and started after the shadow. He listened for the snow crunching under its feet but heard none. As if it hovered over the ground. He quieted Lottie behind him and took out his knife.

The shadow moved toward the direction of the sleeping dragons. Two more had appeared that he could see; the deep red one he recognized. It was the one that had carried him in its long talons from Mount Ignis. The other one he did not know—a smaller green dragon with a glowing belly of orange flame. The shadow was heading for that one.

Without a thought he ran, dragging the girl behind him.

"He's getting away," Taren huffed.

The shadow noticed the attention and sped toward the creature, leaping high onto its haunches.

Taren and Lottie were close but not close enough. The dragon reared up, ready to take flight. Its wings spread like a giant rook, the grace of a bird in flight. It locked eyes with Taren, brilliant green and darkest black.

And Taren understood without communicating: this creature knew magic and knew him.

It did not take flight. Instead, the head of the dragon stretched down to the earth near Taren's feet like an obedient dog. Its hot breath steamed from its flaring nostrils.

Taren stood, speechless, admiring the animal. He'd never felt so connected to anything. His magic compelled him to touch the ridges on its large snout. The fire-eater exuded energy in all forms.

And the magic came back to him, one firebrand to another.

His eyes lifted, and he caught sight of the rider, as astonished as he was. Naomi sat on the ridgeback staring at him. Her eyes betrayed everything, reading his unspoken questions.

"Don't leave!" The yell didn't come from him, but from Lottie. "Don't leave without us."

"No." Taren turned to her. "You need to go back."

"She needs me," she yelled at Taren. "And I need her."

Naomi continued to stare for a moment. Then she snapped back and tried to get the dragon to move, but with little success. It still bowed its head to Taren.

"We're coming," Taren informed Naomi, placing his knife back into his sheath. "And I'll be the one steering."

CHAPTER THREE

Ferra stood with her back toward the entrance to the underground of SisterElm, anxious to start the journey. Mother had packed everything she and Browneyes might need to break into Southwick; each had food and supplies, enough to get them there. With how difficult Browneyes had been since they first arrived at SisterElm, the Louving girl was strangely delighted with the adventure, for what reason Ferra couldn't figure.

It hadn't been long since Browneyes first stalked her and Micah through the heart of Parbraven. The experience of being hunted by the Louving was not a treasured memory. The shapeshifter had used the form of a black wolf to sniff them out, one of several collections of blood she wore around her neck. Those vials were still a worry.

Ferra felt she had to keep close to Browneyes at all times. Now in the shadow of the SisterElm, Ferra just didn't trust her, and every time she disappeared, Ferra would worry about the safety of the dwarves.

Paolo, Ferra's bear protector, romped up the hill to sit near her feet. Ferra's heart had soared when he returned to her. It gave her great comfort that he would be with her this final leg of the journey.

"I know," she muttered to his unspoken question. "I want to go too. Mother's just finishing up something."

Ferra poked her head back inside the hollow of the tree. The SisterElm stood tremendous and strong, filled with little nooks and crannies for the working dwarves. Mother became a leader to them, and as a caretaker in UnderElm, she was the life blood keeping the community together.

A few were busying themselves with whatever provisions Mother had instructed them to find. The inside had become a hive of activity. SisterElm had always been a safe-house for dwarves, but Mother expected something else might happen. Scouts had brought word of soldiers arming themselves, along with demons from the underbelly of the world. Something sinister was about to happen, and Mother directed the other community of dwarves in preparing for the worst of it.

Ferra knew she couldn't stay to help and had to trust that no harm would come to the SisterElm and the dwarves. The time had come, the fate of her and her sisters in reuniting the stones together would come to pass. She knew this. All her sisters would be in Southwick, and though she was anxious, there was no knowing what would happen to them or to the world when the magic combined once again.

She wished Browneyes wouldn't have volunteered to come, preferring to face this alone, but it felt best to get her away from Mother and the other dwarves. To see Mother become so trusting of Browneyes sent a wave of uncomfortable anger into Ferra's heart.

Ferra skipped down the worn stairs to the cavernous room among the roots where the two sat. "The sun is going down. Time to get going."

Mother looked up at her, her gentle eyes smiling. "Yes, it is time."

"Thanks, Mother, I'll keep it safe." Browneyes bent down and placed something in her pack.

"What is that?"

Browneyes just glared at her as she cinched up the bag.

"It is a fairy, my dear," Mother explained.

"A fairy?" Ferra huffed. "Fairies are trouble. We don't want one with us."

Browneyes stood up. "Obviously you don't know anything about fairies."

Ferra gritted her teeth. "Well, it's possible. I can't talk to fairies."

Browneyes let out a laugh. "Or fairies won't talk to you."

"I've never cared to know."

Browneyes shifted her pack. "Well, let's get this over with." She walked up the stairs and out the archway.

Ferra turned. "Mother? Is there something I should know about her?"

"She is kinder than she may appear."

"Yeah, but I still don't trust her."

Mother looked off toward the door. "I didn't say anything about trust, dear. Be careful. The fairy is a good idea. I was surprised she asked." She hugged Ferra with all her strength. "Now, go find your sisters, find this Reynolds, and go protect my boys. Hix and Thornock I don't worry about, but Brandell is so tenderhearted. Watch for him."

"I will." Ferra kissed her on the cheek. "Thank you for everything."

Mother couldn't speak, the tears welling up in her eyes, but she smiled and shook her arm.

Ferra turned and walked back up the stairs. She found Browneyes near Paolo, her hood shielding her from the rain.

"So, are you ready?" Browneyes asked with very little enthusiasm.

Ferra was not one to filter her words. "You don't care about these people. Why are you going to save them?"

Browneyes stared out at the falling darkness. "A kind deed can go a long way in someone else's eyes."

"Are you talking about Reynolds again?" Ferra remembered Browneyes' mention of her infatuation with the ranger.

"No." She turned. "I'm talking about me. Now, let's go before it really starts raining. I don't particularly like smelling like wet dog."

This comment piqued Ferra's interest. She'd forgotten how Browneyes would transform into the large black wolf for this journey, the same that had chased her and Micah on their trek to the SisterElm. "How does it work?"

"What? This?" She lifted out her necklace lined with small vials of blood. "I don't think you really want to know."

"Why is that?"

"I'm drinking blood, that's why." Browneyes took off a small bottle, revealing the black sludge stuck to the inside. "See this? This is the wolf blood. Not too pretty now. Blood's only good for a little while before it turns all sticky. Fresh is best." She shook the little vial, trying to thin the goo.

"Do you have to kill them?"

Browneyes looked at her curiously. "If you want to get their essence—yes, but to get their appearance—no."

"What's the difference?"

"Trapping their essence traps their soul, and you could fool anyone. But when the person's still living, you can't have the same manipulation, and others can see through the disguise. Make sense?"

Ferra's mind quickly wrapped around the idea. "So, let's say I gave you some of my blood. Would it work then?"

Browneyes tilted her head. "No one's ever given me blood before. I don't really know if it would work."

Ferra smirked. "I'm just thinking ahead. It could be useful having a Louving on my side."

Browneyes looked amused. She popped the cork and swallowed the last of the wolf's blood. "Here we go." She pivoted on one foot and began to spin like a leaf falling from a tree—an elegant, graceful spin made transfixing by the illusion. Her long braids wrapped around her body and sprung out in all directions. The spinning abruptly stopped, and wolf paws pounded to the ground. It looked over to Ferra, the same dark eyes blinking at her.

"Okay, Paolo." Ferra climbed up on the back of the large bear. "We don't have much time, so let's make this count."

Together the bear and the wolf raced across the rain-soaked ground toward the secret entrance to Southwick.

They rode on, plodding through the muddy terrain. The day passed on as they traveled farther south. The skies darkened, and the rain grew heavier. With each pad of the ground, the earth slipped from under Paolo's feet. The path they had followed disappeared in the darkness, and soon they were blindly following Browneyes' trail.

Mud splashed as they trod, coating the long hair of the bear with thick clods. Ferra could tell that Paolo felt irritated: his mood changed and he continually stopped to scratch or shake.

Ferra steered him near a cluster of trees. He stopped and began shaking out his fur. The agitation whipped her off. She knocked into the tree, a brief ring of stars spinning in her vision. She blinked a few times and couldn't see much but the large bear snorting and grunting.

"Oh, Paolo, you big oaf." Ferra stood, clearing her head. She patted his mangy, wet fur. "Are you done with the rain?"

She knew the animal had hit his limit and wouldn't venture further.

Below them, she couldn't see much, just black shapes in the rain. Ferra pulled her cloak close and slumped near the bear. Her head ached, but she would manage.

"Do you think Browneyes will come back?"

Paolo made a deep, rattling breath.

"Me, too. Why stick around here?" She cuddled under his big haunch, near his warm heart. "I don't know. I thought she had changed and would help us."

"Stop whining," a voice came from behind.

Ferra turned to see Browneyes, dripping wet, no longer in wolf form, wringing out her braids.

"I couldn't smell you with me, so I headed back."

Ferra could see her shivering. "Come," she beckoned. Browneyes trotted over to the other side of Paolo, snuggling under the big arm.

"Thanks," she muttered, her lips quivering.

"How close do you think we are to Southwick?"

"Not near enough to make a difference. We'll have to see when it's light."

"Then what do you think that is?" Ferra pointed to black shapes in the distance which looked like mountains with yellow flecks of light. It didn't feel like it could be the glorious city she had heard about. Browneyes had been there more recently than Ferra, and she hoped she might have a better idea.

Browneyes squinted. "I'm pretty sure that's not Southwick. I think it's moving."

"Really?" Ferra sat up. She had very good night vision, but the rain hampered her smell and clouded her sight. She concentrated on the mound. Browneyes was right; it was moving, like a slow procession, up a hill. "What do you think it is?"

"Demons," Browneyes said, flicking dirt from her nails. "That's what Sharrod wants."

"How do you know?"

Browneyes turned toward her. "Hello, I'm a Louving. I was part of all this plotting. Sharrod has the support of the Underworld. It was only a matter of time before they crawled up to the surface."

"But I don't understand what Sharrod wants. He would control all the elements, sure, but what's the point of it?"

Browneyes leaned back. "It's not for him, as far as I know. Sharrod is the servant of Shon."

"Who's Shon?"

"You know, Shon, the god of the Underworld, banished for eternity for killing his sister. The War for the Sky."

Ferra frowned. She knew nothing about the history of Parbraven. It had never seemed important.

"You surprise me, Ferra. For being a daughter of proud King Prolius, you sure don't know your Histories."

Ferra raised her head. "To be fair, I'm the youngest of the six. How would I know anything about it?"

"Thought you would care." Browneyes yawned, bored with the talk. "It's only a hunch, really. But I bet you anything that the stones are the gateway to getting him out. If that happens, the world we know is over."

CHAPTER FOUR

Naomi stared at Taren and Lottie, not believing they had caught her trying to run away. Seeing them elevated the terror she felt inside. "Go, Taren. You can't be here."

"Naomi. Come down!" he shouted, but she sat there, frozen with fear.

Taren stood by the foot of the fire-eater, watching her. She could see his impatience. "Are you coming?"

Naomi looked at him without answering.

Taren lifted the little girl onto his back and started scrambling up the neck of the fire-eater. As he climbed, the fire-eater straightened his back, as if helping him along. Little Lottie clung on like a grumbear. As they neared the top, she lifted her small hand and waved.

"Hi, Naomi."

Taren set her down in the comfortable fold between the dragon's neck and body. "Be careful." He stood towering over Naomi, his hard eyes blazing with confusion and disapproval. "What are you doing?"

Naomi's mouth went dry. "Leaving."

Taren took a seat on the ridge of the animal, catching his breath from all the climbing. He turned his head, evaluating her. "Do you know how to ride a fire-eater?"

"It couldn't be that hard.'"

Taren made an audible *humpf* before he answered, "This is a fine creature, but impulsive, stubborn."

"How would you know?"

"*Really?*" Taren's expression wiped away any doubt about him as a dragon rider.

Naomi returned to her senses. "We have to go—before the others find out I'm gone."

Taren's expression changed. "No. We can't. We have to stay here."

"There's nothing for us here—"

Taren silenced her. "No, Naomi, you don't understand. They're in danger. Jack isn't Jack. He's a Louving. I know I'm right. It's not Jack. If we leave tonight, Linnonbury could be in real danger. Everyone in your house could die for their blood, including your mother and your sister."

The word "Louving" shot prickles down her spine. Naomi's heart pumped with the possibility of one in such a protected place. She looked down, ashamed of her thoughts. "But I can't stay here. I can't. Jeanus will see through the disguise. And I trust Sera and Arie. They're both trained fighters. I'm not. That Louving might be waiting for me. I need to talk with Lytte and—"

"Naomi, don't torture yourself. Lytte's dead."

"Don't say that." Naomi huffed. "We don't know. If he is, his stain will be there. I know it."

"Are you ready to see him like that?"

Naomi's eyes glazed over. No tears; there was no time for them. "It doesn't matter what I'm ready for. I have to go. It's time."

Taren's hand gripped the back of his neck, smoothing it back and forth as if trying to take away the tension in the conversation. "Okay. Then we're going too. All of us."

Naomi watched the sweet girl sitting before her as she curiously examined the dragon's scales. "No. We can't bring Lottie."

"Hey," Lottie protested looking up. "I'm right here, you know?"

"It's too dangerous."

Taren pointed toward Lottie. "We need her." He tilted his head thoughtfully. "She's tough, much tougher than either of us."

"That's right," Lottie returned. "And I've got the magic touch."

"See?" Taren clapped his hands. "She's coming." He glanced at the distant fires where Lottie's caregivers waited for her safe arrival home. "Please forgive me, Elian."

Taren stood and took a place behind Naomi. He sat so close, too close. She could feel the heat of his body, the tremble of his touch.

"Hold tight to Lottie," he whispered in her ear.

Naomi wrapped her arms around the girl, who cuddled into her.

Taren leaned into the fire-eater, stroking his scales. "Okay, Sebastian, let's fly."

The dragon huffed and stamped its feet. They rocked at the sudden motion, securing themselves between the bones of the wings and the folds in its skin. The dragon let out a loud cry which echoed around the mountainside, stretched out its wings, and with three long strides it heaved itself upward, airborne and free.

It didn't take long for Sera to understand that something was wrong. Taren had gotten up rather quickly and exited without a word. She knew him as a thinker, a problem-solver, so something had to bother him enough to leave.

Maybe it had been the wrong thing to bring Jack here.

No. She quickly talked herself out of that thought. She couldn't leave him there by himself, without food or care. But maybe she should mention it to Jeanus.

Andriana was tending to Jack's needs, while Jeanus sat on the couch, studying.

Sera assumed a place beside her. "Jeanus, can you answer me something?"

"You might not like the answer I have." Jeanus always spun around words in a loose, mystical way.

"What do you think of Jack's tale?"

"I find it very interesting." She furrowed her brow. "What do you think?"

Sera grimaced. "I just want to get to Southwick already. I don't mean to be insensitive, but I know where the threat is, and it's not here."

"Are you sure about that?"

Sera stared at her light eyes. "Linnonbury is the best kept secret. There is no safer place."

Jeanus' eyes narrowed. "Evil always has determination on its side." She turned to face Sera. "Magic is light, and I can see light. I can see everything around me, but," she turned her head again, "but this person named Jack is red, not light. He is red."

Sera got very still. "What does that mean?"

"Where is Arie?"

Sera looked around. "I'm not sure."

"Make sure he does not go far. I may need him."

As if Jack could hear every word said, he sprung up and lashed at Andriana, pushing her back onto the ground.

Sera instinctively ran for her whip near the side of the wall. "Arie!" she yelled, but he was already there, protectively standing in front of Jeanus. He had no weapon, just his bare knuckles.

"What's going on?" he asked of Jack.

Sera stared at the standoff; he didn't know the problem. The whole way there, Jack had twitched, but she knew nothing of his usual manner. Now, within the magic of Linnonbury, she could see the flashing eyes and strange movements of a Louving façade.

Sera watched her mother closely: she moved but kept pressing her chest. Something was seriously wrong, but she couldn't get to her.

"What do you want, Jack?" she yelled, seizing her whip. "If that is your real name."

Jack started to snicker, a pathetic whine. "I fooled you. Stupid mortal. You can't hide her. Sharrod wasn't convinced she was dead. And I spied, and I killed them all, and they had no idea."

Arie was on him before he finished the words, pounding the kid like an adult.

Sera rushed over. "Stop, Arie." She pulled on his arms, but he had the struggling teenager by the throat.

"He needs to die."

"No. Not here."

"How could you?" Arie kept asking. "We trusted you."

Jack only laughed more. With every punch or jab or kick he laughed, as if the pain were good for him.

Sera turned to Jeanus, who stood watching near a window. "What is it?"

"We need to secure Linnonbury." She met her eyes. "Do not worry about Naomi, she will be fine."

"What do you mean?"

At that moment, a scree from a fire-eater shook the room.

"Sera." Arie's voice woke her from the noise. He had the boy in a tight grip he couldn't escape. "Your mother."

Sera rushed over and found the sharp claw marks in her chest, a deep gash exposed near her neck.

"Quick," Jeanus ordered. "We have very little time."

The ground disappeared, and all Naomi could see were stars in every direction. She didn't turn back to look at Linnonbury. Instead, she looked ahead. Her cheeks cooled at the night wind, and she thought of being free once again. Saying goodbye would only make her sad. Now was not the time for farewell, but time to act.

She found herself leaning against Taren for support. The ride was not as comfortable as the one with Sera at the helm. The fire-eater maneuvered in sharp angles against a torturing wind. Her ankles ached from the constant bracing of her feet against the ridges.

"You need to relax," Taren told her, as if reading her mind. "Linnonbury is far from the Willows. We won't be there 'til morning."

"I don't know how."

"I won't hurt you." His voice carried off with the wind, far away and distant. "I will never do that again."

Naomi softened at his words. She did trust him but hadn't truly forgiven him. She found herself turning toward him so her back and legs could rest.

"Sebastian," she said once they hit a gentle patch of air. "You called the fire-eater Sebastian."

"Yes." Taren lifted up his head. "It's his name."

"How do you know that?"

"We are the same. He is mine."

Naomi angled herself to see his face. "You don't own a dragon."

"Sebastian is a youngling. He belongs with Sera's fire-eaters." A look of sincerity shone in his eyes. "You won't remember but you walked right into a den of fire-eaters. I communicated to him. We share the same magic."

"So, how did he know to come to Linnonbury?"

Taren's eyes lifted. "I don't know."

Naomi turned back around and watched the clouds from above. It grew cold in the air. Taren must have noticed her shivering and pulled his cloak around both her and Lottie. His protective arms held them safe from the distant world below.

Naomi felt a comforting security that she hadn't felt since Reynolds first found her. It was a different tenderness but welcome all the same. Taren was not as easy to be around as Reynolds had been, but Naomi could feel his sorrow, his pain, resonating through every decision he now made. She never felt that with Reynolds.

She found herself resting her head near his chest and felt peace.

A tree . . .

> *Taller than any before it*
> *and since . . .*
> *Calling to her, a small whisper*
>
>> *But*
>> *louder than a*
>> *drum.*
>
> *Vibrating emotion with every course of energy*

It breathes
It thinks
And through its eyes
It sees . . .
She is there.
Standing all in white, glowing heavenly white.
Long black hair swirls about as if by wind
The star on her crown shines bright as if night.
She whispers, "My beautiful Everstar."

>> *"Your test is about to*
>> *begin."*
>>> *"Come find me."*

The sun came earlier above the clouds. Naomi's eyes lifted to the light. She didn't know how long she'd slept but she felt the jolt of energy and sat up. Lottie slept quietly in her arms; the girl hardly moved in her sleep. She turned to see Taren, silent and distant, his eyes blurry from lack of sleep.

"Where are we?"

Taren met her eyes. "I don't know above the clouds."

"You need rest."

"No, I'm okay."

"Please," she begged. "I'll need your help. Sleep will help."

Taren just stared without saying anything. She couldn't understand him and felt her cheeks flush. She turned back around, facing ahead, quieting the storm she felt inside. Soon after, Naomi felt Taren's head rest against her shoulder, sparking another wave of confusion but she pushed it back.

They rode on through the earliest morning across the sky. Naomi reached her palm out to communicate with Sebastian the fire-eater. The warmth of his skin felt good on her cold hands. The magic within the creature blazed, alight with excitement at her touch. Magic to magic, she told him to slowly descend. She showed him her memories of the Willows, of the kindness and the terror. She wanted him to know everything in order to protect them.

Through Sebastian's magic, Naomi understood his loyalty to Sera and to Taren. Sera nursed him when he was young. Taren understood his rebellious heart.

"We are ready, then."

Skimming the cloud, she looked for any sign of mountains and saw none. She looked toward the sun, a glow of orange reflected on the clouds. With one last glance, she said goodbye to the sun, knowing there might not be a chance of seeing something so beautiful again.

The fire-eater angled his wing and curved into the clouds. Nothing but foggy white filled her vision, a muggy humidity saturating her clothes. Loud snaps echoed around her, like something alive bouncing around within the sky. The ground slowly became visible: first trees, then a river. A pattering of rain fell on them, cool and soaking.

Taren lifted his head, as did Lottie, both awakened by the rain.

Naomi wasn't familiar enough with Parbraven to know where they were, but Taren pointed toward the western mountains and an unmistakable patch of black forest.

"The Blackwoods," Naomi uttered. A dreadful fear fell over her. The haunted forest of dark magic. The Willows lay on its edge to conceal all the magic within. From this height, it looked rather peaceful, but its façade could not decrease the panic inside her.

Taren stiffened behind her. She remembered how much he detested this place. "Returning to my prison."

"Your prison," Naomi commented. "My garden."

"How could you call it a garden?"

Naomi grinned at her own memories. "This is where I first discovered magic and how to talk to it."

"Magic is evil, Naomi. I thought you realized that by now."

The warmth beneath her chest told her otherwise. "I don't see it that way."

"With everything you have endured so far, you still side with the magic?"

She looked at him through her peripheral vision, close enough to see his confused expression. "I don't have a choice."

Naomi held his glance, trying to communicate the unspoken complication of what the magic had done to her and for her. She walked a very fine line, and the magic would know.

Sabastian descended through the rain as Taren directed him to a clearing near a large cluster of willows. The large wings swung out in front of him, pushing the air under for cushioning. Its large talons gripped the soft, rain-soaked earth.

The dragon's legs wobbled under the pressure and collapsed. The motion rocked everyone on its back.

Taren collected himself before scrambling off the creature. "He's okay," he said from below. "I pushed him too hard."

Naomi helped Lottie to her feet before attempting to climb down. Lottie slid down its belly. Taren tried to catch her but missed, pushing them both to the ground.

Lottie giggled. "That was fun."

Naomi didn't want to fall on her face and carefully inched her way down.

Taren stood up, mud covering his backside. "Here. I'll catch you."

Naomi looked at his outstretched arms and considered what she was doing. If it were Reynolds, she would tease him and jump around just to irritate him, but this was not Reynolds, this was Taren, and his gestures meant more. He cared about what he did and thought about every action.

She jumped, and he caught her around the waist. "Thank you."

He held her there for a moment before letting her go. He didn't say anything, just turned and headed back toward the fire-eater.

The soft earth molded around her small, bare feet with gentle kisses. The rain fell in droplets on her head. She looked up and watched the drops fall one by one on her nose. This place felt like home: the sweet, earthy rain, the fresh moss, the rain-soaked trees—she loved every moment.

Lottie moved next to her, looking up. "What are you looking at?"

"The rain. Isn't it wonderful?"

"Like I'm flying through the stars."

"Yes." Naomi turned around, looking at the patterns, feeling free and alive. She glanced back and saw Taren watching her, an unabashed look of amusement written on his face.

Naomi wouldn't be embarrassed about this. She smiled.

Taren walked forward. "Sabastian can't fly without fire. I can build one."

Naomi looked around. "Everything is wet. What about your magic?"

Taren's face went cold. "I don't want to use it. I don't want to hurt him."

The magical walls inside Taren had fallen, but the barriers he'd built on the outside had not. He didn't trust himself with the magic anymore. His world had been shaken, and it had happened because of her.

"Let's find the camp. Sabastian can rest for a while, until we can find some firewood. It will be okay."

Taren nodded. "Agreed."

She turned to Lottie and grabbed her hand. "Let's go find Lytte," she said as she walked toward the trees.

The day continued to drizzle. The three traveled through the trees, carving a pathway between the brush and briars. The large willow branches, saturated with the rain, hung low like long arms reaching for the ground.

They wandered around in the leaf jungle, searching for any sign of the camp. It seemed hopeless.

Naomi stopped.

"What is it?" Taren asked.

"I have an idea." And without explaining a word, Naomi wrapped her wrists around the hanging fronds, backed up and ran. She began to swing. A branch came into view. Her bare feet found it easily. She slid her arms from the thin willow fronds, and she hopped from branch to branch, looking from above to see any remnants of the camp.

"See anything?" she heard Taren's voice from far below.

Naomi squinted, and she saw it. "Yes! Something red." Her arms wrapped around another branch, and she sank to a lower part of the tree. Taren and Lottie ran to meet her.

She heaved a breath of excitement. "I know where it is. Come."

They followed her as she maneuvered between the trees and branches, searching for that dark object which stuck out amongst the green. The energy quickly pumped through her as she inched closer, not knowing what to expect.

The red object came into view. It stood out in the clearing. Naomi stopped, the breath knocked out of her.

The dark object wasn't red at all but white stained with blood.

They had found the camp.

Naomi couldn't move. Shock rippled through her body. Before her eyes stood splintered posts, the charred remains of the barracks where the boys slept. Only sticks remained of Aristotlis' hut, his calm retreat amid the chaos of magic. Bits of glass and debris lay strewn along the pathways, obstructing any visible resemblance to the place Naomi had lived. And near the end stood the white tent, Lytte's tent, the smear of blood painted as a banner for the victor. The sight physically pained Naomi.

She sank to her knees, a heavy anchor pulling her down. She placed her palms to the earth and felt the shudder of the magic left here, the lives missed. A flash of its memory took hold of Naomi, expressing its sorrow and loss. Like Micah, her friend there in the camp, the earth had many things to share, and she experienced the suffering of the poisoning magic.

Taren walked forward, silent, as if stepping through a graveyard. The camp had been his home for years, the growing pains of youth now fractured and scattered in charred remains. Each step he took marked the reality that no one was here. What Jack spoke was true.

Naomi knew where Taren was heading and had to build her courage to meet him there. It took all the strength she had left to stand.

"Are you okay?"

Naomi turned, nearly forgetting Lottie standing behind her. She didn't know what to say; instead she just took her hand so Lottie would know all she felt.

An overpowering fear consumed Naomi's thoughts. "I don't know what to do," she uttered, so soft the words fell short in her mouth. The Vivatera—usually so warm in her chest, felt heavy, like a stone, a burden she couldn't remove. Her head began to swim, and her vision blurred.

"No." She stumbled. "No. Taren!" she yelled after him, about to lose consciousness again. "Help me."

Taren ran to her. "Whoa. What's happening?"

"The magic . . ." Naomi tried to form words. "It's taking me…"

Everything went black.

CHAPTER FIVE

T he churning waters reflected the gray skies in mood and temper. The voyage had been rough for all involved, but near the dulling horizon, Katia caught a glimpse of orange-red sunset. She sat on the edge of the bowsprit as she had as a child, mesmerized by the continual motion of the waves and watching for distant land.

A song came to Katia's mind as she felt the wind on her cheeks, a song she remembered her mother singing when she was much younger, before her brother was born and the world she understood disappeared.

A song of hope we sing thee on,
As ye sail beyond the dawn.

> *Brave as knights, in wars and fights*
> *But see thy heaven come, ye be*
> *A braver lot than we.*
> *As ye sail beyond the sea.*

The song was sweet but sad and reminded her of her mother more than before. Was she also a trapped soul like so many here, or did she make it to the other side?

Her outlook had changed, but the way she felt for the sea had not. She loved it, every moment—the rocking, the spray. She felt as if she could live on the boat forever like her father, Briggs. She turned back to watch the person who had raised her until she was ten—a gruff, bearded man standing near the mast, calmly steering the ship into the wind. Her anger toward him had quieted. His actions when he left her to be taken to the camp had proven to be justified. And when she'd found out that her brother Vanya was still alive, after so many years apart, her bond with her father became stronger than ever.

The tall parapets of Southwick came into view midmorning. Katia didn't recognize them at first, but Wenlock Brighton, Landon's eccentric uncle, pulled out his eyepiece and identified the billowing flags of the capital. Reaching the outskirts of the seaport without suspicion would be tricky, especially since they were sailing in a government ship.

"Kat?" Her own name startled her, and she grabbed the hull instinctively. Landon stood on the deck below, drenched head to foot.

"What happened to you?"

"Did you not see that big wave crash overboard?"

Katia looked and saw the water pooled on the spar deck. The boat wobbled again with the sea. Katia was so used to the motion that she no longer noticed. Carefully she slid down the bowsprit and back to the deck just as another wave hit the side, making her stumble right into Landon.

"Sorry." She straightened.

"You should be."

"Stop teasing me."

"Who's teasing?" Landon looked affronted, but his smirk couldn't hide his playful nature.

"Did you need something?"

"Yes. Come with me." Landon snatched her hand and led her down to the living quarters below deck. In a large cabin, at the end of a long table, Wenlock had his head down, a drinking glass sliding back and forth in front of him. He wasn't much for traveling by ship and drank to cover the misery.

In the corner by the windows covered with panes of colored glass sat Fontine, one of Naomi's sisters. She quietly spun her medallion around her neck, the gentle magic inside shining like sea glass.

"Here she is," Landon stated as they walked in.

Fontine looked up, a slight smile on her face. "Looks like the water got the best of you."

Landon shook his shaggy hair with his hands, spraying the girls with little droplets.

Katia brushed herself off. "You're such an ogre sometimes."

Fontine didn't flinch, just sat in her quiet way, observing. She looked far removed from the ship, the motion, everything, and kept to herself a lot—very different from her sister, Ferra, the only other daughter of King

Prolius Katia knew, not counting Naomi. Fontine was difficult to get close to or understand. She didn't have much of a sense of humor nor did she like expressing her opinions. Landon mentioned that she had a temper, but Katia had yet to see that come out. For Fontine to ask to see her was unusual.

Fontine sat up, resting her medallion in her hand. The colored glass spread light on her sandy brown hair and fair face. "I have an idea, but I don't know how to do it."

"And it involves me?"

"It involves us," she clarified. "First, we can't arrive in this ship. I think we should leave your father here and take the raft."

"But the waters are so choppy—"

"Umm," Landon interrupted. "I think she can handle the water."

"Yes. Sorry." Katia flushed with embarrassment. She remembered Fontine had the stone which could control water, but she forgot that she could use it.

"And we should enter through the seaports to the west, not east."

"Why? That might take us another day to get around."

"I know." Fontine placed her hands in her lap and looked at both of them. "This is the commodore's vessel, and they will recognize it in the east. It's too risky."

"Briggs will be fine with that," Landon returned. "Will you know how to get into the palace?"

Fontine fumbled with her hands as she talked. "No. There are certain memories I have of fleeing the palace. I remember a dark tunnel smelling like rotten eggs, and I remember a tall archway that we ran under and a tree with lights in it."

"Well, it's better than nothing."

Katia furrowed her brow. "I don't know. It sounds like nothing."

"I'll recognize it if we see it."

Landon shrugged. "Well, it's the best plan we have."

"It's the only plan we have."

"Right." Landon flashed a toothy grin at which Katia tried to be mad but couldn't.

"And Wenlock should come with us," Fontine added. "He has to get off this ship."

Wenlock stirred a little at the mention of his name. He started to lift his head, but the motion of the ship swept him to the ground. "Oh, good gracious." He put his head back on the wooden planks. Snores soon followed.

Landon looked away from his uncle. "Should I go talk to Briggs?"

Fontine nodded. "I don't want to get too close to the shore."

"Got it. I'll be back." Landon left, and the room went quiet, the only sound coming from the battering waves outside.

Katia turned to leave.

"Wait, Katia. Could you stay?"

Katia looked back at Fontine, who had a strange pleading in her eyes. "Uh, okay." For weeks Fontine had said only a few words to her. She couldn't imagine what she would say. Katia took a seat at the table. "What do you need?"

Fontine took the chair across from her. She hesitated several times before she spoke. "I want to know about your magic."

"Oh." Katia paused. She hadn't expected this. "Well, what do you want to know?"

"Everything." Her eyes lit up as she twirled her precious medallion in her hand. "Can you show me?"

Katia closed her eyes and connected with her magic. Swirling brilliant-white behind her eyelids, it was much easier to connect now than it had been in the camp.

She opened her eyes again and knew what to do. Crystals had already formed around her fingertips. She slowly started knitting the ice patterns together until she'd formed a fragile, intricate ball of ice. She handed it to Fontine, whose eyes were wide with delight.

"I couldn't always do this." Katia smiled at her creation. "Naomi is the one who taught me how to connect with the magic."

"Naomi," she said, reaffirming the name. "I'm intrigued by your ice magic. Water magic is complicated to use and, honestly, is very particular in who it chooses."

"Chooses? Are you saying the magic chose me?"

"Magic always has a choice in how it acts." Fontine took the ball of crystal in her hand next to the medallion. The crystals began to melt and reform. Drips ran down the spindles of ice, collecting together before spreading away in different patterns. The ice moved in motions back and forth until a winged water-butterfly took flight, rising in circles, then vanishing in a spray of mist.

"Oh, that was wonderful."

Fontine bit her lip. "Here." She lifted her medallion and handed it to her.

Katia stared. "What? I can't take that."

"I'm not giving it to you, but I want to see what you can do with it."

Katia's fingers trembled as she picked up the chain, afraid to touch it.

The stone swirled blueish-green, as if liquid hid inside. The energy surrounding it felt alive and excited. It invited her closer, familiar and friendly.

"It's okay." Fontine took the medallion from around her neck and actually placed it in her hands.

A shock of excitement ran up Katia's arms and through her body. Her trembling hand cupped the stone, and like lightning, a bright light shot out and filled the room. The suddenness startled both girls so much that Katia tried to remove her hand, but Fontine held it tight.

"Look," she said.

Katia's eyes hadn't yet adjusted to the brilliance, but she focused in.

It was snow rather than light—snow slowly falling around them, dusting the table with baby-fine flakes, newly formed with tiny crystals.

Fontine couldn't help herself and caught a few on her tongue, tasting the magic.

Katia softened her grip around the stone, and the brightness lessened.

"Good heavens." The girls watched Wenlock's awed expression. "Is this snow? I'm not dreaming?"

Fontine laughed and went over to the man to help him sit up. The tiny flakes fell on his nose. "Isn't it wonderful?"

"But how did I do that?" Katia looked down at her hands, still trembling with energy.

"The magic is pure within the stone," Fontine tried to explain. "I was so impressed with your ice magic, I wanted to just see. I think the stone is more powerful when a magic user has it."

Katia handed it back to Fontine. "I don't know if I want that kind of power."

Fontine's fingers wrapped around the medallion, and she focused on it thoughtfully. "I understand. But now we have a real weapon we can use. Real evil is out there, and I feel so unprepared."

Katia felt a strange kinship with Fontine at that moment. Not that she had forgotten how difficult the magic could be, but it came with such responsibility. Water elements were hard to control and befriend. She understood her completely.

The western dockyards jutted out into the sea like a long stretched arm to Southwick's giant body. Tall stone watchtowers stood out like fingers, snaring those who trespassed. Ships could not reach land without first crossing the dangerous waters, trapped in the spider's web.

The small raft floated near the docks of the seaport. Several larger ships loomed over the tiny boat and its cargo. They had now been adrift for two days within the same raft. Tempers were high, and the sea-worn travelers ached to be on shore again.

The presence of the Southwick guard could be felt everywhere. Even the porters had emblems on their sleeves.

Landon felt a large lump in his throat form.

"Landon," Katia whispered in his ear. "We can't get in this way."

"Ho!" a man from the dock hollered to the ship, catching the rafters' attention. He was stout and weatherworn, with the appearance of an old seadog forced into a porter's uniform.

Landon turned to Katia. "Do you trust me?"

"Of course not," Katia returned.

Landon winked at her. "I got this." Harnessing his charm, he yelled back, waving his hands to signal the man.

A thick rope landed in the center of the raft. Landon anchored it to the hull, and they were slowly towed back to the dock. The others on the raft tensed as they drew closer and closer.

"Ho, there. Need your papers," the gruff voice repeated.

"We don't have them," Landon returned.

The porter looked down at the crew in the raft, checking their condition. "You look worse for wear, bunch a' sorry souls."

"Our ship capsized in the storm." Landon grabbed the porter's hand and climbed onto the cobblestones. It felt strange to stand on a firm foundation, and he began to sway.

"Easy, now." The porter steadied him.

"Everything's gone." Landon took a step, hoping to feel his legs again. "Just devastating. The storms have been so rough. We're all battered and starving."

The porter patted his arm, feeling the charm of Landon's magic. "Let's set you right." He extended his hand to the others in the boat. Landon pitched in and helped Wenlock onto the dock.

"Sweet, merciful ground. I will never leave you again."

"Come on, Uncle." Landon helped him up again. "This is my uncle, my beautiful wife Kat—Kath—Katherine, and her cousin."

"Southwick's closed to visitors." Landon could feel the porter's sincerity. "You're going to have to travel west."

"We worry about our family," Landon explained. "I'm afraid for the city."

"Aye," said the porter. "As we all are. With no king, the council has appointed a devil of a man. Forced the sea out of me and slapped an emblem on my shoulder."

"Sorry to hear that, my good man."

The porter eyed him before he gripped his shoulder and shook his hand. "As am I." He leaned in close. "Dangerous things are happening. Dark, unnatural things. Travel west. No harm will come. Take your family and leave as fast as you can."

"You're a good man, and I thank you, but we have no option. We are here to help, you see. Please help us get inside."

Whether the porter felt Landon's charm or if he was tired of the upheaval, Landon couldn't tell. "Listen close," the seadog whispered. "The patrol is near the gate. Take a left around the wall and find the sewer grate. You can get in there undisturbed."

Landon patted him on the back. "Thank you."

With no other words, the porter dismissed them and went to help others.

"Trust me now?" Landon grinned at Katia, who was trying not to show how impressed she was. He took her hand. "Come. We need to get out of here."

CHAPTER SIX

"Naomi?" Taren snatched the fainting girl in his arms. He carried her swiftly to the remnants of Lytte's tent. A blood-soaked stain covered the entrance, but he pushed down any feeling he had toward it. He would find out soon enough. Now was not the time to think about it.

The tent looked haphazard, as it did when Lytte had lived there, scrolls and books thrown about, though now wet from the saturating rain: the precious manuscripts of old now lost to the world of men. The trunks had been rifled through by whomever had pillaged the camp. Not much remained of the glorious alchemist's life there.

Naomi blistered hot, a fever flushing her cheeks and neck. Without asking, Lottie found an old sheepskin from the corner and laid it out.

Taren gently set Naomi down, her head falling to one side. "Naomi? Come on." He rubbed her hands to help rouse her, but she lay quiet. "I don't know what's wrong."

Lottie looked around. "Maybe it's that?" She pointed to the glow coming from her chest. The Vivatera, where it rested inside her, blazed with swirling light.

Seeing the brilliant scar embedded inside her skin, painful memories rushed back from that night when Taren had taken his father's knife and shoved it deep inside her, killing her to save her. He recalled the horrified look on Reynolds' face, helplessly pleading with the magic.

"No." Taren woke from the vision. "Focus."

The medallion's scar rested just beneath her collarbone. He reached down to touch it. A flash blazed out and zapped Taren's hand, sending him backward, a warning. His hand stung from the energy.

Lottie looked frightened, the first time he had seen fear in her eyes. "Are you okay?"

Taren heaved up again, shaking his hand for feeling. "I'll be fine. But I don't know what to do. I don't know what's wrong with her."

Lottie looked down. "She's too hot."

"The magic won't let me near her."

"Will it let me?" Lottie touched Naomi's shoulder and nothing happened. "The heat is drying her clothes. Look."

Lottie pointed to the steam rising from her cloak.

"I don't . . ." Taren brought his hands to his head. "I don't know what to do."

"Get me something cold," Lottie directed. "We need to bring the fever down. Sweet Mum would get fevers, and I would help her. Do we have anything cold?"

Looking around, Taren saw some shreds of fabric. He ripped part of it and soaked it in a pool of water, then handed it to Lottie, who placed it on Naomi's head.

Rubbing his arm and flexing his fingers, Taren stood to the side, watching the magic escape and feeling he had done something terrible.

Naomi blinked in the bright light. She stood alone in a wandering field that stretched out as far as she could see. Rolling hills of grasses yellowed by the sun waved like tides of the sea. Wind swept around her, carrying cotton seeds and dandelion wishes—

Everything white and yellow.

She looked down at her arms, delicately draped with sheer silks and sparkling lace that continued down to her toes. Her long hair fell in curls about her head, ruffled by the swirling of the wind.

A bright star shone through the midday sun, brighter than any object Naomi had ever seen. It glided through the air, pulled toward her. As it came closer, Naomi noticed it wasn't a star at all, but a person—delicate features and limbs, like her own, a golden halo of hair wrapped around her. The woman stopped on a nearby hill and gazed upon Naomi with wise green eyes. She looked identical.

Naomi stepped closer, not believing her eyes. The sharp nose, small chin, white face with tiny freckles. Everything was the same.

"Naomi," the woman spoke, her voice echoing around the valley.

"Who are you?"

The woman's gestures were slow, belonging to the air and wind. *"Look upon me, Naomi. See what has been created. I am the magic which resides in you. I am the Everstar."*

Warmth covered her body, the glow of life within her speaking of the truth of this ethereal beauty. The feeling so overwhelmed Naomi that she lost speech. She could only stare with unbelieving eyes, captivated by the light which surrounded her.

"You have housed me, trained me, and befriended me. I honor you for your courage. But the eternal darkness is upon us." The Everstar held out her hands to Naomi.

Naomi's trembling fingers reached for the comfort the Everstar offered, tiny like her own.

"Our time is ending."

Naomi looked up into her own eyes, finding the courage to speak. "What do you mean?"

"You must find Pera, mother of all."

Naomi felt confused.

"She is calling to us. The dream tells us where she is. She is guiding us there."

The clarity of her dreams came into focus. She knew Pera; the Guardian had shown her. Pera, the sister whose sacrifice was told in the War for the Sky.

"What will happen to us?" Naomi dared to ask.

Wild wind swept around the Everstar in tremendous power. *"We will separate, and I will return with Pera."*

"But will I live without you?"

The Everstar's eyes turned down. She did not answer.

A darkness covered the sky, causing the vision to fade. Violent wind came from the east, pushing Naomi back, clouding her sight.

"Find Pera," the Everstar insisted in a rush. *"Trust her."*

"But where do I find her?"

"*I will lead you.*"

Naomi watched her magic turn away and vanish, leaving only darkness.

Taren felt the madness take him, the inescapable knowledge that Naomi's condition was entirely his fault. The magic demanded he do it. The Vivatera had to return and combine back with the magic. He knew it, and did it, and now he regretted it.

He watched Naomi, unconscious on the floor, fighting the fever that took her. He was helpless, unable to touch her, to make it right. "I have to leave."

Lottie looked up. "What? But I need your help."

"I can't help. All I do is hurt her."

Lottie turned back to Naomi. "Go take a walk. Clear your head. I'll wait here for you."

Taren watched Lottie wring out the cloth before placing it back on her head. "I'll be back."

He stepped outside into the drizzling rain, each bead more refreshing than the last. Before him lay the desolation of the empty camp. His memories filled with running boys, laughing, playing, thumping on the ground to wake the magic, the continuous sessions learning the art of swordplay . . . and for what?

Taren marched to the sticks that remained of where Aristotolis once lived. A small triangle still marked the entrance, the tattered canvas black and burned. Inside lay fragments of his wooden weapons—staves, clubs, whatever he would make out of the materials around him. He picked up an intricate wooden figurine, a fat cat holding his belly. His fingers brushed across the carving. He had never hated Aristotolis; rather, Taren felt envious of his talent. He'd understood the magical dimensions so well, something which Taren had no respect for at the time. Now, he wished he had paid closer attention. Naomi might be trapped between worlds, and he couldn't understand how to get her back. He placed the little figurine in his pocket and moved on.

Down the rows, all the buildings were destroyed. It looked as though the whole camp had been torched by fire. Hardly any supplies were in usuable condition. He scavenged through a pile near the water well and came upon something blacked by the fire. He picked at it and stopped. It was bone.

Taren bit his hand as the horror overwhelmed him. It was true. People died. The boys, those children lost their lives here. He couldn't stop the tears from coming. How selfish he had been. How uncaring and egotistical. He stood and wiped his face, the despair draining him away.

Near the edge of camp, Taren saw the barracks empty and broken. He feared what he might find inside, but he went all the same. Only the wallposts stood with bare frames where the makeshift bedding had once been. His was no longer visible. A memory struck him: Landon and Katia talking about Naomi when she first arrived. His jealousy of the magic stung once again and mixed into incredible, overwhelming sadness.

But that was a different person. He had grown. He didn't want to be that person anymore. Defiantly, Taren kicked a large post, sending it down to the ground.

"You should care more than you do."

Taren whipped around, his eyes searching through the rain. "Who's there?"

Near the forest's edge, a black form took shape, tall and lean, a man without a face.

"You disappoint me, Taren Lockwood. I thought you would know me."

A haunting familiarity struck him in his heart.

"How . . . how is this possible?"

The shadow moved soundlessly between the trees. *"Magic does not die, it lives forever."*

Taren walked closer, astounded to see a stain—but not just any stain. His own former magical self, coming back to haunt him. "No. You were gone. Naomi banished you. You are not me. You do not exist."

"Dark magic lives in the Blackwoods—and for that matter, lives here. After my banishment I was sent here, free to walk and to poison. There is no protection over this place. Not anymore."

Suddenly the black shade had him by the neck, strangling his life out. Tiny specks of light appeared in his vision as he lost breath. He collapsed on the ground, struggling for air. Every second increased his pain. He couldn't think. He couldn't speak.

He tried desperately to get to his magic, to harness the power to push it back, but he couldn't. The shadow knew his weakness, knew he had his doubts, and attacked with more power than before.

Taren's vision began to fade, but not before he saw two figures, one on each side of him. A thunderous crack vibrated the ground and a blue light swallowed all his vision.

He heard voices, higher pitched and musical. Like shadows themselves, cornering the dark magic like prey.

The grip on his throat loosened. Air filled Taren's lungs as he gasped, his throat contracting, swallowing again and again.

As his vision cleared, he saw a hand stuck out in front of him, offering help up. "My wandering friend, I mean you no harm. Are you in danger?"

Taren looked up at him. He had never seen this person before, but his dark skin and pale eyes looked much like the blind Arenma people who lived in the Echoes. Much like…

A small person came from behind and smiled bright and wide. Taren couldn't help himself. "Micah . . ."

Taren coughed as air filled his lungs. "Micah? Please. Let me up."

Micah looked down at him, his sapphire eyes seeing past his terror. "Taren. Can I trust you?"

"You trusted me once. We fought together in the Echoes. We beat the Louvings."

"But you betrayed my friend."

Taren shook his head. "She saved me, Micah. She saved me from that poison." He angled toward where the shadow had been sucking away his life.

Micah smiled in his strange, cheerful manner and offered his hand. "It seems the fates bring us together again to fight."

Taren took it and stood, the breath stolen from him slowly returning, his head swimming from the effort. He looked back to the spot where the stain—his own dark stain—had stood only a moment before. The trees looked empty of anything unusual. He looked back at Micah and his companion, who had the same small stature and eccentricity in dress. However, unlike Micah, he held a staff in each hand for balance.

"Spotswood Shadower," the man introduced himself. He turned his hands in circles as he bowed. "I am young Micah's uncle."

"I've heard of you." His mannerisms were very similar to Micah's, though he projected an understanding of the world and how it worked within his simple expression. "The dark magic. Did you see it?"

"It vanished into the Blackwoods to hide with its brothers," Spotswood answered.

"How . . .?" Taren struggled, several questions coming at once. "How did it know I was here?"

"There are several magical strongholds, like compass points in this world—the north in Ignes, the Echoes to the east, the Musungu in the south, and the Blackwoods to the west. But the Blackwoods harbor enemies, traitors, tyrants—creatures hungry for it. It was that magical concealment which made the Willows the ideal placement for the camp. The dark magic is talking. I'm sure it sensed you near. Stains are still connected, even if banished."

"But you released me."

Spotswood's imp-like smile curled at the edge of his mouth, proud and gratified. "No one should suffer at the hand of something so pitiful."

Taren stared past where the stain had appeared to the dark forest beyond, searching for any sign of shadows. At last he turned back. "We shouldn't have returned. It's too great of a risk."

"We have come to assist. That is why we are here." Micah became excited again. "We have come to take you back with us. We are here for Naomi."

The name brought back the panic. "Naomi . . . Yes. Come. I need you both."

Taren bolted toward the tent, the others following behind him. Spotswood moved faster than Taren expected, propelled nimbly forward using two staffs to assist him.

The torn flap lay open to the afternoon rain. Lottie sat quietly next to Naomi as they entered the dilapidated tent. Naomi's color had not changed; she lay on the mat in feverish sleep.

Spotswood immediately bent down and placed both hands near her temples. A steady hum emanated from his lips.

"Is she—" Taren cleared his mind again, shutting out fears he could not let himself dwell upon. "What's happening to her?"

"She is in the Netherealm." Spotswood rolled up his long sleeve. Fresh scars were still visible on his arm.

"Netherealm?" Lottie repeated. "Where is that?"

"A dimension between this world and the next. She should be safe there."

Taren's mind clouded with doubt. "But the Blackwoods are so close. I know the magic can sense her here. Are you sure about this?"

Spotswood closed his eyes and concentrated. "She is protected. I feel her protection. She is not in danger. She has—" And suddenly his eyes snapped open, and he withdrew his hand.

"What is it?" Taren watched the look on the old man's face, the confusion crossing his brow. "What did you see?"

"I will not reveal her secrets."

A rush of anger flooded through Taren. Spotswood had obviously found out something dangerous. He wanted to know, but more than that, he felt envious of the power to know. He'd once had such power, but it had vanished from him, and he couldn't press past the barrier he'd created around it. Focusing his mind, he tried again to reach the magic, to emerge from the darkness and step back into understanding.

Spotswood stared at him, seeming to sense the block in his mind. "Why do you fight so?"

"What do you mean?"

"Your magic is wounded. You need to let it heal."

"Heal?" Taren snapped back. "You saw that shadow out there attack me. I don't have time to heal. All I know about magic is pain."

"Magic should never cause pain," Micah spoke up.

Spotswood looked more curious than injured by Taren's sharpness. "But we have never known dark magic as Taren has. Healing and trust come with time."

"Well, time is one thing we don't have." Taren walked out of the tent again, afraid of his own anger. The rain sprinkled down in pathetic spats, cooling his skin and simmering his temper. He slid around the corner until he sat on the wet ground, his head resting against the tent's tethered poll. Scouring the misty gray haze for any movement, he thought wildly about walking through the forest and never turning back.

Surrounded by black, Naomi searched the voices in the dark. A thick curtain shielded her vision and muffled all sound—an argument in the distance, far away in a different world. Her mind searched for it, like running backwards through water. A pain, violently sharp, split her head, but she pressed forward, still searching.

A scream shattered the darkness, a sound of years spent wandering and lost. The ache of longsuffering filling her soul, the black ever-consuming throughout eternity, trapped in the hollow space forever.

And then silence . . . and breath.

The first thing Naomi felt was a soft hand resting in hers, squeezing so gently as to almost not be noticed—delicate, little fingers, cold but caring. She heard the soft murmurs of speech, not arguments; rather, the gentle way one talks to a loved one, soft tones and warm inflections. Naomi didn't know who spoke at first—a musical lilting voice—something she could hear beyond the screaming in her ears. The sound filled her heart.

"Several residents of Southwick have disappeared turning refugee. Others are trapped. The shifting of the magic within the earth confirms my worries. The demons will come from below through the tunnels. It will not take them long."

"That leaves us little time, Uncle," a different voice answered, one higher with a gentle squeak at the end of his phrases. "Dark and light, the two worlds fight. My heart will not sing the morning."

"The magic is preparing. See the calm within her countenance. She is still, while the magic is wild under the surface."

Naomi's eyes slid open a fraction. A gray film clouded her vision. She couldn't find her voice. The words inside her ached to communicate, but not even a cough came from her throat, only breathing—even, silent breathing.

A face loomed down in the haze. "Naomi?" The soft voice rang in her ears like bells. Then she saw the sweet little face looking down at her.

"Naomi? You're awake. She's awake." Lottie turned back to the others in the room. Two dark faces emerged out of the corner of her vision, immediately recognizable.

Micah's bright, wide smile came closer. "Naomi, shining as ever. Careful. You are not well."

Naomi struggled to move her body, a dizzying sensation falling over her when she lifted her head. Every muscle in her body felt tired. But she finally felt her mouth, her tongue at last forming words. "I'll be all right, just faint," she whispered. "I'm glad to see you both." She turned to see Spotswood, anchored on his canes. "I didn't know what happened to you."

"I am not hurt, little one," Spotswood stated with a smile, though she knew it wasn't entirely true. "We are here to help you."

"How did you find me? Tell me everything."

Micah did just that and filled her in with details from the moment they separated from Naomi in the Durundin and traveled with Ferra near the Ravian River. Naomi had forgotten Micah's charming lyrical speech. She smiled inwardly remembering how he looked at the world with such refreshing eyes. She wasn't actually concentrating on his words until he mentioned something that jumpstarted her heart.

"Wait, who did you say?"

"Browneyes," Micah repeated. "She has joined us in the fight."

"Browneyes? The Louving?"

Micah looked at her, concerned. "What is the matter? I like her. She is carefree and world-loving."

Naomi reflected on what she knew about the Louving who had once tracked Reynolds and her through the Blackwoods. Reynolds had admitted persuading her into loving him once. Naomi couldn't remember enough about the battle in the Echoes to place her there, yet there had been a brief conversation with other Louvings when Naomi had heard Reynolds was dead, though he was not. She remembered Browneyes then, the hurt and anger.

And now Browneyes had joined with Ferra to fight alongside the dwarves? An uncomfortable feeling rushed through her stomach and compressed on her heart, squeezing the air tight around her lungs. She had never felt such jealousy before, but it was obvious to her—Browneyes was still in love with Reynolds. It was only logical.

"Where is Browneyes now?"

"With the others at SisterElm."

"Where is SisterElm?" Lottie asked.

"My heart," Micah clasped his hands together. "It is the most wonderful place. Fairies and pixies dance at its feet. And the soil is rich from the days when it was first formed. I've never seen such magic."

Spotswood knelt down closer to Naomi. "The SisterElm is where we must take you before you face the demons in Southwick. It is the heart, little one."

Naomi looked around, still confused. "Is it a village?"

Micah's face brightened. "No. It is a tree."

Naomi's breath evened out, even as the image flashed across her memory. The vision of the woman, the words repeating in her mind, *"Find Pera . . . I will lead you."* Her head cleared and her heart eased. So many unknowns faced her. "I will go," she resolved, trying again to sit up. Her strained effort caused stars in her vision, and she leaned back against the cushions. "I have to rest. I can't move. Where is Taren?"

"He's here, ma'am," Lottie spoke in her quiet voice. "He was just talking to them."

"Can you go find him for me?"

"Of course." Lottie popped up and went through the opening.

Naomi turned her head to Spotswood. "Tell me the danger, Spotswood, now that Lottie is gone. What do you know?"

Spotswood knelt near her. "I traveled from the Durundin to the camp the night we all separated. Lytte knew of the breach in magic and worried for the safety of the camp. We made preparations to leave, but the Louvings came before we could get everyone safe. Several boys perished. We have but a handful of courageous young men ready to aid our quest."

"Where is Lytte?"

"He awaits you at the tree."

Naomi's heart lifted. "He knows what I need to do."

"Magic knows magic." Spotswood smiled, then abruptly asked, "How is your heart?"

The small question brought about a strange quivering, like a tremble within her chest, a sensation she didn't care for and wished would ease. Naomi knew he spoke of her magic. However, confusion blocked a clear answer.

She looked up into his sapphire eyes. "I'm too weak. The magic is draining me. I can't believe how tired I am. But I'm afraid to sleep. Can you help me?"

Spotswood reached into his robes and pulled out a long, thin vial. "This will help you heal and strengthen. Darkness comes quickly, so do not take it until you are ready."

Micah looked around. "I'd like to spend a few days here. I'm surprised that I miss the camp."

"Good memories are good for the soul."

Lottie returned hand in hand with Taren. The look on his face held both terror and relief.

Spotswood stood and headed for the door. "Rest, Princess. We will prepare while you sleep."

Relieved, Naomi faintly smiled. "Taren? Come sit by me."

Micah and Spotswood bowed and exited, leaving just Lottie and Taren again.

Taren hesitated before sitting next to her. "Yes?" His voice was quick, sharp, as if he needed to go and do something else.

Naomi held up the vial. "Help me with this?"

Taren looked at the strange blue liquid before uncorking the vial. His hands trembled as he lifted it to her mouth to drink.

Naomi swallowed hard and then turned her head so she could see him clearly. He would not look into her eyes, just away at some distant thought. "Taren? I'm scared." This admission came out effortlessly in her weakened state. "I'm so scared to sleep. I'm afraid to dream. She will come again. She will take me."

Taren frowned, not comprehending. "Who is she? No one will take you away."

Naomi reached for his hand. "Please. Stay by me. Don't let me leave. I'm not ready."

He grabbed it without any hesitation, a firm grip that curled around her delicate fingers. The heat from his skin warmed her immediately, confusing her again. "You aren't going anywhere."

"Stay by me. Watch me. Your magic can find me. Bring me back."

Taren looked more scared than Naomi felt. "I won't let anyone take you. Never again."

Naomi held his gaze, the warmth in her chest easing before she fell into a deep, dreamless sleep.

CHAPTER SEVEN

Brilliant magic swirling . . .
       White heat in red veins . . .
Elegant rapture of joy
Peace
        She heals strong.
    Her wisdom grows.
    She has no fear. She is the wind, the ocean, the sky.
She hears all, she is all.
    Hope within intertwining light, streaking through visions of those
she loves.

                        Zander
                Landon
     Katia
                   Ferra

. . . Reynolds
. . . Taren
The clear voice resonating through bone.
"Sleep now, little daughter of evening."
"Be troubled no longer."

Taren didn't leave Naomi's side. He stayed just as she'd wished and watched her as she slept. The magic that still rested within the Vivatera hovered in thin, wispy spirals around her body, circulating protectively. Changing like a butterfly from its chrysalis.

Lottie wandered in and out as Naomi slept, checking to see if she was awake before exploring the ruins of the camp. Eventually she returned with something in her hands.

"The rain dried a little. I made her this." She lifted a circlet of petals and placed it gently around Naomi's head. "I collected little spirit leaves and the tiny white flowers growing by the well." She brushed away a stray hair from Naomi's face before leaving the tent again.

Taren looked down upon Naomi's sleeping form. The crown made her look lovely, angelic, ethereal—like a vision from a heavenly plain.

And that was the truth of it, Taren thought. Naomi didn't belong in this world. She wasn't real, more like a dream. The magic would destroy her, and the beautiful woman lying before him would be erased from this world.

Taren knelt close to her, watching and waiting. These might be his last moments with her.

"I'm sorry," slipped from his lips, even knowing she was not awake to hear the words.

The memory of Naomi removing the dark magic from him struck like a painful blow to the chest, knocking away his breath. She'd forgiven him freely. Forgiveness, the one thing he couldn't understand, she taught with selfless acts every day. For that he couldn't stop thinking about her, and for her to be in a state of perpetual sleep haunted him. He felt helpless and useless.

Taren gently took her hand in his. He pressed the back of her palm to his cheek without any jolt of energy as before. Feeling the warmth of her skin renewed his will. She was alive and strong, growing stronger. The magic would understand if she wasn't.

"Please come back."

A surge of energy came from her hand to his, and a white magic blinded his vision. He dropped her hand and stood up. "Naomi?" He had never before felt pure, intense heat like that. He shook his head, but the vision stayed clear in his mind—something he couldn't understand. A wind of intense feeling beyond his comprehension fell upon him. "Naomi? Are you there?"

Taren felt his legs buckle, and everything went black.

The long echo started soft. A whisper grew louder and louder until it surrounded him, filling his head with murmuring voices over and over.

"She belongs to the earth. You cannot have her."

Taren saw a bead of light within the darkness. He felt propelled forward through the tunnel. The light grew closer until it surrounded him.

A woman stood before him, dressed in sparkling gold. The person took on the appearance of Naomi, but it wasn't her. There was no heart, no life-force like the voracious energy he felt within her skin.

"What are you?"

"I am the Everstar."

"No." Taren felt his anger rise. "There is no Everstar. It's not a person—"

"It is what I choose to be." The woman stared down with piercing eyes. *"I am a protector, and I choose to protect her from you. You are a threat to her safety and to her heart. The Everstar combines the six elements. I feel every danger, every feeling, every emotion within each I touch. You are not to be trusted. You understand dark magic and corruption. She is pure and should not know such evil."*

"But I won't hurt her. Never again."

The Everstar reached out her arms, rippling waves of gold shimmering with majesty. *"You are hurting her now. Her pain grows deeper."*

"I-I . . ." Taren stammered. "I'm trying to understand her."

"You are a destroyer and do not understand the delicacy of magic. You exposed her to dead souls. You stabbed her. You bled her. She knows sorrow and pain. You have created this in her."

Taren felt her words like a knife in the chest. "When did I . . . I didn't know what would happen."

"Your actions were thoughtless. You have corrupted her."

"But, the magic . . ." Taren fought for breath. "It told me to act. It told me to stab her. The Vivatera needed to be whole."

"You are wrong!" The last word rang like a bell in his ears. The Everstar grew in size, her anger glowing. *"The Vivatera*

acted in desperation because of your selfish magic. You, who cannot understand the balance of the world, followed foolish instructions and used your dagger to pierce her heart. Her heart that beat strong in her chest bled because of your revenge. That is not understanding. It is your naïve answer to the catastrophic events which have plagued this world. You have caused her too much pain. She should not have suffered at all."

"I didn't . . ." Taren shook his head. "I didn't know. How could I? I knew nothing beyond my own magic." He whispered, almost to himself, "Naomi understands."

"Your love is foolish. You have cursed yourself. You love her out of guilt."

"No!" The Everstar smoldered in his glare. "I don't know how not to love her. She took away the dark magic. She believes in me when I can't believe in myself. She is perfect—"

"There is no one on this world who deserves her."

"That doesn't matter." Taren felt his determination rise. "She has a choice."

Heat shone in her expression. *"She has chosen. There is no way you can save her. She will choose regardless of your love for her."*

Taren went to speak but felt a tug backward and tumbled away from her, down through the tunnel into black.

"Taren?"

He heard the voice surrounding him. His body felt heavy, weighed down by exhaustion.

"Taren, are you okay?"

Taren opened his eyes. He saw the face looking down at him. Her face. Was he still in the dream? But almost immediately he knew this was not the Everstar. The kind warmth and concern in her eyes told a different story—and the circlet of flowers still sat like a crown on her head.

"Naomi." He blinked and tried to sit up. She moved to help him. For a moment he just stared at her, trying to come back from the vision of the Everstar. His mind was still filled with her anger toward him. "Are you all right?"

Naomi smiled. "I feel amazing."

"How long have you been awake?"

"Not long." She examined Taren, looking in his eyes, searching for something. "I thought I saw you in my dream. I saw you, but then you vanished."

Taren couldn't hide his desperation. "Tell me. Tell me about your experience."

"Not yet." She smiled and looked away, lost in some deep thought. "Can you stand?"

"I'm fine. I'm fatigued, that's all."

Lottie came rushing in. "You're awake!" She hugged Naomi fiercely. "I'm so happy you're okay. I made you this." In her hands was a string of snow berries and pine nuts. "It should bring you luck."

Naomi placed it around her neck. "Do I have you to thank for the wreath as well?" Lottie curtsied awkwardly. "You are so thoughtful. Thank you, Lottie."

"Now can we go? I'm terribly bored."

Naomi laughed. "I'm ready. Here. Let's help Taren stand up."

"No!" Taren protested, recalling how Lottie could find out his secrets with her touch. "Sorry, no. I can do this."

He pressed his palms on the ground and lifted himself. He felt drained but shook it off.

He looked back at Naomi, who focused on him with a peculiar gaze.

"Are you okay?" she asked again.

"Yes." Taren brushed off his clothes and walked out of the tent.

Spotswood and Micah had searched the camp for anything useful. They had found several items which might be handy. When Micah saw Naomi walking, he jumped up and ran to her. "How did you sleep, my princess?"

Naomi held him quick. "I'm well. Spotswood is wonderful. I'm rested and ready for anything."

"We have readied the fire-eater as well," Micah stated with enthusiasm. "We filled his belly with warm coal, and he is anxious to fly."

"I worried that we wore him out in the flight here."

"A little warmth and he will be fine," Taren said from behind him. "Sebastian and I understand each other."

"How far is SisterElm?" Naomi asked.

"Two days' journey on foot, but with a dragon, we will be there before supper."

"Good. I don't want to waste any time." She took Lottie by the hand and walked toward a grove of trees.

Taren watched her. The sight of her hand in hand with little Lottie tore at his heart. She glanced back at him. Her eyes met his for the briefest moment. Something had happened in her sleep; he couldn't tell what, but the weight of the world no longer rested on her shoulders. She had focus and determination. She was fearless.

They walked with Micah and Spotswood into the trees. Taren followed but stopped and turned around for one last look. The camp that he had known for years no longer stood. The buildings now lay in piles of broken wood and ash. He had no love for the place. He'd hated his time there, pining and waiting, dreaming of escape. He only regretted not taking the opportunity to understand more about the magic which had shaped his life. He could have learned it there, but instead he suffered silently and focused on destroying his enemy. In the end, his enemy had proven to not be Reynolds, but the magic within his soul.

The camp should burn and all the memories with it.

Taren turned his back and walked into the forest, hoping never to see the Willows again.

Sebastian lay in a field close by, the embers of fire smoldering in a small pile next to him. Spotswood had taken the camp ruins and burned them, feeding what he could to the creature. When the dragon saw Taren, his head rose like a dog obeying his master.

"Firebrand," Spotswood identified, looking up from the cinders. He nodded to Taren respectfully. "The gift of fire is an honor."

Taren looked at him, a question that had plagued him springing to mind. "How do you understand magic so well?"

"Outlanders know many things we should not know."

"So, you didn't study with Lytte in Southwick?"

"No, I did not. I am Arenma. I am the earth, and I will return."

Taren listened for the truth in between his words. "The earth. You are earth?"

"I talk to the earth, and I listen. It knows everything. It knows how we got to now. I will not rise from ashes. I will return to the dust under my feet."

"I . . ." Taren didn't know how else to say it. "Do you think Naomi is made from the earth?"

Spotswood's wise eyes landed on him. "Magic is organic, and she is very magical. It makes up you too."

"But not like her. She's different."

"Yes." Spotswood's face told the truth within the wrinkles. "If you would like—she is life, all three: earth, surface, sky. You . . . you are not."

"So, she can die because she's part of the earth? But I will—"

"Earth is not an enemy, Firebrand. Learn of your gift. Death is not an end, but a beginning," Spotswood finished. With that he made a simple, sad nod, ending his communication, and hobbled away toward the others.

Taren stared blankly, confounded by his words. Walking to Sebastian, he laid his hand near his snout, feeling the hot breath steam out. "Did you hear that, Seb? Fire is a gift." He patted him like any other animal and felt glad he had someone else who understood him.

CHAPTER EIGHT

Ferra tossed and turned all night. The tree cover wasn't enough to keep the rain from soaking through. Paolo seemed unaffected by the moisture, hunched into a ball, unaware she needed comfort.

When light started to appear on the horizon, Ferra sat up and was surprised to see Browneyes already awake, staring at nothing.

Ferra stood and looked toward the south. The tall flags of Southwick stood in the distance, surrounded by high rock barriers. They could be there before nightfall. Last night they had seen a moving mountain with glowing eyes. Now out in the distance, trees and grass dotted the hillock, nothing out of the ordinary. She looked down at

Browneyes, who sat cross-legged and looking as ornery and tired as she felt. "What do you think?"

Browneyes raised an eyebrow. "I think they travel at night."

"But you definitely think it was demons?"

"Yes. Or something like it." She pointed to a blackened trail, now soaked through, which traveled up and over the hill.

Ferra leaned against a branch, thinking. Whatever Sharrod was planning would be bigger than she anticipated. They had to hurry.

"Do you think Paolo can carry me?" Browneyes asked.

"Yes, but he's rather grumpy in the morning if he hasn't eaten."

"Does he like rabbit?" Browneyes held up a carcass dangling on a stick.

"Yes, but that won't be enough."

"Well, do you like rabbit?"

Ferra smiled and sat down. The ground was too wet for a fire, so she took what care she could in chewing the raw meat. After a few attempts, she couldn't eat any more and went in search of food in her pack. She found a few soggy biscuits and felt satisfied.

Paolo bristled awake and galumphed around, scavenging for food.

Ferra patted the big brute before he lumbered off, then took a seat against the trunk and watched the rain. It had lightened considerably since nightfall. Only the faint *tap tap* on the leaves would make it through the branches.

Browneyes finished her rabbit leg and went back to her pack. She pulled out something Ferra had forgotten about:

a small velvet bag. She opened it very carefully and whispered.

Ferra sat up, watching a tiny fairy as big as her small finger climb onto Browneyes' hand. "And what are you going to do with that?"

"Feed her." Browneyes took out some sesame seeds from her cloak. The tiny fairy glowed bright red with excitement and took a quick buzz around before landing in her palm, picking at the food. "Shouldn't you have more compassion for living creatures?"

"Well, a fairy bit me once. I've never forgotten it."

Browneyes snickered. "You probably deserved it."

Ferra shrugged. "But seriously, what do you think you can do with a fairy?"

Browneyes walked over and presented the fairy to Ferra. "Well, this is Thayda, and she is extremely rare, from the vriessa lily that grows on the Butterfly Islands. She is a seeker."

Ferra bent down closer to see the vibrant red petals wrapped around the gentle body and laced wings. "And I'm guessing a seeker finds stuff."

"Very good," Browneyes quipped.

"So, let me guess, you want to use this fairy to find Reynolds?"

A sly grin crossed her face. "All you need is something of the person you want to find, and she will lead you to them."

"Makes sense, but do you have something of Reynolds'?"

Browneyes reached around her neck and pulled out her chain with the different vials of blood. She had four vials: one empty and three completely full.

Ferra paled. "Wait, you have his blood?"

"Yes, of course."

"When . . .?"

"Oh, I chased him down after he stashed that girlfriend of his in that magical camp. He knows I have it, but I never intend on changing into him. I just wanted something to remind me of him."

Ferra stared at the vial, not knowing what to think. She'd dismissed much of her anxiety about traveling with a Louving, but it all came rushing back.

"And that's another thing," Browneyes focused on Ferra. "I've been thinking about your idea."

"My idea?"

"About me taking some of your blood. I have an empty vial now. Might as well use it."

An uncomfortable pit grew in Ferra's usually calm stomach. "I knew you were up to something the moment I let you come with us. You've wanted my blood all along."

"It was your idea." Browneyes straightened up, frightening the fairy from her hand and sending her streaking in flight. "I've been thinking about it. What a ruse. There will be two of you."

"But there's no point to it."

"Sure there is. Southwick knows me. Louvings have been working for the king for years. They won't know you."

"How long does it work?"

"It varies. The older it gets the less useful it is, but fresh blood lasts the longest. As long as the blood lives within me."

"That could be days."

"I know." Browneyes' smile widened. "Let me try."

Ferra's hands went to her face. What had she gotten into? She quickly tried to think. She hated the plan, but what else could she do?

"Okay, but I need to set up some rules."

"Of course." Her sly eyes batted with anticipation.

"It will only be the image of me, right?"

"I'll look like you, but my voice and actions, that's all mine."

"Okay. I don't want you saying you are me unless you're trying to protect me or my sisters. Got it?"

"Cross my heart." Browneyes made the action with her hands.

Ferra huffed. "Oh, merciful gods, what am I doing?"

Browneyes rummaged through her pack until she uncovered a thin blade wrapped in strips of cloth. "Okay, stick out your hand."

Already second-guessing her decision, Ferra stuck out her hand and looked away.

A moment later, the knife pressed down firmly into the center of her palm.

"Ow!" Blood dribbled down Ferra's hand. Browneyes already had her vial out, catching the delicate stream as it traveled down her skin.

"That should do." Browneyes evaluated the newly filled bottle. "Here." She threw the cloth to her. "Bandage it up tight. I don't want any of that precious magical blood spilling unnecessarily."

Ferra wrapped the cloth around her hand and stuffed it under her arm to dull the pain. Her eyes focused on the red blood, *her* blood, settling in the vial. A drop or two covered the outside close to Browneyes' fingertips. "Well?"

"Now?"

"Why not?"

Browneyes couldn't hide the excitement in her eyes. She took the tiny vial and tipped it to her lips. She only used a small portion before corking the bottle and hanging it on her chain.

She stood and began to spin. The magic reacted differently than with the wolf. Instead of black fur, she saw yellow light spinning around. The threads of her clothing transformed to browns and greens. The sticks and leaves which surrounded them rose from the ground, gathering in her hair and skin. The spinning slowed, and Browneyes stood across from her laughing.

But it wasn't Browneyes, it was Ferra—a copy just like her.

"That's amazing."

Browneyes arched her eyebrow, still in her usual manner. "I'm very observant. Using leaves around was my own personal touch." She blew on her nails before she examined her hands and arms. Thayda, the seeker fairy, returned to her hand and grabbed onto her thumb, unfazed by the difference in appearance. "Look at that. She doesn't seem to care that I look like you."

"Hopefully she won't bite you." Ferra didn't know if she could get used to this. The blood had made a very good illusion, but it couldn't fool everyone, much like Reynolds' medallion, which he had used in the Echoes. It was thin-layered magic, and she could tell the difference.

"Show me your neck?" Ferra asked.

Browneyes turned. Right below her hairline was nothing: no star on her skin, no medallion hang around her neck. Instead, it appeared as it would if Ferra hadn't been touched by magic.

Paolo returned, happier and ready for a run, and before long Ferra and Browneyes were racing up the hillsides toward the palace. Browneyes, every so often, would lift her hands to the sky, thoroughly enjoying the ride.

They rode on for a while, only stopping for a drink in a shallow pool. Soon Paolo began to grunt as if he sensed something.

"What's wrong with your animal?" Browneyes complained at the sudden irritable huffing.

"Someone's near." Ferra stepped off Paolo in order to look around. She crouched down near the slope of the hill. Brushing past the shrubs, she could see the outlining wall at the border of Southwick. Several tents lined the edge, military tents like the ones up by the Durundin. Men in uniform worked, guarding the wall. At the back corner stood many creatures, black as night with brilliant, fiery eyes.

Ferra watched as Browneyes surveyed the scene. Before they could decide what to do, someone yelled.

"Right there!" he shouted, pointing in their direction. Both girls ducked their heads.

Paolo gave an enormous growl, a sound Ferra had never heard coming from him. He tromped down away from Ferra, away from safety. She stood to run after him, but Browneyes grabbed her arm, holding her back.

Several soldiers ran after the beast, weapons in hand.

Paolo . . . Ferra had been separated from him before, but this felt different; the danger pressed against her chest. *Be safe, my friend.*

"Come on." She felt a tugging on her shoulder. "Hurry, before they come back."

Browneyes pulled her to her feet and pushed her forward. They quickly dashed around the trees and down to the nearest tent. Those occupying it had left after Paolo. Inside was rather empty—only cots to sleep on and water to drink. Browneyes helped herself.

"What should we do now?"

"Can you see an opening?" Browneyes asked between swallows.

Ferra opened the door flap and searched. The only archway she could see was near the black demons. "I don't want to go that way."

"Well, do you have any magic you could use, or something?"

The medallion around her neck felt heavier than usual. She couldn't use it, not when she was so close to Southwick.

Then again, she was sick of being the daughter everyone expected. Seeing Browneyes, the exact image of her, without the mark, made her realize what a hard life she had lived to get her here. She had already allowed Browneyes to change into her. What could using her medallion do?

Ferra took both hands and grabbed on to her medallion. The magic surged through her, the energy cautiously waiting, anticipating action.

A hot spasm of pain ripped through her back. She gasped and stumbled backward to the ground. Blood—she tasted blood in her mouth as she struggled for breath.

"I'll take that." Browneyes stood over her, her foot rotating Ferra onto her side. In her hand she held a thin blade, her other hand yanking the medallion free from Ferra's neck. "It took some time, but it worked perfectly."

Ferra's eyes went blurry with pain. Her medallion. Lost. Everything.

Lost.

CHAPTER NINE

Reynolds woke to his cell door swinging open. Dim light filtered across his face from a distant torch hanging far down the dungeon corridor.

"Up, you!" demanded a gruff voice. A large shadow stood over him, kicking as he lay in the dark. "Someones wants to talk to yas."

Reynolds lifted up on his elbows and stared at the guard. "I'm not interested in talking."

"Don't matter. Up!" He sank his foot in his ribs.

Reynolds heaved in his breath, a sharp pain running up his side. He gathered his strength and stood again. "Another round of beatings?" The routine was getting a bit tiresome.

"Not today," the gruff guard snapped. "Bigger plans for yas."

"Ooo, scary."

The guard punched him in the gut for his smart mouth. Reynolds buckled again, coughing for air. When he bent over, someone threw a blindfold over his eyes and tied his hands behind his back.

A rough hand shoved him, and he stumbled forward, scraping his shoulder against harsh stone. He then felt the tug of someone leading him through the tunnels and stairs that made up the dungeon. This was his fourth time, and he began to memorize the directions: the stair pattern with the small steps near the end, the narrow passage, then the sloped wall, and finally the clicking of boots on marble.

Once he reached the marble, Reynolds knew where he was. He'd grown up in Southwick. While in the shroud of darkness behind the blindfold, Reynolds recalled tender childhood memories searching out the palace for every secret it held. True, some of the stone walls had been rebuilt over time, but the skeleton of his old adventures still remained, and this pleased him very much.

Instead of being led right to the torture chamber, Reynolds felt his body shoved left and dragged up a rounded stairway—*The East Parapet*. No one went up that way unless he was royalty. With the king nicely out of the way, he might finally be taken to see Sharrod.

The stairs felt never-ending. The pain in his shin from the kick he'd received became a throb. Finally, he reached a landing and headed forward. The blindfold was ripped off, and he saw he stood in the Hall of Kings, a place he knew but was forbidden to go as a child. It was a large room full of portraits of the great kings and leaders. Now, several of the images had burn marks through their faces as if etched out from history, Reinoh's included.

Near the large glass window stood a girl about sixteen. She wore a long green cloak which matched her flashing eyes, her red hair tied up in a knot to highlight her pointed ears, markings of a Louving.

"Well." Reynolds took a look around. "I should have been prepared to meet someone like you messing with the likes of Sharrod."

The girl stared back, evaluating. "He pays well."

"Not as well as you think."

The girl flicked her nails, bored. "I'm Audra, and I've been waiting a long time to meet you."

"And why's that?" Reynolds wasn't intimidated by this girl, even if she was a dangerous ally to the enemy.

"Seems like you cause trouble." She stood tall, evaluating him. "I like trouble."

Reynolds laughed, at least outwardly. "I've been caught up with Louvings before. Yeah. Not interested."

"That's not the kind of trouble I mean."

Reynolds grew tired of the back and forth. "Look, what do you want?"

"I want information." Audra walked forward, dragging her hand across the layered stone. Reynolds watched her eyes intensify, narrowing like a snake on its prey. "Sharrod is keeping you around because he knows you can tell us where to find the missing stones."

The emptiness returned to Reynolds' heart, the kind of pain he couldn't get over. "I won't tell you anything. I'm prepared to die with my tongue tied. I gave up this war. The only reason for it died, as Sharrod knows."

The girl stopped before him. Her look and manner reminded him of Browneyes, of the evil, twisted heart that knew nothing of kindness, only revenge. "He blames you, you know, for the death of his soulmate."

She was referring to the fight in Mount Ignis and the destruction of the goddess of fire, Alene.

"I was there, but it wasn't my knife that sent her back to the Under-realm. That knife belonged to Lockwood. Not me."

"Lockwood's son was useful in killing the girl." Audra gave a small, delighted laugh. "A pity, losing such an ally."

Reynolds' blood began to boil. He tried to reach for her, but the rope held his arms tight together.

"Get to the point," he demanded, sick of playing her game.

"We've run into a few problems." Audra took a seat on a large bench and kicked her feet up. "Everyone knows that the daughters of Prolius are planning to return to Southwick and restore the magic. But it looks as though there's missing text from the Histories that talk about how this can be done."

Reynolds knew all this but didn't know it had reached the ears of the capital. He said nothing.

She continued, "He had men search the Willows, but they found nothing about it in any of Lytte's scrolls."

A new pain started in Reynolds' heart; this time it felt fear. He calmed his pulse and revealed nothing.

"And with Lytte's suicide, we can only turn to you, his prodigy, for answers."

"Lytte's dead?" He couldn't help the words.

Audra gave a mocking pout. She twisted in her seat to look at him better. "It hurts when we lose the ones closest to us."

Reynolds felt fire beginning to burn beneath his skin. "Louvings are heartless. Why would you ever think I would help you?"

An odd smile crossed her face. Audra snapped her fingers. A guard near the door shuffled in someone: a small boy, no more than ten, with auburn hair and almond eyes. Reynolds looked at him in confusion. Why would she send in a boy?

A guard shoved Reynolds into a seat and placed the boy in front of him. The look on the boy's face was distant, far removed from the world. His eyes were the lightest blue he had ever seen—nearly white, like Jeanus' eyes, the sight of the plane of magic.

The Louving stood up and placed her hands on the boy's shoulders. "Say hello, Vanya," she commanded.

The boy looked Reynolds in the eyes, then away. "You are Reynolds Fairborne," he stated without any hint of a Salt Dune accent, though his eyes slanted at the corners like the people of the region.

Reynolds frowned at him, curious. "How do you know this, Vanya?"

"I can tell a lot about you."

"Surprise me."

Vanya rubbed his fingertips together, like a nervous twitch. He went to place them on Reynolds' forehead, but he flinched away from the child's hand. What could this kid do?

A guard from behind grabbed Reynolds' head and forced it still. The little boy came forward, ready to touch him.

With every effort he had, Reynolds raised the magic inside him to shield any information from betraying him.

Vanya's hand felt warm on his temples. Reynolds gritted his teeth, holding in the secrets.

"I see you are sad," the boy explained. "You have lost many people in your life. And you fear you have lost a treasure."

Reynolds strained to hold the shield in place. He tried to push Naomi as far from the surface as he could.

"What treasure?" Audra had a greedy look in her eye.

Reynolds' heartrate tripled. He didn't want to hear about his failures. He couldn't let his mind dwell on her. He forced it back, staring into the boy's eyes. Letting the magic scan him, fearing nothing.

The boy blinked, amused. "You believe it is lost, but it is not."

Reynolds started. "What?"

"The treasure is glowing brighter than before. I can see it."

This was just a trick meant to make him lose focus—though a tiny flicker of hope kindled in the base of his heart. "Prove it."

Audra's hands tightened.

Vanya's engaging eyes changed, transfixing Reynolds, pounding him with vision upon vision.

Naomi flying on a dragon, standing on the top of an ancient tree, running from an unseen enemy . . .

Reynolds lost his breath. He couldn't hold the shield any more. It crumbled inside him.

He tried as hard as he could to communicate to Vanya through thought.

"Please," Reynolds heaved. "Please, don't show me any more."

Vanya lifted his hand, taking away the visions.

Audra snickered. "He's very handy. He can see the world of magic and spot things that you can't."

Reynolds feared what Vanya might say next, but the boy lifted his eyes and looked toward the window.

"Gaythor?" Audra shouted at the guard behind Reynolds. "I think poor Reynolds Fairborne has lost his spirit today. Let's keep him locked in the East Corridor until we can get all his secrets."

Reynolds felt his body move upward. Audra was right; he had lost his spirit to fight.

He looked back at Vanya. A sharp pang of jealousy ran throughout his body, wishing to see the visions again, just one more time.

Reynolds studied his small accommodations. It was better than the cell in the dungeon but it still left him with the same predicament. The room had a small window, too high to climb to and too small to fit through. Layered brick closed off the room from the rest of the palace, sealing it tight with a thick door, latched and guarded. Figuring out the lock wouldn't be a problem, but the heavy metal bar would require strategy.

It had been a few days since he had first met Vanya and felt the piercing invasion of his magic. The experience continued to haunt him. He had never before felt so exposed.

Reynolds let his mind wander instead to Naomi. She had made it through the fire and survived. He remembered once again all the idiotic things he'd done to drive her away, all the precautions he'd taken that only drove her further from him. He had treated her like a little girl, something fragile, but she was strong and beautiful and smart. Regret washed over him again, every wave accompanied by a bitter sting.

The room closed in around him, trapping Reynolds in his thoughts. The only time he could be released from his haunting memories was when someone came to the door, and every time he hoped it would be the boy. Reynolds' mind dwelled on questions he couldn't answer, but the boy could, the biggest one—why did he refer to Naomi as his treasure?

A knock came at the door, shattering his current thoughts. "Good morning, Reynolds."

Audra's voice set his plan in motion. He sat up, ready. "Is it? I wouldn't know."

The creaking of the door echoed off stone as Audra entered and slid into a seat at the small table.

"Well, look at you." She propped her back against the wall. "Looks like you've made yourself at home. Much better than your old home, don't you think?"

"I don't know. I had fewer Louvings to deal with."

Audra pouted. "You should be nicer to me."

"I see no reason." Reynolds hated her childish banter. "You came here. What do you want?"

"Oh . . ." She stirred her finger lazily over the dust on the table. "Well, maybe Sharrod wants to see you."

"Fine. Perfect. Let's go."

Audra sat up. "But don't you want to know why?"

"Nope." Reynolds stood, preparing to leave. "I wouldn't waste that conversation on you."

"But what if he wants to kill you?"

"I understand that. A lot of people do."

Audra slid off the table. "You're very peculiar, you know. Don't you care that you're about to die?"

"No. I'm always about to die." He cracked a half smile. "Oh, Audra, are you of so little consequence that you have to make up lies?"

"Lies?" She looked like a cornered cat.

"I know you have nothing to do with Sharrod. He doesn't want to see me."

Audra's jaw dropped. She attempted to collect herself. "Yes, he does."

Reynolds stared down at the girl. "Sharrod doesn't know I'm up here, does he? He wouldn't trust you with such an important job. I think you're working for someone else."

"I don't know what you're talking about. Of course I'm working for him. He trusts me with his life."

"Then why hasn't he asked to see me until now?"

Audra shuffled. "He's been busy."

"Busy? I don't think so. Lying again. You're terrible at it."

"No! I can't reach him. None of us can right now. It takes a lot of energy."

"Energy? He's already a demon, what would he need energy for?"

"Because he's trans—" she stumbled on the words and bit her lip.

"Trans . . .?"

Audra visibly flinched. "Transforming."

Reynolds couldn't contain his triumphant grin. "And why would he have to transform?"

Audra paled. "Because *he* is coming."

"And who is *he?*" Reynolds shot back. "I thought Sharrod was the one controlling the elements, the one who needed the stones. There is no 'he.' "

Audra began to tremble. Reynolds had struck a chord within her.

She started to say something but looked around first, then motioned him closer. "It is *he.* The one you fear in the dark corners of your room, in the mist when you are in the forest alone. He is the reason Sharrod is seeking the stones. With all the stones, Sharrod can open the portal to bring him back from the Underworld."

Reynolds' face fell. She was serious. He began putting the pieces together. "Are you telling me Sharrod is trying to bring Shon to the surface?" He couldn't believe it—Shon, the creator of evil, the ancient demon who murdered his own sister to gain control of the world. The old histories sounded too much like a folk story to actually be true. The information was a game changer, bigger than Naomi's life and combining the magic. "I don't believe you."

"It's true. I've heard Sharrod talking to him."

Reynolds tried to imagine it, but couldn't: the thought was inconceivable. "Do you know what Shon will do?"

Audra looked frightened. "I have an idea."

"Tell me."

"Forget it." Audra smacked away his hand and walked closer to the door. "I'm never going to help you."

"Then why are you helping Sharrod?"

"Because I know I'm on the winning side."

"There is no winning side. Shon was banished to the Underworld for a reason." Reynolds' mind started reeling with the possibilities.

Audra went for the door, but Reynolds darted forward and grabbed her wrists. "I thought you were taking me to see Sharrod."

"Let go of me."

Loosening his grip, Reynolds softened his expression and tried to play nice. "Audra, don't leave me in here when I know I can help."

"I don't need your help." She struggled to free herself.

"A favor then, please, before demons take over the world. Send Vanya in here. I want to talk to him."

Audra slipped through his grip and pulled on the door. The two guards came to attention at the sound. She looked back at him, and the door slammed shut.

It was near nightfall when Reynolds heard the knock at the chamber door. He sat up, staring toward the lantern light.

Audra entered. Behind her the little boy followed, silently peering in the darkening room with eyes as bright as stars.

Reynolds looked to Audra. "Can I speak to him alone?"

"No. Whatever gave you the idea that you could?"

Reynolds didn't have the energy to fight. Time was running out. "Fine. But if anything gets back to Sharrod, you are dead. I will see to that personally. Understand?"

Audra glared but remained silent.

Vanya sat cross-legged in front of Reynolds, looking distant and ethereal. "Reynolds Fairborne, you have asked to see me."

"Yes. I have questions, and I hope you can answer them."

Vanya straightened his back. "I am ready."

Reynolds bit his lip. "I want to ask you about your magic," he began. "How were you introduced to it?"

Audra piped up. "He's not going to know—"

Reynolds shushed her.

Vanya looked at Audra and then back to Reynolds. "I will tell you. I know where my magic started. I have memory of it."

Reynolds focused on his questions. "How old were you, Vanya?"

"I was an infant."

"How do you remember?" Audra asked, but Reynolds stared at her and quieted her questions.

Vanya turned back to Audra. "The magic is much older than I. It knows how to remember."

Reynolds sat back, listening. "Tell me about it."

"I was given it medicinally, to make my cough go away, by my mother. I remember her crying, thinking I would die. I think of those sad tears of hers on my cheeks. That is the only memory I have of her. A wet nurse, a woman who did not care for me, raised me while I lived in the palace. When I was five she presented me to the king. I became a strategic advisor to King Reinoh and Commander Lockwood when I was seven. Now, I am nine."

"And why have you stayed?"

Vanya tilted his head, contemplating. "Where was I to go? I know that I have insight but I am still a boy."

Reynolds acknowledged the question had been foolish. "So, you advised them where to seek the stones."

"Yes. I can see them. They are traveling closer. When they were separate, hidden, I couldn't find them, just the feel of magic within an area." He closed his eyes. "As they unite together, the magic grows stronger and more brilliant. I can see them, all but one. Sharrod has just obtained another; I can see it close to the first lost."

"Another one?" Reynolds despaired at the thought. He ran his fingers through his hair. "Why did you tell Sharrod where they were?"

The boy looked through him, as if he knew the answer. "It is time, Reynolds Fairborne. It is time for the mistakes of the past to be refastened and become whole once more."

Reynolds frowned, switching directions. "What about your magic, Vanya? Will you tell me how it works?"

Vanya bowed in respect. "I can see the plane where magic is visible. I can read magic in people, much like you, but my knowledge is greater."

"And why is that, do you think?"

"I was an infant when I received it. It grew as I have grown."

Grew as I have grown. This information folded around Reynolds' heart. An infant, just as Naomi had been when he sealed her fate. Memories stirred his emotions until he lost focus. He sat in silence for a moment until he realized his composure had dropped, then quickly pushed back his feelings and moved on.

"The other day, you hesitated when you talked to me about my treasure."

The boy's chin raised, his eyes narrowing. "I know what you ask, and it is impossible. I cannot tell you the future. The chain of actions has begun."

"Then what can we do about it?"

Vanya's eyes intensified. "Act with them."

"If, like Audra says, the Underlord Shon comes to the surface, then no one will be safe."

Vanya placed his hand on Reynolds' arm, an odd gesture for the boy to comfort a grown man. "Then we need to be prepared. The Everstar is the only way, and it is because of you that we have her."

Reynolds felt shame wash through him. "I didn't know about that."

The boy smiled the awkward grin of a growing boy. "The world will remember you as a hero if she succeeds."

"Is she safe?" Reynolds couldn't help but ask. "I didn't know. I should have been there. I was so stupid—"

"Safer than any being alive."

Reynolds exhaled. Peace entered in his chest at his words. He believed him without question. "Will you join me?"

"I will help as I have."

Reynolds turned to Audra, who had heard everything but remained oddly silent. "And what about you?"

"Me?" she spat back. "I'm not going to do anything. Just like I promised."

Hunching her shoulder, Audra moved to the door and snapped her fingers. Immediately the guards rushed inside the chamber, grappling Reynolds to the ground.

Reynolds braced himself. The massive weight of the charging guards pushed him back into the brick. His magic acted on instinct, predicting every move and counter-move. He quickly dodged each blow that came for him. He slid away from the wall with precision. Parrying around one guard, he pushed the other sideways and grabbed a knife from his sheath. He positioned himself between the guards and Vanya, the knife posed to strike.

Reynolds backed toward the door and grabbed the boy to his side. One guard started to charge but Reynolds edged out of the door, slamming the latch down in place.

He searched the corridor. Audra had completely vanished.

CHAPTER TEN

Katia lowered her head and crawled through the small stone arch. The smell of stagnant sea water, thick with briny, dead waste stung her nostrils. The stink overpowered her, and she felt her throat tighten, forcing back whatever was left in her stomach. She covered her nose and mouth.

The sea water came in and washed out through small portals near the bottom of the stone walls. The still water gently lapped against the rock, echoing the fall of wave on wave. A delicate ridge of brick lined the singular archways to the opposite side, where water and other foul garbage collected from the exiting drains.

"Are you kidding?" Her whisper carried around in echoes. She turned to Landon. "We have to crawl over there?"

Landon's toothy grin could be seen in the dark. He didn't reply, just kept crawling. She followed, Fontine and Wenlock trailing after her.

She concentrated on her movement, hand over hand, grabbing the rock edge. The hard surface hurt her knees, and she wobbled time and again, afraid she might fall into the congealed sea water. The harsh memory of crawling through the muddy sludge out of the Durundin came to her mind. Next to that experience, this seemed tame.

A narrow path above the arches led to a tiny staircase. Landon grabbed ahold and pulled himself up, then helped the others reach the ledge. Wenlock dangled briefly, but Landon had the strength to pull him up.

They sat and rested.

"Look familiar?" Landon asked.

Fontine stared at him, not knowing what to say.

"He's just making a joke," Katia clarified.

Fontine stood up without responding and examined the stone around them. "Do you see this?" She pointed to the wall right behind where the narrow staircase started.

"We can all see the stairs," Katia replied.

"No, the stone." She smoothed her hand around it. "This stonework is different from that one."

"What are you getting at?" Landon asked, studying the differences.

"Southwick is built in layers. Every time there was a war, they didn't remake it, they built over it." She pushed against the staircase wall, testing it. "This one is older than others. A wall was built right in the middle. So these stairs may not lead anywhere."

"Or they might lead to secret passages."

Katia frowned. "Do you really want to test it? We may all get stuck."

"How else do we get into the palace?"

Fontine got on her knees and bent her head down to examine the stone. "The tunnels underneath us would eventually lead to the palace. I don't know how long we would have to walk through the sewer to get there."

"Well, if you say it that way . . ." Landon stood. "Who else is in favor of the stairs?"

Katia looked back at Wenlock, who was polishing his spectacles. "Landon, my boy, I'm ready to start this adventure and get away from that blasted sea."

Fontine's eyes lit up.

"Am I the only one who thinks this is a bad idea?" Katia asked, but no one else listened. They scampered up the stairs without a word. She sat stewing, trying desperately to think of a different plan.

Landon hollered down, "Kat, come here. I need you."

Katia dusted herself off before venturing up the stairs to see what he wanted.

Landon stood with his back against a wall, looking down the tunnel. "Kat, it looks like it gets smaller. Go and see if it opens up."

"Me? You want me to do it?"

"You're thin and willowy."

"Is that a compliment?"

"Sure. If you take it that way." He flashed a quick smile. "You could manage better than anyone."

Katia took a deep breath. "You owe me."

"I know." Landon kissed her on the cheek, and she softened just a bit. His charm got her every time.

"Here, my girl." Wenlock pulled out a small pocket-lamp and lit it with a strike of flint. Landon grabbed it and handed it over to her.

"But what if there's spiders?"

"So, there's spiders." Landon rubbed her shoulder. "You're so much bigger than them. You know that? You'll be fine. We'll be right behind you."

Katia grimaced and held the lamp out before her. She could see the narrowing ahead. "Okay," she said to herself and worked her way up.

The masonry on the left side of the passage jutted out in interesting configurations, like it had once been smashed on the opposite side, pushing out the stone. Katia maneuvered past, examining it as she went on.

The ceiling dropped suddenly, sloping downward and twisting around another way. That opening took some thought, but she managed. It might be tricky for Landon's broad shoulders, but she decided to continue on.

Katia climbed a few more stairs before they leveled out. Above her, a long hallway stretched out ahead, looking cavernous, with no end. Katia held the lantern high, probing deep down the corridor. Shadows of black appeared, either connecting corridors or covering windows. Dirt lined the cobblestone floor. Her footsteps slid along the dust, sending particles through the air. Cobwebs hung around unused sconces. Katia unconsciously brushed her shoulders. The thought of spiders around her neck made her tense.

Katia turned her attention back down the staircase. "Landon?" Her voice was a whisper, hoping for an answer. All was silent around her. Slowly, she turned again and crept forward, her eyes wide as she went. A black archway came closer and closer. She stopped, her lamp held out to see anything inside.

White webs spread across the arch, thick like cotton.

She gasped, fixing her eyes on the enormity of the webs. "Stupid Landon. Make me go first. Willowy. Ha! How did he charm his way . . ."

Katia stopped mid-thought, knowing exactly what Landon had done—tricked her into going first. She thought about turning around and giving him a good old punch in the gut when she heard a noise, not from behind her, but from the dark corridor. She gulped and gripped her lamp tighter as she stepped forward as silently as she could.

The noise sounded like a cough or a laugh. She listened closer. She heard it again. Someone was coming closer.

Fear spread through her body. She stepped backward, pulling her hood up tight, and scurried underneath the web-infested archway. She crouched near the corner and sent dust up which extinguished her lamp.

Everything went black, blacker than she had ever experienced. She felt as if tiny spiders crawled all around her. Her cool fingertips crystalized, ready for anything.

A faint blue light grew in the corridor. Katia shrank smaller, hoping the cobwebs would hide her. *Just go away. Just go away.*

A shadow crossed the wall and stood right outside the arch. She strained to see the outline. The reflection of the metal on the sword sent shards of light across the masonry.

Katia's magic shot out before she could think straight. Icicles hit the wall and shattered like glass. The man in silhouette turned toward her. She scrambled to her feet, stumbling backward in the empty tunnel behind.

The man dashed in. Her scream echoed before long fingers cover her mouth.

Landon heard the scream from the staircase. He jerked, knocking his head sharply against the stone. Letting go of his uncle's arms, he sent Wenlock stumbling backward.

"O-oh," Landon stammered, struggling to stand. "Sorry."

"That was Katia," Fontine stated from his side. She had fit easily through the overhang. "Go. Go to her. I can help him. We'll catch up."

Landon rubbed his head clear. He grabbed the sunsparks from her hand and clambered up the rest of the stairs. The long chamber was dark and silent. "Kat?" he yelled, though the sound didn't travel. "Kat!"

Landon's heart leapt to his throat. Panicked, he reached for his knife. He studied Katia's footprints in the dust where another set joined from the opposite direction. He lifted the light and saw the snow crystals along the wall. Gripping his weapon, he stepped forward.

He heard a small scuffle and began to run, his sunsparks illuminating everything around him. The stone path turned sharply and opened in three different directions, three escapes. Katia could be down any one of them. He looked on the ground for footprints, but this floor didn't have any accumulated dust—rather, smooth stone, as if it had regular use.

But something caught his eye . . . Ice!

"Kat!" He ran down the corridor, searching wildly for any trace of Katia's magic. He heard a soft mumbling down the third archway. Inside were circular stairs leading downward. He jumped down two at a time. A light became visible, like torchlight flickering. He reached the bottom and stopped.

A large room opened up, full of people—men and dwarves, women and children, all staring at him. Some mothers clung to their little ones, scared. Other dwarves brandished axes, ready to fight.

Landon glanced over to his left. Katia stood next to a man she had trapped in ice shackles, his mouth frozen together. Her breath was quick like she had just finished a big struggle.

"Kat. Thank the gods. Are you okay?"

"Yes," she huffed, still holding the man hostage.

"What is happening?" Landon looked around at the scared people and then back to Katia. "Kat, let him go."

"What? No!"

"Look around you. He's not going to hurt you."

Katia turned, looking at the others, but didn't lower her guard.

Landon walked over to the man. "Hi, Landon Rhees. This is Katia Ravenmoor. She tends to get overexcited about strangers."

"Overexcited." She turned to him. "You idiot. This man tried to kill me."

"Did you?" Landon asked the man. A muffled sound came from his frozen lips. "See? He didn't."

Katia's shoulders relaxed a little.

Landon bent down and tried to shatter the ice shackled around his feet. "It hurts. I know. Trust me. You hang around her long enough—" The ice cracked and broke apart. "Kat. Run up and find the others, please."

Katia still looked like an angry hornet, but she backed away. He handed her the sunsparks. Though still confused, she went back upstairs.

"Really sorry about that." Landon loosened the ice roped around the man's wrists until it fell to the floor.

The man still couldn't speak. Landon looked around. "Does anyone have any water?"

The stunned crowd remained silent until a woman came closer and filled a cup from a barrel. She handed it to him, and Landon lifted it to the man's mouth. The brown water melted away the frost until his lips parted.

"Thank you," he exclaimed, moving around his mouth, loosening the muscles. "I didn't know you would help us. I thought we were in danger."

"I understand."

"Why would you come here?"

Landon gave a little laugh. "It's complicated. Tell me, why are you here?"

"My name is Salvador. We are refugees hiding from the city guards."

"You're not the only ones. What's happening here?"

Salvador did not answer. He looked to the others in the room, making eye contact with a woman sitting next to a little girl. The young woman had striking features, like those in a dream: short black hair around a heart-shaped face. She was dressed plainly, like everyone else, but she still commanded attention.

She stood as if called and walked over to him. Landon stood as well, mesmerized by a familiarity he didn't understand.

"What do you know of Sharrod, Landon Rhees?" she asked calmly.

"About Sharrod? Actually, not much. I probably know a very different story than yours, and he's involved somewhere."

The woman's eyes slid from one side of his face to the other, analyzing his features. "We are in trouble. Southwick is not the same. Sharrod has begun poisoning people with magic—dark magic. It takes over their senses and keeps them from thinking. The walking sleep. This is not a good place to be."

Landon looked around to the others, trying to piece information together. He raised his finger to his lips. "Wait a moment—you're one of them . . ."

The woman took in a deep breath. "I'm not sure I—"

Scuffling from the stairs announced Katia's return with Wenlock and then—

The woman gasped as Fontine turned the corner. Their eyes met and without hesitation, Fontine ran to her. "Silexa!"

CHAPTER ELEVEN

Katia stared, mystified, as Fontine nearly collided with Silexa, as they spoke over each other in their familial excitement.

"Wait." Landon looked over at Katia. "Another sister? We're bringing the whole family together."

Katia evaluated Silexa. She was a statuesque, willowy beauty, sharp and strong, quite different compared to Fontine's quiet demeanor. Silexa had to be older; she treated Fontine with almost motherly affection.

Each spoke of their journey and escape so fast that Katia almost missed some of the key points—Silexa had fallen in love with the prince of Southwick, a man named Bryant, who, with a boy named Zander, disappeared in the Musungu to find Vespa and bring her back. The sisters continued on talking about protective animals, their sister Ymber's separation from the magic, and her unfortunate passing as the result.

Katia suddenly felt very uncomfortable. Death was a real possibility in their journey. What they were doing was dangerous. She had nearly killed the man who had searched them out. She took a deep breath and brushed it away, not ready to tackle that feeling.

Silexa changed the subject to her modest escape from a shapeshifter and the destruction of the palace.

"That is where I met Salvador." She gestured to the man Katia had frozen.

"Yes." He stood and bowed his head. "She saved us from the black smoke, my family and I. I sent my family north to the get away from here but I couldn't forget my princess' kindness. I never will forget. I came back to protect her from the changeling."

Landon stuck out his hand and shook Salvador's. "You're a good man, Salvador. Glad to have you in the fight. You said changeling—do you mean a Louving is here?"

"Yes. And she is vengeful against Silexa."

"Aren't they all?"

Silexa turned her head. "Do you have experience with Louvings?"

"Yep." Landon smacked his lips. "Several were down in the Echoes with Harrow, that sly underdemon, and one tracked us to Tapoof and followed us to find Fontine. Slippery fellows. Never know who to trust. I'd like to think that the one who followed us is gone. I don't know for sure."

Fontine quickly spilled out a short version of their escape from the Spring of Sephar and the journey on the commodore's ship.

Silexa listened without much expression until the last part. "Wait. You have a ship?"

"Well, it's actually Katia's father who has it." Fontine gestured to Katia, whose face turned red.

"We could use it to get these people to safety." She began to pace as she thought. "We're trapped. We are too many, and I worry about the little ones. There's nowhere close enough to go, and we're running out of supplies. Sharrod's spies are everywhere."

"What's happening here?" Landon came closer. "What is Sharrod doing?"

Silexa's expression turned grave. "Unspeakable horror. I've never seen anything so evil. He can use them as pawns and can control their thoughts and actions. After so much exposure, the soul turns and becomes—" She couldn't speak the word. "They don't know what they are doing. I don't think we will be safe for long."

"And you think a ship would help?"

"If we could get a message to her father, he could help these people."

"But Landon," Katia muttered, "there isn't a way to do that."

"I can do that," Fontine volunteered. "Let me do it. Please."

Silexa shook her head. "No. No medallions. If you use your magic, Sharrod will find you."

"There's not much choice, and I could do it faster than anyone else. Wenlock can help me."

At the sound of his name, Wenlock raised his head, confused. "What? Me?" He looked at Fontine, completely flummoxed. "LeAndra, my dear. I don't think I am the best seaworthy—"

Fontine rushed over to him. "You have the Meridian, don't you? That will work perfectly. Help me. Do it for Mae. She would want you to help these people."

Wenlock gave in. "Yes. Yes, you are right. But I hate that confounded ship."

Silexa sighed, clearly distraught. "I'm not ready to lose another sister. You have to be careful."

Fontine looked back. "Of course I will."

"You must be starving. Come eat with us. We'll discuss the details over food."

The soup was spread out to the new guests. It was simple, yet satisfying.

Katia stared at the small bowl and sipped. She didn't feel much like eating. Her stomach turned from guilt at attacking Salvador, and the small amount of soup entering her throat couldn't soothe her soul. She looked over at Landon, who was in discussion with Wenlock about his instruments. A brief thrill went through her at the memory of his kiss on the boat. The thought made her blush, and she quickly brushed her hair around her ears to distract herself.

"Katia?" a voice interrupted her thoughts. Fontine sat cross-legged in front of her. "I know this is a new plan, but I have a great idea about how to get everyone out and to the boat. I think with your ice magic, we could make a bridge—"

"I can't," she interrupted.

Fontine looked confused. "You can't?"

"I'm really sorry. I'm not here to save these people. I'm not going."

"They need our help."

Katia's fingers fiddled around the bowl in her hand. "Right, I understand that, but—"

"Please." Fontine's voice began to shake. "I've seen what we can do. The ice magic could make—"

"Let me talk to Landon. Can you send him over?"

Within a few moments Landon came close. "Kat. What's going on? Fontine says you're not going with us."

"I can't go, Landon." She looked down, afraid of his brown eyes.

Landon sat next to her and reached for her hand. She pulled it away. "What's wrong? What did I do this time?"

Katia sighed and set down the broth. "Nothing. Promise."

"Then help us."

"This isn't what I came here to do."

Landon moved in front of her so she couldn't escape his gaze. "But it's the right thing to do. These people are starving, and we can help them."

"I'm needed somewhere else."

Landon nearly laughed. "Where else could you be?"

"Really, Landon." His words infuriated her. "Do you need me to freeze you again? I'm here to find my brother."

Landon stopped smiling and looked at her. "Well, I am too. Did you forget that?"

"This isn't funny."

For the first time, Katia actually saw anger in Landon's face. He looked seriously hurt. She didn't know how to take it—a real reaction. "He's with Sharrod—in the lion's den.

You can't go there alone. We're a team. *After* we help these people."

Katia felt her face redden. She felt scolded like a little girl. "I'm going to find my brother."

"No!" The statement echoed around the stone walls, startling others and making them turn. "Now listen to me, Katia Ravenmoor. It's too dangerous. I need to be with you."

"Then come with me."

"Kat," he whined. "Wenlock needs me. We will find Vanya after—"

"I'm not going."

Landon clenched his fist, his face turning red, then he breathed and let it all drain out. "Ah, Kat. Why do you always have to be so stubborn? I'm on your side. Don't you know what's important here?"

Katia felt the heat in her face and the coolness in her fingers. "And why do you always need to be the hero? I'm not a little girl. I've figured out my magic and how to use it and don't need you there to tell me to calm down. You're such an idiot sometimes."

Landon bit his lip, started to speak, then just stood up. He began to walk back, but turned. "So much time wasted. And you still don't understand me."

Katia watched him return to Wenlock. What did he mean? Her stomach turned again. She had hurt him, but at that moment, she was too angry to care. She stood up and walked away from all the staring eyes and found a quiet, dark corner away from the lit room.

She sat for a long time without moving, just thinking and processing her conversation and the decision she had made. Her head rested on the old brick as her fingers traced delicate circles in the dust. The tiny ice from her fingers mixed in the dust and melted it into a smooth paste.

A gentle hand settled on her shoulder. "Can I sit?"

Katia looked up and saw Silexa. She only shrugged and went back to drawing. Silexa quietly took a seat against the opposite wall.

Katia turned and watched the silhouetted beauty, still not saying a word.

After an awkward silence, Katia finally spoke. "So, do you want to change my mind too?"

Silexa's head bent slightly. "No."

Katia waited for a reason and got nothing. Silexa only stared wistfully off in the distance. There was something so intriguing about her stare, seeing the storm in her blue eyes, belonging to a different world. "Why?" The word felt so small in her mouth.

Silexa didn't answer, her arms sliding over her knees. "Tell me about your brother."

"My brother?" Katia had forgotten she'd said so much in front of all the refugees in the room. "Well . . ." She didn't know what to say. It was odd to remember the little baby Vanya, crying and sickly. He wouldn't know her, though something pulled her to him, an invisible string attached within her chest, and she felt the tug stronger as she grew closer to the palace.

Silexa's lip curled. "Blood is peculiar, isn't it?" she asked in her soft voice. "There is a strength that is given to you just by having family. It's noble and sacrificial and troubling." She pointed toward Salvador. "You know the person whom you froze today?"

Katia felt ashamed again. She looked at the man tending to an older woman as she tried to rest.

"This man shared with me the tenderness that comes from family. His littlest daughter is the sweetest, most precious thing I've ever beheld. I see her when I close my eyes, holding her little doll in her hands. I hope in my heart that I might have a child like her one day."

Katia considered her words, curious why she was opening up to her.

"This man saved his family, then came back to find me. And I've often thought what an odd thing to do, after you and your family are safe and have escaped the dark magic, why come back to find me?" She looked at Katia again. "I don't have the answer either, but Salvador tells me that he is doing it for his family. It's strange how sacrificial one becomes when it involves the ones they love most."

"I . . . don't know my brother," Katia felt the words spill out. "I only found out that he is still alive before we came on the ship. I need to rescue him. I can't escape it."

"And he is with Sharrod?"

"I don't know. He was with King Reinoh, that I know for sure."

Silexa's eyes grew very still. "Reinoh?"

"Yes. He took him as a baby."

"So how old would he be now?"

"Maybe nine."

Silexa's expression changed to worry. She sat still a while before she spoke again. "I think the best thing we could do is find Reinoh."

"But, I thought . . ." Katia trailed off. "Outside, someone said that the king was dead."

Silexa tapped her finger. "I wouldn't count on it." She again fell into thought, then stood without saying anything.

Katia watched her as she walked over to Salvador. Many of the refugees had fallen asleep. She glanced at Landon from behind the wall. He looked angry as he fiddled with something of Wenlock's. How she wished she could walk over and curl into his strong arms. Nothing was stopping her but her pride. She pulled her head back into the darkness.

Katia sat and closed her eyes.

A tiny tap woke her. Silexa stood over her again, a small pack on her shoulder.

"Come with me," she whispered, helping her up.

"Where are we going?"

"Into the dark," Silexa stated, giving her a pack of her own. "I have a hunch. Pray it is right." She started walking down a tunnel, away from the refugees.

Katia glanced quickly back. Most everyone had fallen asleep, Landon included, who rested against the brick wall. She watched his sleeping form before turning to follow the princess.

Part Two

Let me kiss you, butterfly.

Show me your colors,

Open your eye.

Let me dance, fairy dear.

The blue lilies open

And you appear.

Let me hear you, little baby goat

Ninny and winny

With your new shiny coat.

Let me embrace you, sister earth.

Change me, my sad heart

For death, for birth.

— Heartridge Valley Lullaby

CHAPTER TWELVE

A strange haze covered Ferra's waking eyes. Distant dark shadows moved about her, speaking with muffled voices, fading in and out . . . in and out . . . Sounds surrounded her ears, the delicate rhythm of her own breathing.

". . . awake, my lord," she recognized among the words.

A larger presence came forward. Her eyes strained to focus. A long, handsome face looked over her, evaluating her eyes before she lost consciousness again.

Ferra woke a second time to the sound of water, a gentle trickle from the rain outside. It ran close by as it carved a way down toward the sea. Something within her stirred, wanting to see and feel the cool wetness. She needed water and strained to drink.

"Wat—" she tried. A shadowed figure rushed over, his side lit only by lamplight.

"Here you are." The man handed her a cup full of cool liquid. Her dry mouth relished in the delight of the fresh water running down her throat. She drained the cup.

"Thank you," she whispered and rested back her head. The water so refreshed her that Ferra began to return to her senses. She could see the animal hide covering the makeshift tent, the weapons thrown haphazardly into a pile, the crates of rations stacked in the corner. Her eyes found the man who sat next to her on an empty crate.

"Who?" Her voice was but a whisper. "I don't . . . Where am I?"

"You're safe," he stated. "Several of us fighters are guarding just outside the wall. We thought you were dead."

Ferra felt the pain in her back. "I am." Her hands convulsively went to her neck, confirming that her medallion was indeed gone. "Did you mean to save me or capture me?"

The man just sat there without speaking, looking at her in weary bewilderment.

Ferra tried to sit up. The pain in her back increased, but she pressed on, pushing through it.

"Careful, careful. That stitching is not the best."

"Oh, so you're a healer."

"No, just a man with mediocre stitching ability." He helped her straighten. "But I've seen my share and learned a few things. The blade pierced your shoulder but hit nothing vital. So, we bandaged your arm—"

"We?" Ferra interrupted. "Where are the others?"

"Well, I volunteered to watch over you. The others are out patrolling."

Ferra looked closer at this man. He was young but not much older than she. His sharp bone structure and smooth, tanned skin showed the marks of Southwick heritage. He averted his eyes from looking directly at her, which she found annoying. "What is your name?"

"Mahoney, Your Grace. Just a footman, and a lousy footman at that."

Ferra stiffened. "Well, I'll be the judge of that. Are you a footman for the Southwick army?"

"Yes . . . er, well, no. I mean, I am, but I have a new commander."

Ferra looked at him in confusion. "A commander who doesn't take orders from Southwick?"

"I can't say exactly." His head bent down low.

She reached for his chin and slowly raised his gaze to meet hers. A long, dark scar ran down his left side, blinding his eye. "I'm sorry that happened," she murmured. "Would you like to look at my shoulder again? I should have a good scar from it, I'm sure."

Mahoney chuckled, not expecting the jest. "I thought you might be afraid of my face, Your Highness."

"Your what?" She laughed. "I'm not royalty." Ferra studied him, trying to figure out if he looked familiar. "Who have you been talking to?"

Mahoney sat back. "I'm sorry. He said you were—"

"Who said?"

"The prince. He said you were a daughter." Mahoney raised his fingers to his own neck, referencing her scar.

Ferra felt the fight die in her. "Someone told you. This prince of Southwick?"

Mahoney's face spread into a grin. "Yes, exactly."

Her mind reeled over this information. She vaguely remembered there once being a prince, but had long forgotten about any monarchy. "Okay. I guess I need to talk with him," she said, ready to stand, then the pain in her shoulder rippled through her body. She gasped and fell forward. Mahoney snatched her in his arms before she could move very far.

"I think it might be better if he came to you." He steadied and eased her back down. "He'll be back soon. A lot is happening here on the front line."

Ferra decided not to fight the pain and instead rested on the cot. Her eyes fell on Mahoney. His scar gave his face a rough appeal she rather liked. It told a story that she desperately wished to hear. "Will you tell me?"

Mahoney adjusted his seat. "Well, the prince showed up here a week ago with several dwarves. He hid amongst us at first, until he learned what the guard was doing to prepare for war. Many of the men have been weary of King Sharrod's plan to begin with. Seeing Prince Bryant was a welcome sight. Now we have a reason to fight again."

A tiny laugh escaped Ferra's lips. "Sorry. I meant about your scar. But I'm glad you told me about your prince."

Mahoney went pink. "Oh, sorry." He turned his head, looking at her quizzically. "Why do you want to know about my scar?"

"Oh, I don't know. I'm curious, that's all. I like that you have one. Makes me like you more."

Mahoney reflectively traced the line which ran down his face. "Maybe I'll tell you one day. For now I think it should remain a mystery."

Disappointment filled her, but she moved on. "Do you know more about the plans of Sharrod?"

"Yes, some."

She waited. "Well, are you going to tell me?"

"Lie down, Your Highness." Mahoney went to help her, but Ferra's hand flew out.

"And that's another thing—this 'your highness' business. Please call me Ferra and nothing else."

"Okay, Ferra," he returned. "Is there anything I can help you with?"

"Yes." Ferra suddenly felt dizzy. "I need to meet with your prince. Go find him."

Mahoney stood. He shifted his weight to one side, amused by her demands. "I'll see if I can find someone to help you."

"No, the prince," she insisted.

"I heard you," Mahoney repeated. "But I can't guarantee he's around, so I hope I can find someone to help. I don't want to give you a promise I can't keep."

"Oh, fine." Ferra laid her head on the cot and fell unconscious from pain.

When her eyes again opened, someone else was sitting on the small stool. She couldn't focus on the specifics beyond the fact that it was not Mahoney, but a girl with black straight hair streaming over her bent head. She listened to her soft sobs and wondered what made the girl so sad, but before she could ask, the girl raised her head.

All of the air came out of her lungs at once. "Vespa . . ."

Vespa looked surprised at her own name. She reached out quickly and grabbed her hand. "Ferra, you're okay."

Ferra looked around again. Mahoney stood in the back, guarding the door, a gentle smile on his scarred face. She looked back at her sister. "How did you get here?"

"Prince Bryant came and found me in the Musungu. I travelled back with him and the dwarves." Vespa looked visibly disturbed. "Oh, Ferra, there is so much evil right now."

"Why? What's happening?"

"Sharrod is poisoning everyone left in Southwick with dark magic, the army included. It's doing horrific things to them. Bryant is doing what he can to save the souls left inside."

"How can he do that?"

Vespa turned her head with a mystified look. "I wish I had an answer." She grasped her hand tighter. "Oh, Ferra, what are we going to do about your medallion?"

Ferra took in a harsh gasp as the pain shot through her but she sat up and attempted to stand. "As I figure," she said as she struggled to regulate her breath, "I have nothing to lose. I'm going to fight. And I'm going to hunt Browneyes down, that worthless, betraying Louving."

Mahoney ran to her side and helped her to her feet. "Easy, Your, er . . . Ferra."

"Now, please, Mahoney, take me to your prince."

Zander examined the carefully folded papers under the cover of branches. He sat quietly watching the patter around him. The never-ending rainfall made him miserable, so pulling out the pages helped distract him from his commitment to Bryant and furthered the ache to see Naomi again.

He ran his fingers over the indentations of her scribbles. One dream after another, each mysterious woman becoming more important to him.

The dark shadows of night gently crept around the corners of the trees. Zander grew used to the long shifts. Though he was much younger than the other men and dwarves, Bryant had agreed to not treat him differently because of his age, so he took watch like the others, serving the prince with valor like the knights did.

Something moved near the side of the tree. Zander quickly stood, ashamed of his careless daydreaming. It was one of the dwarves.

"Bucklingdown," a gruff voice called Zander's name. "Prince Bryant asks for you. I'm here to relieve your post."

"Y-yes sir." He gathered his things and carefully folded the dream journal back into his satchel. Raising his hood up over his head, Zander nodded to the dwarf and trudged through the rain back to camp.

His soaked boots splashed through puddles, dampening pant cuffs that no longer covered his ankles. The muddy water slid down the holes in his boots. Zander shook his feet out of habit. The rain never stopped, and as much as Zander missed the sun, he did his best to endure these conditions.

The small camp lined the eastern wall of Southwick near the forest. The prince had seized the encampment with very little effort. Many of the soldiers were willing to help him, being loyal to Bryant, but something else had frightened them, though Zander was kept out of those conversations. He might be young but he wasn't stupid.

Something strange was going on in Southwick, something big enough to frighten grown men.

Zander reached the prince's enclosure deep in the forest. Bryant often invited him to dinner to check how he was doing within the resistance. He flipped up the tent flap and found several men deep in discussion in low voices.

"Oh, here he is." Bryant smiled as Zander walked closer. "Zander, my boy. Come here."

Zander immediately felt the eyes of everyone on him. He hesitated near the door.

Bryant stood and came closer. "Zander, I have someone who you need to meet." He placed his hand on his shoulder. "I've just spent a great deal of time talking with her. And I think you will understand her story better than I do. Excuse me," he said to the other men. They bowed their heads and then turned back to their discussion.

Bryant guided Zander out the door and down toward the end of the row of tents. He heaved a big sigh as if he was about to say something but remained silent. It wasn't like Bryant to keep quiet. An uncomfortable pit began to form in Zander's stomach. They stopped before a small medical tent. A man stood near the opening, chewing on a long, black stick. A visible scar ran down his otherwise handsome face.

"Mahoney, I brought the boy," Bryant said.

The man half smiled. "I think she'll be delighted. Come on in."

He opened the flap and led them in. A small, single candle lit the tiny space. Vespa sat near the flame, her sleek, dark hair reflecting the flickering movement like a halo. The expression on her heart-shaped face looked grave, a sadness Zander couldn't identify. She nodded to him as he entered but flipped her head back to the girl sitting on the edge of a makeshift cot.

Zander turned his attention to the bright-eyed stranger. A large bandage was wrapped about her shoulder, accompanied by traces of blood on her clothes. A pile of knotted hair twisted around her head like a woven bird's nest. She looked up and smiled, capturing him with her gaze.

"Well, I wouldn't mistake you for the world," she stated. "Naomi talked as if you were a little boy, but I don't see it. I'm sure you've outgrown her by now."

Zander's tongue stuck to the roof of his mouth. He tried to spit out the words but only could say, "N-n-n . . ."

"Naomi." Bryant cleared his throat and took a chair near the cot. "Zander, this is—"

"F-f-ferra," he finally got out the word. "You're F-ferra."

"Yes. How did you know?"

"The j-journal. N-n-n—" He still couldn't speak her name, so he grabbed the pages from his bag and presented them to her.

"This is Naomi's?" Ferra took it and analyzed the writing. "Amazing. That girl didn't miss anything."

Zander felt the questions form in his mind but didn't know if he could speak them. He looked to Bryant for help.

Bryant read the expression. "Yes, Ferra has seen Naomi. She spent weeks with her, I think. Is that correct?"

"Yes." Ferra tried to straighten but groaned. Mahoney started to her side, but she held up her hand to stop him. "Yes. I met her near the Echoes and fought beside her. I was there with her recovery and helped her find her magic."

"Magic?" Zander felt the connection burn through him. Of course Naomi had magic. She had to be the most powerful of them all.

Ferra smiled and continued. "We hid in an underground lair until the army found our hiding place and destroyed it. We separated then. I haven't seen her since."

Zander felt the words fill his mouth but couldn't speak his gratitude. He hoped she could see it in his eyes.

"She's amazing. She's alive, I know it. And she'd be so proud of you, Zander. Bryant's told me a lot of what you've done here. How you rescued Vespa. Naomi will be so proud to hear it."

"Thank-k you," he spoke, still shaking. "I thought sh-she was—"

"We know." Bryant patted his back. "Now, with formalities out of the way, let's talk about what we're doing next. Zander, take a seat." He gestured to a place next to Ferra. Zander sat on the cot and felt a reassuring hand grasp his. Ferra winked and looked again to Bryant.

Bryant motioned to Mahoney to join in the conversation. "Mahoney here is the leader of the refugees outside this camp."

"Leader?" Ferra said, directing her gaze toward Mahoney. "I thought you were a lowly footman."

Mahoney didn't acknowledge her statement—just stared at Bryant as he continued. "I don't want to label him as the leader unless he accepts it."

Bryant gestured to Mahoney, who nodded in respect.

"Thank you, Your Honor."

"This man helped rescue many of these soldiers from the Darkening."

"Darkening?" Ferra questioned.

Mahoney stepped forward. "We talked about the dark magic, Your . . . Ferra."

"Will I always be Your . . . Ferra?"

"Possibly?" He continued, "Sharrod is poisoning the men of Southwick with dark magic—so dark that it has turned their hearts black. They are no longer thinking humans but mindless drones seeking to destroy anything or anyone in their path."

Vespa sat up. "But why would someone do this? It seems a senseless act, poisoning people just to control them. Fear works better than magic."

"You're right," Bryant agreed. "So there must be a bigger picture we're missing."

The room fell silent as everyone pondered the information.

Zander was the first to break the silence. "Wh-what happens when you t-touch d-dark magic?"

Mahoney turned to him, looking surprised by the comment. "It spreads like a sickness, infecting everything it touches—the trees, the grass, everything."

"It poisons the earth?" Vespa asked.

Ferra turned to her sister. "Like in the Blackwoods, remember? That whole area is poisoned, and the roots reach down deep in the soil. Father warned us not to hide there."

"But the Musungu is much the same and also different," Vespa thought out loud. "It's haunted by stains, but nothing grows there. The trees and plants have all died. It's more magic than life."

"So, dark magic needs living things," Ferra concluded. "If that's the case, then what can protect the living from the dark magic?"

"The f-fairies," Zander said with perfect knowledge of the danger. Ferra squeezed his hand at his answer. Zander looked again at Bryant. "The fairies can save us."

Vespa's eyes shone bright as she slowly stood. "He's right. The fey cannot be touched by it."

Zander felt the grip of Bryant's hand on his shoulder. He beamed down at him. "I knew you would have a place in this meeting."

In that brief moment, Zander remembered the spirit of the fairy who sacrificed herself to save the prince. Little Lovely had cured Bryant of fatal dark magic, and now he stood tall, prepared to battle an army that could not harm him.

Vespa smiled. "They will help us. I know it. I can find them."

Ferra suddenly gasped. She grabbed at her chest, fighting for air. Zander stood looking at her, not knowing if he had done or said something wrong.

Vespa came to her side and held her as she struggled through the seizing.

Mahoney rushed forward, a pained look in his eyes. "What's happening?"

"Her medallion," Vespa explained to the others. "We need to find it. She may not last long without it."

"She'll die?"

"Like Ymber," Zander whispered.

Vespa didn't answer, just rocked her sister gently as her breathing returned to normal.

Ferra's skin felt tighter than Browneyes' own. A new shape always felt uncomfortable at first, but the Louving didn't care. The satisfaction of getting her way overruled any discomfort on her part. The green medallion bounced playfully around her neck as she advanced on the nearest entrance to the palace.

Her plan? Just walk right in.

When she got to the trees, she ran, testing out her new body. Ferra was flexible and agile. She started jumping from rock to rock, tree to tree. It felt good. This body wasn't sluggish like the old man or restrictive like the crippled fish merchant. This was young and fit and fearless.

The wall to Southwick was high with not many entrances besides the main gates, but she knew of an entrance which not many had discovered. She had used it before in her travels. It lay near the eastern side by the fishmongers . . . not far now.

The bridge came into sight, and Browneyes quickly stepped underneath. The once-bustling bridge of activity lay rather quiet. No street merchants or fish mongers called out their sales. The gate was locked, and nothing stirred. The gap lay around the right on the bridge wall. She just had to climb the tree and sidle through.

The climb was easy in Ferra's body. Just up and around until she stood on the ledge. She inched her way along the stone, seeing the light on the other end.

When she made it through, Browneyes turned and faced something completely unexpected. Thousands of people, still as stone statues, a black aura covering each man, woman, and child, all gazing like mindless sheep at one thing . . . her.

How horrible, was her first thought, then she smiled with delight at the distraction.

Browneyes lifted Ferra's green medallion. "Take me to Sharrod," she demanded. "I'm a daughter of Prolius."

CHAPTER THIRTEEN

"She's gone?" Landon felt the anger die out of him, replaced by worry. "Katia's gone?"

Salvador nodded again. He'd already explained what had happened once Landon woke, but he couldn't believe that she'd just left him without a word.

Landon slunk down to the ground. "Not even a goodbye. She must have been mad at me."

Salvador placed a hand on his shoulder. "I trust Silexa. She knows the underground well. And she told me where to meet her once we have everyone safe."

Landon sighed. "At least she didn't freeze me this time."

"Come, come, Landon." Wenlock offered his hand to stand up. "Stick to the plan."

Gripping his wrist, Landon heaved himself upward. "Fine, but only if I get to use the instrument with all the spindles."

"The Meridian?" Wenlock fumbled through his coat and pulled out the small timepiece. "It's yours."

"Okay. Now I'm ready."

They departed at what Landon presumed was nightfall to the outside world, leaving nothing and no one behind.

The plan was to make it back to the water, and Salvador knew the perfect entry. The refugees organized themselves and followed as silently as they could. Nearly a hundred men, women, and children marched behind in groups of ten. They weaved along rounded staircases and through the narrow corridors and old halls of the ancient fortress. Both Fontine and Wenlock helped within the lines to the rear.

"Through here," Salvador whispered. He pointed to Landon to enter first with the torch.

Landon held out the light in front of him. The light traveled far up and around, not reaching the far corners of the great room. A few tall windows near the top were boarded or bricked over.

Salvador entered after the other refugees in their group had safely arrived. "Over there." He pointed to the far corner.

Landon followed. The sound of shuffling boots on stone filled the room. A dark circle came into view. "What is that?"

"It is our fishing hole," he explained. "This room is an old storage bay for fishermen."

Landon stepped closer and looked down the hole—large enough for a man but not by much. The dark water slapped against the brick, rolling with the waters from the sea. "There isn't much to see."

"The outside wall is several layers thick, but if we follow the water, we will be safe."

"Are you sure about this?"

"Yes." Fontine walked in from behind, her sea-blue stone glowing through the darkness. "I can part the water so we can walk under."

"Brilliant!" Landon loved the idea.

"But Sharrod will know when I am using the stone. That's why this is so much harder without Katia. She could have frozen it and—"

Landon shook his head. "You got this. Okay?" He handed off the torch to one of the men in the company. "So, I guess we shouldn't waste any time. I need to get Briggs the message before you make the tunnel."

"And you know how to use it?"

"*Psh*, of course," Landon waved her off, though his furrowed expression told a different story. He pulled out the instrument Wenlock had given him, the small box sitting quietly in his hand. "Where is Wenlock?"

"Here!" A hand shot up through the crowd. "Confounded stairs turned me around. But we made it, every one."

"Good. Listen, I'll need your help scaling a wall." Landon pointed to the tall brick wall in front of them. Near the top of a boarded window was a solid stone ledge. "I think this is the best place to use the meridian."

"Oh, quite right." The old man rubbed his hands. "I have just the thing." He licked the tips of his fingers before he began rummaging in his bag. "Let's see . . . where is it?"

He continued mumbling to himself before he finally shouted, "Aha! I found it."

In Wenlock's hands lay a contraption full of gears and wheels wrapped around a steel barrel. "Yes. I think this will work nicely. I've been dying to try it out. Mae never liked it much. Thought it was impractical since we lived in a treehouse. Now, let's see here."

He began to wind the gears with a metal crank, pushing back the spring.

"What will it do?" Fontine asked.

"Well." Wenlock held a steel pin in his mouth, reconfiguring a widget. "I've never actually used it." He moved the pin into a different slot and cranked the handle again. A click on the wheel set the pin in place. "There."

He handed it to Landon, who examined it. "So, what do I do?"

"Aim it right there." Wenlock pointed toward the boarded window high in the corner of the room. "Spun from violet spider silk. Quite strong. It should hold you."

Landon looked at the contraption again. Feeling the weight of the metal on his palm brought back the magnitude of his mission. He pulled his arm straight, wrapped his hand around the metal latch, and released it.

A pop rang across the walls, and something like an arrow shot toward the board, followed by a trailing glowing string. It hit and spread its silver claws deep into the rock, sending tiny fragments splintering to the floor.

"Perfect!" Wenlock clapped his hands. "Now, hold onto the latch and let the spring go."

"Okay." Landon's casual manner toward his uncle's invention soon changed as he felt his body yank forward, flying through the air toward the grappling hook. He couldn't slow his momentum, and his side slammed right into the rock frame.

Pain shot through him, but he held fast to the grip. The ledge of the frame was not far from the grappling, so Landon swung his leg out, leveraging his body until he could grip the stone with his hand. He slid over until he felt more secure and rested his back against the boarded space behind him. He seemed so much higher than it looked from below. He rubbed his shoulder to dull the pain. Wenlock should have prepared him.

Landon found the small torches illuminating the faces of the refugees below. The mechanized glider bounced gingerly as it slowly edged back down the spun silk string. Wenlock waved, saying something, but Landon couldn't hear it and wasn't interested in listening. He knew what he needed to do from here.

He pulled out the knife strapped to his boot and shoved it in between the wood and stone, prying at it. The wood only budged a fraction. He tried again and again, straining with the effort.

"Oh, this will take forever," he grumbled with frustration.

Bracing himself against the stone, he kicked it, but the force propelled him backward near the edge of the frame. Landon reflexively forced his knife into the mortar. It stuck and held. He caught the stone with his other hand. Tiny pebbles tumbled down. He heard a few gasps from below. Carefully, he turned again and rested, taking in a few deep breaths. He slowly waved his hand, indicating he was all right.

Landon's heart continued to pound. "Okay. Don't kick it. Bad idea." He wriggled his knife loose from the stone and set it back in its sheath. He looked closer at the dark boarded window and where he had kicked. A gap had appeared that he swore hadn't been there before; maybe the kicking worked. Landon took his boot and wedged it between the wood and stone. This time it moved. He got his knee, then leg, and then body through the crack. With one final push, Landon rolled out into darkness.

A thick layer of dust covered his hands as he landed on the floor. Landon stood, weary of the darkness. He couldn't see anything but the faint light coming from the torches outside.

A mechanical winding sound came from behind him, followed by a loud *thump* and a slight groan.

Landon peered through the wood opening. Fontine's trembling form had hit the wall. He quickly offered his hand to help her inside.

"You okay?"

Fontine pressed her hand to her head. "I will be."

"Why are you here? You need to help those people."

Fontine looked up. "I came to help you with the Meridian. Do you know how to use it?"

Landon thought about the instrument in his pocket. "No. Not really. But I can figure it out."

"I've used it before, to communicate with my sisters."

"Is Wenlock coming up, too?"

"Salvador needs his help. They are staying back with the others until we return. It shouldn't take long."

Landon's gaze fell to the luminescence coming from the medallion she wore. It hung loose around her neck, casting soft blue waves around her like underwater turbulence. "Can you hold that out?" He pointed to the stone.

Fontine clutched the chain protectively. "I don't want to use it yet."

"I mean, use it as a light. Let us see what's around."

Fontine's hand slowly pulled it upward. The glow cast shards of light through the shadows.

Landon watched as she moved forward, revealing forgotten hallways and old framed portraits. A stone column stood tall in the midst of darkness, an old picture spider-webbed and forgotten, the people long dead.

"Come," Fontine beckoned as she started down the stone tunnel.

Landon followed close behind her, tracking the dancing light as it traveled around the walls. Fontine walked slowly down a hallway, the light brightening as the space narrowed, the walls closer together.

The moldy stench of sea water and time hovered around the old stone masonry. An uneasy feeling fell over Landon. He turned around, double-checking behind him to make sure no one was actually following them, but the darkness swallowed all shadows.

"Are you sure—" he started, but the words dropped out of his mouth. An intense feeling, dark and powerful, crept over him.

Fontine stopped and looked at him. She had to have felt it too.

The stone vibrated, sending the light into a frenzy.

Fontine quickly wrapped her hands around it, smothering the light. The two stood in silence, waiting for something to happen, but nothing did and soon the suffocating feeling disappeared.

"Should I go on?" Fontine asked in the smallest whisper.

"We'll be okay," Landon said to reassure her but honestly didn't know. "Tell me about the Meridian."

"The Meridian? Why?"

"I don't know. Maybe it could help."

Fontine's voice calmed as she spoke. "The Meridian creates a pathway of communication from one position to another. That's all it does. It's not magical, more mechanical."

"So, if it's not magical, how does it work?"

"It uses energy."

"Like from a crank?"

"More like the sun," Fontine clarified. She pulled away, becoming more animated. "Do you still have it?"

Landon reached into the pocket of his cloak and pulled it out.

The box was no bigger than his hand, the silver gears faintly glowing from what energy it had absorbed. The tiny widget clicked in repeating motions.

"Is it working?" Landon could see gears whirling about.

"It's responding to the energy within you. That's all. It needs much more."

"So, if we get it outside?"

Fontine shifted. "It's rainy all the time. I don't think it would work."

Landon heard the despair in her voice. "But, magic has energy. If it's not magical, could magic fuel it?"

"My stone is not the answer."

Landon squared his shoulders a little tighter. "Well, I have magic."

Fontine placed her hand on his. "I don't think you have enough."

"Why does everyone think my magic is lame?"

The little Meridian whirred in a vibrating spin. Both stopped and watched it.

Landon grinned at the instrument bursting to life. "See?"

Fontine's hand went to her face. "Oh, Landon."

"We can do this." Landon looked closer at the mechanism. "I mean, it's worth a shot, right?" He closed the Meridian and shoved it back into his pocket.

The two crept forward. Landon slid his hand across the uneven stone until it hit the wooden beams of a door. A large metal ring hung near the keyhole.

"Do you think it's locked?" Fontine's timid whisper fell flat.

Landon grabbed the ring and pulled.

The door groaned, moving slightly. Hope ignited in Landon's heart, and he pulled again. It was evident that no one had come that way in years—its tired hinges moaned with every effort to open it. Fontine tried with all her might to help. With one final yank, the door widened enough for him and Fontine to slip past. The dull gray light of day pushed through cracks somewhere beyond.

Landon slid through the opening and into an empty hallway. The muffled sound of the waves crashing near the rocks told him enough about his location and where they were in the palace.

Fontine grabbed his arm, securing her fingers in a tight grip. Her tense body told Landon how scared she was. He had no light and relied only on his sense of the dark. "Which way, do you think?"

"Find the Meridian."

Without a thought, Landon slid his hand into the side pocket and grabbed the small instrument. He lifted it up, examining the finely crafted metal before resting it delicately in his palm.

"Turn in over three times."

"Huh?"

"Three. Over end." Fontine motioned with her hands.

"Okay." Landon took the box and rotated it as she instructed. On the third time, they heard a small click. The top flipped up, exposing the tiny gears. A faint beam of light shot out and down the corridor like a moonbeam.

"Follow it." Fontine latched herself to his arm again. "The light will reveal any channels."

Landon took a step forward, watching the blue lines trace the archways revealed before him. The two walked cautiously, looking for any sign of others within the corridor. Small slats between windows revealed daylight outside.

Down they walked, following an unknown path which led nowhere, all the while straining to see a clear indication of the channel Fontine mentioned. The corridor cornered slightly, leading them into a dead end.

A flash startled them both: a bright spark and then it disappeared.

"It's there." Fontine pointed near the corner.

Landon guided his palm in that direction and again saw a spark.

Fontine ran forward, investigating the corner. She bounced like an excited little girl.

Landon looked closer. Wooden planks blocked any light from entering, with only the smallest traces peeking through the imperfections in the beams.

"If we can get enough light," Fontine stated, "I think this could work. I could send a signal."

"Here." He surrendered the Meridian to Fontine's care before investigating the boards. Pulling and jarring the wood did very little. "I've got an idea." Landon reached into his boot and pulled out his short knife—a sturdy hunting knife, less flimsy or fragile than his short sword. He placed it between the slats and began to pry. The wood creaked with every nudge but inched slowly until Landon had a side of the plank exposing light.

Excitement rushed through him. He grabbed his knife and stuck it into the board, ready to use both hands to pull it away from the window. Using his foot as leverage, the board gave way, letting the hazy light of day spill into the room.

CHAPTER FOURTEEN

"You did it!" Fontine flung her arms around his neck.

Landon was surprised but elated and hugged her back.

They were interrupted by a dreadful, foul howl that echoed around them.

Landon froze. On the opposite side of the wall, the small light touched the darkest hidden corner. A spark ignited and furiously ran across the ground, tracing something that had been invisible and soon forming the image of a horned beast. A loud cry shook the walls as it pulled its massive frame forward.

Landon panicked. "Do it!" he ordered Fontine, who stood petrified. "Quick!"

He grabbed his knife from the plank, taking in the hulking form excavating itself from the wall, smoldering embers lighting up its massive frame composed entirely of stone.

Landon threw the knife. It caught in between the rocks in the center of its chest, heating with the rest of its body. Slowly the blade melted, as the handle burst into flame.

At that moment Landon knew he couldn't stop it; he could only distract it. He turned toward Fontine, frozen in place.

"Can you make contact?"

"I . . ." She couldn't finish. Her eyes connected with Landon's, revealing her inner terror.

"Fontine! You can do this!"

Fontine held out the Meridian before her and began directing it toward the light. The brilliant flash sparked brighter than before.

Briggs puffed on his tightly bound seaweed smoke, staring at the waves. The sea had calmed enough to cast out in hopes of finding a succulent dinner. His mouth watered at the thought of a sweet, tender fish instead of dry bread and flavorless broth.

He began reeling in the net near the side of his boat when he heard his name. The sound startled him so much he lost balance. Being alone at sea messed with his mind, but he'd become used to the solitude.

This time was different. He looked around. Nothing but water in all directions.

"Briggs!"

He turned. The voice was urgent. And slowly, like a beautiful mirage came the unmistakable image of Fontine glowing like an angel. "Fontine?"

"Briggs. Help us!"

He staggered back to his feet, his cigar fallen from his mouth. "Fontine? Is that—"

"Briggs. People are trapped. You can find them at the western fishing hole. The western shore. Take them to safety."

"Uh. Yes! But how can—"

"There's no time." A large rumble sounded behind her. "Landon and I are in trouble. Please save these people. Find the western gate. Western shore. The fishing hole is near the grate."

"Fontine! Let me help you!"

A sad smile covered her face. "Please help them. You have done so much already. I know I won't survive."

"Yes, you will—"

"Briggs. Tell Katia I'm sorry. I tried to save him."

"Wait! Fontine!"

The image vanished and the quiet returned, leaving him alone again with the sea.

Briggs sat back on the deck, stunned. He stared at the small smoke rising from his fallen cigar. Picking it up, he analyzed the smoldering ash and extinguished it with his fingers.

The beast let out a snarling growl, reclaiming Landon's attention. Rubbing his palms, he called his magic, which answered quickly, excited to act.

He slammed his palms to the ground. A rumble shook the floor beneath him and the beast, opening up a chasm between the two of them which dropped into a deep abyss. It was all an illusion, but the rock monster didn't know the difference. It started forward and stopped, looking down. Then it roared its heated breath toward Landon, burning his face.

Landon stumbled backward, a searing pain burning across his cheeks and forehead. He looked back, but the beast remained fooled by the cavernous drop and held steady on the other side.

Behind him, Fontine had opened the portal, like a mirror to another world. He stared, captivated by the magic, though he couldn't see beyond the frame. He didn't know if she had Briggs in her sight.

Another heaving breath came towards them both. This time Landon held his cloak up between them. The heat sent smoke through the cloth, and small ashes created pockmarks in the fabric. It wouldn't withstand much more.

With a brilliant flash, the portal was gone, leaving Fontine holding the tiny instrument once more. She turned toward him, tears staining her face.

"What?" Landon asked.

Fontine didn't answer, just placed a gentle kiss on his burned cheeks.

Landon stood dumbfounded, lost for words.

The ember-glowing beast stepped forward with a hard thump. The illusion faltered.

Fontine took the Meridian and directed the light toward the creature. The light sharpened to a point, blinding its sight. It stumbled backward, clawing at the beams.

Landon watched the anger rise in the beast, its large mouth screaming at the light. In retaliation, it shook its rock body like a wet dog. Fist-shaped rocks, hot as coals, flew toward them.

"Fontine!" He ran to shield her, but she pushed him away, holding the light steady.

He huddled down, the rocks burning holes in his cloak and clothes.

Fontine flinched and dodged but couldn't block everything. She gasped and yelled as the blows came, burning and smashing. The beam grew and began destroying the creature rock by rock.

"Shield yourself!" she shouted to Landon.

"No! Stop!" Landon cried out, right before a large rock knocked her to the ground. The Meridian flew from her hand and skittered across the ground.

The beam died, and the beast howled in anger. With one big thud, the illusion between them dissolved.

Landon acted without thinking. He scrambled on his knees to where the Meridian lay. The tiny gears still whirled around. He snatched it in his hands and held it to the light.

A beam struck instantly, and he guided it again toward the demon. Landon's magic, still warm in his hands, reacted within the beam, sending a sharp, alarming blow. The beast staggered back. The embers around it grew larger, swelling to the point of bursting.

Landon saw what it was doing and closed his eyes. *Come on, magic. You can do this.* His magic ignited, sending a magnificent stream directly at the chest of the creature. The creature cried out before it burst. Flaring brick and rock shot everywhere. Landon shielded himself as best he could. Rock hit him hard on his temple, and he grew dizzy.

He hit the floor as the rocks fell around him. Landon forced his focus to Fontine, her still, quiet form lying among the fiery debris. The stone still glowed upon her chest. His hand stretched to reach it. Blurred vision obscured his sight. The darkness was coming.

He knew Fontine was dead.

Zander stayed calm and held his head high, though fear ran around his insides in a mad frenzy of nerves. His bravery was just a front for the prince. He would do as Bryant asked—always, even if this might be the last time he saw him alive.

Zander secured his small pack, filled with anything he thought he would need, plus Naomi's journal. He may not need it, but the mismatched pages brought him luck. He would carry them until he died.

Bryant ruffled through his scruffy beard. "I still don't like this plan."

"I-I know," Zander returned. "But it's a g-good plan."

"Yes." Bryant sighed and turned away. "Keep those girls safe. I'm entrusting their care to you."

"Of course."

Bryant looked back with something new in his gaze— a pride that couldn't be measured. "Zander. You are the closest person I have right now. I've come to rely on you. You are my compass without Silexa by my side. What will I do without you here?"

Zander felt his throat tighten. He tried to make a sound, to reassure the prince of his role and how he would succeed in leading the army to save all the people affected by the darkening, but nothing came out.

Bryant didn't need the words. He grabbed him by the shoulders. "Be safe, my friend. Go save the world." He quickly embraced Zander before sending him out the door of the tent.

"Ready?" The voice behind sounded coy. He turned to see Ferra standing upright and stiff but looking ready to go on an adventure. Vespa stood by her, dressed in her usual black robes, holding some white flowers in her hands. Mahoney stood impatiently behind Ferra like a protective watchdog.

"Here." Vespa came closer and placed a flower in the pocket of his tunic. "The fairies are brave too. This should protect you."

Zander glanced at the star-like petals and the memory of Little Lovely sprang into his mind again. The fairy had given her life to save Bryant. Such a beautiful sacrifice. A pain swelled around his heart thinking of her. For someone so small, she had strength he couldn't imagine. The flower gave him hope, and the thought made a smile cross his face.

"Well, look at that," Ferra noticed Zander's grin. "Do you have a secret, Zander?"

"Yes," he returned, still grinning.

"We should go," Mahoney suggested. "It will be dangerous in the light of morning."

Zander nodded.

The four quickly moved through the forest, working their way west. The secret tunnel they were heading for would only appear at first morning light, just as the fairies had designed it.

Zander followed Mahoney's lead in and out of the trees and bushes. He lost track of the time, just walking with his head down, watching his footsteps carefully.

Hazy gray light could not penetrate the thick clouds. The only indication of it being morning had come from the commotion of waking birds. A startling caw of a crow woke him from the monotonous march.

The city wall appeared in the distance.

Zander stopped. Soon the others stopped as well, noticing he wasn't with them.

"What is it?" Vespa asked.

"I-I don't know?" Zander pointed to a dark sea of perpetual movement.

Vespa placed her hand on her medallion. "They are not creatures of night, like you see. They are not fey. I feel . . ." She stopped and looked at Ferra.

Ferra came closer, staring. "They're human. What did they do to them?"

"It's beginning," said Mahoney.

"But it's too early," Ferra protested. "Bryant isn't ready. We have to go back to warn—"

Mahoney grabbed her wrist. "There isn't time. Up into the trees."

"What?"

Zander wasted no time. He grabbed onto the nearest low branch and swung upward as far as he could. He kept climbing until he felt safe and watched the others scramble up to him, Mahoney helping Ferra as much as she would let him.

The sea of black came closer and closer, like thousands of swarming flies. The dark army marched over the land, leaving a poison on anything they touched.

"We should be protected," Vespa whispered, tapping the lovely flower she wore.

Yes, the fairies would protect them, and hopefully they would warn Bryant for him.

As the mass came closer, Zander fixed his eyes on the first line. The people didn't look normal; the magic had changed them, altered them into gruesome mangles of their former selves. The pink luminosity of life had drained away, replaced with a gray color, making them look like walking corpses, the eyes of each sunken and glowing yellow as day. They walked in unison, pounding the ground as one, controlled by something or someone. And in their hands each held a sleek, black blade.

Zander pointed it out to Mahoney, who whispered, "Ebony blades. Poisoned. One touch." He shook his head, and Zander didn't need an explanation. *How could Bryant defeat this?*

The marching went on eastward—hundreds of men traveling mindlessly toward an unknown destination.

Zander leaned over for a better view and the branch cracked underneath him. He slipped off, frantically grasping at anything. Another few branches snapped before he hit a thick limb, knocking out his breath. He gasped, holding onto the harsh bark of the branch, dangling freely.

Mahoney rushed down to him, trying to reach him before he fell more. Zander's arms felt scratched and bruised, aching from the grip. Mahoney grabbed his forearm and pulled him back to a sturdy branch.

"You okay?" Ferra asked, checking his arms.

Zander nodded but he was visibly shaken.

"Looks like they heard us." Mahoney scanned the dark army. "Several have left and are coming closer."

"I see the door." Vespa pointed to the wall where the army moved past. A curling archway of vines threaded over the rocks, weaving between each other in stunning black against the gray stone. "It will only be open at first light. We have to hurry."

Zander watched each expression in their little group change. The time to act was now.

Mahoney took in a deep breath. "Do you want me to make a plan or are we good with just running?"

Vespa looked at Ferra. "Will you be okay?"

"Of course." She winked at Zander. "We got this."

Vespa grabbed hold of her medallion. Zander's eyes widened as the magic swelled between them. The power felt stronger than before.

A vicious roar escaped from someone, like the dark army had been waiting for the magic to appear. Several came toward the tree, relentlessly pursuing it.

"Drop on three," Ferra instructed. Mahoney grabbed his sword and motioned for Zander to do the same. Zander only had the small dagger, no match for the black-bladed warriors. Still, he found it and held it tight. "One, two . . ."

They all dropped.

Zander landed harshly on his back. It took a second for him to find his feet, disoriented from the fall. He felt Mahoney pull him up and away. He quickly found his stride and ran with the rest.

The dark soldiers were quick. He couldn't see how many were chasing them, but it felt like thousands. They were close. Mahoney turned around to face them. He slowed, raising his broadsword before him.

Three lunged. Mahoney swung the heavy sword in attack right at the black blade, clanging the sharp metal against the other weapon. He dodged again and again, cutting off hands holding the black blades.

"Go!" Mahoney yelled.

Zander pulled his cloak, and he began to run again.

Ahead were more.

Zander felt fear race through his heart. He held strong to his dagger, hoping this was enough to save him.

Suddenly, something appeared next to him, a creature running in stride. He turned to see a badger scurrying alongside them. He looked and beheld more woodland animals accompanying them, protecting the crew as they pressed forward. Even without her medallion, animals were loyal to Ferra as if commanded. It gave them the chance they needed. The creatures fought, confused at the herd coming toward them. This gave Zander and his friends a chance. In one bound, all the animals headed right for the mob of fighters, ripping and gnawing as best they could.

It slowed down some but not all.

Ferra raced toward the secret entrance, the first to arrive through the doorway.

"Come on!" she yelled. "The flower will let you enter."

Zander dodged away from the grasp of the dark army and rushed as fast as he could. He entered, grabbing at the stitch in his side. The inside was cold and dark, but he could see the outside world like through a window. He turned to see Mahoney still battling off more knights. He could hurt them, maim them, but not kill them.

Vespa stood clear in the plain. She held tight to her medallion, its magic swelling around her hands. Something was happening.

Mahoney rushed through the archway, immediately safe from the herd of creatures. None that had been following him could see or penetrate the wall.

"Vespa?" he called as he entered.

They all turned to see her. She had stopped. Several of the ebony blades were pointed at her. But the lavender magic springing from her hands kept them at bay. Something in it made them afraid.

Her little flower she had been wearing floated upward to her shoulder, twirling for a moment before revealing itself to be a tiny fairy.

Zander tried to walk out, but the archway would not let him leave. His own fairy prevented it. "But she n-needs us," he protested, banging on the invisible wall.

A dark guard crept behind Vespa, his blade pointed toward her back.

"No, no, no." Ferra rushed to the wall. "Vespa!" she yelled as loud as she could.

Vespa's fairy started flying in a frenzy as the dark knight approached. Several of the creatures fell but some still moved forward.

The man with the blade swung forward just as the fairy's purple magic ignited, sending everyone flying backward—and suddenly a solid wall appeared where the window had been.

Zander, Ferra, and Mahoney were sealed behind the wall, away from the dark army, without Vespa, and without any way to help her.

CHAPTER FIFTEEN

Katia followed Silexa through different pathways and passages, eventually losing her sense of direction completely. She felt like the walls were closing in around her.

Silexa didn't talk much. She explained the directions and layout of the palace and where they were heading but nothing about how or why she knew the place so well.

They reached a dark tunnel, and Silexa stopped.

Katia looked around, confused. "What?"

"I'm thinking." Silexa fidgeted with her fingers. "If we travel through UnderElm it would take us right to the grate. But it's risky."

"What's UnderElm?" Katia asked. "Why would it be risky?"

Silexa continued mumbling to herself but then turned toward her. "You are about to find out. Follow me."

"Wait!" Katia grabbed her arm. "What kind of danger?"

Silexa did not answer but slipped away through a small tunnel chiseled in the rock.

Having no choice but to follow, Katia crouched down behind her and entered the dark tunnel. She felt the carved jagged stone sharp on her palms. The passageway had been carved out by hand with painstaking effort. She could feel the different layering of brick on brick, from the rebuilds of so many wars.

The tunnel sloped downward, nearly vertical, and each step became more precarious. She slipped once, sending small bits of brick tumbling. Her hands gripped the sharp edges, scratching up her arms and fingers. Silexa continued on, not missing a step. Katia grimaced through the pain and followed.

The passage was uneven and jagged, sloping in places and smooth in others. It narrowed and curved unnaturally and seemed more of a rough path through random wall gaps than planned architectural design. Several times Katia felt closed in, the panic of dying under the earth catching her breath. Her only thought was to get out as fast as she could.

A strange purple light traveled upward toward her, a soft nightlight, like mist across water in early morning. Katia stepped out of the tunnel and took a deep breath in the open air, glad to be away from the confining tunnel.

Silexa sat near a rock ledge, peering over into a chamber below.

Katia started to speak, but Silexa quickly waved her silent. Her lips read, "Not now."

Out of curiosity, Katia stepped closer to see this UnderElm. It was dark and vast, an empty hollow beneath the palace. Block shapes in the hazy light revealed themselves to be small homes and buildings, a miniature town left abandoned. No torches were lit in the lanterns and no fires blazed in the hearths. The place was completely empty.

The only light in the entire cavern came from a tree, crooked and old, standing tall in the midst of a courtyard. From what Katia knew of trees, it seemed impossible for it to grow in a dark brickyard with no sun and no earth, but there it was, its wondrous limbs stretching outward, capturing the abandoned village in its long arms.

Within the branches and leaves, tiny lights appeared like little starbursts twinkling one after another. Katia knelt at the ledge, leaning in closer to see the strange phenomenon. She presumed they were star bugs living within the tree.

The dazzling spectacle distracted her from realizing Silexa had begun climbing down the rock wall. "Under—what?"

"Elm," Silexa answered. "Come on. We don't have much time."

Katia watched from the ledge as Silexa reached the cobbled floor and nimbly navigated her way toward the tree until she disappeared from view. An eerie feeling came over her. She felt both alone and not alone, like others were there watching them. Unsettled, she began climbing down after Silexa.

Katia felt exposed walking through the vacant village, hearing her own movements on stone. To distract herself, she focused on the rows and rows of homes, smaller than they looked from the ledge, miniature, like they were made for children. Her uneasiness intensified, looking for faces in the small windows or overhanging doors. The large tree still in her sight, she picked up her pace and ran to the town center.

As she drew closer to the tree, Katia could see the magnificence of the amber elm, its leaves full and red. The lights inside weren't bugs at all. She couldn't tell what they were. The charming miniature homes hanging from the branches made her think of birds or fairies.

Silexa stood over a mound beneath the tree.

"Silexa?"

She turned. Her eyes soft with tears, a delicate drop sliding down her cheek. "This is my sister, Ymber."

"Oh, no." Katia's cheeks flushed. "I didn't know she—"

Silexa wiped her cheek. "It's all right. Her stone was taken, and she suffered. I just wanted to see her grave once more."

"I don't understand this place." Katia turned herself around. "Why is it here?"

"The dwarves took refuge here, but they deserted it. It's not safe anymore."

Dwarves. All the random details began to click into place. "Well, how long do we need to stay?"

"Not long." Silexa's calm voice sounded unnatural. "There is a sewer drain at the end of the village. That's where we need to go."

"There's something wrong with this place."

"Yes." Silexa stood up. "Look in the shadows for anything strange."

Katia turned her head. Shadows were everywhere. She focused on a building, a small marketplace, the canvas overhang covered in shadows. Staring so intently was playing tricks on her. Were those yellow eyes?

She whipped her head back to Silexa. "What is it?"

Silexa moved her hand toward the chain around her neck. She didn't answer, just stood still as stone, watching the eyes glow in the dark purple hue of shadow.

Katia felt the frost on her skin, the dancing energy of her magic swiftly moving through her body, thrilled it might escape soon.

The eyes of whatever creature it was watched them. Silexa moved very slowly back to Katia's side. "The grate to the sewers is on the edge of town," she whispered.

"Do you think we'll make it?"

The question was never answered. At that moment the eyes surged forward from the shadows, hurtling toward them.

"Run!"

Katia swiftly followed in Silexa's wake.

The creature was fast, and she could feel the intense evil emanating from it as it chased them.

"Don't let . . . it touch you!" Silexa yelled with staggered breath.

The creature was covered with the dark magic Katia had sensed before. She could hear it trailing close behind. Katia turned to see its approach, running like a man.

Her magic kicked in, and she aimed her fingers toward the floor, sending slippery frost over their trail.

They turned down a side street facing the back row of the dwarven houses. Katia caught a glimpse of the creature sliding on stone. Her heart leaped at the thrill of the pursuit—then she caught sight of more yellow eyes, many more in the shadows.

"There's more!" she yelled to Silexa.

Silexa picked up her pace. They were nearing the end of the village. Bars appeared across the sewer grate, the entrance to the underground tunnels.

Katia glanced behind. The shadows were upon them. "No!" she shouted and raised her hands in a cross, protecting herself. Ice shot forward, bouncing off the brick homes, forming a barricade of ice. It should slow them down, she thought.

The pounding coming from the other side confirmed it would not. At first she'd thought the creatures were spirits, but these were flesh and blood. Real people. For some reason this affected her more. She didn't want to hurt people.

"Katia!"

Katia staggered back and began to run again as fast as her legs could move. From behind came a sound like shattering glass. They had broken through.

Running in the dark, she tripped again and again, stumbling into unknown objects in her path. The presence of the dark magic crept close around her, suffocating her will.

Above, Katia heard what sounded like the buzz of bees. Purple lights illuminated the dark space overhead. Distracted, she fell over a crate, sending her tumbling. She looked up to see the darkenings mere steps away. Her cold magic clung to her fingers, ready to act, when a streak of purple dropped like a falling star, burning brighter as it hit one of the creatures, who then fell to the ground.

Suddenly a shower of purple streams pelted down like rain, taking out the creatures one by one.

Katia felt someone at her shoulder tugging her arm. She flinched, though it was only Silexa helping her to her feet.

"What—?" Katia tried to speak but failed.

Silexa didn't say anything, but stared at the weird phenomenon, just as clueless.

"My lady," a voice cried from the crowd of fallen darkenings. "Please."

Silexa paused.

Katia grabbed her arm, pulling her away. "It's a trick."

"The fairies," Silexa said, her voice soft.

"Leave them. We need to get away."

Silexa turned to face Katia, the look in her eyes bright with understanding. "A fairy's bite."

"A what?"

"Who are you?" Silexa asked the crowd of the fallen.

"Bremin," a voice answered. A man stood in the midst of the other fallen, who were now awakening like the first, as if reborn. "Of the court of Reinoh. I . . ." The man stumbled and looked at his hands, a small red drop of blood visible on his thumb. "I do not know what happened nor where I am or have been."

Katia gaped, astonished at what she just witnessed. She turned to Silexa. "What's going on?"

"They are waking up."

"But how?" As she said the words, Katia connected the meaning. On the ground she saw it: the little purple wings of a fairy.

Silexa bent down and scooped it up. Its tiny body clung to her arching fingers. A rhythmic pulsing of the fairylight steadied to her own breathing. And then within a moment the light faded and was gone.

Katia gasped. "They're dying?"

One by one as the men shook out of their mesmerized state, the purple lights that were once so brilliant in the sky blinked and were gone.

"No. Silexa. Don't let them die."

"I have no choice." She kept the fairy in her hands. "They saved these people. Their sacrifice has saved us." She turned back toward the crowd. "Sir Bremin."

A man walked forward. "Yes, my lady."

"Do you know me?"

He bowed. "I am part of Reinoh's inner circle. I know of you."

"Gather the bodies of the fallen fairies. Find any alive and see if they will speak with me."

The man bowed again and did as she bid. The tiny flickers of fairylight extinguished one by one and were placed in a wooden crate found in the alleyway. A few fairies were still alive, flying about. Silexa sat away from the others and spoke to them.

Katia's heart felt heavy. The tiniest things in the world could win the battle between light and dark.

Once all the dead were found, Katia watched a moment of quiet reflection among the men who'd survived. Caps were removed to honor the little saviors. A strike of flint sparked the wood and the crate began to blaze. The intense magic within the fey changed the fire to purple, transforming the atmosphere to a lovely twinkle-like sunset.

Katia's eyes were wet with tears. She had never been so touched by a divine act.

"Are you all right?" Silexa asked, returning to her side.

"It's beautiful."

"Fairies only know valor. They are bound to it."

Katia wiped her eyes dry. "It doesn't seem fair."

"No." Silexa raised her hand. "Bremin. Gather the ash in a jar. It may become useful."

"What are we doing now?"

Silexa steadied herself on the uneven ground. "The fey will do what they can to alert others of the darkening. Bremin will lead us to the dungeons."

"And what's in the dungeons?"

Silexa's eyes brightened. "The king."

CHAPTER SIXTEEN

Reynolds looked down the dark corridors near the winding staircase. Audra had simply vanished. The only sound came from the guards pounding on the barred door of his cell.

"Come on." Reynolds tugged at Vanya's shirt collar. "I need some answers."

"But what of the Louving?"

Reynolds registered where he was in the palace. "As you said, it's time. If she tells Sharrod, there is nothing that can come of it."

A room near his cell stood open. Something caught his eye. He ran there and found the abandoned blue cloak of one of the guards strewn across a high-backed leather chair.

He snatched it and flung it over his shoulders, fastening the hood tight. "There. This should help."

Vanya gazed at him with unreadable eyes. "What answers are you seeking?"

"It's more like pieces to the puzzle." With that, Reynolds started down the stairs, Vanya close behind him.

Reynolds hadn't run through the palace in years, not since the explosion at the ceremony, the fating of the daughters of Prolius to the stones—the same night he forced Taren to help him create the Vivatera and both were exposed to magic.

The atmosphere of the place had changed though the clicks of his boot heels on the stone floor felt as familiar as if no time had passed.

"Tell me what you see?" he asked Vanya, who had an eager gait but could not match the stride of Reynolds' grown legs.

"There are black shapes in corners. There are traps."

"We have to avoid as many as we can. Can you direct me?"

The boy reached up and touched Reynolds' arm. A sight flashed in his mind: the guards patrolling around the perimeter, on the balcony before the Grand Hall, under stairs and doorways—all with the same energy, a purple-black aura surrounding each body.

"Hold on." His instructions to Vanya were unnecessary as the boy had gripped his wrist with all his might. They charged around the winding stairs to a vacant floor where they quickly slid behind a long drape next the large window overlooking the city. Guards slowly moved past, monitoring the floor. Looking out, Reynolds noticed how the city did not sparkle as it had. The lights were dimming.

The guards turned the corner, and Reynolds could see the path clearly.

They sped down the corridor, their hearts steady with the pace. The black shapes were ever-present in his peripheral vision. The east wing lay hidden within the walls of the palace: that is where they had to travel—to the built-up ruins surrounding the war-broken stone—where he and Taren first experimented with the magic.

Frequently, Reynolds pulled Vanya out of sight, down hidden backways, and through secret doors. The boy provided the insight he needed.

A harsh voice entered in his mind. "*. . . I found you . . .*"

Reynolds stopped and turned toward the voice. The corridor was empty. Only Vanya stood near him, confused.

"It's all right." Reynolds patted him on the shoulder with reassurance. He looked down each empty corridor, unsure he had heard anything at all.

"*. . . Hawk . . .*" The voice now had a face. It was not the demon horns of Sharrod as he feared. This face had eyes deep and soulless, black as night. It came to his mind like a flash of heat, a sharp pang piercing the image.

Reynolds reached for Vanya. Heat seared through his hand and up his body. It felt as if a bolt of energy sparked before him and everything went white. He let go of the boy. The pain disappeared, but the burning remained.

"Vanya?" Reynolds whispered, searching for the boy. His hands touched a matted mess of hair. A sphere of blue light surrounded Vanya, who was huddled into a ball. "What's happened?"

"He knows," Vanya whispered. "He knows I have betrayed him."

"He's not after you. He used you to get to me. " Reynolds looked around, trying desperately to see. He sensed the walls around them—he knew they existed. However, he could not see them. Extending his hand, he grazed the rough stone with his fingertips. "I . . . I can't see."

"You are in the plane."

"What do you mean?" Reynolds bent down and analyzed the light coming from Vanya. He could see the magical energy flowing through his body. The life-force circulated with each heartbeat. Beyond him was vast, empty space. He now understood sight as Jeanus must experience it.

"But you have sight, Vanya? You can see beyond the plane?"

"Yes."

Reynolds looked at his own hands, not as brilliantly white as Vanya's aura, but a cool blue. "Is there a way to fix this?"

"I do not know."

"It's okay. It's not your fault." Reynolds lifted the boy back to his feet and placed his hand on his shoulder. "You'll need to be my eyes right now. I'm going to tell you how to get to the apothecary."

He closed his eyes, filling his mind with the memory so Vanya could use it. He'd run down this hallway so many times. "A doorway is at the end of the hall. Do you see it?"

"Yes."

"That leads to a winding staircase." Reynolds walked forward, trying not to be alarmed at the empty space below his feet. "And let's hurry. I don't like this feeling."

Vanya picked up the pace, and they sped through the corridor.

Reynolds kept blinking, trying to restore his vision, but the strain sent pangs to the side of his head. White streams of energy trailed after them like shooting stars in the night sky. He felt trapped in space and time.

The magic reacted strongly within him, heightening his peripheral senses. Dark magic crept around like an unidentified mass, reminding him of the danger. Losing his sight scared him more than anything. If that was Sharrod's endgame, it was a strong retaliation.

Reynolds watched Vanya turn left before him and felt his body move down the familiar steps, though he couldn't see anything around him. "Follow the tunnel at the bottom of the stairs. It will lead you there."

Vanya stopped and looked around before proceeding.

In the distance was a faint glow. The stain of magic still held strong after so many years. Behind walls of stone, he could make out the hearth, the caster, the melting pots. So many years ago, he had experienced something incredible and made the biggest mistake of his life.

"Do not think of it," Vanya interrupted Reynolds' thoughts. "You should not blame yourself for fulfilling a prophecy."

"It's not that easy."

Vanya looked up at him. "The Vivatera is not finished. It has one more thing to do."

"And you know this . . . ?"

"I see it."

Reynolds closed his eyes to the white. In his mind, the flashes of memory sealing themselves around his heart—the brilliant streams of magic combining together in the apothecary, the terrible explosion, the burns, the scars, the look on Naomi's face as Taren's knife plunged in her chest, the magic swirling around her, protecting her, the image of her walking into the fire, the shock and horror as she fell into the River of Souls fighting the fiery temptress . . . The pain of remembrance flooded every fiber of his being. His decisions, both good and ill, shaped the fate of this magical world, though he could not save it. The only thing he had was hope.

Reynolds knew Naomi would act braver than she was. She no longer had innocence. She had knowledge. Naomi had walked full stride into the fire to save him and Arie from the Mountain Trolls. She would do it again—she would do whatever fate demanded of her. Naomi would come here, he knew. The noble, brave girl, not caring one fraction about her own life, just for those around her. She would save others because she loved.

"The Vivatera won't work again." Reynolds knew in his heart there was no way to save her. "And even if it tries, Naomi has a choice." He sighed before he opened his eyes again. "And I know what she will choose."

Vanya stared at him with blue eyes filled with deep sympathy and said nothing.

"I see the light of the room. Take me there."

Vanya navigated. However, Reynolds knew the corridor well. As they came closer, the room sharpened in his focus, every detail preserved, just as he had left it. He didn't need Vanya's sight anymore. He could see the stain of magic as visible as torchlight.

When Reynolds walked in, it smelled like home. The apothecary lay quiet and undisturbed in this isolated corner of the palace. It was in the older part, a secret to the uninitiated. The accumulated dust made him feel more at ease. No one had touched any of the instruments, bottles, or books since he had been there with Lytte eighteen years before. His fingers trailed through the dirt on the wooden tabletop, finally stopping on the collection of different vials. Reynolds picked up one, reading the inscription.

"Sunsparks." He smiled, turning it over. It was clearly empty: he had used the last of what he had. He handled the others with just as much wonder. The last was an iron cast with a hole in the middle, a mold for the hot metal to form. He touched it without thinking. It was cold to the touch, but he still could feel the singe of heat, the burn to his skin. He examined his hand, and the spiraling scar around his palm. His eyes traveled to his loose shirt front. He reached up and spread the fabric away, seeing the red rash of scars tightly knitted with his own flesh.

His eyes closed . . .

Boom!

Red sparks shooting from the fire. The purple swirls of magic tightening like a snake.

The heat . . . the burning . . .

Taren's terrified young face. Reynolds' shock, the horror of what he had just done.

"Reynolds?" Vanya's voice woke him from the haunting. A pile of books spread out before him. "Is what you are looking for in these?"

Reynolds collected himself. "Yes." He returned the cast back to the table, never intending to touch it again.

Among the different descriptive manuals on the elements was a small, leather-bound notebook. Reynolds grabbed it and started thumbing through it.

"Lytte's journal." He skimmed the different pages, mumbling as he went along. "Here," he stated at last and read aloud.

" *It is of my opinion that the girls must be separated. The effects of the magic are too great while together. Though seared to the spirit of each girl, the magic cannot act alone. It must have a conduit. The girls are that as of now . . .'* " He skipped ahead, looking for something else.

" *If the stones of magic were to be brought together, I fear this would not be enough. The instability of the elements could rip the fragile balance of the world. Without the elements, nature would not survive.'* "

Reynolds frantically looked through the next pages. "Come on, Lytte," he mumbled. He stopped on the last journal entry.

" *The child is a surprise to us. I am delighted. It is prophecy fulfilled in my lifetime. She has the mark as the others do but without the binding. She is a conduit. She has the power of this world and the ethereal plain. She will have the choice, unlike the others. We must keep her safe. If she is safe, the power to restore balance is hers.*

" *It is advisable to keep Reynolds as close as possible to her. I fear his involvement in the beginning has left its own mark. I fear he will also be needed—'* "

Reynolds slammed the book shut.

"Reynolds." Vanya's voice calmed the atmosphere. "Someone is coming."

He could hear it now: soft footsteps still a distance away. Reynolds' eyes focused on the three shapes heading their direction—two with magical auras unlike each other, one cool as ice, the other gray as stone, both dangerous, alight with energy. The third was the least magical but wore a stain of old magic. Reynolds could see he wasn't a magic user but knew the old ways.

Reynolds unsheathed his long sword and shoved Vanya behind him protectively. They slid into the corner near the hearth, silently awaiting the intruders.

The first came to the entry, hooded, with a sword equal to his own. He combed through the knickknacks thrown on the ground.

The next two were slighter, one with an unmistakable mark. It so surprised Reynolds that he nearly lost his grip.

He raised his sword with two hands. "Don't move any farther!"

The third walked with no fear toward him. He stopped and stood, staring first at Reynolds, then at the boy behind him.

"I do not think you will need that sword, son of Cornwallis," the man's voice slid like ice through the air.

Reynolds looked closer at the face; only a hint of magic traced the lines. He wore the appearance of a king, one claimed to be dead.

CHAPTER SEVENTEEN

The tree stood unmistakable in the midst of the rolling hills and forest glade. The large branches stretched out like a protective canopy, a shield from the rain. The beautiful dragon carried its crew with grace, gently gliding them down to the softened earth amidst the hillocks.

Naomi kept quiet the entire ride, knowing Taren's eyes stayed on her the whole time, heating the back of her head with his penetrating gaze. She didn't turn but stayed focused on the journey. Taren was perceptive and understood her silence. If he didn't know already what she had decided to do, it would not take long for him to figure it out if she let him. It took all the strength she had to not fall apart.

As the dragon settled, Naomi's bare feet slid to the ground, the grass cold on her skin. The earth yielded to the slightest pressure, but she wanted to remember the feeling of the dirt between her toes, the connection to the minerals igniting her senses.

"Naomi?" Taren's voice awoke her from her reverie.

She continued walking without turning. "Yes, Taren."

He ran to her side and grabbed her shoulder. "Please, we need to talk."

Naomi looked ahead, spotting a small woman, possible dwarven, at the base of the tree. Micah and Spotswood greeted her as they made their way up the slope. Lottie stayed close to Naomi, swinging their clasped hands back and forth.

Taking in a deep breath, Naomi forced herself to smile at Taren. "There is time, I promise."

Lottie took off running up the hill, leaving Naomi's hand bare. Taren grabbed it as it swung back.

"Let me go." She tried to pull it out of his grasp. This slowed her down, and she made the mistake of looking at him. His eyes were red, like he hadn't slept in days. He looked fatigued and weary. She saw the pleading in them and felt her heart splinter away from her.

He knew. She didn't know how he knew, but he knew. It wouldn't change her fate, though.

"You have a choice," is all he said.

"I don't."

Taren attempted to grip her hand tighter, but her fingers slipped through his grasp with a magical pull he clearly hadn't expected. Naomi used what charm she could to leave him stupefied as she walked to meet the others.

The small woman had tears in her eyes. "Oh, you are Naomi." The woman placed her hands on Naomi's face and kissed her cheeks. "You are even more beautiful than Zander described."

Naomi lost her breath. "Zander?" She grew weak with surprise, her voice trembling. "You know my Zander?"

The woman smiled. "Come inside, and I will tell you a story."

Inside the tree, surrounded by wrapping, twisting roots, the hall led to a wide open room enchanted by tiny glowing fairy lights. The warmth pleasantly surprised Naomi, enveloping her skin like a blanket of heat sweeping between the chambers.

"Please, take a seat." The woman gestured to the generous stools spread around the room. Naomi and Lottie sat near a large root, Micah and Spotswood opposite. Taren never entered, completely absent.

The woman cleared her throat before telling her story. She was simply called Mother, and she spoke of a home under a great city. A boy named Zander had come with the Prince of Southwick, a man named Bryant, who was in love with Silexa, a daughter of Prolius and one of Naomi's sisters. She told about the death of Ymber, another sister, and the charge to the haunted swamp called the Musungu. So much information rushed out of her lips, Naomi lost track of the details, all but a few: Zander, the boy who had been raised as her brother, was alive, and her sisters were all heading to Southwick.

Naomi's grip tightened on Lottie's hand, grateful for something to hold and keep her grounded. Her emotions bubbled to the surface, but she smiled and held in the tears.

A small stream or two trailed down her cheek. She didn't wipe them away. Instead, she wore them in honor of those involved, all those who were affected by her life, her decision.

When she had finished with her tale, Mother stood up. "I have food and places for you to rest."

Naomi looked up at her. "Where is Lytte?"

"After you rest, my dear. He is preparing to see you."

"Do the fairies sleep?" Lottie asked.

"Of course." Mother smiled. "Let me show you."

Lottie followed Mother into a different chamber, leaving Naomi to her thoughts.

Micah came near her and wrapped his arm around her. "Come, Goldie. You must eat."

"I don't feel like eating."

"And that is why you must eat. Tomorrow we leave for Southwick, and you must be ready."

Her stomach pitted with fear. She would never be able to eat now. "I'll be in soon."

Micah let go of her and bowed. "Dear princess. I respect your wishes. Your heart is bright, and yet it seeks for release." He touched her forehead with his hand. "You will have peace. That is a promise."

He left the room, and Spotswood bowed and followed. Naomi had no interest in joining the others. Instead, she stood and turned down the opposite archway.

In the next room, other dwarves worked on goods and supplies, some sharpening blades, others forging weapons. A few stopped as she entered, gazing like they had never seen anything like her. Several pointed and said her name. Clearly "Naomi" had become a word which harbored much talk.

Soon, though, the room became silent, with all eyes turned to her.

The nearest dwarf sank to one knee and bowed.

Naomi frowned, confused. "No, you don't need to…"

The two dwarves behind him quickly repeated his actions. Like a ripple in water, dwarf after dwarf stooped to honor her as their princess, the girl of prophecy here to right the world.

Naomi lost all words. She didn't know what to say or do.

"Dearest Naomi," a voice entered her mind. She knew the voice and turned around—to nothing. All the dwarves still bowed, not saying a word, but across the room lay another door.

Naomi quietly tiptoed through the room toward the arched opening, her bare feet navigating the rough ground. The dwarves' low bow kept steady as she walked past.

"Please," she said to one. "Please, there is no need to bow."

The nearest dwarf said nothing, just looked up into her eyes. *"But he needs you,"* is what she heard.

She stopped, looking around again. No one was there. *"Come through the door."*

Naomi wiped away the strands of hair that stuck to her face, clearing the sweat from her brow. Her hands grasped the thick roots which framed the archway, and she entered the narrow pass, dark and deep, smelling of rich earth. She felt along the way as it turned and twisted, a small light at the end of the passage guiding her. As she reached it, she turned and gasped.

Alone in a small hovel amongst the roots of the great tree stood her mentor—though he was not fully there, an incomplete version of the man he used to be.

"Lytte?"

"My beautiful girl," he said with his arms outstretched.

She ran to him, embracing him as best she could in his incomplete state. "What happened?"

"A sacrifice, my dear. I am still as sound as I can be but am only a mere shape."

Naomi pulled back to examine him. A sad, longing look covered his face, that mystic forlornness worn by the shades left on earth to roam. She'd seen the same expression in a man named Dobbins Foger, the stain who'd possessed the form of Nobbs the Grumbear in the Netherfields. And again in the souls trapped in the river in Mount Ignis.

"How?" was all she could say.

Lytte sat wearily on the curved end of a large root. Naomi took a seat on the ground by his feet, patiently waiting for him to speak.

"I could not let the Louvings have me." His voice quivered. *"If they killed me, my dear, they could use my blood. And I could not be used like that."* His eyes bore into her soul. *"If I took my life, my blood was useless."*

"Oh, Lytte." Naomi touched his ghostly feet. "I'm sorry."

A gentle smile crossed his face. *"Death is a strange place to be. I do not wish for life. I lived long and well. There is no place for me here."*

"Why are you here and not at the camp or Southwick?"

"I came to help you. That is all."

"Help me?"

He touched her shoulder. *"You are here to meet Pera."*

Naomi immediately knew Lytte had something to do with her preparation—the visions, the Everstar, all happening while in his tent.

"What do you know?"

"The danger is escalating in Southwick. Sharrod is preparing a way to bring Shon to the surface and, with him, open the gates of the Netherrealm. Do you know any of this, my child?"

"I was instructed in a dream."

"Pera is the only one who can release Shon from his exile. The gateway will open tomorrow night during the blood moon. That is the only time Pera can appear in physical form. I know she has strengthened you to handle it, but there is much mentally that cannot be prepared. I wish we had time."

"Tomorrow, then." She sighed. "How can you help me?"

Lytte smiled at her. *"Such a brave girl. I am not worried about your heart. It is so strong. Let's work on your mind."*

His gentle fingertips touched her temples, and Naomi closed her eyes.

Taren began to follow the others into the tree but stopped, watching Naomi alone. He reflectively looked at his hand that had just touched her. There was nothing unusual, but something changed.

Not since he had first met her had he been able to read her magic, except in this last moment, and he was mesmerized by the clarity in which it spoke to him.

She had a terror within her that couldn't hide behind the protective shield of the Vivatera. She was scared, absolutely terrified about what she was going to do. So calm on the surface, but that emotion could not be hidden.

Naomi was prepared to die, and soon.

What could he do? Taren picked up a nearby rock and threw it as hard as he could. He threw another and another. He began to run after them until he reached the edge of the hillock.

There, he sank to his knees, and in his desperation he cried out, "What do I do?" All the frustration came out in a rush of heat, his magic igniting his soul. The grass around him quickly dried from the rain, warming with every moment in contact with him. The fire surged to his hands like it had for so many years.

He looked at the embers smoldering into his skin, ash flakes rising away.

Astonishment replaced his sadness. He patted his palms together to calm down the magic. He was not broken. He could feel the magic reconnecting inside.

He closed his eyes, letting the renewed energy surge through his veins to his skin. He knew how powerful it had once been, the instant connection he'd had. Except this magic was different; it filled the measure of its power. It had no darkness, only the rush of energy pushing forward.

"I am ready." He opened his eyes. The rain still fell around him.

The feeling of the magic was indescribable. He wanted to tell Naomi—and the thought halted his breath. Naomi was going to be leaving this earth, leaving him. His magic retreated in despair.

She couldn't leave this world without knowing how she had changed him, how he had found himself again, how he loved her beyond any earthly reason. She had to know. She had to know everything.

He didn't have long. Taren wiped the rain from his face and walked back to the tree.

Inside was quiet and dark. Taren wrapped himself around the tangles of roots protruding from the dirt. A feeling of something familiar surrounded him, the warmth of an unspoken memory creeping into his thoughts. This place had an enchantment around it, an old magic that swelled within every branch and mineral. This was no simple tree, but much like the one Naomi visited in Linnonbury. He knew this tree had a purpose, though he didn't know what it could be.

He found a dirt path which led to a set of carved stairs. At the bottom was an empty circular room. Illumination came from small patches of fairies dancing from one tiny fairy home to another. He quickly dismissed them and searched the adjoining room.

"Oh, good greeting to you, Taren," Micah said as he entered. He sat at a long table with Spotswood, Lottie, and a kind-looking dwarf.

"Taren is it," the dwarf addressed him. "Come have some soup, freshly prepared."

"Yes. Come sit," Lottie insisted. "This is Mother. She lives here."

"I am staying here, my girl," Mother corrected. "I could never call this home, but it will do for now."

Taren had no interest in food. "Where's Naomi?"

"Come, come," Mother insisted, pouring him a bowl. "We need to get you warm and well."

"Please," he implored. "I need to find her."

Mother placed the bowl down before him and looked at him, her eyes betraying sadness. "I believe she is with Lytte."

"But Lytte's—"

"He is a stain," Mother interjected. "She still needs instruction from him."

Taren sat in the chair, staring at the swirling pattern steaming from the broth. "Can I see her?"

Mother offered a crooked smile. "Give her time. And be patient." She looked over the state of him. "Goodness. You are soaked through."

"No. I'm fine."

Not listening to his protest, Mother grabbed her own shawl from around her shoulders and paced it on his back. "Eat."

Taren took the spoon and stirred his broth. The others ate vigorously and lightly chatted. Mother, though, watched his every move, still smiling kindly. He slowly brought the spoon to his lips and tasted the savory liquid. A few more spoonfuls and his head began to clear. He couldn't remember the last thing he ate.

Taren looked up from his bowl. "Thank you."

Mother rested her chin on her hands and looked at him. "I can tell when someone has never had a mother. You're as stubborn as they get."

Taren's mind flashed to the only memory he had of his mother—a brief moment so hazy it almost could be a dream. "I've not had many tell me what to do."

"And you want answers that I cannot give."

Taren stilled. "But you know more than you're letting on."

Mother lifted her head. "What would you like to know, my dear?"

"Something is wrong about this tree."

"Very perceptive." Mother sat back in her seat. "What did the tree tell you?"

Taren understood her words and thought about the feelings he'd experienced when he touched it. "Tremendous sadness."

"The trees are the storytellers of this world," Spotswood interjected. "They record our history without saying a word."

Mother nodded to Spotswood. "This is the SisterElm, planted first on this world. It has been here since the beginning of it all."

"Planted first?" Micah asked. "Are you talking of the Histories?"

"Yes," she returned. "I know Lytte has taught you this in the camp. Do you remember?"

Taren never forgot anything. "But Lytte only told us some of the story, what he wanted us to hear. We were merely boys. What does this tree have to do with it?"

Mother caught Spotswood's eye. "I don't know what I'm allowed to say."

Taren noticed the exchange. "I will find out the truth, if not from you, then from the tree itself, so there is no need to protect us."

Mother patted his hand and did not speak. She instead turned her attention to Spotswood, and he nodded in understanding.

"You are asking about the War of the Sky."

Taren scoffed, "That old story? It has nothing to do with a tree."

Mother eyed him. "Tell me the story you know."

Taren thought back. "A father gave a kingdom to his two sons, but in order to keep it, they needed to work together. They didn't and both were banished. It's just a legend, like many of the Histories. None of it really happened."

"You are close, Master Taren," Spotswood clarified. "Histories have seeds of truth, though several have evolved over time."

"You know the real story?"

Mother's kind expression confirmed it. "Yes. We know the story."

"How? If every text is corrupted?"

Mother seemed to sense his agitation. "Do you remember why the brothers were banished?"

"It was the sister," Micah answered, his funny voice full of excitement.

Taren looked at them, puzzled. "I don't remember a sister."

Spotswood looked around the table. "The story you know is true, although needs explaining. On the first morning, before the mountains had shadows, the father, Undal, gave the breath of life to the world we know."

"Breath of life?" Taren was immediately skeptical.

"It was this entire world, not just a kingdom, as the story you know speaks. He made the world for his sons to construct and rule together. His two sons were named Yulin and Shon."

Taren stopped him. "Wait. Shon? Of the Underworld?"

"The very same." Spotswood continued, "The brothers were given this world. This is their kingdom, and they could not agree on how to manage it. Shon did not like waiting for the natural process of life, where Yulin would work patiently for exactness. Shon infused the elements within the world. He is the father of magic in Parbraven."

An amused smile crossed Taren's face. Everyone knew of Shon, the master of everything dark in this world but didn't understand the depth of his malice. "Shon is the creator of the stones, the ones King Prolius found and crafted into those medallions."

"Correct," Spotswood returned.

"Why would he create them? There's no logic behind it."

"We do not have the answers. Shon is a figure of lore, and not much is known about him."

"So, who is Sharrod, if not Shon's lackey?"

"Oh, he's a smart one, Spotswood." It was Mother this time who answered. She absently brushed the table for any crumbs. "Do you think Sharrod has been a ruse the entire time?"

The idea never crossed his mind until now. Taren turned it over and over. The intimidation Sharrod had used on him to bring down Naomi was nothing that he couldn't handle—just a demon from the Underworld who wanted power.

However, Shon was something else, something unknown, brewing in banishment since the beginning of time. Shon was death to the world as they knew it, malice and destruction to everything living. If he was the creator of magic, what would stop him from using it?

A tremor ran through him as all of the thoughts connected. Shon created the stones—they belonged to him—for a secret purpose.

And Naomi . . . Naomi was a key that could unlock everything.

His heart sank in his chest, and he struggled to collect himself. "So, Micah mentioned a sister. How does she enter the story?"

"Ah." Spotswood grinned. "Her name was Pera, most beloved of Undal and cherished by both her brothers. In the fateful argument, Pera came between the two of them. With a valiant, pure heart and only love for her feuding brothers, she was wounded by a blade made of slate stone...Shon killed his own sister."

"Wept in his tears, for years and years," Micah sang the rhyme.

"She died on this very spot. And the tree that has grown over her is blessed by her spirit."

Mother looked around the hollow. "There is magic here. The tears of her father, the God of the Sun, consecrated this ground."

Taren could feel the truth of it within his magic. "Has Pera talked to you?"

"I have seen her, yes," Mother answered.

"And do you know the plan? Can she do anything?"

"Pera will speak with Naomi tomorrow during the blood moon."

Taren sighed, aggravated by his feeling of helplessness. "Do you think Naomi has spoken to her already?"

Mother slowly nodded.

"I need to find out." He said this aloud, not speaking to anyone but himself. Naomi's decision had something to do with Pera. He had to find out more.

CHAPTER EIGHTEEN

The night grew long, and still Naomi had not returned. Taren listened to the talk between the few in the room about different legends and folklore. He had heard much of it before, and his thoughts wandered back to his own troubles.

"We have beds for you," Mother told Taren, waking him from his reverie. She had cleaned up the dishes without him noticing. "We had a few leave us recently, heading to Southwick, you know. I'm sure it will be comfortable for you."

Taren absentmindedly followed her around the twining roots and hollowed earth. Several enclosures were filled with small dwarf families, all preparing for a night's sleep. The fairy lights lit the pathways like torches. It wasn't far from the main room, Taren gathered; he always needed to know his bearings.

The room spread out, wrapping behind a large root. Straw mats lined the walls and around the corner. Taren wasn't interested in sleeping but slunk behind the root, a private place to mull through his thoughts.

As the night wore on, Taren remained still in his mind, but his magic circled around his body, fueled by his new knowledge. The room filled with sleeping people, and Taren's anxiety deepened: Naomi had not returned.

A hand brushed his shoulder and made him jump back until he recognized Lottie's small brown eyes, her curious smile still visible in the darkness. "Sorry I scared you."

"You could never scare me. I wasn't expecting you."

The girl sat down right across from him. She didn't speak, just stared.

Taren knew something was troubling her. "You can tell me."

Lottie sighed. "Naomi is planning on doing something stupid."

"You know this?"

She nodded and held up her hands. "I know everything. I don't know if she forgot that I can read magic if I touch her or if she did it on purpose because she wanted me to know."

Taren rubbed his forehead as if it were painful to process. "Please." His voice was but a whisper. "Please, I need to know."

He could see the concern on her face, and her little voice shook. "She's going to take her life."

Nothing had changed, but the simple confirmation of his suspicions brought Taren's magic to a heated boil. He smacked his fist on the ground, tiny sparks flying from his hand. "When?"

"Tomorrow, I think. Whenever she meets Pera."

Taren stood up. "I have to find her. I have to stop her."

"Wait." Lottie tried to touch him, but he pulled away. "Don't leave me here, Taren."

He shushed her, not wanting to wake the others. "Fine."

Lottie continued to watch him, her face haunted with secrets. "There's more."

Taren turned. He hadn't expected anything more. "What?"

At this, Lottie trembled. "She . . . she—"

Fed up with waiting, Taren stood and aimed for the door.

"She . . . loves you."

Taren stopped at the entrance and looked back at Lottie. A lump formed in his throat. "No, she can't."

Lottie shook her head, afraid to say more. "Sorry." The poor girl burst into tears. Taren still felt the shock of her words. He knew she needed comfort, but he was not the one for it. He couldn't help her. He took a fairy light from the wall and left the room without a word to her.

Not many moved in the night. The hall lay empty, as did the first room surrounded by chairs. He held the lamp high before him, lighting the way around the cavernous root system.

"Lookin' fer sumthin'?" a voice from behind asked.

Taren turned to find a bearded dwarf standing at the ready with a strong axe in his hands.

"Naomi. Where is she?"

"With Master Lytte, sir," the dwarf returned. "Not to be disturbed."

"The hell she is." Taren stood defiant. "Lytte knows me. I'm not a threat to him. Please. Show me."

The dwarf shook his head. "I'm sorry sir. I have me orders."

Taren felt his anger bubble. "Look. I don't care what orders you have. This is bigger than you and me. This involves the end of this world, which includes you and me, so you can just let me pass—"

"Taren?"

Naomi stood in the archway, accompanied by Mother. The sight nearly drained his energy. She looked more radiant than ever, strong and brilliant, nearly glowing like the fairy lights. He exhaled her name, "Naomi."

"Naomi is very tired," Mother stated. "She will be staying in my chamber tonight."

"No!" Taren didn't mean to sound so demanding, but his anger still resonated in his voice. "I need to talk with you," he pleaded with Naomi.

Naomi looked him square in the eyes. "I'm tired, Taren. I need to rest."

Taren saw the sadness in her eyes, and something hurt inside him, like he could feel the pain as well. "Please, just a few moments. Not long." He turned to Mother, silently asking for this one chance.

Naomi whispered something to Mother, who patted her arm. "I'll make up the bed for you, dear."

"Thank you." Naomi kissed her lightly on the cheek. "Thank you for everything."

Mother didn't say anything and turned to the guard and escorted him from the room, leaving Naomi and Taren alone.

Naomi stood still as a statue, not saying a word, but watching Taren. She looked calm, but Taren could see her hands clutched together in tight fists.

Taren thought of the words he wanted to say, yet nothing came out.

After a moment of silence, Naomi spoke up. "I don't want to hear what you have to say."

"What? You don't know—"

She held up her hand, stopping his explanation. "I am so drained. I have no fight left in me—"

"I love you, Naomi." The words spilled out and immediately felt wrong in the air, hanging in the still silence with only the fairies to hear. The look on her face told him nothing of her surprise or delight; she just continued to look at him with haunting sadness. He had to finish the words. "I couldn't let you leave this world without knowing."

Naomi slid her eyes away from him, gazing at the fairies as they flittered about. Her face held back any emotion she felt, her voice coming out barely a whisper. "Why do you think I am leaving?"

"Because—" Taren staggered forward toward her. She still stood as stone. "You are. I know this. It's no secret."

A silent tear slid down her face. "You shouldn't have told me."

Taren stopped and took in her beauty as he hadn't before, transfixed by the sadness in her eyes. "I'm sorry."

Naomi's lip trembled. "Me, too." She looked away. Her exhaustion was evident, and she began to sway. Taren grabbed her arm and led her to a stump to sit. "Thank you," she uttered in an airy whisper.

Taren sat next to her, wanting to comfort her, to help her in what little way he could. His courage grew as he felt the energy around her. "Please. You don't have to do this."

Naomi's cry turned into a laugh. "I am not that selfish, Taren. My life means very little compared to the magic."

"I . . ." Taren's heart raced. "I think you're wrong. The magic means very little. You are what's important."

"You can't say that—"

Taren cut her off. "The magic is selfish. I know exactly what it wants. You took me away from that darkness."

"Taren. Don't speak any more." She stood, waving off his assistance, and began to walk away. "It hurts me to hear these words . . . and you've hurt me enough."

The words stung. She walked away, leaving him alone with his thoughts.

Naomi did not return to the room with Mother. She wandered outside into the rain. The world was dark, but she knew where the branches hung. She pressed against the tree with her palms, listening to the life-force beat strong within its roots.

"Help me be strong." Her words carried over the pellets of rain, through the air, surrounding the tree with warmth. She felt the gentle branches move at her will, gliding to where she could grab on, lifting her high until the limbs cradled around her body. The leaves shielded her from the rain, providing coverage like a blanket.

Naomi thought of nothing but peace, breathing in the sweet smell of rain on wet, living trees. Her last thoughts weren't of the task ahead or of the people she loved, but the drifting memories of being a child and sleeping in a tree.

Taren sat alone on the earthen floor. His body nearly collapsed under him, his fight drained from him with her last words. He sat in the dark, unable to sleep, listening to the deafening quiet and feeling the magic pulsing around his body.

He stared wide-eyed, blank of all thought, until something grabbed his attention—a sound he knew better than any other sound: the screech of a dragon.

Taren stood and found his way to the entrance of the tree. The outline of gray began to appear near the eastern horizon. The rain drizzled fresh on his hot skin. High above the branches, he saw the warm underbelly of the fire-eater circling to land.

Another cry, husky and dry—distinctly Sebastian's call—rumbled low, shaking the ground. Taren tore off through the grass toward the grove where he knew Sebastian would be. He pressed past the scrub and brush until he stood near the clearing, just in time to witness the long tail whip the trees into splinters. Its harsh thump shook the ground.

Taren had forgotten the enormity of an adult dragon. The red scales reflected like armor in the sparks of light. The dragon snuffed in the chilly rain. Her breath steamed through her teeth, coming from the fire in her belly.

So taken by the beauty of the creature, Taren hadn't noticed the two figures scaling down the beast. Sharp pangs shot through his numb heart, and something new swelled within him, unfamiliar in his current state.

It was hope.

Sera's unmistakable hair shone copper in the hazy half-light. She moved with the grace of the fey, gently gliding down the back of the fire-eater until she lifted off and landed nimbly on the soft earth. Arie, on the other hand, fumbled near the top, sliding past its haunches until he fell downward and hit face-first in the mud.

"Nice." Arie sat up and wiped his eyes.

Sera ran to help him up, pulling the bruised man to his feet. She brushed off some of the dirt before she turned and saw Taren standing alone.

"Taren?" Her voice shook. "Blazes. It is you!" She ran and embraced him before he was prepared for it. "I can't believe it." Her whisper softened his reaction, but he held still.

"How . . . did you find us?" Taren finally spoke.

Sera pulled back. She didn't answer but looked into his eyes. He read her magic quickly, with no hesitation, like she wanted him to know. Her sadness ripped her up inside; she couldn't speak it. He knew that her mother, Andriana, was dead, truly dead, and that Jeanus was injured.

"The Louving," Sera confirmed out loud.

Arie joined her by her side. "Taren, good to see you." He shook his hand with a grip. "You left at the perfect time. That boy was a shape-shifter."

"No." Taren shook his head. "I could have helped. I suspected, but Naomi, she was about to leave on her own. I couldn't let her go alone."

"Then you were where you needed to be," Sera returned. "Oh, monstrous things. Jeanus knew, of course, but I couldn't tell. She was quick to secure the village. But, there . . . there were a few . . ."

Taren knew what she meant. "Do I want to know how?"

"It won't matter." Sera looked distant. "My mother should have died years ago. She was injured while living in Southwick. She never talked about it, but I saw the scar on her stomach. She fled to Linnonbury partially to keep us safe but also because she knew she could prolong her life there. Jeanus could help her." She looked him again in the eyes. "At least she can be with my father again once this stupid fight is over."

Sera walked away toward the dragons, not interested in continuing the conversation.

Arie stayed by him. "I think she is feeling guilt."

"Why?"

"You see, the Louving went looking for Sera. The medallion was what he wanted. Andriana took the hit, right before Jeanus burned the nasty creature. Those beasts are soulless."

"Yes." Taren thought on his own experience with the Louvings. "I couldn't agree more."

Arie gripped his shoulder. "So, tell me the plan."

Taren turned toward the brightening horizon. "There is no plan."

"We flew here to help you. There must be a plan."

"Well," Taren turned to him, "if you consider preventing Naomi from killing herself, I guess that's my—"

"What?" both Arie and Sera cried out at the same time.

Sera came back from tending to the creature. "What do you mean? How could she possibly think that's the right thing to do?"

Taren looked down, abashed. "I thought you would know. She seems to think this is the only option."

Sera grabbed his arm. "Where is she?"

Taren pointed to the SisterElm, its large frame highlighted in silhouette. "I believe she is asleep inside."

Sera took off running, and Taren followed.

"Wait!" Arie yelled after them but was soon left behind.

As they reached the tree, they saw a few dwarves had woken to the cries of the fire-eaters.

"Quick! I need Mother," Taren ordered one of the stalwart dwarves near the door. He turned inside without hesitation.

Spotswood and Micah appeared at the entryway.

"Oh, dear lady," Micah bowed. "The morning greets us with a surprise."

Sera bowed back. "Yes, Arenmas, I am delighted as well. Tell me, where is Naomi?"

"I'm sure she must be resting," Spotswood stated. "It is a blood moon tonight." Seeing Taren's confusion, he explained, "The night the sky weeps."

Mother came rushing to the entrance, out of breath. "I've searched. Taren, help me. I can't find her."

Taren swore before tearing inside. All the dwarves were on alert. Every inch of the place, down to the smallest root, was searched.

Mother wept. "She can't have just disappeared. She didn't meet Pera. It was all planned. Tonight is the only night Pera can appear to us. Naomi wouldn't abandon us."

And then Taren knew. A vision of Naomi flashed through his mind, the wind sweeping her hair as she stood on the crest of Linnonbury near the tree she'd visited so often. The tree knew secrets of the world and shared these with her. Why would this tree be different?

Taren ran back outside, daylight now filling the gloomy skies. He began to scale the tree. He heard voices shouting at him from below but continued climbing with no other thought but to find her. He huffed as he reached each new limb, never feeling any confidence in his balance but continuing anyway. He spotted what he thought would make the best perch and where he suspected Naomi would be hiding.

"Naomi?" The branches shifted with the wind. He wrapped his hands around a branch near the spot. With every ounce of energy left, Taren pushed off to swing up to the cluster of branches, but instead, a limb caught him from behind and held him in the air.

A woman stood before him, an aura of heaven encircling her, with hair as dark as night, though her eyes shone like stars. She stood clothed in gold, matching her jeweled crown. In her hands, she cupped a floating six-pointed star.

The woman's voice echoed within his mind. *"Your Naomi is gone."*

Part Three

Rain, Rock, River

Earth and stone

Fires, Fairies

Garden grown

Count the sisters

One by one

First are six

But now there're none

—Six in the Garden, Nursery song

CHAPTER NINETEEN

Bremin pried at the bars of the grate, an echoing peal bouncing around the shaft walls until they gave way. Katia looked down at a void that seemed to go on forever.

"This goes someplace?"

"Yes." Silexa had already fastened a harness from spare rope. "The underground sewers will get us to the dungeons."

Bremin sparked a torch and threw it down the shaft. It lit the tunnel as it traveled downward. Bats flew upward, away from the light and right in Katia's face. She squealed and flailed her arms, sending them out into the large underground cavern.

"Sorry." She quickly composed herself. "I didn't expect that."

Silexa tied the rope into a secure knot around one of the bars of the grate. "It doesn't look too deep. I'll go first. Katia, you can follow when I'm halfway—"

"What about the others?" Katia asked.

"I need them to go find Salvador."

"They'll never make it up that passage."

Silexa frowned in agreement. "You're right. What do you suggest?"

Katia hadn't been expecting that. "Uh, I don't know. I've never been here before. The fairies would know more than me."

Silexa smiled. "Yes, you're right. Bremin. I need to talk with the fairies again."

Bremin obeyed and sent a messenger who brought forth a fluttering of wings—only a few from the large swarm that had existed before.

Silexa sat cross-legged on the ground and motioned for Katia to do the same. One of the fairies broke from the pack and buzzed around Silexa before landing on her finger.

Katia took in every graceful wing, every spin in her petal dress. The little fairy glowed vibrant purple, revealing her emotion. She had been crying, grieving their loss of lives.

Silexa's voice filled with sadness "Thank you, brave ones, for your sacrifice. I will honor your kindness forever."

The little fairy curtsied, pulling the delicate fabric of her dress to its length with her arms. It was as thin as cobweb and as fine as lace.

"Help us once more. Guide these men whom you have saved. Find Prince Bryant. I don't know where he is, but I will share a secret with you if you do."

The fairy buzzed.

"I do not know where he is, but he is with Brandell, the fairykind."

At the mention of the name, the fairy turned a bright white and flew around her hand with delight. Katia's eyes widened, watching the spinning light in the darkness.

"It's settled, then." Silexa went to stand, but the fairy buzzed around. "Oh, yes, sorry. The secret." She took the tiny thing in her cupped hand and whispered something Katia could not hear. When she opened her hand, the little fairy flew away, like releasing a captured butterfly. "Come now, time to get going."

Katia stood, dusting herself off. "What did you say to her?"

Silexa grabbed the rope, securing it to her waist. "That I will die in this fight and . . ." She took a deep breath. "And to tell Bryant I love him."

Katia stood frozen. "Die? You're not going to die."

Silexa's smile looked serene. "I'm giving up my stone, regardless of what happens." She jumped backward and into the pit, the rope suspending her fall and keeping her close to the wall. Katia watched her push off the side, lowering herself little by little.

Katia knew very little about ropes and climbing, but by watching Silexa, she knew enough to get down. She fastened the other rope around her waist and slowly inched her way down.

Her hands gripped the harsh rope, and she began her descent. The bristles cut into her palms, and her muscles tensed as she struggled to hold on. Silexa made it look so easy.

Halfway down, pain shot up her arm, and her grip slipped. Her other hand clutched onto the rope burning into her palm as she slid.

"Find a hold!" she heard Silexa shouting.

Katia found a crack in the wall and jammed her fingers into it. Her hand stung. The skin had rubbed off, leaving fresh, oozing sores were blisters had formed. She flicked her wrist, trying in some way to lessen the pain, and found another hold. She couldn't hang there much longer.

The light from the torch still flickered against the wall. It grew in brightness as she worked her way to the bottom of the shaft.

"Ah!" Katia's hands slipped, and she fell. But then didn't. Stairs appeared below her that she hadn't seen before. She stood on the top step, perplexed. "I swear these weren't here."

She looked toward Silexa, who had her hand on the medallion she wore around her neck.

"Wait, did you make these?"

Silexa didn't answer, but her expression told Katia enough. "We need to go. He'll know we're here."

Katia ran down the stairs to join her. "Okay. Where now?"

"How's your hand?" Silexa asked but without a reply, she wrapped a piece of cloth around Katia's open sores. The stinging cooled immediately.

"Thanks."

Silexa nodded to her, tying a knot on the back of her hand. She turned, picked up the torch from the ground, and held up the light. The dark tunnel stretched out into blackness. "Here. Take this." She handed over the torch.

Katia took it without question, watching her fumble around with her medallion again.

"Sharrod will recognize my magic. I've used it before." Silexa sighed, looking far away. "But we are at the end. And if this is the last thing I do, I want to use my magic the best way I can."

Silexa raised her stone necklace with one hand and pressed her other hand directly on the brick. She stood there with her eyes closed.

Katia waited in silence, watching the intensity on Silexa's face increase, but nothing happened. A spark of ash fell from the torch and hit her hand. "Ouch."

Silexa didn't react. Her head bowed, and her eyes were still closed.

Far down the tunnel, something flickered. At first, Katia thought her eyes were playing tricks adjusting to the dark. But then she saw another flicker and then another.

Silexa still had her eyes closed.

"Silexa." Katia nudged her but got no response. She shoved harder. "Something's coming."

A smile broadened Silexa's face. "It's working."

"Working?" Katia's eyes widened. Flash. Flicker. "What is it?"

"A trail." Silexa suddenly opened her eyes. "I know the way." She started running down the path.

"Wait!" Katia started after her and slipped on the loose rocks and fell to the ground. The dying flame hit a pool of standing water and extinguished completely.

But the tunnel wasn't dark. Within the walls, a soft glow lit a few stones here and there the entire way down the tunnel. Katia gathered herself up and followed Silexa.

She brushed her hands against the lit stones. They weren't hot. It looked as if the heart of the rock burned on the inside. The magic was mesmerizing. She continued on.

The sewer split into different paths. Katia turned again, following the illuminated path. Silexa was not far from her now. A light surrounded her like a fairy glow. On and on she followed her down several tunnels, once again feeling trapped.

Ladders appeared along the way, leading to various places within the palace. Some alleys were completely devoid of water, but the patterns in the rock remained.

Then Silexa stopped. The glowing stones came to an end, and she stood at the bottom of a ladder.

"I guess this is it," she told Katia, and started up.

"Wait." Katia grabbed her ankle. "What are we doing? I mean, what's the plan? You haven't told me anything about where we are or what we're doing."

Silexa stared back as if she knew everything. "The dungeons. That's where the king is."

"So, we just go get the king?"

"Yes." Silexa began climbing again.

"This is crazy," Katia said under her breath but started after her.

The bars were cold to her fingers, dirty from lack of use. She climbed hand over hand, methodically moving upward. Brick surrounded them, a slim cylinder closing in around her. She looked up, watching Silexa's agile feet ascending.

"I think this is it," Silexa whispered down to her, stepping out of sight.

Katia passed the last rung and climbed off the ladder. The stone floor was covered in a thick layer of dust, untouched for years. A large steel door stood bolted before them.

Without any discussion, Silexa took her stone and pressed it next to the lock. The metal grew hot and began to melt, and the lock dropped with a loud thud. Then she began prying at the door with her fingers, working with a furious energy.

"Silexa, please." Katia pulled on her arm. "Let's make a plan."

Silexa looked back at her, wide-eyed. "There's no time. My magic is everywhere. He will know."

"So what? Let's hope Sharrod has bigger problems than us."

The color returned to Silexa's face. "All right. What is your idea?"

Katia pursed her lips, her nerves suddenly rattled. "I haven't thought of anything."

Silexa's lips thinned. "Just trust me. Act with your instincts." She gave the door a hard yank and entered.

Sighing, Katia inched out after her. Farther down, the shadowy hallway was lit by low burning torches. The dark stone walls were layered with cobwebs. A stench worse than the sewers overpowered her, and she had to cover her mouth to keep from gagging. The air felt thick around her skin, hot and humid, suffocating her body like a shield.

Silexa crept cautiously ahead of her, watching for any sign of guards. She stopped near the end of the corridor and peered around the edge.

Katia couldn't contain her anxiety and took a glance. Two guards sat in quiet conversation. Apparently not much was happening within the dungeons. Both wore long black robes.

Silexa pulled her back and looked her in the eye. She had a plan, though she didn't communicate what it was. Katia couldn't do much but trust her.

Taking her medallion in her cupped hands, Silexa slowly pressed it to the stone wall. She closed her eyes again. A small rumble moved through the rock, forming a slight crack which slid up the wall.

Katia quickly whipped her head back to the two guards. Both looked around, unsettled and confused by the sudden quake. One stood, raising his long pole axe at the ready. As the sound of splitting rock grew, the other jumped. Before they had time to react, large boulders toppled from the ceiling. A large chunk of rock came crashing down on them, knocking out one and sending the other cowering for cover.

Katia grabbed a nearby rock and threw it. It knocked the second guard on the head, and he stumbled backward. A small avalanche of dust and debris covered both.

"It won't be long before they crawl out of that." Silexa was back, adjusting her medallion around her neck. "Head that way." She pointed down a dark bank of cells. "I'll take the other side."

And she was gone.

Katia acted immediately, following Silexa's instinct to hurry. The hallway before her had very little light, and she tiptoed through the dark, unsure of her footing. Each cell she came across, she peered in, only to see the dust and ruin of old beds no longer used. On and on, each like the other. Old, forgotten, hidden away.

She found one that had been recently used. The straw mat had not withered away as the others and was still yellow from the sun. It was free from dust, and the water in the dish nearby had not completely evaporated.

The cell door stood wide open. Katia cautiously walked in, her boots marking a fresh new path in the straw.

"He is not here," a cold voice echoed around her.

Katia gasped, turning in a circle, looking for anyone around her. Her hands came up in defense as ice grew at her fingers. "Who?"

No one answered at first, just silence, with nothing but her own heartbeat to quiet her nerves. She heard a gasp, air trapped in someone's throat, searching for breath. "A ghost."

Across from her was a small cell, much smaller than the one she stood in. She could now see dirty hands grasping at the bars so tightly the knuckles had turned white. She inched forward looking for a face.

The prisoner let out a wail like he was in physical pain, and she stopped.

"Hush," she tried calming him, looking over her shoulder. "Quiet, please, I'm not a ghost—"

He began to clank his cup back and forth, making a loud vibration around each bar.

Katia ran to him, grabbing his fingers to stop the noise. "Stop it. You'll send the guards here."

"Ghost!" he kept saying over and over. He stopped clanking and grabbed his knees. Now she could see his face. He was an older man but not as hopeless as she imagined. His shabby clothes might have once been refined. The once-rich velvet hung in tatters on his frail body. He would not look her in the eyes.

"I promise I'm not a—"

"Irina . . ."

Katia froze. "What did you say?"

He began mumbling, clearly shocked. "I'm sorry, Irina. I'm so sorry, I'm sorry."

"No. Stop. Please. I'm not Irina. Please."

His hands slipped from the bars, and he moved to cower in his corner. His mumbling became a whine, a cry that nearly hurt to hear.

Katia felt a pull like string inside her, wrapped delicately around a treasured memory. "Please. Stop. Irina . . . my mother's name was Irina."

The man grew quiet. She tried to see his face, but it was blocked from view.

"Do you . . . did you know my mother?"

The silence grew. Katia peered into the cage but couldn't see any movement.

"Please. If you know anything about my mother, then maybe you can help me. I'm looking for my brother. His name was Vanya—"

The man's hand slid through the bar, shoving a dirty finger toward Katia's face. "You haunt me. Why must you haunt me?"

"Because you killed her," Katia stated without doubt. "You killed my mother."

The man's face came into focus. His hollow eyes were empty of any feeling. His long, greasy hair clung matted to his head, hiding any regal quality. He did not react to the accusation but looked at her with pity, gaunt from endless self-inflicted torture.

"Irina." Her name fell out of his mouth like liquid. "I loved you, Irina. I could have made you happy."

Flashing hatred for this man made the cold in her fingers rise. All she had thought about was taking revenge, but now she felt pain instead, unbearable sadness. "She . . . I was happy before you took me away from my family." Her voice was but a whisper. "Why couldn't you have left us alone?"

"No. No. Irina. Please forgive me. I saved your son. He's alive, Irina."

"Where is he?"

"He sees. He is a seer. He is close to Sharrod."

"Can you take us?"

The man grew silent, looking at her. Soft contemplation covered his expression.

Katia couldn't deal with his self-pity. "Listen. We need you. All Southwick needs you. Nobody wants a wallowing king. We need someone strong to follow."

"I am not that king." He retreated back to the shadow.

Katia grew frustrated again and took a seat, leaning on the bars behind her.

Soft footsteps startled her, causing her to reflexively jump.

Silexa stared at the cage, a kind expression on her face. She sat before the bars and began to hum. Katia didn't recognize the music but sat and watched her quietly.

> *"Of salt and sea the earth remains*
> *A playful garden gay*
> *And on the rocks the waves regain*
> *The capturing light of day.*
> *'Come play,' said she, 'among the tide*
> *Where seatrim and flower lay.'*
> *'I will,' said he, 'but here I'll hide*

My treasure among the fray.'
Forever they lie, together they die
On the banks of foamy gray.
But the treasure of spoken nigh
True love's continuous stay."

With each verse the man came closer and closer, until Katia could see his full wide expression. A look of awe over every wrinkle.

When she finished, Silexa's eyes were full of tears.

"That is the song of Southwick," the man said softly. "How do you know it?"

"My father sang it to us."

"But only those of royal blood know it."

"Yes."

The man's hand came to his face. "Who are you?"

Silexa's countenance changed. She sat tall. "I am a daughter of King Prolius and Queen Andriana. I am Silexa, and I'm in love with your son."

The man's hands went to his face. "I have killed him."

"No. He lives." Silexa touched his hand with hers. "I promise. He is alive. But I don't know for how much longer. We need your help desperately."

The man withdrew his hand. "I am not the king I was."

"But I know the king you can be." Silexa placed her medallion on the lock, sizzling it clean through.

The man looked shocked.

Silexa stood and offered her hand. "Will you help us?"

The man looked around, unsure at first, but with a deep breath, he grabbed it and rose to his feet. "I will."

Katia was so transfixed by the exchange, so taken by the tenderness, she was nearly left behind.

CHAPTER TWENTY

"No!" Ferra wailed. "Vespa!" She pounded on the brick. "I have to save her. We have to." She began frantically searching for a door or passageway but found only solid wall.

"I don't think we can—"

"Don't tell me we can't. We have to."

Zander saw her desperation and wished he could help. *What would Naomi do at a time like this?* He walked over to Ferra and took her hand.

Ferra seemed startled at first but grabbed it back. Then she lost her fight, and she sat down on the cold stone and began to cry. Zander sat next to her and wrapped his arm around her shoulder. Both stared helplessly at the brick wall between her and her sister.

"What do I do?" she repeated over and over. "Mahoney, help me."

Mahoney came to her side. "I don't know if there's anything we can do."

"But we need her. The fairy magic. It's the plan. The only plan. I can't leave her there to die."

"Ferra, I don't think she escaped the ebony blade."

Ferra punched him in the arm but didn't have the fight within her to continue. "Don't say that."

"Vespa is s-strong," Zander came back. "We n-need to trust her."

"I'm living a nightmare." Ferra put both hands over her face. "This isn't fair. Another medallion gone. Another sister . . . gone?" Her voice faded to a whisper.

Zander looked up at Mahoney, who looked utterly confused about what to do. He finally knelt down beside her and rested his hand on her back. "I'm . . . I'm so sorry."

Ferra turned to him and curled against his chest. He gently wrapped his arms around her and held her as she cried.

Zander watched her for a moment, feeling rather helpless, then stood and walked away, leaving Ferra and Mahoney alone.

He wandered around the room, finding an archway. The gentle light of his fairy flower revealed the rich red brick of the adjoining rooms. Stacks and stacks of crates lined the walls like a warehouse. He walked closer, investigating the storage area. One room had bottles of wine, different ages and tastes; another room had barrels of mead.

A grin crossed his face. Zander ran through other rooms until he found the steep stairs leading up . . . to a door he remembered seeing near the kitchen.

Excitement propelled his legs, carrying him back to Ferra and Mahoney. "I think," he caught his breath, "I think I kn-know where we are."

"Really?" Mahoney raised his head.

Ferra sat up and wiped her face. "How would you know, Zan?"

"From when I worked h-here. Bryant gave me a r-room and everything."

"Do you think anyone is still here?"

"Mildred," Zander said without hesitation. "She ran the k-kitchens."

"Is she trustworthy?"

"Oh, yes." Zander nearly beamed with the idea of seeing her again. She was rough, but he admired her greatly.

Ferra tried to stand and lost her breath.

Mahoney lifted her by the elbows. "Are they getting worse?"

Ferra didn't answer, just straightened herself and began to walk forward.

Mahoney stared after her. "It's okay to ask for help, you know?"

Ferra smirked and stuck out her arm which he hooked around his. "I'm trying."

Zander quickly led them through the rooms and to the stairs. Mahoney climbed first, rattling the trapdoor. He took hold of the handle and pushed up. A hazy gray light filtered down from the room above. Zander motioned to Ferra to climb next. She ruffled his coppery hair before starting, working through her pain with every step. Zander watched her carefully and then followed her.

They entered a storage room full of sacks of wheat. Zander couldn't help but smile. He knew this room. He pulled at the door, which opened to several hallways with different rooms. He practically skipped on the stone looking for anyone, but the passage was empty.

The stillness felt unnatural. While he had been here, not that long ago, the kitchen had been filled with constant bustling hubbub. Where was everyone?

The large kitchen came into sight, and Zander rushed in. The tables, which were usually filled with rows of food in preparation for whatever meal came next, were bare. Near the stoves, pots were overturned, dried sauce clinging to the inside. Rotting fruit and stale bread lay scattered on the floor where rats feasted cheerfully. A saturating, pungent smell of sour apples combined with the overpowering waft of rotting meat and moldering tomato stew.

The place was deserted.

Mahoney looked into the pots. "Does no one eat around here?"

Ferra kicked some of the dried bread away from her feet. "This place is filthy. They just fled."

Zander's worry grew. Mildred would never leave. She lived to cook for others and ran the kitchen like a ship. Becoming frantic, he rushed from the kitchen and down past the different storage rooms. His heart pounded with each discovery—spills, ripped wheat sacks, broken wine bottles.

He ran down the hall where he remembered Mildred's room to be. She stayed so close to the kitchens. The door was opened slightly. He pushed against it, but something blocked it.

With all his might, he slammed his body again and again, wedging the door wider open every time until he hit it hard enough and tumbled in, landing against the bedframe. Instantly the smell overwhelmed him, and a sharp gag came to his throat. Zander shook his head and turned to see what had blocked the door.

There, propped against the frame was Mildred, dead, the color completely drained from her face. Dried blood stained the corners of her mouth. Her eyes were still open from whatever shock had come at the moment of her death.

Zander turned, no longer holding back, and vomited at the side of the bed.

Ferra entered the room. Horror crossed her face, and without hesitation, she tenderly wrapped her arms around Zander. Mahoney followed her and went directly to investigate the body.

"She's been dead for days." He respectfully closed her eyes. "Looks like a blow to the head."

"S-she," Zander tried to speak but started sobbing.

"I don't understand why anyone would do this."

Mahoney picked up her wrist, examining it. "There was definitely a struggle."

"And how do you know that?"

Mahoney looked at her with his eyebrow raised, indenting the scar on his face. "I don't think I need to answer that."

Ferra shifted, her hand pressed to her forehead. "There has to be other people here. Right? Not everyone could be in the dark army."

"I—" Zander wiped his eyes with his sleeve. "I can take you."

Mahoney bowed his head. "You are braver than many I have fought with."

Zander tried to smile at the compliment but just didn't have the heart. He couldn't take his eyes off Mildred. Death still confused him. He hadn't seen his father dead, only heard about it from Bryant. Witnessing Curtis ripped apart in the Musungu had been horrifying, but nothing was left. And though Ymber passed away in Mother's home in UnderElm, she had been at peace, as if she were sleeping in a dream. Mildred didn't deserve to be left to die alone and in pain.

Zander quietly left the room. A fire lit within him. He hadn't felt angry about the different things that happened so far, just calmly accepted each and dealt with the consequences. Anger was a new emotion, and he snapped. It was time to end this, time for a normal life.

Wenlock grabbed the instrument back from one of the refugees. "This is a sensitive tool. Not to be handled like a grumbear."

The kid laughed at his old wizened ways but left.

"Sir." It was Salvador. He had paced restlessly about, skulking like a cat waiting for its master. "Sir, I think something has happened to them."

"And why do you say such things?"

"It shouldn't take this long."

Wenlock began cleaning his eyepiece with his tunic. "Come now, they are not lost. Landon is a smart boy. Takes after his uncle." He winked in jest, but the man was in no mood for it. "Well, then. What do you propose?"

"I don't know." Salvador began to pace again. "I don't like it in here. We have nowhere to go. And I am not protecting Silexa as a promised I would."

"So, you need to get back to her. I see." Wenlock walked back over to the water hole and looked down. The water level had fallen. "What's this, then?"

"What do you mean?" Salvador looked as well. The level had definitely lowered. "It must have worked. They must have done it."

Wenlock laughed. "No. There's no magic that did this. The Meridian doesn't use magic, just numbers. Calculations. It's an instrument, not a magic wand."

"Then how did it lower?"

Wenlock couldn't believe it. "Are you saying that you have lived in this city all your life and never experienced the waning of the tide?"

Understanding, Salvador quickly measured the hole. "Here. Help me."

Wenlock took the man's arm and braced his feet, helping to lower him down. Within a few feet, he jumped down. A small splash of water echoed off the wall. Wenlock looked down. "Can you see the tunnel?"

"It is too dark to see."

Wenlock quickly rummaged through his satchel. It took him a second to find the little lantern. He hit it a few times with his palm. Nothing. The wick fell limp, but with a twist and the tiniest bit of air, the light began to glow again. He got on his knees and gently lowered the lantern down.

Salvador reached for it, grabbing it at the base. "Ooh." He jerked his hand from the bottom and took the handle instead. "It is more like a cavern than a tunnel." He walked down more. "Wait! I see light!"

"Well, we better hurry. The water will return eventually."

After a few miserable minutes trying to yell for everyone's attention, Wenlock just began quietly talking to people and asking them to go over to the hole.

"What do we do?" someone asked.

"Jump in."

"There's no water?"

Wenlock raised his finger. "Exactly! Now go before it fills, my boy."

One by one, the refugees who were stuck within the walls of the palace now had the magnificent chance of escaping without detection. Salvador would lead them and then return.

The water began to rise slowly, trickling back in, nearing Salvador's ankle when only half of the people were gone. "We must hurry."

Wenlock rushed to get the rest of the people herded toward the watering hole. When he came back, the water was up to Salvador's knee. "Hurry! Come!" he urged.

The people wasted no time. Still, with each moment lost, the water level climbed. Salvador helped each one until finally Wenlock was the last.

Though rather hesitant about the strange hole in the ground, he gingerly began to climb down until Salvador could grab his wrist and help him in. The water was now waist-high.

"We don't have much time." Salvador rushed out before him, leaving a wake of water behind with each stride. Wenlock followed the tiny light in front of him. He heard splashes from the people around but couldn't see them.

The dark space widened into an underwater cave. Light from outside crested a thin line of hope near the end of the cavern. The rock beneath his feet became softer, full of sand. The ground began to sluff off, the water continuing to rise. He began to tread.

"Salvador. I can't swim."

"Almost there!" Salvador's yell echoed.

Wenlock tried to paddle, tried to stay afloat. He kept bobbing under, gasping with each rise. When he sank, the water looked cloudy with sand and movement. Daylight spilled into the sea. His arms flailed above him. He couldn't breathe. His panic increased his flapping, but he still was sinking deeper into the sea.

He felt a force pull him up, strong arms lifting him through the water until his head broke the surface. He gasped for air.

Salvador and another man pulled him to the rocks. He felt a gentle tap on his back. "You all right?"

Wenlock shivered at the wind from the sea wrapping around the coast. "Yes. I am indebted to you, Salvador."

Salvador grinned. "Not as much as I am to you, good sir." He patted him once again on the back and stood to help the others.

They were not on a beach but on harsh rocks, battered over and over by the sea. Tiny pools littered each rock with sea creatures trapped from the exiting tide. And off in the distance, a rumble of thunder rolled around in the clouds. A storm was heading their way.

As Wenlock contemplated the calculations in the patterns, something shot out—a beam of light heading southeast. He stood, looking closer. His eyes followed it back to a tall window in the palace. "The Meridian . . ." he said to himself.

Wenlock felt a hand on his shoulder. Salvador, too, had seen the beam and wore a large smile on his face. "It worked!"

From his memory, Zander mentally traced back the steps from the kitchens to his room to Bryant's room to the courtyard—and finally to the Grand Hall. That's where they would get the answers they were looking for.

The halls were completely empty of people, something Zander had never experienced. The palace had once been a bustling hive of activity. Seeing the place completely deserted created an uneasy feeling with every echoing step on the marble floor.

He could sense Ferra and Mahoney not far behind him. At every hallway, he stopped to search for signs of life. As he approached the Grand Hall, things began to change. He finally saw someone—a sentinel standing guard at a staircase. He peeked around the corner and saw more. These were not like those possessed by the dark magic but were real people with real faces. They were dressed in Southwick uniforms, the best men in the army. These were hired men trained in combat.

Zander had no idea what to do. He turned back to tell Ferra and Mahoney, but neither had followed him. He panicked and started back to find them. In his haste, Zander forgot to quiet the click of his boots.

"Stop!" he heard behind him.

Zander glanced back and saw the guard charging after him. Two more followed.

He ran back down the corridor as fast as his legs could carry him.

Mahoney came into view. He was kneeling over someone. Was it Ferra? Had she fainted? "Mah—!" he tried to yell.

Mahoney heard him and sprang into action. He grabbed something from his boot and threw.

Zander heard a *whizz* past his ear. An anguished cry echoed behind him. He turned and saw the front guard grabbing his face, a knife embedded deep in his eye. The man grappled with the hilt before toppling to the floor. Zander's breath quickened as he watched the man writhe and bleed, too distracted to know the other two guards had each drawn their swords.

"Zander!" Mahoney yelled. "Zander! Move!"

He didn't remember stopping, but the shock of watching the man die had stunned every muscle in place. Hearing the panic in Mahoney's voice, he picked up his feet.

As he approached, Mahoney unsheathed his sword from his back. "Help get her out of here!"

Zander crouched down. Ferra's eyes were open, her breathing fast and gasping.

"No," she kept repeating. "No. Not yet. Help."

Zander grabbed her arms and lifted as best he could.

The two guards charged toward Mahoney, both fueled for the fight. These men were ready to kill Mahoney and him, and Ferra as well.

Mahoney countered and dodged each swipe with the quickest agility but he couldn't keep up the pace for long. His deflection of each attack made him vulnerable to the other. He kicked one guard against the stone wall, knocking the sword from his hand. The other struck with fierce power, slicing into Mahoney's arm.

Ferra slapped Zander's arm, snapping him to attention. She leaned back on him, her weight pushing against him to steady her feet. "I'm fine. I need my staff."

The bo staff lay a few yards away where she'd originally fallen. Zander ran to grab it.

The guard who had fallen rose to his feet and charged at Ferra.

Zander ran straight for him with all the strength he had, swinging the stick in front of him. The action drew the attention of the guard, who mostly looked annoyed. He swung his long sword, knocking Zander off balance and hurling him toward the wall.

With all his might, Zander swung toward the guard's legs, hitting him hard in the shin—not stopping him, but distracting him just enough.

Ferra was now up and recovered from whatever had taken her down. She seized the bo staff from Zander's hands and balanced herself in a low crouch, ready to attack. She sprang. With two quick snaps of her stick, Ferra rounded both sides of the guard. He swung, nicking her staff with his sharp blade.

She pulled back and stood with her staff at the ready.

Feeling helpless, Zander pulled out the dagger Bryant had given him, prepared to act. His hand shook, but he gripped it tightly. Mahoney pushed the guard back and dodged the sharp back-and-forth swing of his blade—the calculated move of a seasoned fighter sent the guard scrambling for his next attack.

But blood dripped down Mahoney's arm. He was wounded, though he moved with all swiftness as if he was never hurt.

Zander gripped his knife tight. It warmed in his hand.

Zander charged toward the guard battling Mahoney, sinking his blade into his side. The man swung his arm, knocking Zander away like a fly.

The thrust gave Mahoney the opportunity he needed, and he slashed the guard across the chest. He fell against the wall, not down, but dazed. Mahoney drove his sword into his chest hard.

The guard succumbed and collapsed as Mahoney withdrew his blade. He grabbed Zander's dagger from the fallen guard, looking it over.

"Good blade, my friend." He returned it to Zander with deep appreciation in his expression, then swiftly turned his attention to the last guard.

Ferra dodged nearly everything the guard sent her way, but she clearly didn't have the energy to last. Every counter left her gasping, but she kept trying.

Mahoney jumped into action, springing forward with his blade ready.

The guard saw him coming and defended against his attack, swinging with furious energy toward Mahoney.

Zander ran to Ferra and grabbed her hand, trying to pull her away from the melee, but she wouldn't budge. Her breath might be quickened, but her stare was determined.

"Come," Zander pleaded.

"No." She yanked her hand away. Grabbing her bo staff with both hands, she joined the fray, battering the guard on his right.

Zander watched the fight play out until the guard was on his knees, Mahoney ready to slash his throat. With one quick action, the last threat was dispensed.

Mahoney stood there, breathing hard. Without a second thought, he grabbed Ferra in a tight embrace, who held him back just as fiercely.

Zander walked to them. "Sorry I—" he tried to apologize for alerting the guards.

Mahoney wrapped an arm around him. "The dagger was a good idea."

Zander felt that was as close to forgiveness as he would get with Mahoney. He noticed again the blood on his sleeve and pointed. "Blood."

Mahoney let go and began rifling through the guard's possessions. He ripped fabric away from the guard's uniform, bandaging his arm. "Here. Throw these on." He threw over the guard's leather padded armor.

"This will never fit Zander," Ferra interjected.

"It doesn't need to." Mahoney began unstrapping other armor pieces unceremoniously from the guard, leaving his body exposed. "It will keep him safe."

"It didn't keep these guys safe."

Mahoney stopped and looked at her, giving her a grievous look as if she were ungrateful to him for just saving her life. "Well, we'll use it as a disguise."

Ferra grinned slightly, enjoying his annoyance.

"Are you all right?" Mahoney's voice turned tender.

Ferra nodded. "Fine. Don't worry."

Zander fumbled with the straps, so Mahoney fit the armor into place.

"Let's see what else we can salvage."

The three made quick work. Soon each had put on what gear they could gather and pulled the hoods up around their faces. Zander wouldn't pass as a guard, but from far away it wouldn't matter.

Mahoney led the way this time, taking every precaution.

As they drew closer to the stairwell, Zander's heart began to hammer, remembering the guards who now lay dead behind him.

Mahoney waved his hands, motioning them to stop. He peered around the corner and returned with a confused look on his face. "Zander?"

Zander crept closer to see what he had seen. They'd reached the Grand Hall for sure. The marble columns stood as he remembered them—tall and regal—but what lay beyond halted his footsteps.

Everything had changed.

In Zander's memory, the Grand Hall had been the center of all activity, surrounded by sleek marble rails looking over the large atrium below. Vines grew up from the center, filling everything with flowers and fragrance. Now everything lovely was gone, replaced with black.

Darkness covered the atrium. A few torches were lit, but nothing could penetrate the depth below.

Zander felt the others alongside him. He crept closer and closer until he could see beyond the railing. It looked as if all the walls had been burned. Black smoke rose in different places around an enormous chasm. The glorious stone floors had been ripped away to reveal a cavern wider than anything he had seen before.

And in the center of everything was a red swirling mass, slowly churning end over end. It hovered in the middle of the chasm, stretching across the space like a cloud of energy.

"Wha—?" Zander started but stopped. People were below. Something was happening. Guards, much like the ones they had just fought, marched in carrying a body.

Ferra gasped. "No. It's Landon," she whispered.

Zander focused closer. The man was sprawled out, carried over the guards' shoulders.

"Place him in the cage with the other one." The voice that spoke was harsh and cold. It came from a man who stood below, his long robes flapping about from the swift whistling winds of the pit.

As instructed, they carried the body over a narrow bridge where someone beyond their sight turned a crank which lowered a cage. Someone else was inside. It was hard to see in the dark. Zander feared it was another sister but couldn't tell.

The guards loaded the unconscious Landon into the cage and raised it again. The cage dangled like bait over the deep hole.

"How are we going to rescue him?" Ferra's voice was filled with panic. "Landon's a good man. We have to do something."

Zander looked to Mahoney, who looked deep in thought. "We are in a good position right now. Guards will be stationed all around this pit. Let's take cover and see what is happening."

"But he could die."

"I know," Mahoney returned. "A lot of people could die. I think this is the best way to prevent that."

Ferra didn't like his words but she didn't argue, either.

It was the best plan they had.

Landon heard a loud clang and flicked his eyes open, his vision filled with black shapes around the corners of his sight. A hot, unquenchable heat seared his skin where the fresh blisters pocked his face. The tender flesh burned with every motion of his body. The raw skin lifted with each pass of wind and sent an excruciating throb around his cheeks and forehead. He gasped and blinked again, straining his eyes to see the objects around him. Above, he saw black iron bars crisscrossing each other. The same metal pressed into the small of his back, warmed by the stifling heat.

His awareness came rushing back, filled with the haunting memories of Fontine falling to the ground. Despair hit him full in the chest. He had failed. Fontine was dead. Her medallion was gone. All was lost.

He closed his eyes, trying to forget everything that happened, giving into his hopelessness. His head hurt, his face burned, his body ached, and his heart filled with pain.

Landon felt the world sway, a slight wind crossing his brow like hot breath. He felt the presence of someone watching him.

His eyes popped open. A shadow loomed over him, bright eyes the only thing reflected from the half-light. He quickly pushed away and banged his head on the bars.

"Ohh!" He grabbed his head and rubbed the pain away.

The person sat back, just watching him. "I didn't intend to scare you."

Landon slowly sat up, propping himself up with his elbows, his ears ringing. He could only see the person in silhouette, but something about her felt familiar. A flicker of flame below hit the highlights of her face. And then he knew.

"Ferra?"

A moment of quiet passed as the person came closer. "Y—" Her voice halted. "Yes."

Landon felt a wave of relief. "Oh, thank goodness." He sat up and grabbed her hands which rested on her lap. The quick motion sent vibrations through the cage, jerking it back and forth.

"Careful." She pulled her hands away.

Landon could hardly control himself. He felt the impulse to leap over and hug her tightly. Ferra was here, alive, joining him in this gloomy place. They were such good friends. He had last seen her by the Durundin when they had snuck into the army camp, and she had charmed horses for them to ride. To have her here with him at what was surely the end of his life was incredible. "Ferra. How did you get in here? Where are the others?"

Ferra's hands clenched the bars. "Too much to tell."

"You mean . . ." His mind trailed off into thoughts he didn't want to imagine. "Is Micah okay? Did he make it?"

"Oh, yeah. Of course. We made it to the SisterElm, and he left to do something else, with his . . ."

"Spotswood is with him?"

"Yes. Spotswood. That's right." Ferra shifted slowly closer to him, minding the weight of the cage. "How did you get here?"

Landon spilled his side of the story up to the moment before arriving here. He stopped mid-thought. What would he tell her about Fontine? "I . . . was knocked out. I don't know anything after that."

Ferra sat, holding her legs, unusually calm. "And the medallion?"

"I'm sure Sharrod has it." Landon straightened up, curious at her reaction. "Sorry . . . I don't know what happened with your sister."

Ferra turned her head. "Right. I wonder." She came closer, whispering, "Wouldn't they bring her here if she were still alive? I'm in here, after all. Why cage me and not her?"

Landon watched Ferra's expressions. Something was wrong. "Are you okay, Ferra? What happened?"

"Magic happened." Ferra sat very still, so still it became eerie. "Do you see that mass below us?" She pointed at the swirling magic visible between the bars. "That's not a good sign. That tells me lots more will die. We don't have time to grieve. To me, it seems the dead got the better end instead of rotting in a cage used as bait."

Landon narrowed his eyes. "Bait? For what—a giant bird?"

Ferra slid back to her corner. "Yes. Exactly."

"There isn't such a bird."

"Boy, Southlander, you know nothing about the danger you are in."

"Southlander?" Landon felt the insult like a slap to the face. "What happened to the funny Ferra who would joke with me?"

Ferra looked through Landon like she remembered nothing of what their friendship was before. "She died."

Landon connected it. "You've lost your medallion. That's it. You've been separated."

"Yes. Of course I lost it. Sharrod's down there with three. Three! It won't be long before he'll have all and then—"

The sudden silence became unnerving. "And then what?"

"And then we die, Southlander. We all die."

CHAPTER TWENTY-ONE

Silexa threw Katia a black robe. "Put it on."

Katia slipped her head through and felt the heat from the previous owner. "Where did you get these?"

Silexa didn't answer, just handed the king one as well.

The king fumbled with the robes, clearly weak from his imprisonment. Silexa took pity and helped him with the arms.

Katia's worry grew. "Do you know the way out?"

"The rocks will help us." Silexa fitted the last cuff around the king.

Katia looked at her. "Wait! What about you?"

Silexa turned and pressed her stone to the rock. Slowly the core of each stone began to glow. "They are coming," she said, quickly putting away the stone.

The rumbling began again. This time it was accompanied by shouts—loud, angry men yelling at some unforeseen fear. Silexa grabbed the king by the arm and ran. Katia swiftly followed after.

The dungeons were a labyrinth of hallways, this way and that. Several prisoners raised their cups and clinked the bars. Many were afraid, some angry.

But once they noticed who Silexa was with, each stopped and watched. The king was being rescued. Something big was about to happen. The yells turned to cries, even cheers.

Katia spotted other guards running down the corridor. An avalanche of rocks came down, blocking their access.

They turned again, down a large tunnel now. The people there were quiet. And Katia saw them—women, even children were locked up. Why?

Katia couldn't help herself. She reached over and touched the bars, sending an ice cold chill through the metal which ran down the locks. Each frosted over so cold that it shattered under pressure. One broke and then another, clink after clink.

The prisoners were astonished. "Free?" some said. There was confusion, then exclamation, then madness.

Everyone rushed through the doors, bumping into each other, all looking for an exit.

Katia could see the lit rocks ahead and sprinted to the stairs. Others followed, and suddenly they were not alone but a hundred strong, bounding up the stairs behind them.

Silexa led the way through the dark, turned this way and that, through narrow turns and corners, until the stone changed to marble and the hallways broadened.

A tall wooden door stood at the end of it all.

"Go behind the door," Silexa ordered Katia.

Katia grabbed the king and did exactly as she asked.

Silexa pulled on the giant rungs, and light flooded the chamber, blinding all that were there. The people poured over the threshold, running into the palace proper. Shouts of exhilaration filled the echoing halls, providing an excellent distraction.

Katia remained protected behind the door as the prisoners rushed out, screaming their freedom. She held the king tightly, though he didn't run with the others. Instead he stood quietly looking at her.

"I know my Irina is gone," he whispered softly. "I knew she was never mine. I'm more sorry than words can express."

Katia stared at him, unable to articulate a proper response. She couldn't forgive this man who had killed her mother. But she had no time for her emotions to get the best of her. She pressed down the awful feeling in her stomach. "Don't say another word about it. I don't want to hear it."

As the last of the prisoners exited, Silexa slid behind the door. "Where do we need to go?"

"The Apothecary," the king stated.

"What's there?"

Silexa turned to leave, but Katia stopped her. "No, I need to know what's there. I've been following you blindly, and I need answers."

The king stood before her now, looking more regal than he had ever appeared. "That is where we will find the answers." He drew up his hood and proceeded out the door. Silexa followed, grasping her medallion.

Katia soon went after them.

Silexa had done something strange with her appearance, almost as if she had disappeared into the background. She was there, as solid as ever, but camouflaged. *That's why she didn't need a hood. She can reflect her surroundings.* Of all the magic tricks thus far, Katia was most impressed by that one.

The king picked up his stride, gaining energy with every step. Silexa didn't move from his side. Katia tried as best she could to act the part of a guard, though she felt deeply inadequate.

Down they traveled through hallways and chambers. Katia tried not to get distracted by the splendor of the palace, the marble floors or stone pillars. She had never been in anything so grand.

Then they turned down a different hallway, something less spectacular. It was much darker, older than the polished palace steps.

A winding staircase took them down to a secret hallway.

Silexa stopped and held the others back. She placed a finger to her lips. Someone else was there. Katia's magic frenzied with the sudden excitement, readying at her fingertips.

The room was covered in dust. Old books, vials, cauldrons, and jars lay strewn about. The clutter only highlighted the large hearth covered in stone. Near it, in the corner, stood a man.

"Don't move any farther," the man shouted. He held a long sword out before him. He hid something or someone behind him.

The king walked up to the man without fear. Katia's heart increased at the action. She raised her hands just in case, protecting the door.

"I don't expect you would listen to me," the king said, his voice commanding attention. "I'm surprised to see you, old friend."

The man slowly lowered his sword. "Reinoh?"

"The dungeons killed Reinoh. I am but a beggar now. Did you find it?"

The man didn't answer, just stood still.

Katia walked a step closer, the face still too dark to see, but something about his sharp profile reminded her of someone. And then he turned toward her, his steely gray eyes lighter than she had remembered. "Reynolds?"

The man's confused expression changed to relief.

Katia came closer, examining his face. The shaggy head and beard looked worse than she had ever seen before. His eyes locked upon her. A wonderful feeling of hope sprang up inside her. She felt like running to him but stayed near the king. "How did you get here?"

"I couldn't explain."

A face appeared at his side, and the peculiar blue eyes struck Katia immediately. "Hey there. Who are you?"

The little boy sidled next to Reynolds. "I am Vanya."

The name. His name.

Feeling the weight of it, Katia's legs buckled. The wooden table couldn't hold her. Her grip failed, and she fell to her knees. She grew cold with exhilaration, the magic within her blistering to the surface.

Vanya's eyes grew wide. "I know you."

She reached for his hand. He looked at Reynolds before he cautiously grabbed hers. Though Katia's fingers were covered with frost, he held it as she tried to communicate what she felt inside.

Vanya took his other hand and placed it on her head. "I knew you would find me."

Katia started to cry. The soft tears rolled down her cheeks, freezing near the end of her chin. She pressed his hand to her cheek. "I thought you were dead."

"Where is our father?"

"He's not here but he loves you."

Vanya's smile lit up the room. "I hope to meet him someday."

Reinoh hid his face as he slouched into a chair near the table. He didn't speak, but Katia knew he was affected by the scene, that his guilt wore on his soul.

Katia turned to Reynolds. "You found him."

Reynolds placed his hand on her shoulder. "Actually, he found me."

"Reinoh," Silexa interrupted the moment. "We need to ready ourselves."

The king looked back to Reynolds, his weary eyes set on him. "I am haunted by your father. He was a good man, Cornwallis. I am only bones and memories. I am tired. Tell me, Fairborne, can you end this?"

Reynolds looked perplexed but nodded. "Yes, sire."

Katia stood but didn't let go of Vanya's hand. "How?"

"He has the key," the king informed her.

Silexa moved closer, softening with interest. "A key? What kind of key?"

"Let me show you." Reynolds began feeling around the room until he came to a spot on the floor. He took out a small dagger and pried at the floorboards. They cracked and splintered at the pressure. Reynolds reached his hand inside and pulled out a dirty rolled cloth. Slowly he peeled it away.

Flashes of light filtered through the room, echoing the brilliance of the stars in each ray. Under the cloth was a single jar. Katia stared, mesmerized. "What is it?"

"The Everstone." The voice was Vanya's. He placed his hand around the jar. "It is the life source, the heart of the magic."

Katia couldn't take her eyes away from the jar. Inside lay a single orb the size of her fist. She stared closely at the magic swirling around—silver against opal, mixing like lava—pulsing as if it had a life of its own. She wanted to reach it, to touch it, but the magic within her grew scared. It was too strong for her.

Reynolds held it up, taking a long look at it before speaking. "This is it. The evil I created."

"You did this?" Katia asked. She sat on the floor, still staring. "This doesn't look evil at all, just beautiful."

"It's not," he clarified. "This is the source of all our problems. This stupid idea."

Reynolds sat on the ground, placing the jar in the middle of the floor. "I didn't know what I was doing. It was just an experiment. It was the same night as the presentation ceremony."

Silexa knelt closer, examining the magic. "When my father gave us the stones." She sounded far away, trapped in her own memory.

Reynolds continued. "I didn't know the repercussions of what happened. The explosion sent the magic out. The binding happened. Lytte found us and we hid it, me and . . . and Taren. He hid it here. But . . ." His voice cracked.

"It wasn't everything," Katia connected. "What about the Vivatera?"

Reyonlds looked at her with sincerity. "You're right. It wasn't everything. The Vivatera was made from this. So was Naomi's power and . . ." He hesitated. "And me as well."

"You?"

"I was so curious about it. The magic called to me. I'm in the same mess as everyone else."

"But what about Taren?"

Reynolds ran his fingers through his hair. "I don't know. He was with me. He was here during the blast, but I did this to myself." He lifted his tunic, revealing scars. "These wounds happened during the blast. I thought if I used the magic as a salve it would help. Instead it bound me to everything, everyone. Naomi's not alone in this."

"But she thinks she is." Katia felt the heat rise in her cheeks. "You let her think she has to sacrifice herself for this, but what you're showing us is that she doesn't. This involves all of us."

Silexa wiped her face. "So, there may be a chance?"

Reynolds turned to her. "There has to be."

"But what do we do? How will it work?"

Reynolds covered the jar again with the cloth and put it into a satchel. "I don't know."

Silexa drew close, looming over Reynolds. "I forgive you."

Reynolds looked up. "What?"

"Do not punish yourself so harshly for mistakes made when you were young. No one could have predicted this. But we have time, and we can change what happens. We have the solution. Everything is coming together. And if we die, then we die, but at least we will have done everything we could at the moment. That's all that matters. Are you ready?" Silexa offered a hand to him.

A half-smile rose in his face. "It's time to end this." He grabbed her hand.

CHAPTER TWENTY-TWO

White, brilliant, covered in gold.
She walks in slow stride.
"Naomi."
Echoes through her mind.

"Born Redemia,
the last of the Everstar Children."
Long tresses roll off her shoulder and down her back.
Unseen wind sweeps about her robes.
"You are Pera."
"I am." Her voice spins of honey and sleep.
"I've been sent to you."

A sad smile confirms the truth.
"My little Everstar. You are prepared for me."
"I'm ready to die, if that will save this world."

Gold tears stream from her eyes.
'My sweet child, you are my vessel.
I need a carrier.
You have the magic in heart and soul.
You will protect me through the journey."
Aching emotions swell within.
"How?"

She comes closer, glowing inside and out.
'I will not harm you,
I will protect you, my sweet one.
Trust me.
I will take care."

Fear rises within.
"I can't face Taren again."

"There will be time."

"Please do it quickly."
Sweeping tendrils caress her arms
wrap in warmth unknown in the living world.
A light outlines radiant,
Shimmering aura.

A burning lifts her heart.
The magic is alive.

"It is time."

One last look and the world vanishes.
A breath taken,
A final exhale.

A sensation spread rapidly through Taren's chest. Each breath left him empty as he felt the full weight of his body hanging on his frail bones. "Please, no," he gasped. "Please, where is she?"

The woman stared at him with starry eyes, motioning with her head to a branch above.

Taren looked and saw it. A giant chrysalis hung above like an ornament, each vein from the leaves glowing with a bright light, making them transparent and highlighting a delicate frame.

"Taren Lockwood," he heard the voice enter his mind. He looked back at the woman, and that same familiarity of magic swept over him. *"The time is come. And I will need you once more."*

Taren felt his heart clench. He couldn't speak.

"Nothing is coincidence, young Taren." Her eyes held him in place. *"Everything has a plan and purpose. You have been very valuable to me."*

His chest heaved. "I don't . . . understand."

"But you do." Wind swept through the trees, tangling the black hair around her body. *"Naomi was fed the elements of magic, and they grew strong inside her, but they alone were not strong enough. The Vivatera was needed to prepare her body and mind, to create the protection I need to shield me from the outside world."*

Taren never wanted to remember what action he'd taken that day. The magic had told him to do it. He'd acted with jealousy, true, but had still been ruled by logic. He hadn't known what would happen, if she would live or die by his actions, but the magic knew better than he. But then, why this guilt that was driving him mad? Why had the magic retreated and left him a shell of himself, of what he could be?

"This was planned?" He felt heavy again and sat in the crook of the branch that held him. "Is this a lie?"

"An opportunity," she clarified. *"You have the talent of understanding what the magic needs. A gift of empathy of the corruption within this land. The magic needed you as an instrument in action. You understood what needed to happen, and you acted, however painful it was to you."*

A frenzy of magic whirled within him, clearing any doubt he had felt before. In this one solid moment, he knew something beyond what he had suspected, and his head cleared with new understanding. This was new. This was truth.

"You had the choice, young Taren, though the decisions were guided. The actions you took to return the magic and then protect Naomi were your own."

"But you still need her."

The woman bowed.

"What will happen to her?"

"What she chooses." The woman held up the floating Everstar with her hands. *"This, young Taren, is her last gift to you."* She moved her hands over and over until the star formed a seed with the Everstar burned into the center. It slowly floated toward him until Taren pulled it from the air and held it in his hand.

"I don't understand."

"There is always a way back, young Taren. Keep this safe. You will know in time what to do."

Taren evaluated the gift. It was warm to his touch, energy held within ready for the earth. He didn't understand it at all. He tucked it away in his cloak.

The woman raised both hands high in the air. The chrysalis in the tree began to glow. Each leaf slowly started to shed away, shriveling into transparent flakes, falling with the wind. With every layer, streams of gold revealed more and more of the body hovering within. Long golden waves of hair spiraled around her small frame, no longer dirty from the hard travel, but brilliant and white. The inner leaves wrapped around her, lacing like fairy wings, dressing her in vivid green.

Taren's breath caught. She didn't look real—but like a dream or vision of a creature so perfect he lost all speech.

Naomi floated down from the center of the canopy, her eyes still closed with sleep.

"It is time." The woman brushed her hands together and the tree shook. *"Tonight at the Blood Moon is the only time I am able to stop my brother and reclaim the magic. You must act quickly. Promise to protect her every way you can. I can protect her spirit; you must protect her body."*

Taren didn't get a chance to answer. Light shot in every direction, blinding him. He looked away until it faded gently, and there he saw the barefooted creature before him. His chest seized. It was her but also someone else. She looked at him quizzically, the bright green eyes vibrant and alive.

"Naomi," he barely uttered the name.

A sad smile crossed her face. "Pera."

Everyone from below witnessed the bright lights coming from the tree. It took every effort Sera had not to climb it herself and see what was going on, but Mother held her in place.

"Just wait, my dear," Mother reassured her. Lottie couldn't wait, though, and began to climb. "Get down, child!"

Lottie soon realized the branches were too far apart and too large to scale for her little frame. "I don't like this." She sat down on the branch. "It's my fault."

Sera came closer. "What do you mean?"

"I shouldn't have come. I betrayed my new family and left to be with her. Why would I do that?"

Sera reached for her hand. "Come on down, love." She helped lift her down. "Why would you say it's your fault?"

"Because I see things. I know things." Lottie sat cross-legged on the ground. "Naomi, she wanted me to know things. So, so . . ."

Sera sat next to her. "Know what?"

"What is about to happen. What needs to happen."

"Because you can read people's secrets."

The girl nodded. "I've seen the place in the palace. She showed me. A giant wide pit. Someone is coming. Not the bad guy, someone else."

"Someone else?"

"Yes. Not the bad guy everyone thinks. This is someone different, but I don't like him. Something bad is going to happen."

Sera grabbed her little hand. "What? Tell me?"

Lottie shook her head. "A bunch of people are going to die. The stone-bearers. All the stones. And then . . ." She gulped. "And then *he* will come."

"The puppet master?"

Lottie nodded.

"That's quite enough." Mother wrapped her arms around Lottie, helping her up. "The poor thing is scared."

"We all are." Arie came closer. "How much longer can we wait?"

"Ah, no. I can't." Sera started up again. "It's been too long." She looked out at the awakening day. "I feel this urgency inside me. Something's happening, but I don't know what."

"It's the Blood Moon." Mother kept Lottie snuggled to her side.

Arie began twisting a blade of grass in his mouth. "What exactly is a Blood Moon?"

Mother came and patted his back. "When this world is closest to the ethereal plane. The day when the rules change."

Arie perked up. "Like rules of magic?"

Mother shook her head. "I don't know. I've never experienced one. This is what Pera has shared with me. A Blood Moon is the only time she can cross through the plane. I imagine it is the same with Shon."

Sera felt a pit form in her stomach. "Today. Everything will be finished today. Do all the stones need to be present for this girl—?"

"Pera."

"—yes, to fix whatever Shon has plans to do?"

"Yes. This I know."

Exhaustion overcame Sera, who sank down to the ground. "How are we going to do this?"

She looked around at everyone's faces, coming to a grim realization of the difficulties facing them. Then she looked at Lottie, who wasn't looking at anyone. In the moment Sera felt the most despair, she saw hope shining in little Lottie's face. *There shouldn't be doubt. There is always hope.*

Two figures came running through the forest toward them, interrupting all their thoughts.

Sera reached for her bow, but Mother raised her hands. "No. Don't. They are scouts. They are friends."

Both were Arenmas, dark skinned with transparent eyes. Sera had befriended an Arenma tribe near Ignis and knew they were good people. She stood to greet them and gave a traditional salute.

The man stood still and greeted her likewise. "You must be the dear Sera, hailing from Ignis."

"Yes, I am. This is Arie, Reynolds' brother."

The second one behind him began jumping up and down. "Oh, good people. We are glad you have joined us. I am Micah, and this is my Uncle Spotswood."

"The infamous land-dweller." Sera smiled.

Spotswood's eyes brightened with recognition. "We must travel fast. Naomi must leave immediately. The darkness is coming."

"An army," Micah clarified.

Arie stood up. "An army, like the Southwick soldiers? I wouldn't think they would be loyal to Sharrod's ideas."

Sera narrowed her eyes, trying to see the army in the distance. A dark shadow of a cloud appeared near the meadow. "Is that it?"

Spotswood came closer. "I believe they are people spellbound by a curse."

"But why come here?" Sera grabbed onto Arie's sleeve. "We need to get Naomi out of here."

Mother didn't say much but looked far off in the distance, as though to another world. "Yes. You must go."

"What about you?"

Mother's mouth hinted at a smile but her chest heaved. "I expect they are sent to destroy the legacy."

"Or they could be a distraction," Arie threw out.

Micah crouched like a cat ready to strike. "Well, I will fight with you."

"Yes, Mother." Spotswood came up behind his nephew. "We will help. Arie and Sera should take the dragons."

Lottie appeared lost in the conversation. "What about me?"

Sera glanced over at Arie. He nodded when he met her eye. "Come with us, Lottie." She reached out her hand.

Lottie's small hand took hers with no hesitation. She giggled and looked up at her. "You are in love with him?" She pointed toward Arie.

Sera peered down at her and then back to Arie, who smirked at the truth. She ignored the question. "How soon before they get here?"

"They are not fast, but persistent," Spotswood stated. "Midday is a possibility."

"I do not want to harm anyone." Micah stared in the distance. "Poor people. Confounded. Pawns."

A rustling from above disrupted them. Sera glanced upward and gasped.

A high branch began to move, lowering itself down to the ground. She recognized Taren's tall frame, his black hair mussed with the wind—the other she didn't recognize.

The limb hit the ground and unfolded. The two passengers walked onto the grass, one leading the other.

Sera walked toward them, then stopped. Both turned. Taren was visibly shaken; the other . . . the gorgeous creature next to him couldn't be Naomi. The light within her radiated from every hair on her head, and every movement she made looked graceful. A delicate dress covered her perfectly, not a thread out of place. Where was the spirited Naomi, driven by her purpose? She was absent from the unfamiliar smile on this person's face. "I don't understand," slipped from Sera's mouth.

Taren grabbed the ethereal girl's hand, who stood tall and magnificent and walked with commanding presence.

At a closer glance, it *was* Naomi, but something was very different, very wrong with the sister Sera had come to adore. A brilliance in her aura, an unearthly majestic quality. And something that completely alarmed Sera—Naomi's charm was gone, replaced by an unknown sense of command. Sera didn't know what to say.

"Sera?" It was Arie.

Sera examined his expression. He looked sad and confused, as well. "Yes. Right." She snapped herself back together.

Lottie reached out to touch the woman's smooth skin. "Naomi?" Her question didn't register. She tried to grab her hand, but Naomi pulled it away, placing it instead around Taren's arm.

Sera looked up at Taren. "What happened?"

"I wish I could tell you." Taren's voice quivered. "We have to get Naomi to Southwick now. Tonight. If not . . ." He didn't finish, but Sera understood the implications.

"I don't think the fire-eaters are ready to fly," Sera informed him.

"I have an idea for that." Taren freed himself from Naomi's entangled arm and rushed toward the dragons.

Sera analyzed the woman up and down. "Naomi? Is this really you? What happened?"

Naomi's eyes stared back into hers, revealing secrets without telling. "Sera, you are a stone-bearer," her voice rolled out smoothly.

"Of course." She grabbed the stone around her neck and lifted it into view.

Naomi gazed at the medallion, seeming transfixed by the way it caught the daylight. "Oh, I've longed to see you," she spoke to the stone and not to her sister. "I believe you were a gift I did not see."

Sera waved her hand. "Naomi?"

Naomi looked miles away. "She is here. She hears you."

"What do you mean?"

Naomi gazed at her fingers and palms like they were magical things. "I have never known a body." She found Sera with a peculiar, penetrating glance of curiosity. "I have never felt the wind or rain or physical touch." She pressed her fingers together and looked to where Taren had run off. "I wish I had time for so many things."

"Don't talk like that."

Naomi looked around her. "This world is an amazing place. Each flower and tree is a gift. Magic doesn't corrupt it, it makes it. It should be celebrated, not destroyed. My father was wrong and should forgive."

Sera didn't understand a word of what her sister had spoken. "Naomi, you're not making any sense."

Naomi bowed her head as if making a silent prayer, then regained an appearance of firm determination. She turned to Lottie, whose mouth still hung open, and offered her hand.

Lottie took it. A smile grew on her face, amazement in her eyes. "You are . . ."

Naomi nodded and returned her gaze to Sera. "Are you ready, princess of fire?"

"Of course, but—"

"Come with me." Naomi started to walk after Taren, taking Lottie with her.

Sera just stood in a stupor.

"You okay?" Arie asked from behind her.

Sera peered back at him. "I hardly know."

Arie came close. He took her hand and lifted it to his lips. The gentle kiss made her heart warm again and returned her to what she knew to be true.

He held on to her hand, looking at it a moment longer. "What do you think will happen to you if you return to Southwick?"

Sera didn't want to answer. "I might die, you know. Leaving this world right when I finally feel happy isn't fair."

"No one considers what's fair." Arie lowered her hand and wrapped his arm around her. "Promise you won't leave me again."

Sera kissed him swiftly on the cheek. "I'll do my best." A hint of a smile crossed her face before she took off running toward the others.

"You already broke your promise!" Arie yelled after her. The thrill of the mild flirtation kept her going, with Arie fresh on her heels.

In the clearing, they found Taren with the large fire-eaters, feeding them hot stones.

"Where did you get the fire?" Sera asked, out of breath.

Taren lifted his ashen hands, his fingertips still blazing with embers. "I talked with them, as well. Both fire-eaters are prepared."

"Do you know where to go?"

"I do if he doesn't," Arie said, finding the reins of the

red dragon's harness. "You ready to get this over with? 'Cause, I'm mighty tired of it."

Sera agreed. Eighteen years in hiding. She was ready to begin life again.

CHAPTER TWENTY-THREE

Landon looked into Ferra's intense eyes. She wasn't joking. They were all going to die, and even worse, they were the bait to lure the other sisters there.

He took a close look below. The cage was suspended near the side of a giant pit where a swirling mass of gas and vapor turned over and over into itself. Near the edge of the pit, near the high palace walls, were six pillars, three of which had marvelous light emanating from the tips—green, blue, and white, the light feeding into the floating energy. Landon knew exactly what they were: a final resting place for the sisters' stones.

He peered closer at the magical mass. "What is that?"

Ferra followed his gaze. "Each time they place a stone the magic grows. I think all the power is being collected."

"Into what?"

Ferra didn't answer, just sat back up and rested against the cage. "This is pointless. No one's going to rescue us."

Landon turned, frowning. "It's not like you to give up."

"Who said I was giving up?"

Landon heard the cheek in her voice. "And your plan?"

"Well, I—"

Footsteps echoed through the chamber, halting Ferra from continuing. Men marched along the perimeter, one holding something in his arms. A girl followed, a red hint to her hair reflecting the fire from the torches.

"What is she doing here?" Ferra spat.

"You know her?"

"Well, of course. Audra's my—" She stopped and cleared her throat. "She's a Louving."

"Louvings. I hate those guys."

"As you should." Ferra sat back again, making the cage swing.

Landon watched on. He couldn't hear what they were saying from the distance, only a few mumbles echoing across to them. A hooded figure entered the chamber, the light from what was clearly one of the sisters' stones visible in his grasp. He seemed very agitated by something the girl had done. A few words bounced around the rock walls: "lost . . . find them . . ."

"This is fascinating. I wonder what—" Then Landon heard a name and stopped. "Reynolds?"

Ferra scrambled next to him, the quick motion causing the cage to squeak. "Where?"

"I don't see him, but that's the reason that girl is in trouble."

"Why, that little brat." Ferra was visibly irritated, talking to herself. "Of course she came to the hornet's nest.

Boy, is she going to get stung. What does she know about Reynolds besides what I've told her? Idiot."

Landon watched her very closely. Ferra wasn't making sense. As she leaned over, a tiny string dangled loose around her neck. "I didn't think you knew Reynolds that well. You only had a day or two with him."

Ferra turned her head as if trying to understand what he meant.

Then her eyes flashed.

And Landon knew. He quickly pushed her away to the other end of the cage. The impact sent a violent jolt through the metal and rocked them back and forth.

"Watch it." Ferra rubbed her arm where she had slammed into the side.

Shock overcame him at the realization. "You killed Ferra. You . . ." He lost his voice. Anger flooded every inch of him. He wanted to throttle her, choke her until nothing came out. But the cage began to spin and every action sent a new tremor through it.

The imposter started to laugh, a low rumble that sounded less triumphant than he expected.

"She was going to die anyway," the fake Ferra mused. "I assume she's dead. Her skin feels great." She shrugged her shoulders. "She could still be alive too, you know. If I want people dead, they die. I just needed her dead enough to take a bit of her soul."

Landon sat stunned. His chest heaved, his mind wiped of any rational thought. "And when did your plan go awry? When you took over her persona or her life? You're in this rat trap as well."

She rattled the cage. "Aware of that, Southlander."

Landon still felt disgusted. "Who are you?"

The Louving smiled. "Browneyes. Heard of me? I sure recognize you, one of those heroic magicians in the Echoes."

"Of course you were there."

Browneyes looked at her fingernails. "I shared space with my fellow Louvings. He's here, too—did you know?"

Landon felt the memory seep in his skin like poison. "Yes. I've seen him, thanks."

"This whole chasm beneath us opened up the Underworld to the surface. Not much time before—" She stopped.

"Before what?"

"The end of everything, smart mouth." Browneyes was clearly irritated with her current situation. She turned and looked back down. "Wait, what are they doing to her?"

Landon focused on the girl whose arms were held tightly by the men—the argument had certainly turned sour. Small yelps and pleas fell unheeded around the rocks.

"What do you think will happen to her?" Landon asked. "You think they will cage her with us?"

Browneyes didn't answer, just continued to watch.

The struggle turned violent. The Louving Audra kicked and fought her way out of the men's clutches. Some shouting was heard and more scrambling and fighting before a shadow crept to the corner of the platform.

"Enough!" The shout echoed around the cavern, silencing every living thing.

Landon had never seen Sharrod before. He had imagined him a big man, broad, strong—but nothing like what they saw below them.

Sharrod was much taller than a man, with cloven hooves and sharp, pointed horns protruding out of his head. His skin was dark, charcoal, like he'd walked through fire. The robes hanging around him were scarlet as blood, ribboned with gold. He was a demon, not a man, and Landon felt small even from so far above.

"Audra." Sharrod's voice slithered from his throat. "One tiny task and you failed to do it."

"But," she struggled, "I've done everything you asked. Everything. I took care of the king, the prince, the boy."

"And yet each is a failure." Sharrod's walk was slow, deliberate, toying with her in each step.

"Please, my lord, I . . ."

Sharrod swiftly grabbed her by the throat. "You're wasting my time."

With his mighty arm, he hurled her over the edge of the pit. Landon was shocked, and even Browneyes uttered a small gasp.

Audra's scream echoed around the cavern as she fell farther and farther down. The wind picked up and carried a large howl with it. Fire from below shot up in a wicked, licking flame, savoring the meal it had been fed.

Landon felt his heart thumping within his chest, loud and hard. He turned to Browneyes, whose eyes were wider than he expected.

Sharrod left, clearly not caring about the horrifying thing he had just done. He vanished back into the dark, a few men following behind. The hooded figure remained, silent.

"I don't care who you are," Landon heaved. "We are not staying here. Please tell me you have a plan."

Browneyes narrowed her eyes at him, then pulled out a black pouch from her side. "Not a plan, an idea."

"Oh, no." Landon expected the worst. "Is that some weird monkey claw, or a virgin's heart? Whatever you guys do?"

Browneyes scoffed, "You only wish. It's much more powerful than the magic you possess."

Landon was about to argue, then shrugged. "Show me."

Browneyes opened the tiny pouch, letting out a small light. She placed it in her hand, and out walked the littlest thing he had ever seen. "A fairy?"

"Don't mock. Your girlfriend did."

"My girlfri—" He stopped. She meant Ferra, and the uneasy feelings came back to the surface. He had to play the upper hand. "I'm not mocking, I'm impressed. I'm familiar enough with them. They love music and would follow the musicians when I was with the Travelers."

"They are the purest kind of magic."

"And did you know they also can see through your disguise?"

Browneyes smirked. "I'm no idiot."

Landon sat back again, analyzing her. "So, what do you plan to do with a fairy? Drink her blood like everyone else?"

Browneyes glared. "I thought of that, but she doesn't have enough."

"Then what's your idea?"

Zander sat in a corner near the edge of the stairs, the large hood from the guardsman's uniform draped over his head. The horror of the fight replayed again in his mind. He rubbed his eyes, trying to dull the pressure in his head. Too many things clouded his mind as he thought of everything that led him to that point. For the first time since his adventure began, he missed his father, his farm, his old life of stability, predictability. And more than anything, he missed being taken care of.

He closed his eyes, hoping to see Naomi's face again, wishing that she could transport him away and rescue him from danger. The only thing he had was luck, and he felt that was running out. The intensity of everything happening weighed down on his worn heart. He didn't want to do it anymore. Maybe if he hid in the corner until it was all over

. . .

Bryant depended on him, but for what? He was just a boy, scrawny and freckled. He remembered back when he'd felt brave, not realizing he was marching into a trap. He had seen Sharrod for himself, the beast who everyone feared. He had seen him face to face.

And Ymber had been there, alive still, feeling the same fear.

And now Ferra would suffer the same fate, the same death.

Zander didn't know how long he sat there dwelling on his own thoughts before he saw the small light outside his hood. He lifted his head to see a tiny dancing glow, almost like a flick of ash, land gently on his lap.

He flinched, brushing it away, but it floated up again and landed back as it had before.

Zander leaned in and noticed the small wings like a butterfly. He checked his tunic. The flower Vespa had placed was still there, the budded fairy in its shelter. This was someone new, a different fairy. "Where did—"

It walked nimbly crossed his arm and then bowed. She smiled. She was so much like Little Lovely that he felt he knew her, that he could talk with her.

Zander's face brightened. He did know how to talk with fairies. "I have a secret," he said in the lowest whisper. "Would you like to hear it?"

The tiny fairy swirled from his arm to his face. He could see her closer now, nearly making his eyes cross. She nodded and turned her head to listen.

"I . . ." He stumbled, thinking of the right words. "I'd give m-my life if it would st-stop this, this . . ." Zander's throat tightened. The words felt different hearing them out loud. But it was true. "I don't want any more sisters to die."

The fairy danced with delight and came to rest on his shoulder close to his ear.

"I know you, good-hearted Zander." Her voice was a tiny whisper. "I am Thayda from the SisterElm. Mother has sent me."

"Mother? I don't have—?" And then he knew. He lost breath. "Mo—Mother."

"Yes."

"How?"

"It is a greater secret," the fairy mused. "And I cannot tell you until it is time. First, your courageous heart is needed."

Zander sat up. "Mine?"

"I was sent to seek for help. The gateway has been unearthed. The UnderGod will devour the world. He breathes smoke and spits poison. He has been trapped since the beginning of time. He seeks to destroy the land with fire and obliterate the sky with ash."

Zander began to tremble.

The fairy left his shoulder and flew before his eyes. "He is coming. The portal has begun to open." She zipped away from him.

Zander scrambled to his awkward feet. He followed her, tripping over his long robes, until he could see the fairy near the pillars, looking over the large pit. The strange mass of swirling magic must be what she meant, the portal. "How do I . . . ?"

The fairy flew close to him. "The monster will need the flesh of the living. The taste of blood will make him stronger. But the cage has a Louving, the blood of many. If he eats her, he will be invincible. You must stop this. Save them, friend of the fey."

"Zander?"

Zander gasped and turned to see Ferra's face.

"Zander, go back to your—" She stopped, seeing the fairy.

"Will you help?" Zander asked the fairy.

"Zander. It's not wise to try. There are too many guards."

The fairy came closer. "I have a gift for you. Close your eyes."

Zander did as he was asked, never questioning the fairy.

"You know your brave heart, young Zander, and it is time to test your courage. This will help you find the truth."

He felt something sharp on his neck like a sting. His eyes popped open, and he reactively reached over and felt the tiny thing. It fell into his palm.

"No." Ferra came closer. "She just—"

Zander looked down at the limp body. "What?" She lay motionless as if dead. His heart pumped faster, not understanding what she had done. *She was going to help us.*

The sting began to inch.

Ferra looked at it. "She poisoned you, Zander."

He began to feel it, the pulse in his veins quickening. The itch spread with every pump closer to his heart. In his muscles, a throbbing, stretching feeling overcame him, his fists clenched tight. Pain flooded his head, a pang so sudden he lost his vision and collapsed.

He heard Ferra rush to his side and felt her drag him away. It inched closer to his heart. He felt the pulsing take over. He heard the scream but couldn't speak. His back arched.

And then it hit. A rush of warmth filled everything, tingling down to his toes, flooding his lungs with energy, tightening every muscle. And a voice came to his mind.

"I'm here with you."

Thayda's whisper.

"Open your eyes."

Zander did, and the world was the same but different. He saw Ferra's sad face looking down at him.

"Zander?"

The warmth stayed with him as he sat up, looking at Mahoney kneeling at his side. Something was different. He saw a bright spot next to him. The fairy flower that Vespa had given him—he could see the magic from the fairy like a shot of light.

He looked back at Ferra. A lovely green aura accompanied her, as well as the luminescent golden spot next to her.

"I can see magic."

"What?" Ferra asked.

"I c-can hear her, sh-she's here." He pointed to his head.

Mahoney grabbed his hand and helped him stand up.

And now he saw it, what Thayda had tried to tell him. The mass of magic was not that at all. He walked closer, trying to see exactly what it was, but even from a distance he could identify what looked like people, bodies of people swimming over each other. The screams of trapped souls wailing for relief.

"Do you hear . . .?" Zander tried to explain.

Both Ferra and Mahoney shook their heads.

"You are strong, Zander. Are you ready?"

"Yes," Zander answered out loud. He took hold of the large hood and turned toward the corridor.

"Wait." Mahoney held him back.

The ground began rumbling, a small pounding of several feet on the hard stone floor.

Mahoney stood protectively in front of the others, but Zander pushed away. They watched as people came running down the hallway toward the gate. They looked like regular citizens, hardened by circumstances.

All the guards in the area dealt with the disruption. They quickly ran after the escaping prisoners.

"Now, little Zander. Find the lever."

Zander ran toward the pit.

"Zander!" he heard Mahoney yell from behind, but Zander didn't turn. He kept running down the makeshift stairs from the heap of rubble. The mass swirling around in the center of the pit seemed to watch him, all eyes staring in his direction. Other ghosts were hovering in the dark corners. It felt like he was back in the Musungu swamp. As long as he didn't disturb them or anger them, he could make it.

The few guards who remained came after him. He heard the scuffle and turned. Mahoney and Ferra were not far behind.

Mahoney fought off two guards. One fell directly in the pit, the other swung out. Mahoney dodged but slid against the rocks, clinging tightly as the guard tried to muscle his way toward him.

Zander began to run back. He grabbed a rock and threw it toward the guard, missing.

And then he saw Ferra lying sprawled against the rock pile. His heart stopped, and he ran back to her.

"Ferra?" He knelt down. Her breath came in quick gasps.

Her eyes glanced toward him, her hand gently tracing the tears on his face.

He couldn't speak, but his heart screamed, *Please don't die, please!*

Mahoney rushed over, blood gushing from a cut above his brow. "Ferra. Ferra." He kept saying it over and over. He grabbed her hand. "Don't you dare leave me. You stay with me, you got it?"

Ferra's eyes flitted upward.

"No, come on." Mahoney rubbed her arms. "I finally found you. Stay with me. I need you, Ferra." His panic was clear. "Come on, come on! Come back to me."

Ferra's eyes searched the air before resting on Mahoney's face. She tried to smile but she was in obvious pain.

"No, please." Mahoney had tears in his eyes. "Please, don't."

Zander watched the pain slip from her face. He collapsed with his face in his hands and cried.

Despite the darkness covering his sight, Reynolds could still make out a few things. Silexa's stone shone like a star in the heavens. Across the room were outlines of enchantment, mere traces, but beyond the room he felt the actual presence of magic. It surrounded them. He wished for his sight back, but he could manage well enough if the magic was there.

Silexa gripped his shoulder. "Are you ready for this?"

Reynolds looked in the direction where he last remembered the boy being. "Vanya." The boy came to his side, his aura waved with both delight and concern. "I need you to be my eyes." Reynolds winked. "Now I can call *you* Hawk. Sound good?"

Vanya didn't reply but lifted Reynolds' hand and placed it on his shoulder.

"What's wrong with you?" Katia asked.

"He's blind," Vanya returned. "I cursed him."

"I'm fine." Reynolds rubbed his eyes, trying again to get them to work. "No time to waste. Reinoh, let's get this over with."

The king spoke up, voice directed toward Silexa. "We are at the end game, daughter of Prolius. Are you prepared?"

Silexa didn't respond immediately, and Reynolds somehow felt she was looking at him. "More prepared than anyone."

"You love my son."

"Yes," her voice fell softly. "And I will always love him, no matter what happens. I've always known this. Love is a gamble. Win or lose."

Win or lose. The words echoed in Reynolds' mind.

The king walked toward the door. "He deserves love. I never loved him or his mother, and she knew it. I loved once." He paused, glancing at Katia before exiting Reynolds' sight.

Katia came forward and shoved Reynolds in the chest. "Is Silexa giving up the stone?"

Reynolds witnessed her magic flare inside, the crystals springing around her body like an instant flurry. He was impressed. "Yes, Katia. That's the idea."

"What do you mean?"

Silexa spoke up from behind. "It's time to finish this."

"No. You have to stop this." Katia grabbed both sides of his face, directing his attention. "This isn't fair. Use the Whatever stone and—"

Reynolds saw the magic in the tears as they froze on her face. "Katia, I promise I'll do whatever I can to fix this. But none of us know how."

Katia fell silent and stepped away.

Reynolds glanced toward Silexa's stone, watching as she carried it out of the room after the king. Vanya took Reynolds with him, Katia following right behind.

Reynolds' new view of his world was disorienting, yet it felt familiar, as if he had seen it all his life, the same ever-presence of the magic around him, communicating to his own magic. He had always been able to predict the movement of others, the actions before they came, which had made him so quick in his reflexes.

He closed his eyes and tried instead to feel where things were. The walls alongside him, seasons old, passed by many lives. The stairs added for convenience, not as old. How did he know this?

"Katia, hit me," he said with his eyes still shut. "Just slug me or something."

He could feel her magic excited at the prospect of punching something. She tried. He dodged, and her fist hit air. She tried again and again, and each time he knew exactly where she would be. At one point, he even grabbed her hand, all without seeing.

He opened his eyes again, seeing the snow white energy radiating from her.

"Well done." Vanya's blue magic shimmered like water.

"I think I can do this." Reynolds felt the energy around him again, the familiar presence of something beyond his sight making itself known.

King Reinoh and Silexa stood near the foot of the stairs.

"We need to get to the ceremony room," Silexa instructed. "It was sealed—"

"No," the king interrupted. "It is destroyed. Unearthed."

"What?"

"Sharrod knew the place," Reinoh continued. "He knew it all along."

Reynolds looked around, sensing where the largest concentration of magic was, though he couldn't see it. Obstacles were in the way. "We need to get closer."

Silexa turned to Reinoh. "What about the tunnel?"

"Several tunnels would lead us there."

"Show us."

The king had barely any magical trace on him, but Silexa was hot behind him. Vanya stayed close, and Reynolds followed, feeling his way.

Through the stairwells and twists of the different corridors, Reynolds felt confident. Only a few times did the space feel unnatural, with an undefined darkness he couldn't see through.

And then he felt it—the evil he had sensed but had not yet seen. He stopped and turned around, looking for an aura, a trace, something that would help him find Sharrod. His uneasiness grew.

"Stop!" he shouted. "Stop! This is the wrong way."

Katia and Vanya halted near him. Silexa stood at a distance, and though he couldn't see the king, his presence was there.

"We are in the tunnel," King Reinoh told him.

Reynolds looked above. Darkness enveloped him, no visible fibers or grid like before, just emptiness. "Vanya, what's above us?"

"It is a tunnel, carved earth, as King Reinoh has stated."

"But there's something wrong. I feel it." Reynolds shifted uneasily. "Something is blocking the magic. I can't see."

"I'll help." Vanya went to grab his arm, but Reynolds shook it off, watching Silexa's stone, like a shadow coming closer, ready to snatch.

The king gasped and fell to the floor.

"No!" Silexa knelt down.

Reynolds went forward and stumbled. "What's happened?"

Silexa didn't answer and started running down the tunnel.

"What? What is it?"

Katia was there. "Oh, no." She knelt near the king. "It's a knife." She tried to pull at it, but couldn't. "Oh, help. A knife in the chest. Someone threw it. I can't—"

Reynolds looked as hard as he could. He scrambled to the side of the tunnel.

A scream echoed ahead.

Katia's aura changed, nervous.

"Run. Go!"

Katia bolted down the tunnel in a flurry of white.

"Vanya." Reynolds could hardly see the king. "I need your sight. Help me."

Vanya stayed calm and approached. His aura betrayed how scared he felt, still only a boy thrown into witnessing the murder of a king. "The knife is too deep. He is gone."

Reynolds rested his hands on the king's chest. No rise or fall of a steady beating heart. He mulled around the questions in his brain. "That was calculated and close, thrown with accuracy."

Katia's fast magic lit the tunnel. A frosty cloud hung in the air, and Reynolds could see through the mist as if the magic were a torch. He took the advantage and ran toward them, focused onward to the scuffle with the girls and a dark shadow. Another blast of ice shot out, travelling away. The air grew cold as he approached.

Then the brilliant starlight from Silexa's stone disappeared from sight like it had been snatched from existence.

Katia was on her knees when Reynolds found her. Silexa lay on the ground, blood spilling from her temple.

"Oh, no." Reynolds pressed against her wound with his sleeve. "What happened?"

"I don't know what it was," Katia said between breaths. "A man in a dark cloak. He took the stone and ran."

Reynolds quickly ripped cloth from Silexa's cloak and fastened a bandage. "The king is dead. Vanya's in shock."

Katia's aura began to change to a strange blue, the light beginning to fade again with her thoughts. "I didn't want him to die. I did at first, but I think he wanted to make things right."

"That may be his redemption in the end."

His attention turned back to Silexa.

"Please save her!" a voice came from behind, a soft female voice.

Reynolds turned and saw a woman standing there, long silver hair running down her back. He knew her as Ymber, Silexa's sister who had passed on, and yet she stood as if in flesh and blood, speaking to him as clearly as if alive.

"Don't let her die."

Reynolds checked her wrists. Her pulse was slow.

"What do I do?"

"She is slipping, Reynolds Fairborne. You must act fast."

Vanya appeared behind Ymber, visible to him as well. "Katia, preserve her."

"What?" Katia looked up. "What does that mean?"

"You have done this once before," Vanya stated. "I have seen it. Preserve her in cold."

"Save her."

The bandage was already soaked through with blood. She needed better care than Reynolds could provide.

"Dammit, Katia! Do something!"

Katia's magic flared into action. She placed her hands on Silexa's chest, and slowly, the crystals began creeping away from her fingers. The ice flowed up and over, creating a perfect cocoon.

The blood hardened around the wound, freezing Silexa's insides.

Katia lifted her fingers, looking down at what she had done. "What if she . . ."

"Then she is." Reynolds placed his hand on the cold ice princess. "Vanya. Watch her. I don't want you entering if there is a fight, understood?"

The boy leaned over Silexa. "Yes."

"Come on." Reynolds grabbed Katia by the arm, dragging her to her feet.

"My poor sister." Ymber tried to touch her through the ice. *"I will stay as well. Set me free, Reynolds Fairborne."*

Reynolds studied the girl's sadness and nodded. "I will."

CHAPTER TWENTY-FOUR

It hadn't been long after Zander and the others had left when Bryant heard commotion outside the tent. One of his men came rushing in.

"Sire." It was Hix, taking his hat off as he entered the room. With a swift bow he returned it back in place. "You must come. The gates have opened."

"The gates?" Bryant ran out the flap and through the forest to the overhang overlooking the great wall of Southwick. The city wall had several entrances, but each was a solid, metal fortress. The main gate near the bridge had been locked for some time now. They had been waiting for any sign of movement, but so far nothing had happened.

As Bryant watched, something struck him as odd. "Those are not soldiers."

Hix glanced at him. "Then they are monsters."

Bryant took a closer look. "I don't see monsters, my good man, I see people. We talked about the danger that may await us, something we hadn't seen before." He gripped Hix's shoulder tightly. "It's like the Musungu, unexpected. It's time to use magic."

"Sire, we don't have—"

"Where's Brandell?" Bryant began bounding down the hillside. "And Thornock. In fact, all who served me in the Musungu. There is a trick to this, I know it. I feel it."

Bryant stopped at a tree, looking closer. Through the hazy, gray light of morning, he saw people marching in synchronized step, but somehow it looked less like marching and more like puppets told to walk. They were all different sizes and shapes, both young and old. In a steady march, each creature had sight of Bryant's small troop of soldiers, slowly moving toward the camp.

"They are mindless," Bryant surmised. "They can't think for themselves. How are we to fight them? They're innocent people."

"But look." Hix pointed to the black blades in their hands. "They are armed. That weapon I am not familiar with."

Bryant ran back to the camp and signaled to one of the scouts to sound the alarm. A horn blew, alerting them to danger. Men emerged out of the trees and tents and hollows, armed to fight. But there were not many, a little over two hundred strong. Those pouring out of the gates and flooding the field with black were numbered in the thousands.

"There's no way we can fight off that many," someone murmured in the crowd. Others voiced their concerns, but Bryant raised his hands.

"Brethren. We do not know what we face as of yet. It's clear they are not under their own power. We need to find what is controlling them and stop it."

"There's no time," another shouted.

"Much like the Musungu, things are not as they appear."

"So, what do you suggest we do?"

"Do whatever you can to spare their lives."

"But you've been training us to fight!"

"Traps!" someone shouted. Bryant looked through the crowd to see Thornock, his withered face standing out among the men. "Use the nets from the fishermen near the docks."

Bryant smiled. "Excellent! Think around the danger."

"There are too many!"

"Do what you can until we solve the mystery. Go, my brethren! Spare as many as you can!"

The men rushed to find what they could in the time they had.

The black mass surged toward them, inch by inch, with black blades held high. Bryant armed himself and searched for Brandell.

Near the edge of the forest, he found the dwarf Brandell holding several different flowers. Bryant stepped up to meet him. "What do you make of this?"

Brandell shook his head. "I know fairy magic, not dark magic."

"Then you recognize it as such." Bryant looked out over the scene. Several trip wires had been secured across the path in order to slow them down.

"It's clearly dark magic." He looked up to Bryant's tall frame. "I don't know what the fairies can do."

"I do." Bryant crouched down. "The fairy that saved my life," he motioned to his heart, "is the bravest creature I know. She saved me from the poison of Shivra. She gave up living to save me." He patted Brandell on the shoulder. "Now, why would she do that?"

"Because," Brandell stammered but pushed the words from his throat, "because she saw the greater good."

"That's exactly what I see here," Bryant pointed out. "These are normal civilians, my people whom Sharrod has poisoned. He is using my own against me, knowing I am defenseless against them. If I hurt my people, I'm hurting myself. How am I to succeed?"

Brandell's eyes drooped in thought. He had no answer.

Bryant straightened. "What do you make of the black blades?"

"I . . . I think they are dangerous. I think we need to stay away from them."

"Agreed." Bryant turned his head in thought. "What about the magic? Who is controlling them?"

Brandell stepped closer. "I don't think they are close. They wouldn't need to be. They could give the order and leave."

And Bryant understood. "It's a distraction. Someone is keeping us busy." Bryant looked harder at the masses. "It's happening today, Brandell." His mouth tightened as he thought of Silexa, afraid he may never see her again. "We need to stop this. We need to get inside."

His heart thumped deep at the thought of her. This fight was for her. He was ready to give his life if it was required of him. Silexa was everything. He looked back at the creeping dark and stepped forward.

Brandell follow suit. "I have a few fairies who will help." He held up the flowers.

"Thank you, dear fellow. They will be perfect."

The black march continued. They were not far away now. Only a few nets had been found to hold them back. Another horn sounded and the men formed a line. Bryant walked to the forefront, his scabbard held tight in his hand.

"Remember!" he shouted. "Spare all you can! The task is difficult but not impossible. Beware of the black blades."

The ever-moving black army was nearly to their position. He unsheathed his sword and raised it high in the air. With a swift downward swing, Bryant led the charge.

A few of Bryant's men moved to the sides of the approaching army with ropes, ensnaring a few and tripping others. The dark soldiers in the army were confused but also angry. Several continued forward, slashing with their dark swords.

A blade pierced one of Bryant's men, and he went down screaming, writhing, and convulsing on the ground. Black smoke rose from the wound, coiling itself around his arm like a snake. It moved up and over his chest.

Another man tried to pull his friend away from the smoke but got sliced with a swinging sword with the same result. In a matter of moments, both men were completely covered with the same thick smoke and got back up again, marching to the same unheard rhythm.

Bryant witnessed it all. Though some men had succeeded in trapping the dark soldiers, it would not be nearly enough to stop the mass of doom.

He didn't know what to do. "Brandell!"

Brandell had already headed into the front line, armed with nothing but his flowers held out before him. In one swift motion, he threw the flowers into the air. As if halted by the wind, the flowers caught in the air, five of them, each beginning to twirl in different ways. An explosion of light and color ignited the air. Various colors flashed around— the fairies emerged and took flight.

In a huge arch, the fairies flew over the crowd, confusing the dark mass, distracting and slowing their march. A purple streak headed toward the bridge, zigzagged between people, and left a trail of dust. Where the dust fell, a tree sprang up from the ground. Line after line followed the haphazard pattern until there was no more space to grow. It was clearly an illusion, but the dark army couldn't tell. They froze as if trapped in the mirage.

Two blue fairies tried the same thing, circumnavigating the crowd round and round. Streams of bright blue wrapped them. Several soldiers howled, and some flailed about, their blades swinging wildly. Then one of the streams stopped as a fairy was hit mid-flight, instantly disappearing into black powder. The illusion faded.

Two fairies, white and gold, streaked past, the white hovering over Brandell's head protectively as the gold one tried something similar to the illusions. Yellow rose petals floated in her wake. The moment they touched the ground, a thorny patch of briars sprang up from the earth. Unlike the tree illusion, these seemed to harm the people, stopping them in place.

But with one blow, the gold fairy also disappeared.

Brandell looked back at Bryant without knowing what to do.

Prince Bryant ran forward, watching the carnage. He had to act. A few of the dark ones came right for him. He dodged the blade of the first and kicked one in the chest. The next aimed for his heart. He swung his sword swiftly upward, knocking the sword out of the attacker's hand and striking him in the jaw.

One came for Brandell, who scrambled backward. Bryant ran and pushed the soldier away, but more were coming. Bryant's army was dwindling. With every life lost, the dark army grew in size, his own men becoming part of the advancing infantry.

Brandell stumbled backward, into the clutches of a dark knight.

The white fairy instinctively flew down, hitting him right in the chest. A puff of white powder fell on the man as the fairy petals disintegrated. The dark knight wobbled at the impact and fell to the ground. Slowly, the color in the man's face turned from a grayish hue to the normal brown of Southwick. He sat up, dazed.

Bryant, witnessing the sacrifice, felt a sting in his chest, the same spot where he had a tiny, bite-sized scar left by his own fairy savior. The unidentified man sat, confused by what had happened.

"Help him!" he yelled to Brandell, who immediately checked on the man.

The stinging in Bryant's chest didn't go away but instead gave him an idea.

Two dark soldiers headed for him, a man and woman. He stood ready to fight, ready to act, but then he took his sword and sheathed it—completely unarmed.

"What are you doing?" he heard Brandell yell from behind him, but he braced himself.

The man reached him first. His blade was sharp, pointing directly at him. In one powerful swing the man's arm came down, the blade disappearing right through Bryant as if it were not there at all.

Bryant's chest heaved and a sly grin stole over his face. The woman attacker tried as well, cutting across and trying to slash him into bits—but nothing happened. No blade touched him.

Some of his men stopped at the sight.

"Fairies . . ." Bryant turned. "We need more fairies!"

"But," Brandell replied, clearly stunned, "I don't have any more."

Sera saw the looming clouds of Southwick ahead. Her heart sank as she remembered why they were flying there in the first place.

Frida, her red dragon, grew agitated, and she leaned in closer. A sea of black appeared below, like the same that had come for them at SisterElm. She steered the fire-eater in that direction.

"What are you doing?" she heard Arie in her ear, his voice mixed with the rushing wind. He leaned in close, squashing poor Lottie sitting between them.

She pointed to the sea of shadows. "What do you think that is?"

Arie straightened up behind her. "Those are people, Sera, innocent people marching to their death, like Spotswood told us about."

Sera flew closer. The dark shadows moved together like ants over prey. A few civilians ran away toward the palace wall, but one brave person remained to fight off the shadows.

Like one soul breathing together, Sera communicated what she needed to Frida, who swooped down, her talon stretched forth toward the floundering creature below. She snatched the girl in the midst of darkness, wrapping her tight within her grasp.

Sera quickly steered Frida to a clear meadow not far from the impending darkness. The dragon made a graceful descent, not unlike ones made so many times near the volcanoes in the Ignis Mountains. Sera threw over the reins and slid down the creature.

Frida's talon was still closed, protecting whoever lay inside. Sera reached over and stroked them until they opened one at a time.

The scared girl looked up, greatly astonished. "Sera?"

Sera grabbed her by the hand and pulled her into an embrace. "Oh, dearest Vespa," she whispered in her ear. She didn't want to let her younger sister go. It had been years since she had vanished into the Musungu. It was the safest place for her, she knew, but she never thought she would ever see her again.

She pulled back, wiping away her tears. "Are you hurt?"

Vespa shook her head. "No, I have protection."

"What in the world is happening here?"

Vespa quickly explained about the dark magic army created as a distraction.

"But what will stop them?"

Vespa lifted her flower from her cloak. She cupped it in her palm, and it danced into life. A tiny fairy broke free from its petals and spun around her hand in streaming yellow light.

Sera watched on. "How can fairies help?"

"Dark magic cannot harm them. They bring light to the world."

Sera turned to her. "Vespa, it's your turn."

"What do you mean?"

"You still have your stone, don't you?"

Vespa reached down and pulled on the chain, revealing the purple stone alive with light. "I'm afraid to use it."

"I can't think of a better time than right now. We need to save those people. They don't know what they are doing."

Vespa held her medallion for a moment longer. Then, without speaking, she took her necklace from around her neck and placed it on the ground. She picked her flower from the front of her cloak and placed it near her medallion. "Okay, little one," she said softly, "time to wake up the world."

The flower began to spin around, hovering over the stone. It increased its speed until light emanated from within the circle. Vespa looked up into Sera's eyes, a trail of tears falling from her own face. She smiled and whispered something Sera couldn't hear, then with a swift thrust, slammed both her palms down on the flower, smothering it on the center of the stone.

A shockwave rippled through the ground with a thunderous boom. The vibration knocked Sera off her feet and onto her back. A strange silence filled the void, an awareness that something in the world was different, something had changed.

And then Sera saw it happen: tiny particles came from the wave, like specks of debris, only falling upward, away from the ground. Little glowing specks of life-force for all fey filled the air.

The flecks dazzled her sight, and she sat up. Her arms waved through the dust, swirling with the movement in the air. Vespa had released life into the world, the gentle organic magic that bound life's precious fibers together.

Sera marveled at the beauty of it all. She breathed in deeply, inhaling the intense floral aroma, like all the flowers she had ever smelled wrapped together. The scent awoke all her senses, surging her magic strong in her veins.

The creeping darkness in the periphery of her vision had fallen, like dying embers in ash cooling in the air. The entire army lay on the ground. Sera stared, watching the phenomenon. A few were now sitting, waking toward the heavenly air. The black ash lifted from their bodies returning them to the healthy color of life.

"She did it," Sera exhaled. She turned and spotted Arie sliding down the dragon's hind quarters, carefully guiding Lottie safely to the ground. Sera stood and ran toward them as fast as she could.

Arie gathered her into his arms and kissed her forehead. Lottie wrapped her little arms around them both.

Sera could have stayed there forever but turned, a thought striking her. "Vespa."

Arie let her go the moment she saw the heap of dark clothing on the ground.

"Oh, no." Sera hurried back to the spot where her sister lay. "Vespa?" She knelt, grabbing her wrist. "Vespa!"

Her sister lay quiet and still, tears wet on her cheek. Next to her lay the tiny form of a small pink fairy, both of them passed beyond this world. A light, warm as a summer evening, outlined Vespa's body, growing and touching every inch of her until she sparkled.

Sera held her breath, the sight both sad and wonderful. With a flash, the light disappeared into tiny flecks of gold, leaving the outline of Vespa's body cradling the only thing left—her purple medallion.

Sera broke down and sobbed.

Micah listened to the tree. He heard unspeakable sadness in its roots. Its heart had been ripped out, leaving it hollow. He felt the ground. It was cold, without energy or life source. "Something has happened."

Mother felt the tree. "Oh, my stars, yes. Look at the leaves."

Micah watched the leaves turn a deep red before shriveling and falling to the ground. The branches hardened as well, shrinking as the nutrients disappeared.

"Lytte must know," Micah stated.

"But what of the dark army?" Mother exclaimed. "We don't have time to worry about the tree."

"But the fairies will die. All the life this tree supplies will disappear."

Mother looked conflicted.

"Run," Spotswood instructed Micah. "Hurry. Speak with Lytte. I will ask the elements to help."

His uncle placed his palms on the ground, and suddenly the earth began to awaken, the minerals springing to life. Time was short. Micah dashed back through the entrance to the tree, running as fast as he could to where Lytte hid.

As he passed by the dwarves inside, Micah spat out warnings of the approaching army and instructed them to gather what they could and find Mother outside. "Quick! The tree will not hold you. It is not safe. You must hurry!"

Their faces reflected mostly confusion until they heard the cracking and splintering of the wood, the roots ripping away from the dirt. Then hurried footsteps and yells filled the air as they rushed from the hollows and caverns.

Though Micah preferred the dark, his sight sharpened as light gathered in the darkness of the corridors. The fairies had come together, fearing the end of everything. Micah didn't know what to say as he passed them by. He entered the far room, the fairies following. He stopped and turned.

"No, you must flee."

The large moving light flew across the room, outlining the doorway he needed to enter.

"Are you coming with me?" he squeaked. "Oh, dear ones, I am with you."

He ran through the archway. Lytte stood in the corner of the cave, listening to the earth buckle around him.

"Master Lytte!" Micah approached, but his mentor looked as if he was in a trance. "Please, Master Lytte. We need your help. Mother is worried. We don't know what to do. The black army approaches—"

"Yes." Lytte opened his eyes and looked at him. His gaze told him everything he needed to know. "Pera has left her home."

"How?"

"With Naomi, as instructed."

"Then you knew what would happen to the tree." Micah didn't know what to think.

"Yes, young Micah. Pera has told me."

"Told you what, sir?"

"The fire." The fairies surrounded Lytte, lifting him away from the wall, lighting his white cloak.

Around him, Micah felt the nervous energy of the minerals, fearing what Lytte just said. "What do you mean? I do not sense fire."

"The tree must burn."

"No!" He didn't mean to shout, but the destruction of something so beautiful did not make sense. "Why?"

"To give new life." Lytte looked at the fairies surrounding him. "It is the rebirth of Parbraven. Pera has left and will not return. We must burn the tree so it can release new seeds, new life to the earth."

Micah felt the flame inside, the burn of sadness within him grow. "Does it have to be like this?"

"Yes."

A large root ripped out of the ground, sprouting up between the two of them.

"Micah, I must trust you to do this."

Micah knew it, too. The fibers all around him told him the same. "What of the fairies?"

Lytte floated toward the exit. "Find a new home."

With a beautiful final glow, Lytte began to burn. It started in his stomach, a fire igniting and spreading until it was a beautiful flame around him. The ash collected around, the embers consuming, then smothering like a withering leaf, smaller and smaller until a single flame hovered in the air.

The dancing light mesmerized Micah. Without communicating, he knew he had to touch it. He reached out with his bare hands, apprehensive. The flame did not burn, nor sting nor singe; it was warm and gentle. He scooped it up within both of his hands. Another large, shattering rumble shook the earth. The fairies filtered out, some following the cracks in the ground, some out the exits, and some loyal to the flame.

Micah carried the fire as carefully as he could back through the roots and crags, following the lights flying before him.

Dirt fell around him, earth piling up with each shift of the ground. The hardened stairs had broken up, and Micah scrambled to find footing. He jumped to the last ledge and started to lose his balance. A cluster of fairies caught his hood and set him right.

"Run." Micah felt the word resonate inside him. Not wanting to chance it, he fled as fast as he could. He saw the opening out of the tree. The fairies burst out before him, lighting the outside world.

A large, whirling tornado stirred along the ground, blocking any attacker attempting to get to the tree. Spotswood stood tall, his arms an orchestra of movement. Mother had gathered the dwarves—some armed, others standing firm against the wind. She was leading them away toward the gully. But Micah knew they would be trapped there.

The dark army came closer, their black swords raised, their march synchronized. Micah listened closely to their collective heartbeat. It was strong and muted of feeling, but each heart string burned bright with life.

None did he care to hurt. They were not what they seemed, he knew.

As they came closer, some were confused by the winds, but theirs was a relentless march, a torment, but an instruction they could not disobey. Forward, always forward. The armed dwarves attacked those on the side, pushing them back.

Micah watched helplessly, holding the eternal flame as black blades sliced into several of the dwarves. Screams echoed through the valley as they were filled with poison.

"Uncle!" Micah yelled through the noise. Spotswood couldn't hear through the wind, his trance-like motions preventing him from seeing the dangerous dark army approaching him and the tree.

What could he do? The fibers of Micah's magic sprang to life within him. He felt the coursing strands surge in power, listening to the earth and its awakening call to action.

'Not yet!' it murmured. He was ready to burst into action, the dust devils wanting to jump to life.

But he still held the flame.

"No!" he shouted as loud as he could, trying to get his uncle's attention. His little heart beat faster as he watched the soldiers descend upon Spotswood.

The tornado ran wild, losing its direction and slowly floundering about. Hearing his cry, Spotswood had turned and was now in combat with a few of the poisoned soldiers. Watching him was fascinating, his frailty lost with each fluid motion, his arms and legs in precise harmony with the elements. One down, two down. Micah smiled.

Then a third lashed out with his sword and caught Spotswood in the arm. The poison worked fast, and Micah watched in horror as his beloved uncle turned slowly into a dark, creeping, mindless soldier.

His heart shattered and his spirit broke. The flame nearly fell from his hand. "No. Uncle!" he cried out, but the army only moved forward.

A light sparked like a shooting star before his eyes. And then another. Through his grief, Micah looked up at the fairies. The ball of light moved, penetrating the dark sky like a shattering star. The lumbering soldiers collapsed to the ground. One after another, each fairy turned to crisp dust in the air.

"It is time!"

Micah's hand shook, his sight weak from his streaming tears. He held the flame high above his head as more creeping people surged forward. Turning toward the tree, he saw its tightened, twisted body stood gaunt, devoid of nourishment.

"Now!"

Micah threw the flame. It left his hand, spun through the air, and landed within a knothole. The flame grew, spreading its gold wings around the trunk, moving along the veins, sparking as it traveled around limbs and branches. The heat began to work, charring its surroundings to black. The tree was set alight, pushing both ash and ember to the sky.

Soon everything he knew about the tree had changed. Something so vibrant only moments before burned with a fury he had never beheld.

An intense, overwhelming heat pushed him away from the fire and back toward the trees. The flames did not spread, only embraced the wood more.

Micah had been so captivated he hadn't noticed the dark army had stopped, all looking at the flame, stunned. The fairies were no longer flying to save them but hovering near the fire like a glittering cloud. They scattered in a quick frenzy, circling the tree, protecting their home.

Buuuuurump!

Micah heard the world shuddering. Something was happening within the ground.

"Energy alive!"

He fell to his knees, pressing the ground for information. It was coming, a ripple through the entire world. Faster, faster, with no time to prepare.

Micah lifted his hands just as the wave hit.

Crack!

The tree split near its middle. Embers flew everywhere, scattering heat in the air and toward the ground.

Wind followed, blowing fast and frantic. The smoke billowed high to the sky, spiraling upward. Micah squinted, watching the black smoke pierce through the thick clouds, pushing the harsh thunderheads apart. A swirling hole ripped through, and a single beam of sunlight hit the tree.

Micah stood in awe like everyone else.

The rays of heaven lit the tree, smothering the flames and spreading gold down every ring, every vein. Leaves twisted into life, green and glittering, stretching out more glorious than before.

Micah stumbled to his feet. Around him stood people—not soldiers, but men and women gazing in dumbstruck wonder. The ash had changed them, cured them.

But what of his uncle? Micah found him kneeling near the hill, as he had before, stunned and hurt but alive. What had happened he did not know, but the world was changing, and he was witnessing the birth of new earth.

Part Four

CHAPTER TWENTY-FIVE

The fire-eaters reared up. Sebastian scraped his claws on the ground and extended his giant wings. Taren held tight to the reigns and patted its side. "Okay, Seb, let's take one more ride together."

The dragon huffed. The wind pushed around him as the creature leapt into the air, gaining flight with each great flap of its wings. Sera and Arie drew up alongside them. Their red dragon was more seasoned, had more grace in flight, but Taren was fond of Sebastian. His temper matched his own.

The cooling wind felt good on his hot skin. Naomi's delicate arms held tight to him as they flew. He pushed away his feelings and focused on the tall parapets far in the distance near the sea. This wasn't Naomi, he had to remind himself. It was Pera. Naomi would come back to him if Pera succeeded.

But Naomi couldn't have disappeared, not entirely. She was still there. She had to be. If nothing else, she could still listen.

"Where are you, Naomi?" he mumbled.

Naomi's form leaned her head against his back. "She is here."

Taren straightened his back, afraid to move or think.

"You are warm." Pera pressed closer to him. "Blood is warm and fast. Bodies are something I do not know anything about. I've never felt curiosity or cold or air. It was well for me to know, to experience before I return."

"Return to the tree?"

"No." Pera pulled back at the question. "To my father. I am returning home."

Taren's heart raced. "And Naomi? Will she return with you?"

Pera let silence answer him.

"Can I tell her anything? Is she listening now?"

"You may speak, young Taren, and she will hear, but she may not answer."

Now faced with the opportunity to speak freely, having a silent audience who had no other choice but to listen to his words, his apologies, he ran through everything he had thought to say to her—all the beautiful moments and the sad memories, the regrets, the hopes, the journey as a whole . . . and came up empty.

"I . . ." he began and stumbled on his words. "There isn't anything I can say." He grabbed the hand that circled around him. "There's not enough time. And now that I have a moment to think, I . . . I don't have words."

All went quiet. He had said too much. He shouldn't have asked at all.

Naomi's hand squeezed his arm.

Taren was overcome by the small gesture. He gently kissed the back of her hand. "I'm sorry," he whispered.

"All is right, Taren," she said. "All is forgiven."

Sebastian jolted, which knocked Taren to the side. He held Naomi tighter, gripping the animal with his other hand.

"What's wrong, Seb?"

As they drew closer to Southwick, he could see dark masses moving about like a plague of locusts infecting the ground.

Taren watched Sera turn the red fire-eater down toward the fray. He began to follow her.

"No," Pera instructed. "We must get to the palace. Keep me safe, young Taren."

Taren pulled up. Sebastian didn't like the sudden movement and snaked his giant body around the other way.

Taren encircled the neck of the beast, calming him down. "It's okay, boy." The words seemed to soothe the beast, but he still turned the opposite direction. With every effort at his command, Taren yanked hard on the worn leather straps, guiding Sebastian up to the tallest tower.

Wind whipped around as they sailed upward, circling the spires. A strange, sinister darkness began to form near the tower, threatening the light of day.

Sebastian fought the air, but Taren held firm, leading him closer and closer to the structure. The dragon stretched out his long talons and grasped the precipice firmly, anchoring them deep into the ancient stone. Taren gripped Pera tightly as they both held onto the harnessed creature.

Crumbling pieces of brick tumbled down, breaking apart the palace bit by bit.

"I feel him," Pera said, a terrified expression her face. "Shon. He is here. He is strong."

Taren took her hand once again. "You are stronger. Don't doubt now. You can face him." He pointed to a window high in the tower. "We can get in through there."

Sebastian whipped his tail and shattered the glass.

"Good boy." Taren patted the dragon.

They began to climb down the tail and around the broken stone and glass. Taren guided Pera into the palace as carefully as he could, sweeping away the bits of glass with his boot.

Sebastian turned his head toward him, his yellow eyes full of hunger.

Taren nodded. "Let me help." He turned to find fallen stones, the heat from his hands turning them into blazing hot coals. The dragon opened his mouth wide as Taren fed him one after another, filling the creature's belly with warmth.

After five stones, the belly of the beast began to glow from the inside. It huffed, and smoke rose through its teeth.

"Now, go my friend, until we meet again."

With one final push, Sebastian swept his wings high and flew into the air. Dust fell around Taren and Pera. In the distance, they saw the bright green dragon flying freely. It turned back toward Southwick and let out a roar, a single streak of flame rising from his mouth, before he disappeared from sight.

Taren looked at Pera. The dust only made her aura glow brighter. "Are you okay?"

She took in a deep breath. "We are fine."

Taren heard an ominous creak from below. "It's not safe. Come." He grabbed her hand and led her through a series of doorways until he found a spiraling staircase heading down.

Together they ran through the tower, seeing firsthand the damage the dragon had made on the structure. Deep holes tore through the brick layers where its talons had dug into the stone.

They reached a landing, and Pera stopped, letting go of his hand. "Inside me—my heart in the center—it thumps hard."

"Yes," Taren answered. "We've been running."

Pera looked at her hands. "They tremble."

"It's fear." Taren held them to calm her shaking.

"I have never known fear." She examined her hands and then looked at him. "I have an uneasy feeling everywhere. Is this also fear?"

"Possibly. Anxiety. Fear. We have emotions. Emotions drive all our actions."

Pera started to shake her head. "I cannot do this."

Taren froze, looking at her. "Pera. You have to do this."

Pera closed her eyes. Her aura increased, growing brighter.

Tunneling . . .

   Magic pull and release . . .

Naomi stands before her.

Glittering gold against the white of magic.

       "I cannot do this. You are strong, Naomi.

         Guide me. Where do I go?"

"Pera, I don't know. I've never been here."

"It is not about knowing.
It is about instinct.
Your magic is strong.
It will know where to go. Use it."

"Me?"

"I am not human.
I do not understand the frailty of life.
Emotions are overwhelming and confusing.
I was not made to experience them.
You must regain it."

"But Lytte warned me against it.
The crossover is dangerous."

"I am afraid.
I have never felt fear, and I cannot control it.
We will not succeed."

Hands gently press on her face.

"You are the strong one.
We have made you thus.
We prepared you to be here.
You will win."

The fibers dance about her, light streaming in vivid color.
Tunneling . . .
Ascending . . .

Breath.

Naomi opened her eyes to dark, filtered light. The air in her lungs moved freely in and out. She didn't know where she was or how she'd gotten there. The instructions were to bring Pera to the palace. And somehow she was there, really there, feeling the air again. She couldn't help but smile.

"Pera?" She turned, startled. Taren stood next to her, his intense dark eyes filled with concern. "Pera, what's wrong?"

Pera. The name echoed. Yes, she felt the light within her burn. Every time she exhaled, Naomi could sense the anticipating spirit, her superior magic waiting securely for her moment to act.

Taren's gaze questioned what they were doing stopped in mid-action. She was at a crossroads. *He doesn't know I am here. What would he do if he did?*

"Everything is fine," Naomi lied, trying to mimic the delicate cadence of Pera's voice.

"I don't believe you. You went into a trance."

Naomi looked around her, not knowing where she was or how to get out. Pera would know. "There is no time to believe," she replied, keeping the game up.

She closed her eyes again, searching her magic.

The world closed in, swallowing her up with black. Pera stood by her, not saying a word, letting her discover for herself. Darkness surrounded her, like floating in the sky at night. Lights appeared like stars moving about, dashing from here to there. She pressed harder at the images. Looking closer, the shapes became people, became magic. Reds, blues, purples, all manner of elements circling about in a world of nothingness.

She had entered the plane of magic.

Far in the distance, near the edge of the blackness, sat a hole like a rip in fabric. It moved like a windy sail, rippling around itself in grays, blues, and greens, each moving independently but harmoniously. Creatures were waiting, red with fire, heated by anger. A man stood on the edge of a platform, siphoning energy from another. Pera sent a burst of magic spilling into Naomi's veins. This was Shon. He was already here. His transformation was nearly complete.

Her eyes flew open. "I know where to go."

Taren grabbed her arm. "You sure you're all right?"

"My heart aches, Taren, but I can't let this go on any more. It's time to end this. I'm ready." Naomi turned down the corridor and headed forward.

Taren shuffled behind her. "Wait. What's the plan?"

"There doesn't need to be a plan."

"Yes, there has to be a plan or we all die." He grabbed her arm again to slow her down. "Pera, I promised to protect you. I need Naomi back. I need her alive."

Naomi slowed and took in his words. Her breath caught, but she tried to remain calm. "Yes. Taren. What do you think?"

Taren's eyes widened. "First, we need to be more inconspicuous. You are glowing like the night star."

Naomi looked at her arms and hands and then noticed her dress. What had happened to her? The old, tattered, adventure-worn clothes were replaced with the kind of elegance she had never worn before. Naomi blinked but tried to hide her confusion. Pera would never act like this.

The light filling the tunnel came from her. The aura had not faded. If anything, it glowed brighter every step she took closer to the magic.

"Here." Taren shed his cloak and placed it around her like a shield. He raised the hood, covering her golden hair. A memory came back to her of doing the same, hiding her hair away from the speculation of others. She felt the curls down her back. It had returned to the length it had been back in Sharlot. The sensation felt so unnatural now, and she had no explanation of the transformation. Her hands flipped to her neck. The shadesilk scarf she received from

Malindra was still there. She relaxed internally, hiding the anxiety of losing it.

"What else do you suggest?"

Taren looked distracted, thinking. "This is no time to act foolishly. We need to be smart. We should wait for the right moment to act. Naomi's impulsive. She always acts with passion instead of thinking everything through. We need to see what is going on first. Understand the whole picture."

Naomi felt her cheeks begin to blush but calmed herself. "Understood."

"And there's something else." Taren leaned in closer, so close Naomi couldn't get away. "Could you give Naomi a message?"

Naomi blinked, acting the part but feeling weak inside, her magic frenzied with energy. "I will do my best."

He leaned in and kissed her. The action so surprised Naomi that she couldn't prepare for it. At first she panicked, but then a sensation beyond what she could imagine filled down to her toes.

He pulled away and looked down. "I'm sorry. I . . . I shouldn't have done that. I'm sorry, Pera."

Naomi blinked, trying to remember what she wanted to say but lost all thought. Did he know it was really her and not Pera? She couldn't hide it. Her cheeks flushed. She took a deep breath to calm her reaction, but it didn't help. Taren would figure out it was her, not Pera. She didn't want to feel what she did, but it was so natural, so much different than when he had first kissed her near the Echoes. The magic had made him curious then, but here it was just Taren. An ache surrounded her chest that she knew would stay there as long as she lived.

Taren only glanced at her, a parting look of embarrassment. "Oh, Naomi, I wish you could feel that," he murmured to himself—not to Naomi, not to Pera. He stood back and brushed his hair with his hands as he collected himself again.

"She does," Naomi said, nearly shaking. "She knows."

"I'm sorry, Pera. At least you now understand a kiss in human form."

Naomi smiled. "Thank you."

"Okay. Let's go save the world."

Naomi righted her shoulders and marched forward with Taren at her side.

"What did I do?" Sera's fingers scraped at the ground where her sister had vanished. "I forced her to do it. I didn't mean for her to . . ." All the air escaped from her chest. She covered her eyes. "All my fault."

Arie stood near her, silent. His presence both comforted and annoyed her, pressing on her soul like a watch dog.

Sera lifted her eyes. All around, people were beginning to wake from the nightmare of dark sleep. Lottie ran around chatting with the confused fishermen and farmers before rejoining Sera and Arie. "They are from Southwick. Many don't remember what happened. She . . . saved them all."

She had forgotten how young Lottie was, still so believing. Sera looked at her, then back at the perfect medallion in her hand. "What do I do?" Her voice was barely audible, the unbelievable shock still resonating through her.

"I know."

Sera looked up to see a tall man towering over her, a dark shadow over his face.

In her peripheral vision, Sera saw Arie grip his sword.

The stranger stood with his palms visibly empty. "I have no weapon. You, however, have a dragon."

Sera looked behind her. Frida's large talon gripped the moist earth, her legs ready to spring. She glanced back at the newcomer. "She won't harm you unless you harm us."

"I have no intention of that," he returned. "I hoped that she might help me."

Arie inched closer, analyzing the man. "Why, you bastard . . ." He trailed off.

Sera took in Arie's expression, confused.

Arie shoved the man hard in the shoulder, which only made the other retaliate and shove him back. Sera scrambled up from the dirt, watching the scuffle. The two wrestled about, still remaining on their feet. Arms flailed around until Arie had the man in a headlock, rubbing his head like a young boy.

Sera placed her hands on her whip. "Leave him alone."

The man raised his arms, as if surrendering. "Enough! Rass. I get it."

Sera wavered. "Wait. What is this? Rass? Get what?"

Arie let the man out of the headlock but grabbed him with his hands. "You sneaky ol' bastard, what are you doing out here?"

Sera stared, confused by the grin on his face. She came up between them, still pointing the whip at the man. He didn't look at all familiar to her, but she knew very few people from Southwick. "Arie, 'fess up, how do you know him?"

"Rass—I mean, Arie—was in my bunk before he jumped ship." The man turned to him. "Where did you go?"

Arie's mouth thinned, and he glanced back at Sera. "Doesn't matter now."

The man extended his arm and shook Arie's shoulder with a firm, reassuring grip. "No, I guess it doesn't." He then extended his hand to Sera. "I'm Bryant."

"That's just fine." Sera didn't take his hand, too upset to shake it. "Why do you want my dragon?"

Bryant grinned. "I mean to ride it. We could get into the palace much quicker—"

"Wait." She pushed back his hand. "Why would you want to get into the palace? Do you understand what is happening in there?"

"Yes. I know everything."

"Sera?" Arie tried to get her attention, but she quickly waved him off.

"And you might die," she continued.

"I understand the risk."

Arie grabbed her arms and spun her around to meet him. "Shut up already. He's the prince. Trust him."

"Prince? Of what? Southwick?"

"Yes."

"You're that scoundrel Reinoh's kid." She pushed him in the chest, though it didn't affect him in the least bit. "He plotted to kill my father. He helped create this mess."

"Possibly," Bryant returned calmly. "But I didn't."

"But how can I trust you?"

Bryant cocked his head and looked her right in the eyes. "Because I am in love with your sister, Silexa. She might not make it out of this, but I'll be damned if I don't try everything possible to save her."

Sera rolled her head back. "If that's not the biggest lie—"

Bryant grabbed her hand hard, shaking her from anger. "Please, we don't have time to waste on this."

Sera tried to wrench away from his grip but then she saw it—the pleading, and the unimaginable pain of losing his love forever. She glanced at Arie again. He was biting his nails and only briefly looked at her, though his eyes held the same pain. Everyone was losing someone tonight.

Sera's limbs lost all strength. "Do you have any idea of what is inside?"

"Yes and no." Bryant let go of her arm. "I've had a few scouts try to find out, but the palace—or frankly, all of Southwick—has been on lockdown. I've only had one man return with any news at all."

"But you know the palace. You lived there."

"Well, yes."

"Do you know where the ceremony will be held? That's where we—"

"Sharrod's unearthed it, the ceremony room. It's exposed. My men have seen it. Your fire-eater is the fastest way there."

Sera turned toward Arie. "What do you think?"

Arie hadn't moved since he let go of Bryant. "I think we're wasting time talking about it." He walked back to where Lottie stood and grabbed her hand, talking with the villagers.

Sera felt the distance between them, but somehow it brought her closer to understanding him. She clasped Vespa's medallion tighter. "Okay." She looked up at Bryant. "I trust you."

"Let me communicate with my men." Bryant motioned to someone standing behind him. "These people don't know what has happened."

A burly looking dwarf came close to him. They spoke in low voices. But Sera's attention was stolen away by someone else walking behind him, drawing closer. It was a younger dwarf, a dull crop of hair sparking his head. He didn't stop to talk to Bryant as she thought he would but instead walked directly to her.

"I know you," he said in a soft whisper of a voice, a slight hitch in his words. He reached inside his tunic and pulled out a flower. "The fairies speak of you."

"Of me?"

"The girl who sings Dragonsong, much like Fairyspeak."

Sera's fingers curled around the red rose offered to her. "What is this?"

"The fairies' contribution to the fight, a Blood Rose."

"I've never heard of it."

The dwarf smiled, and a great sparkle came to his eyes, like he was about to the reveal the most precious of secrets. "The fairies demand that you use it when the time comes."

"But how will I know?"

The man shook his head. "They didn't tell me, only that I had to deliver it to the one who knows Dragonsong."

"What is your name?"

The dwarf's voice caught before he spoke. "Brandell, Your Highness."

Sera bent down and kissed him on the cheek. "Tell your fairies I will do what they've asked."

Brandell blushed.

"Sera?" Arie stretched out his hand to hers. She grabbed it and followed him to the dragon, Bryant walking solemnly behind.

"Wait for me!" Lottie yelled from across the field. She ran as fast as she could to meet them.

"Lottie, no. Stay here with Brandell." Sera gestured to the dwarf.

The girl stamped her feet. "No. I have to help Naomi. I have to help Katia and Landon. This is why I—"

Sera felt a tenderness toward the girl, and the emotion rose to the surface. She quickly choked it down. "I know. I know, Lottie. It's too risky. These people need help."

"Please. Don't." Tears flooded the little girl's eyes. "I'll never see anyone again. Everyone will die. Katia doesn't know I'm alive. She doesn't know Naomi saved me. It's not fair."

"I can't watch after you during this fight."

Lottie's eyes narrowed. "Who said I needed to be watched? I can take care of my—"

Sera grabbed her and held her as tight as she could. "If you die, I will never forgive myself."

"I won't," Lottie spoke into her clothes. "I promise."

Sera pulled her back. "You're right. You won't, because I can't let you come."

Arie grabbed Sera and hoisted her up on the dragon's haunches. "Sorry, kid."

"No!" Lottie screamed. Brandell came to the girl's side and held her as the dragon prepared for flight.

Sera watched the girl violently fighting the dwarf as she, Arie, and the Southwick prince took off toward the castle, riding on the wings of a dragon.

The sky grew unnaturally dark. The sun was steadily falling, and it felt as if she were falling forward in time. The clouds thickened as they neared the palace parapets, a ring of darkness swirling near Southwick's center. Every sweep of wing, every push of air, brought them closer to the danger.

Sera tapped the fire-eater, communicating her trust. She turned to Bryant. "I don't know where to go," she called over the wind.

Bryant pointed at a tower mid-height to the rest of the large palace. "Fly toward the ocean side. There is a garden where the fire-eater can land. That's the quickest way to the Grand Hall."

Sera steered the creature around the giant spires. The harsh wind pushed against them. Sera wrapped the leather straps around her hands securely.

A strong pelt of rain hit them. Sera focused hard on the approaching turn. Frida's speed waned with the cold. Her belly was running out of fire.

"Come on, girl, just a little farther." Her encouragement pushed the fire-eater onward.

In the distance was a long set of windows near several archways. Sera concentrated there. A deep green garden sprawled out before it, perfect for landing.

"There." Bryant pointed.

Sera pulled on the straps to control the beast. The creature began to carve through the wind, maneuvering through different archways in their descent. She aimed carefully through the last one and . . .

Smack!

The dragon hit the stone structure on her side, throwing Arie and Bryant off. Sera flew through the air like a ragdoll, remaining tethered to the dragon.

Below her, Arie and Bryant hit the earth. Frida twisted around, sending Sera flying through the air again until she landed on the other side of the fire-eater's belly. She caught a glimpse of the heavy stone, barely enough time to brace herself before Frida smashed full into it. The ancient rock cracked and broke apart, bits of rock splintering around them. Sera felt the barrage of stone on her skin, ripping through her cloak, smashing against her bones. A large piece hit her upside the head, blurring her vision.

The massive weight of the animal hit the floor, but her momentum kept her moving. Frida flailed around trying to turn her massive body, but her wings flapped in vain. She arched her back as she tried desperately to right herself.

Sera had but a moment to act. She grabbed at her wrists and pulled at the twisted leather straps. They cut into her skin, her hands white from lack of blood. She worked frantically to free herself. The dragon continued to push and arch underneath her.

The dragon's scree of pain reverberated against the stone. She slammed her claws to the ground, knocking Sera onto the floor. Scratching and scraping against the marble, the dragon again tried to fly, this time through the palace.

Knowing seconds were precious, Sera hurried to free herself. She felt the massive weight of the creature pushing her down to the floor before it tried to get off the ground. The dragon stumbled, smacking Sera again and knocking her head.

Sera's ears rang and things started to blur together.

She heard voices. Men. Angry men. A long cry from Frida. She stamped the ground, dragging Sera along with her.

A hand slipped free and Sera tried again to focus, forcing her vision to clear. She had to get free. Frida could kill her. Around her, she saw others screaming and wailing, ordinary people being hunted by the guards of Southwick. Torches raised around the dark palace halls.

And then she saw it—a hole in the floor, a giant chasm where the Grand Hall used to be, now an empty pit.

The two medallions around her neck began to glow. Their chains yanked hard around her neck, choking her. Vespa's slipped from around her neck and flew toward the pit. Sera reached up with her spare hand and held onto the other. The chain dug deeper into her neck, slicing as it twisted.

She felt as if she would rip in half, one arm on the medallion, one wrapped around the dragon. She yanked hard, trying to loosen the chain, but the pull was too strong. The chain inched up her neck.

Frida kicked off into flight, slamming against a pillar. Sera lost her grip, her medallion whipping away from her head and toward the invisible force. The leather unraveled away from her other wrist, and she felt herself weightless, tumbling away into oblivion.

CHAPTER TWENTY-SIX

A thunderous noise echoed through the cavern. A terrible vibration shook the rickety cage, sending both Landon and Browneyes toppling to the side. Then another noise: familiar but unbelievable.

"Is that a—" Landon started but didn't need to finish. A dragon came sliding across the intricate marble floor toward the grand staircase, its speed broken only by columns. All the soldiers' attention diverted to the enormous intrusion.

As the beast tried to regain its balance, several of the men attacked it, arrows deflecting off its tight skin-armor. It grunted and howled, digging into the floor and splintering away the ornate patterns of stone.

More men arrived, surrounding it. Spears flew, impaling its side.

The dragon let out a roar and stretched its wings. With a few steadying flaps, the great fire-eater rose in the air, scattering soldiers in all directions—some behind, some down into the chasm.

Landon watched through the tremendous swaying of the cage, his knuckles turned white as he gripped the bars tightly. Browneyes curled into a ball, waiting for the motion to stop.

As the creature flapped its wings, the resulting wind pushed the cage into a spin. Landon's hold tightened. He watched the magnificent animal push upward. He had never seen a dragon. Only in his wildest imagination did he believe he'd ever see one. It was wondrous and terrifying.

But then he saw something that brought his heart to his throat—a woman trapped beneath the fire-eater, hanging by leather straps, the harness barely attached.

A huge throbbing pulse resounded throughout the room.

Landon looked downward to see Sharrod. He stood near a platform, his hands outstretched, sending out a shock of magic.

The magic around her neck came free and whizzed across the hall.

The purple medallion flew through the air and landed on its pillar.

A beam of light shot high up in the air connecting with the other streams of magic. A loud crack echoed as the fifth magic touched the others. Like an exploding fire, sparks flew in different directions.

Another one of the sisters. Landon gulped at the truth.

"It's happening," he whispered.

The creature attempted to fly away, but the surge of power kept it from leaving. The invisible force pulled against the girl. Landon saw a different light, red in color, come loose.

"No," he said to himself. "It's another medallion. That's two."

Browneyes finally looked up, her face as horrified as his.

The light flew away toward the side of the chasm opposite from the other. The magic below swirled with obvious excitement as the red glow shone out.

And then Landon heard the snap as the harness was freed and the woman fell freely down into the pit.

"No!" He was so engrossed in the fall he didn't see the fire-eater's large wing collide with the cage, the impact so harsh it sent both him and Browneyes toppling over each other. A loud crack echoed as the iron arm holding them aloft buckled. The cage plunged downward.

Landon and Browneyes slammed into the bars as the cage twisted mid-air.

Then a horrifying cry shattered the room. Landon lifted his bruised head, now eye-level with the swirling magic. It had tangled itself around the dragon, squeezing away its life. Like liquid metal, it siphoned life from the creature's open mouth, smothering its scream. The sharp sound of snapping of bones made Landon's hairs stand on end. He was terrified, yet fascinated.

"This is what you were talking about," Landon breathed. "It is going to eat us."

Browneyes didn't lift her head.

He looked closer. Browneyes lay crumpled in a heap. Any trace of Ferra's appearance had faded, replaced with the Louving girl he remembered from the Echoes. Behind her long, dark braids he saw blood running down her face. A long gash ran across her head where she had smashed into the bars. "Browneyes?"

Should he even care? The girl had caused the death of several people. A menace like a Louving should die. But his instincts took over, and he quickly wrapped cloth around her head to stop the bleeding. "Browneyes. Wake up."

She still didn't respond.

"Come on, girl."

A loud screech came from above.

Landon looked up and saw how damaged the chain holding the cage was. The slightest movement could snap it, sending them down into the eerie abyss.

The fear that had waited calmly behind his mind rushed to the surface.

Bryant brushed off the dirt from his clothes. His side ached, but it was nothing he couldn't handle. He looked around him. Arie lay in a crumpled pile near the grass.

"Arie!" Bryant rushed over. Arie grimaced, grabbing his shoulder. Bryant could see the awkward angle of the bone. "It's dislocated. What would you like me to do?"

"Do your worst," Arie grunted.

Bryant pressed firmly on his chest, then lifted on his shoulder until there was a sickening pop. Arie yelled at the pain.

"Better?"

Arie grimaced and fell forward, the agony clear on his face. "It will be. Make sure you never do that again."

"Try not to move it." Bryant offered him a hand. "We must hurry."

Arie accepted his help and stumbled to his feet.

The two men stood at the edge of a stone platform, staring at the massive hole within the palace's wall. A few people were tumbling out, frightened for their lives.

"Good sir!" Bryant hailed to a youngish man picking his way through the rubble. The young man froze, staring as if seeing a ghost.

"Are my eyes playin' tricks?" The young man pointed at him. "You look just like the prince. But you can't be—the prince is dead. Everyone knows that. The prince and his lousy father."

Bryant walked toward him. "Do I look like him now?" His voice was kind, but regal.

The young man immediately bowed. A mother and her son did also, then others followed, all muttering, "He is the prince. He's alive."

"Please. We have no time." Bryant motioned to the man to stand. "What have you seen in there?"

"Dark magic, sire, very dark." The young man wiped the sweat from his forehead. "We was in the dungeons. All the kitchen staff, they hid us away there. They said it was to keep us safe, but that ain't it. It was to let us die away from whatever they was doin' in the Grand Hall. Broke it to pieces and dug up the earth."

"Why would they do that?"

Arie, still holding his shoulder, replied, "Must be the place where the stones were originally given. Sera told me something about that a while ago."

"It's awful, sire," the young man continued. "Did you see the fire-eater, sire?"

"Yes. We came here on it."

"Oh, no, sire. Something's happened."

Arie ran past the two, searching inside for it. "What do you mean? Where's the girl who was riding it?"

"Didn't see no girl," he replied. "But the dragon got caught. I couldn't watch and ran away."

Arie took off toward the dark broken hole in the wall.

"Thank you." Bryant touched the young man's shoulder as a sign of respect and rushed after Arie.

The signs of destruction continued inside the palace. Gouges where the claws had scraped along the floor. Staircases were gone. Floors were damaged and open to the hall below. Smoke and dust obscured their view, specifically of the Grand Hall.

Bryant met up with Arie, who was searching wildly. "She must have gotten away."

Arie's look on his face told something different. "No, something's wrong. I feel it. Something happened."

A noise came from ahead—a sharp cry, a shrill scream, and then it was gone, ringing left in their ears. Both ran forward through the tangled debris. The haze cleared enough for them to see they stood near a platform, looking out over a very large, very vast pit where the Grand Hall used to be.

"What in the name . . ." But Bryant lost speech. Here was his home, the place he had lived since he was twelve, when his father took the throne after King Prolius was assassinated. The once-beautiful marble façade now lay streaked with dark marks and lined with cracks. The lovely gardens that had grown in the center had been ripped away.

Bryant saw a strange shape twisting in the air, the violent figure of a creature's mouth forming, but he didn't want to focus on what he couldn't understand. His eyes searched for answers near the edge of the pit.

Sharrod had summoned the strange demon from the Underworld. Wide wings stretched out from its back, and it had a ferocious gaping snout bearing long rows of teeth. Yet, it didn't have talons like a dragon, and instead it had what looked like arms and legs with sharp clawed hands. The hide burned red, every inch scaled, with demon-yellow eyes that pierced Bryant through. Sharrod surrounded himself with several guards who were faithful to him, the black cloaks of rebellion hanging around their shoulders.

And behind Sharrod, behind the chaos, stood a hooded figure, General Lockwood. Bryant felt a sharp stab of pain, remembering the jolt that had gone through his body the last time they met. The shock had paralyzed him, would have killed him if Silexa and Zander hadn't been there.

The thought of Silexa sent his eyes roving again, searching for her or Sera or any of the sisters. But as his eyes adjusted, he noticed the pillars of light, each with a different color. Did that mean they were too late?

"Where's Sera?" Arie's eyes swept the arena, a frantic look on his face.

"This does not bode well," Bryant answered.

Several things started happening at the same time. A large cage hanging near the left began to swing as a strange whiz flashed across the pit toward it. Two people were near the cage—one of them was Zander.

Bryant started in their direction when Arie held him back. "No, wait. Look over there."

Near Sharrod, of the guards who were protecting whatever he was doing, several had sprung into action.

Arie snagged his shoulder. "Look. The guards are leaving Sharrod vulnerable. Go after him. If you can catch him mid-chant, maybe this whole thing will go away."

"Good idea." Bryant considered. "How should we get down?"

Arie pointed to a mound of crumpled debris not far from them. The pile was near the left side of Sharrod. They could navigate a path around the other side of the mound with little chance of detection.

"Yes," Bryant agreed. "Let's go."

They swiftly moved along the marble floor until it fell away into the pile. It was tricky, two broad men working their way clumsily around an unstable heap of masonry.

A large crash sounded, like metal hitting rock. The anchored cage swung down and hit the edge of the large crater. It knocked loose the unstable debris they were crossing. A small avalanche of brick and dust toppled downward.

Bryant clung close to the stone as large boulders bounced down, cutting off the path between the two.

"Go!" Arie waved him away. "I'll search for Sera."

Bryant nodded and carefully moved away from the loose rubble and jumped to the bigger, heavier, more stable rocks. He bounded from one to the other, scattering tiny rocks below.

He neared the bottom when a tremendous roar echoed around the expanse. The vibration sent shockwaves through everything. Bryant couldn't help but cover his ears. Whatever creature Sharrod had summoned had arrived.

A strange force within him pulled his body forward so he could behold the dragon-like creature. The transformation was complete.

Sharrod lowered his hands, satisfied.

This was his chance. His only weapon was a broadsword. He unsheathed it and prepared himself. "For Silexa," he whispered, and ran forward.

Zander shoved away Mahoney's hands, forcing his eyes wide. Mahoney had protected him from the debris from the pillars, but he couldn't keep the sight of a fire-eater entering the hall a secret. Its wings flapped courageously, blowing dust around.

Fire-eaters were myth, but here was one. Zander fell into schoolboy enchantment, not comprehending what he was seeing. A spark inside him saw something.

"There!" Zander shot his arm up at the girl tied to the creature. The colored magic pulled away from her body, like a soul being ripped apart.

Then he heard the scream coming from above. The woman was no longer bound to the creature but falling.

Zander took off toward the edge. The wind from the flap of the dragon's wing pushed her away through the air, hurtling her toward the rocks.

"Zander!" he heard Mahoney cry out, but Zander dashed to where she would hit.

Before he could stop and see what had happened, Mahoney had run past him, making it to the boulder right before the girl smashed into them. She collided, and they both tumbled backward.

Mahoney was dazed but unharmed. *He must be indestructible.* The woman was clearly hurt, open scrapes on her body. Her eyes flitted open and then closed again. She was too weak to move or speak.

Then a scree echoed loud around everything, shaking the very inside of Zander's chest. Since the fairy's bite, he could see the magic act, and like a snake it curled around the body of the flying dragon in a pulsing squeeze, slowly devouring it.

"The dragon!" He pointed at the sight.

Across the pit, a man stood, his arms stretched out. The magic began pouring between him and the dragon, arching like a bridge.

"It's Sharrod," Mahoney stated, still attending to the woman.

Zander took a deeper look. He had seen Sharrod with his own eyes, had been in his presence. "No, I don't—"

A large squeal of metal interrupted his thought. The structure that held the cage winch was going to snap. Zander searched Mahoney's face for direction.

"Nothing else will save them." Mahoney looked toward the dangling bars. He placed his hand on Zander's shoulder. "Go my friend, I believe you are their only hope. I'll stay with her. Be safe."

Zander turned away from the sudden commotion and shouts of men. He gathered his strength. With a deep breath, Zander took off running.

Katia huffed, her breath catching every few steps, her side aching from the run. She saw someone up ahead. She could almost see the outline of the shadowed figure standing near the edge of the tunnel. Just a little farther. Her ice magic was ready at her fingertips.

Her emotions were so high that the air grew cold around her, the ground slippery. She couldn't calm down.

"You'll never escape," she shouted.

The figure stopped and turned. His strong profile told her immediately of danger. Katia's magic reacted, sending shards of ice toward him.

The man covered himself against the barrage, though the pelting ice melted mid-flight, hitting him with droplets instead of sharp, stabbing blades.

Katia's frustration mounted. She was nearly there.

"Stop, my dear!" An older man geared with eccentric weaponry came running toward her from one of the openings leading into the tunnel.

"Wenlock?"

"Cease and desist, my good woman."

Katia slowly lowered her hands. "Then who is this?"

The man standing near the opening lowered his hands.

She saw him and blinked, thinking her eyes were playing tricks.

The bushy, unkempt sailor stretched out his arms. "My Tia."

"Papa." She fell against him, overcome with a rush of relief.

"You are ice cold."

"Yes," Katia returned, her face in his shoulder. "I'm ready to fight." She pulled back. "How'd you get here?"

"By ship." Briggs cocked his eyebrow. "I received a message from Fontine. She and Landon were in serious danger."

"Of course they are." Katia threw back her hands. "And it's my fault. I ditched them and left with Silexa. Wenlock probably told you that."

"He filled me in, yes." Briggs looked around. "Where's my son? Is he with you?"

Katia shook her head. "He's back with one of the daughters. He's protecting her . . . Reinoh. He's dead, Papa." She broke off, not knowing what he cared to know.

Briggs' eyes turned hard. "I've waited years to face him and squeeze the life out of him with my bare hands." He turned to Katia. "Irina wouldn't want me to do that."

Katia felt her anger mix with sadness. "No, Papa. Go find Vanya."

Suddenly, a thunderous rattling shook the underground, interrupting her speech. Katia held to the wall for balance.

"What was that?"

The three rushed toward the growing light. The tunnel opened to several broken walls from previous foundations in the palace. The darkness in the tunnel was a stark contrast to the red light now spilling around the cracks.

Katia picked her way through until she could finally see the vast room before them. She looked on with horror and shock at an enormous mass that engulfed a red dragon with its energy. What in the world could do that?

Her answer came in the form near the edge of the chasm. Though she had never seen Sharrod before, he was every bit as massive as she had imagined, an intimidating creature with ancient markings of magic. At the top of his head were two devilish horns. Near him stood the cloaked man—the one she had chased.

Six different spots of light shone out of the mass, feeding its magic as it began to change and morph. Her heart raced. *This can't be happening. This can't be happening.*

What could she do?

Each of the stones stood on a pillar, generating its own color of light. The color of blue frost rose on the other side—Fontine's.

"Fontine's," she exhaled. Katia grabbed her father's wrist. "Forgive me." Without another thought, she raced toward the pillars, looking for a way to reach it.

Wenlock couldn't take his eyes off the strange mass hovering before him. "This is not what I expected."

He turned, thinking Katia was next to him, but she had run toward the debris, Briggs watching after her. "Let her go."

Briggs took a step forward, but Wenlock pushed him back. "No, my good man, find your son."

"She's going to run off and get herself killed."

"And so are you." Wenlock pointed behind him. "Trust her. Go find your son."

Briggs stumbled backward. His head turned toward the tunnel. "Yes." He grabbed Wenlock's hand. "Be safe."

Wenlock clasped his shoulder and nodded as Briggs retreated to the tunnel.

CHAPTER TWENTY-SEVEN

"We are close," Vanya stated as they neared the end of the tunnel. "Can you see yet?"

Reynolds held tightly to the boy. How ever the tunnel had been made, it hid all magic from his sight, but the closer the boy brought him to the exit, the more he began to see traces of it again. It didn't make sense to him yet but it would.

"Thanks, Vanya." He clapped the boy on the shoulder. "I can find my way out from here. Now, go back to Silexa. Stay with her, just in case."

Reynolds felt Vanya stiffen. Someone was there. He instinctively pushed Vanya behind him.

"Who are you?"

The presence didn't speak, didn't move, just stood there.

Reynolds could feel Vanya come from around him to stand in view.

"It is my father," Vanya spoke in his all-knowing voice. "What?"

He could feel the presence stumble forward, falling to his knees. He heard an audible gasp, a stifled sob.

Vanya walked forward. Reynolds could only see a trace of magic touch the presence of the father grasping his son in a sad, exhausted embrace.

"My son, my son." The man gripped tight.

Reynolds could not see the agony and joy expressed from Vanya's father. The reunion was short, much like the brief encounter Reynolds had with his own father while searching for Naomi in the Echoes. Haunted the same by mistakes made in the past.

Vanya's father's voice broke. "How do you know me?"

"You wear the ghost of Irina, my mother," Vanya stated. "She sacrificed her life for me."

The man pulled back. "Do you see her?"

"Yes. She is waiting for you." Vanya glanced back at Reynolds. "We are here to fix the balance of souls. When you are ready, she will carry you."

"My wise boy." The man embraced him again before standing. "Help me. Tia—Katia is in danger."

He pulled the boy forward. Vanya reached his hand back for Reynolds, who snatched it and followed.

Ahead, a strange but compelling light outlined the exit of the tunnel. Reynolds released Vanya's hand and walked to see the plane of magic for himself.

He stood on the edge of a different world. The view did not stop with walls but endless streams of light traveling away in the distance. Different colored light radiated in a large ring several yards before him. Huge cauldrons, swelling with liquid at the basin, spread out in a circle; a guardian stood near each of the six pillars—visions of the daughters of Prolius each protecting the colors, the stones. Darkness blurred the outer lining of the plane. Streams from the cauldrons filtered up to the center of the space…

And in the center stood a man.

Reynolds glanced at those below. Other men with magical traces, flashing beams of light, fought their own battles. Sharrod stood in the midst of the action, though through Reynolds' magical eyes, he looked like nothing more than a man—no red, tattooed demon, but a simple human with a brooding expression. His long dark hair whipped around in the invisible current. His body wasn't monstrous, but lean and muscular with broad shoulders, good for wielding heavy swords. This was the first time Reynolds could see vulnerability, weakness, exhaustion.

"Katia's run off toward one of those pillars," Vanya's father stated. Reynolds found her easily, her magic detectable to him now.

"Katia's strong," Reynolds said. "She can handle this fight. Sharrod's the one to stop."

Reynolds pointed to the center. Energy streams filtered between Sharrod and another through a connection between them. He concentrated on their connection and understood quickly what Shon had done.

"No, wait." Reynolds stumbled forward. "That clever bastard. If you want to help," he stated, "go after Sharrod. We have to break his connection with Shon."

Vanya turned to his father. "I will wait and watch." And though Reynolds could not see it, he understood the shared moment between father and son before the man turned and valiantly did as he was asked.

Vanya pressed his hand to Reynolds' chest. "Don't trust your eyes. Use the plane and take care, good friend." He turned back down the tunnel and scurried away.

Reynolds watched the boy's light travel away from him, then turned and pressed his palms to the rock wall.

A strong gust of wind hit the cage. A loud creak sent Landon's eyes upward. The arm was barely hanging on, the metal bent and twisted. The chain continued to swing back and forth, each motion bending the bar more and more.

Browneyes moved her head. Her eyes opened. "Reyn," she croaked. "Reyn. You came for me. I knew you'd come."

"But, I—"

"I did awful things, Reyn." She couldn't look at him anymore. "I shouldn't have killed the girl. It got me nowhere. You were right."

"How?" Landon asked, compelled to know her secrets.

"Regret." Her voice became quieter. "You told me I would. I never killed a human before her. And now . . . I die hollow."

"No." Landon grabbed her cheeks, forcing her to look at him. "Browneyes. I'm not Reyn. You'll have to tell him yourself."

"My Reyn," she mumbled, looking away. "I just wanted to see him again."

Landon didn't respond as there came a sickening twist from above, and the metal began to give. He couldn't bear it. He grabbed Browneyes' hands, clasping them in his own, and closed his eyes, waiting for the fall.

Wenlock returned his attention to the pit and took in everything that was happening. He picked his way through the rubble of debris until he had a good view of everything. He searched through his pack for a weapon that he might use to fight. Inside were only useless instruments and gadgets, no small knives or grenades. He grabbed his specs, hoping he could get more insight about the magic.

As he looked through them, everything went dark except for a few spots of light. Katia's spot followed the perimeter of the hole. He focused on a few strange dots and gasped. "That's Landon," he said to himself.

He raised the specs off his eyes and rested them on his forehead. Looking back toward where he'd seen Landon's light, he saw a cage dangling at the side of the chasm. Landon had been captured. And it was Wenlock's fault. "Oh, my dear boy. I knew something bad had befallen you. Mae would never forgive me if something happened to you."

He thought quickly. The grappling.

Wenlock felt at the side of his bag and found the device he had used earlier to send Landon and Fontine to the window. Rummaging through the bag, he found a new tip. He fitted it and carefully wound the string properly around with the crank.

His eyes were diverted by the sudden changing of the floating mass in the room to the forming head of a dragon. The sight sent a tremor of fear down Wenlock's spine.

"This is no time to lose your courage, Wenlock Brighton." He shook his shoulders and grabbed the grappling, looking carefully through the sight. The swinging cage was impossible to target. He looked upward and saw the arm was damaged, holding on by one piece of metal in the broken crane. He couldn't aim for either. It was too weak. And he had no anchor.

Then he saw what he needed.

Down near the bottom was a crank. Someone was already there, trying to turn it.

Wenlock had no time for precision. He had to act immediately. He quickly aimed and shot.

Zander tried again with all his might. The crank was jammed. He pulled on it again. "I have to . . . keep . . ."

Something whizzed through the air. It struck deep into the wooden frame, trailing a string that was attached to something across the chasm. Zander scrambled away and grabbed at his weapon, ready for anything.

The dark shape hit the frame with a quick *thunk* and dropped to the ground.

"Wait," it said, holding up its hands. It was an old man, small and clearly dazed as he stumbled to his feet. He wore strangely made bits of armor, with long eyepieces on his head. "Wait, stop! That's my nephew up there."

Zander lowered his dagger. "You've come to help?"

"Precisely." The old man straightened his jacket. "But there is no time. Another gust and we'll lose him."

Zander sheathed his weapon and ran to the crank. "I-it's jammed."

"Jammed, eh?" The old man looked around the cogs and wheel. Zander watched on, completely fascinated. "Good thing I'm an excellent mechanic."

The old man fished through a bag around his body. "Hold this, would you please?" He beat it with his hand, and it illuminated like a torch.

Zander held it as the old man rummaged some more before pulling out a small wand.

"Point it right in the center there."

Zander did and it lit the place up. The old man flicked the wand, and it grew in length, with a tiny clamps near the end. He stretched it over toward the center of the cogs, and its minute fingers began to work rapidly, mending the wheel.

"Try now!" he shouted. Zander scrambled back to the crank and pulled with all his might.

The arm moved slightly.

A thrill moved through his bones. "It's w-working."

Zander pulled again, feeling the strength surge though him, something that wasn't there before. The fairy had renewed his energy, sharpened his mind, and given him strength he never thought he had. The old man came over and started pulling along with him.

With their combined effort, the cage turned more and more, but with every movement, the arm of the metal whined.

The bottom of the cage was nearing the top of the cliff when something snapped, sending the two of them backward.

The cage began to fall, the last link severed.

It dropped and hit the wooden frame. Splinters flew out in every direction. The cage rolled forward toward the edge where the two had landed. Zander scrambled and felt a force inside him pull him away as the large metal frame hit the ground.

Zander could see the people inside. Two of them, a man and a woman, thrown around.

The frame of the platform began to crumble away into the pit.

"It's still attached to the cage." Zander ran to see the people inside. The door had a heavy metal lock. He began pulling on the bars.

Inside the man was coming to his senses. "Wait . . . We didn't fall."

Zander didn't know how to answer. Another whine of the wood and more fell away. They had precious few seconds. He frantically pulled on the door, but it wouldn't budge.

"I need something metal!" The man reached for Zander's shirt. "Find me something, anything."

Zander grabbed a long nail and shoved it through the bars.

Inside the cage, the man rubbed it with his fingers, and it began to glow white. He then inserted it into the lock. Within a few turns it broke apart.

Zander wrenched the cage door open and tried to take the man's hand. He pulled on the man's arms instead, but he held the limp body of the woman inside.

With all of his might, Zander helped the stranger from the cage, who lifted the girl over his shoulder just as the cage jolted away. The entire structure made an awful breaking sound, the arm tumbling over and over against wood and stone and earth. The cage attached yanked hard on the chain and pulled it down to the fire below.

Zander was so wrapped up in the sight of it falling he didn't notice what was happening behind him.

He heard the groaning and turned.

The old man lay on the ground, his legs twisted. Zander came closer. The cage had fallen and crushed both his legs.

The man from the cage rushed over to him. "You crazy old man." The young man quickly knelt near the man's injured legs. "Wenlock. You saved us."

"Glad I could help." Wenlock muttered through his pain. He looked at his battered legs. "Oh, now . . . let's not tell Mae about this."

Katia was close now to Fontine's stone. She recognized the light blue streams feeding away to the center where the magic churned. Time was critical.

She had passed three different pillars, each a unique pedestal with burn marks scarring the ornate marble carving. The floor around them had intricate spiraling gold patterns designed to reflect light from the shining stones. Katia had to wonder what the floor had looked like before the gaping hole was created. But the precise placement of the pillars had to be designed for something like this, to open a gateway or something like that.

The bluish pillar was tight against the wall. It skirted a vast cliff that fell into blackness, bottomless and empty. Katia worked her way around, deliberately not looking down, but concentrating on her feet and not the black.

Directly on the other side of the pit, a long, metal arm crashed down to the surface, shaking the ground where she stood. Her balance wavered, and she braced her hands against the wall. Her heart pounded hard as she watched a few rocks come loose near the edge. The heavy iron cage toppled off the edge and fell into the pit, taking the chain and arm with it.

People were near the cage, people she almost recognized. But she couldn't think of them now. She was only a few feet from the pillar. She slid sideways with her hands bracing the wall. What was she going to do once she had the stone? All she had thought about was getting to it, not about what would happen once she had it.

Katia flushed and her magic flared. Little crystals lit her fingertips, and the wall became slippery. "Calm down," she told herself. "Not yet."

She was there. She had reached it. Katia wrapped her hands around the pillar. The beautiful medallion lay imprisoned in a perfect circle at the top, surrounded by the same polished marble as the floor, the same scarring around the top. It somehow looked more enchanting than before, like it belonged here at a place of rest and not around someone's neck.

Katia fell transfixed by its splendor, watching the rough ocean inside swirl like a restless sea. She wanted it. It called to her, claiming her as its new bearer. And she heard it, her name, like a whisper. Katia shook her head, clearing it out, but the same voice came again, this time with a flash of memory. It was Fontine, handing the stone to her in the ship.

"Water magic is complicated to use, and honestly, is very particular in who it chooses."

"Chooses? Are you saying the magic chose me?"

"Magic always has a choice in how it acts."

Katia closed her eyes and envisioned the power she had when she used the medallion. It was a choice—and it chose her.

She opened her eyes, her hands trembling to pick it up.

A loud cry shook the ground, knocking Katia off her feet. She clung to the pillar. Her boots struggled to find a hold and slid to the edge. Her fingers gripped the carved stone tightly around the corners, and her feet tried to find footing she could use to push herself back.

The wind rose, pushing up from the belly of the earth—hot, like exhaled breath.

Her magic was there, unwanted, loosening her grip. She held tighter, her arms aching as her fingers pressed harder into the stone. Her foot grazed over a boulder. She pushed her weight against it and tried to use it to level herself. She slipped, nearly losing her grip. She tried again, but it was too awkward an angle.

And then she knew: if she wanted to use the boulder she had to let go of the pillar. There was no other choice. Her magic would melt in this heat. It couldn't save her. And with every second dangling, her grip slipped more.

She took a deep breath and pushed, letting go of the pillar and using it as leverage. Both of her feet felt the boulder underneath. Her hands grasped out for anything to cling to. Her feet anchored on the boulder, she pushed up again, her body now dangling halfway off. Katia slid her body forward until her weight kept her from falling.

And then she found her breath, inhaling deeply. Her heart raced. She had nearly died.

Then the ground shook again.

Katia looked at the flying creature in the middle of the room. She had precious little time.

Then she heard a cry, a scream. It was human. Katia whipped around to see a fight between her father and one of Sharrod's men.

"No!"

CHAPTER TWENTY-EIGHT

Reynolds tried to move forward but stumbled. Rocks blocked the path that he couldn't see. The physical world didn't make sense. He closed his eyes again, sensing everything around him, listening to the magic, finding a way to get closer.

"Hey, you!" he heard from behind him. Guards had spotted him. Though he opened his eyes, he didn't use them. Rather, he sensed their movements like he had always done.

Quickly, he shot out his arm as hard as he could, catching the one closest in the stomach. The man buckled but swung his sword. Reynolds caught his arm. He twisted his body and held onto the guard, taking him down to the ground. He stomped his foot into his throat, crushing his windpipe.

Reynolds snatched the sword from the body in time to sense the next soldier at his side, higher than the other, on a ledge ready to jump. He readied the weapon for the attack. With two quick slashes, right then left, he took the man down.

A third approached but didn't dare engage.

"Take me to Sharrod, and I will spare you." Reynolds' steady arm brandished the sword before him.

The guard raised his own sword and pointed it toward Reynolds. "You aren't in a place to bargain."

"I think you're wrong about that." The man lunged. Reynolds dodged to the side, grabbed the aggressor's wrist, and twisted it hard. The guard pivoted, kneeing Reynolds fast in the back, but Reynolds had already rebounded with two quick blows—an elbow to the chest and a swift jab at his throat. The guard lost his grip and struggled to breathe. His sword dropped from his hands.

Reynolds locked the guard in a chokehold, ready to crush his windpipe. "You're going to take me to Sharrod, you'll pretend like you captured me, but you won't tie my hands. Do all this, I'll let you live. Do we have a deal?"

The guard struggled against his tight grip. "Yes," he choked out.

"Good." He slowly loosened his hold.

The guard backed away and looked at Reynolds. "Why?"

"I need your eyes."

"What can mine do that yours can't—"

"Don't always trust what you see," Reynolds interrupted. He groped around until he felt the hilt of the fallen sword. "This should do," he said and slipped the man's sword through his belt. He held out his hands like a captive.

The guard accepted his surrender.

Reynolds did his best to pretend to see everything, even as he stumbled on the unseen rocks beneath his feet. If he looked down, all was emptiness, an abyss to the center of the earth. Then the uneven ground leveled, and he could see everything happening around them.

A strange band of energy hung out to the left of his vision. Within this force field he saw a dark cloud. He recognized Landon's aura immediately.

"Wait." He stopped. "What has happened there?"

"The cage fell," was all the guard said.

"Who was in the cage?"

"Two captives, one a Louving."

"But why?"

"To feed to the beast."

"Louving," Reynolds repeated to himself. He changed his plan. He needed an ally. "I knew she'd catch up to me. Here's as good a place as any. Take me over there."

The guard didn't move.

"Quick. Something's wrong."

The guard tried to kick him in the chest. Reynolds sensed it and reacted quickly enough to avoid it.

"Reyn!" He heard someone calling after him. The shout gave the guard enough time to turn and run. "Reyn. Thank all the stars."

Reynolds watched the trickster's aura brighten as he approached. "Landon?"

Landon met him in the middle of empty space and clapped him around the shoulder. "Good to see you, too."

"How did you get in this mess?"

Landon shook his head. "I wish I had time to tell you, but here is what I need."

He led him over to the other people, including an older man sitting on the floor, his legs twisted below him. Browneyes was crumpled on the ground. A growing boy assisted with her wounds. Landon made quick introductions to Wenlock and Zander.

"Zander." Reynolds couldn't help but admire. His magical trace was faint but obvious. Though he didn't have magic himself, the evidence of Naomi's aura made him shine white. "You've grown since the last time I saw you."

The boy stared, confused. "I don't . . ."

Reynolds moved on. "Landon. What happened?"

"The cage." He started toward an older man on the ground. "It dropped and crushed his legs. And she—" He pointed to Browneyes. "Well, I don't know what's wrong with her."

Reynolds tried to take a closer look, but the world of the living was difficult to see. The man's face was bright with pain, but he seemed capable of bearing it. "See to the girl, would you?" he sputtered. "I'll survive this, but she may not."

Reynolds' attention turned to the Louving with whom he had such an unpleasant history. The aura hanging over her was like dark velvet fog, waiting for something. He knelt beside her. She didn't look menacing at all. Her head had a gash at her temple. He took his sleeve and dabbed it, seeing how deep it was. His touch made her stir a little.

"Reyn," she said with her eyes closed. "Reyn. I know you're there. I see you."

Reynolds looked around, but the velvet fog still hovered. He looked down. "Open your eyes, Browneyes. I need you."

Browneyes kept her eyes shut. "I just wanted you to love me. And you didn't . . . You never did—"

"You were selfish, Browneyes," Reynolds broke in. "And so was I. We used each other. It was the perfect arrangement."

Browneyes' eyelids slid open to look at him. "Perfect for you, not for me. I was mad, hurt, ready to claw every last bit from you." Her pointed chin moved only a fraction when she spoke, as if it pained her to remember. "In the Echoes I thought you were dead. And I'd never felt regret before, and I didn't like it. And you—you made me feel that. You tricked me. It hurt. I don't like being tricked . . . And so I wanted to hurt you back. And I wanted to take your heart like you took mine, and rip it in half. But I never found her, Reyn . . . Your princess. She's probably dead . . . like I will be."

Reynolds didn't want to talk about Naomi. "Seriously, come on. If you want to help me, get up."

"I'm dying, Reyn."

"You are not." Reynolds shoved her. "I know how resilient Louvings are, and I know you, Browneyes. You're scratched. That's all. Now stop playing this stupid game and open your eyes."

Browneyes raised her arm to her face. A dramatic sigh escaped her lips.

Reynolds bent close. "What do you need me to do?"

Browneyes' eyes remained closed, the faintest tear appeared in one corner, threatening to drop.

Reynolds knew. "Okay. Fine. I'll let you kiss me."

"Seriously?" she whispered, one eye open.

"Ha!" Reynolds smiled. "Yes. Promise. But I have a question. What vials do you have?"

Browneyes opened her eyes and leaned up on her elbows. "I still have it, if that's what you're thinking."

"Yes. Exactly." Reynolds helped her sit up. "How's your head?"

"Stings, but I've had worse."

Landon looked flabbergasted but offered her a hand as well. "What do you need us to do?"

"Keep the boy here with the wounded man," Reynolds said, looking around. "Use your strengths. And Browneyes, don't hurt any of my friends."

"I'm stealing that kiss now." She quickly planted a salty, wet kiss on his mouth. He felt the heat behind it, the emotion and passion she still harbored, that she always would. In that moment, the guilt of using her and leaving smarted, but he could never join her world, even if there was something real between them.

A loud sound broke them apart.

Bryant ran right toward Sharrod, ready to strike, when a force pushed him back into rock.

Sharrod turned. "You think your weapon will kill me, mere mortal?"

Guards approached. Bryant hopped to his feet, dodging the first. The fairy blood inside him sprang into action, keeping him light on his feet, sharpening his instincts. He downed the first and headed for the second, catching him in the arm before feeling a pulse of magic pushing against his body.

Bryant's body began to stretch. He felt his chin rise and his arms tighten as he was pulled in different directions.

Sharrod grinned as he pressed the magic again and again, forcing his victim hard against the stone. Bryant's leather armor held, but the continual battering hurt his insides.

A guard rushed forward and cut him with his dark blade. Like in the battle outside, the blade disintegrated. The guard stepped back, stunned. The other guards dared not approach.

"You are not immortal as I am," Sharrod jeered.

"You're the fool!" Bryant yelled. "Your attack on the outside did not work. The people are free."

"A mere distraction from the real work, dear prince." He spit the title out as if it were acid on his tongue. "I have blinded the strong." He looked deep into Bryant's face now. "I have killed each bearer."

Bryant heard but didn't want to believe it. The wretch was talking of his dear Silexa, his love, his future. He felt the pressure in his chest build. "You lie!"

Sharrod merely sneered, moving forward. "I do not." He pointed to the pillars. "The magic is there." He whipped back to Bryant. "I care not about any living. I have returned and will reign. I have taken my world."

With another blast of power, Sharrod pressed against Bryant's chest, squeezing the air from his lungs. "You lose."

Bryant gasped, searching for air.

The magical dragon creature cried out with intense fury, shaking everything. It stretched upward, wings arching and flapping. Hot wind hit Bryant's face, suffocating him further.

Surprising everyone, a man came rushing forward with great speed toward Sharrod, a man Bryant had never seen before, an older sailor with a long ginger beard.

Sharrod raised his other hand and pushed the man away.

"You spineless piece of filth!" The bearded man stood, fighting against the power that held him at bay. And he was winning, inch by inch. Sharrod stood his ground and pushed back. With his focus diverted, he loosened his hold on Bryant. Air filled the prince's lungs, but the binding on his arms continued to hold him in place.

Lockwood was not far behind the pirate, a knife gleaming in his hand. Without hesitation, the general plunged the blade into his back.

"No!"

Katia's voice came out like ice, a permafrost covering everything it touched.

"No, no, no, no." Her fear took over, and the cool pushed through her veins stronger than she had ever felt. She had no tears, just anger. She didn't know how to contain the flurry taking over her body.

Her fingers fumbled over the medallion. She couldn't pry it loose. "Come on, come on," she kept muttering. Sharrod would soon find out what she was doing.

From behind her came an enormous sniff, like a large dog scrounging for food.

Katia lifted her head. It was not Sharrod as she had presumed, but the dragon-like creature. He was right behind her, his eyes blazing like fire. He hovered close, the steady flap of his wings bringing him closer and closer.

Panic moved through her. She scrambled to get hold of the stone but couldn't.

The creature hissed out words so low they sent vibrations through her soul. "Gurrrl with maahgix," it hissed through its forked tongue. "I smell you, gurrrl."

It snatched at the pillar, at Katia. She screamed as she pressed back against the wall. It tried again, but Katia dodged away.

Her magic shot out of her fingers protectively, sealing her within an ice ball. The creature's long claw clamped on the ball and squeezed until its nail snapped through, narrowly missing her stomach.

It tried with its other claw, sending cracks up and down the sphere. The ball shattered, ice shards bursting around her, melting under the creature's hot breath.

Katia wrenched forward, pressing her hands to the medallion. Instantly, a large blast of cold erupted. A cloud of frost blew over everything and everyone, making it difficult to see through the flurry of snow.

Katia braced herself against the pillar, her hands still firm on the stone. Two hands grabbed her, yanking her forward. She felt as if she might fall into the fog forever, but the grip tightened around her waist.

She used every fiber of magic to free herself. Ice crystals formed around Katia's hands but melted. She tried harder, pushing her magic to the limit.

The beast began to laugh. "Good. Use it. Let me smell it."

Katia began to feel the drain. Like a pump, pushing and pulling. Then she stopped. He was draining away her magic.

"No," was all she could muster. She beat on the tough leather hide of the creature, but he would not let go, stealing away every bit of magic she had.

Katia closed her eyes.

Her magic was still there, scared like a lost child. It didn't dance with dizzying happiness but nervously jumped in terrified motion.

"*Help.*" The sad echo broke Katia's spirit. "*Don't let him take me away.*"

Katia scrambled. She reached but couldn't touch it; the swirls kept falling farther and farther away.

"*Help.*"

Katia opened her eyes again, feeling the tight squeeze against her ribs. The flurry cloud around them was clearing. The monster was inhaling the magical snow. With every second, every moment, more magic disappeared from her body.

She reached for her knife, the one Landon insisted that she wear, wrapped at her inner thigh. The beast squeezed her again, pushing her breath out, until her rib snapped and pain erupted around her middle. She screamed, but the monster only laughed.

She gasped, needing air, but with every intake of breath, Katia felt the fire within. She couldn't see through the haze of cloud. She fought to reach the dagger, bending herself lower to find the leather strap and sheath. Her fingers fumbled with the fastening until she tugged it free.

Something was happening beyond the cloud. She heard voices yelling. The draining of her magic slowed as the creature took interest.

Katia grabbed the dagger with both hands and plunged it down into its thick muscle.

The dragon head turned toward her and merely smiled. "Mortals kill mortals." His eyes flamed. "I am a god." His voice shook the walls, the ground, and everything it touched.

Katia felt the vibrations down to her core.

He tossed Katia out of his hands into the frosted air.

Above Landon a swirling, powerful magic exploded in the center. Strings of energy pushed out, the magic growing red with anger, with fire. A girl who stood on the other side of the stone circle feebly dodged his blows. It was Katia.

Landon turned pale. "He's going to kill her."

Reynolds looked behind him. "Quick! We need to make it to Sharrod."

Landon couldn't take his eyes away from Katia. "But we need to stop the dragon."

Reynolds turned. "Dragon?" He looked again at the man swirled by magic—just an angry man with wings going after Katia. He couldn't see what Landon saw. He placed his hand on his friend's shoulder. "Trust me on this. We need to destroy Sharrod. We take out Sharrod, the dragon will disappear."

Browneyes still looked disappointed that the kiss hadn't been long enough. Zander also stood ready to go.

"Naomi would kill me if anything happened to you," Reynolds said to the boy. At the mention of her name, their eyes met. "Stay. Look after the old man."

Zander sat back down and held his knees. "Win," he called after them as they scurried over the fallen debris and toward Sharrod.

Reynolds had Landon guide him through the broken debris, but Landon grew more distracted by what was happening around them. Time was critical.

"We need to hurry," he prodded Landon, who kept glancing at what was happening to Katia.

"Is he going to kill her?" Landon's voice was quiet, unnerved.

Reynolds pressed on. "Browneyes, are you ready? I'll need your sight."

Browneyes had already taken out her vial. From his magical perspective, Reynolds could see the little vials of blood were echoes of people. He saw the missing part of their soul, trapped, each one emanating an aura. The one she held in her hand was familiar, like an old friend. His insides churned with excitement to see what might happen.

"Do you think the guard will alert the others?" Landon stated.

"Probably," Reynolds returned.

Three guards rushed toward them even as he spoke.

A surge of power rang through the air. White, like someone had turned on the sun. Reynolds could see again. He could see everything in the world of magic and the world of stone. He looked down at solid ground. Something had happened—he didn't know what, but just then, he didn't have time to think on it.

Reynolds swiped at the leg of the guard, and he went down, only to turn and counter with a clumsy jab with his staff. Reynolds gave a few swift kicks before darting forward, running hard on the solid ground.

From the corner of his eye, he saw Browneyes keeping pace. He didn't have far to run, but he didn't know how long his complete sight would last and had to make the best of the sunlight.

At the side of his vision, a man came to aid Landon, a burly, strong fighter. He wore the garb of a guard but didn't fight in the same way. Reynolds looked ahead.

Before him was a large pile of boulders which crested the pit. He had to cross it somehow. He began stretching from rock to rock, only staying but a moment on each one.

After a few more boulders, he made it to the top.

And saw everything.

Across the pit, Katia struggled with the levitating man, but now, seeing both worlds, he could make out the large wings and dragon head Landon had feared. The man's claws snatched her up and dangled her in the air. But it still wasn't real. It was an illusion—magic.

Down near the bottom, Lockwood stood over the corpse of a poor man, someone who had to have fought valiantly to his death. The blood of the innocent victim pooled near his feet as Lockwood stood over him with a knife, laughing, mocking the dead. The spirit of the man had risen from the body, and Reynolds could see it clear as anything. And as if the spirit could see Reynolds, too, he saluted before stepping toward the pit, sealing his fate with the other doomed souls.

Reynolds also recognized Prince Bryant, the good man he aspired to be, forced against the wall by a blazing amount of energy. A wild spark ignited within the prince, though, resonating through his skin in a way that told Reynolds not all was as it seemed. Sharrod was using a very strong force to block him, to shield himself from whatever magic the man had—could it be fairy magic? Reynolds wondered.

So many mysteries surrounded his eyes, mysteries that would have to wait.

The quick plan he hatched in the back of his mind wasn't very refined, but it didn't matter; he just needed time and instinct.

Reynolds grabbed a rock and threw it toward Sharrod. It skittered past him, and the man looked up to meet Reynolds' glare. The energy he had pushed on Bryant was redirected at Reynolds who bounded down the rocks, sending shards of debris out with each step.

The prince moved forward with a jolt as all of his own strength returned.

Guards from the outside perimeter flooded in. Reynolds landed with a *thump* on the ground floor, the prince nodding to him with his weapon drawn. He drew his own sword and prepared to attack.

He knew he didn't have much time. They were all a distraction from something else, something Sharrod was waiting for.

Reynolds charged without fear and began fighting with intense precision. They were seasoned fighting men, the best Sharrod had, and fought hard.

A sound of yelling came from behind him, a diversion. This gave Reynolds the opportunity he needed.

Another swift swing and a kick to the outside guard, and Reynolds made the leap out of the fray and into the open. He ran right toward Sharrod.

"Ah, the little scrapper," Sharrod said in a plain droll. "Want to play Blind Man's Bluff?"

Reynolds smirked at the reference. "I can see just fine. Better, actually."

"Let's test that theory." Sharrod stood and threw energy toward him. Reynolds dove across the ground until he was clear of the magic. Again Sharrod shot, again Reynolds dodged. He felt invigorated with each test of his skill, his agility heightened, his magic increased.

"Is that all you got?" he yelled toward Sharrod, wiping his brow.

Sharrod thrust his hands toward the ground, a slight rumble shaking under Reynolds' feet.

Behind Sharrod a strange glow began growing around the circle. A ghostly aura swirled until a skeletal hand appeared. A form followed, hair black as night, eyes white as stars. He took his place near Lockwood, staring toward Reynolds with heat in his penetrating gaze. "The bastard son returns." Harrow's hollow eyes sent a piercing glare toward Reynolds.

"I knew they would drag you into this, Harrow." Reynolds steadied himself, pulling out his sword. "The Underworld has no need for a keeper."

"Yes," Harrow agreed, and before Reynolds could come back with a retort, another desperate soul crawled to the surface, its mouth gaping wide, eyes dead and haunting.

Another came, and another, and another, all dragging themselves forward toward Reynolds. The army grew massive—an army of starving souls.

Above them came Katia's scream.

Reynolds looked up, watching Katia flail as the dragon captured with Sharrod's soul tossed her away into the air.

Then, like a still moment in time, magic so intense erupted in a glow so brilliant Reynolds could not shield his eyes from every detail of beauty radiating from it—for at the edge of the destruction stood Naomi.

Through the distraction Reynolds didn't see the energy force coming. It hit him square in the chest, knocking him back into the debris, dropping him like a stone straight to the ground.

CHAPTER TWENTY-NINE

The world around Naomi grew dark, the edge of her vision narrowing. A powerful pressure came over her, seizing her chest. She gasped and dropped to her knees. She felt sick, dizzy, as everything went black around her. The only thing she could see was Pera standing before her.

"Naomi. Shon has come. We do not have time. Events are moving faster than I can prevent. We must gather all your strength. Hurry."

The torchlight returned to Naomi's vision. She stumbled back, pressing her hands against the wall, trying to steady her feet.

"Pera?" Taren's voice was tense. He took her by the waist to help her stand.

Naomi's vision cleared, and she saw Taren's concern. "There's trouble."

"What kind of trouble?"

"I don't—" She shook her head and looked down the hall, then began to run.

"Wait!" Taren ran after her.

She took a few deep breaths, returning her focus. "Something's wrong." Naomi dashed toward a staircase, then doubled back, confused about which path to follow.

Taren grabbed her arm. "Stop, Pera. Tell me what's happening."

Naomi held her head as the echoing returned. She started down the stairs again, panic-stricken, but Taren held her fast. "Wait. You don't know where you're going."

She turned. "Do you remember the palace?"

"What?" Taren analyzed her for a brief moment. "Yes. Of course. What do you need?"

"Something is here. I can feel it. In a great, open space. If we don't hurry, I'm afraid something bad will happen."

Taren nodded. "It must be the Grand Hall. This way." He pulled her down the rest of the stairs and through another corridor.

A large rumble shook the ground and knocked Naomi off her feet. A loud roar accompanied it: chaos paired with screaming. Naomi threw her hands over her eyes. Looking beyond what she could see, she sensed the sounds, the screams, the movement, the way the air waited for instruction, the flicks of ice, the dramatic heat. Her memory stirred—of the being in the depths of hell, the souls near her, wanting her. She felt as if they were close, anticipating what happened next.

The lost souls. All of them could be freed tonight. Then the stains caused by this magic would be gone. All the suffering, all the hurt could be healed. The kingdom would be stitched back together. She could do this. She was there, at that moment, ready to face the demon and give Parbraven its world back. A feeling of gratitude and empowerment overwhelmed her heart.

"Come." Taren held out his hand to help her up. She hesitated, having nearly forgotten she wasn't alone. Naomi looked at his face, the concern painted like a picture across it. He felt the same urgency she did.

"We may be too late," Pera's voice warned. *"He has transformed."*

"No. It's not too late. Tell me what I should do."

"I have endangered you."

"He won't get me. This is why I've come." Naomi's magic flared into action inside her, overpowering the feeling of dread that had consumed her. She felt every fiber moving with her own, synchronous fluid motion which thumped with her own heartbeat. "I'm stronger than him."

Taren still stood, waiting for her hand. His eyes wore concern down to the corners. "Naomi?"

Naomi took his hand but then let go, feeling the magic within her resisting his touch. "I'm ready."

"Naomi." Taren's voice was quiet. "I know it's you, not Pera. It's you, isn't it?"

Naomi looked through him to the magic core, her memory struck by sadness. Taren's eyes held her, a soft forgiveness and terrible grief. "You need to let me go," she stated as strongly as she could.

"I can't do that."

"You have to." She felt the sorrow within her, the overwhelming grief she never wanted to feel. "I'm so sorry, Taren." She clenched at her chest where the Vivatera steamed with heat. "This is so much bigger than us. And Pera needs me. I have to try, and you need to let me."

Taren stood back but his expression held firm. "I can't watch you give your life for this."

"Pera is with me, Taren." She felt the despair but held back any tears. "I'm her carrier. And it's time to end this."

"This doesn't feel right."

"I can't tell what it should feel like anymore."

Naomi tried to stand, and again Taren held out his hand to her. She waved him away. "Don't touch me. My magic has flared, and I'm worried what it will do to you."

Taren clenched his fingers into a fist. "Then this is it. Naomi. I'm sorry."

Naomi stood. She caught Taren's eyes, the eyes she had been avoiding, fearing what she would see. The torches lit his dark pupils, and she understood so much about his sadness. She couldn't focus on everything she would miss or how she would never see him, how she would never see Reynolds, or have him understand her respect for him, her friends she would never see.

So many who left this world never got the chance to think about what they were leaving behind, but there, in that moment, she thought of everyone. "I'm sorry too."

Grabbing her fingertips, Taren bent down and kissed the back of her hand. The simple gesture said everything he had wanted to say without a single word. His head fell to the side. "Come." He turned and led her onward.

Browneyes took one last look at the blood vial, its beautiful dark red liquid still filled to the top. She popped open the bottle and downed the contents in one gulp. She could feel the transformation instantly, the stretch of her muscles burned as they grew. She spun, feeling the wrap of cloth around her skin, her hair disappearing from its long braids to a messy amount of unruly curls.

The spinning stopped, and she looked at her hands and body. It was only his image, but a tight-lipped smirk came across her face. The disguise felt just as good as she imagined.

Naomi followed Taren through the corridor and down another set of stairs. They turned toward a strange brightness filtering through the broken stone.

The glow of white became clearer and clearer, like daylight reflected off snow.

Then everything came into view. The palace's walls had fallen in piles of rubble surrounding the large pit. In the midst was a gruesome monster she immediately knew as an enemy.

She was vaguely aware of others in her peripheral vision, but Naomi couldn't take her eyes off the creature. Pera's instincts synchronized with her own. She knew the dragon-creature was not what he seemed. It was not Shon but an illusion meant to distract their attention. Shon was here, but where?

Naomi looked to the floor and saw a demon. That's when she knew. It was a disguise. Shon was disguised as Sharrod. Shon—demon ruler of the Underworld, banished underground for eternity—was here above the ground, let out of his cage by his loyal servant, Sharrod, who was masquerading as the dragon man.

Naomi had been so distracted by seeing Shon in the flesh that it took her a moment to recognize what was happening around him. As soon as she did, she gasped, struck by a deep pain. The intake of breath hurt everything it touched, swelling within her chest until she remembered to exhale.

Reynolds stood facing Shon. Her Reynolds, alive and facing the enemy. There was no way her Reynolds could defeat him. He would die. Her Reynolds was going to die.

A scream distracted her. The dragon-creature had a person clasped in its claws, struggling to breathe, the magic being sucked out of her like air.

"Katia," she whispered to herself.

Taren held her arm. "Something's wrong. The magic is wrong. Don't do anything."

Naomi tried to pull away from him. "It's an illusion. Look at the source."

Taren continued to hold her. "Naomi, you're not safe here. You'll die. There has to be more—"

"I can't wait. Katia's going to die." Naomi pushed him away. The force slammed him backward to the ground. Taren grabbed at his chest. "Taren." Her eyes spoke everything. "I'm sorry, Taren."

The end of the word shook the walls with vibrations. The sound stole her attention and she turned just as the dragon-creature cast Katia into the air.

"No!" Naomi flared into action. Her hands and feet surged with power, the magic pushing out in all directions. Light engulfed her vision. Though she could still see forms of people, everything else became background, obsolete; all the distractions disappeared and everything important became clear.

Streams of magic stretched out around her like vines full of light and energy and warmth. Her magic reached and caught Katia mid-air. Naomi could feel the trembling, terrified girl as if she caught her with her own hands. Briefly, she caught Katia's eyes, filled with a surprised, thankful expression.

Within her, Naomi could feel the heartbeats of those watching, the power of each living soul, the amazing magic that created each one. Prickles of light spread out around her—every movement followed her action, every wave, every breath. Heat and cold, wind, love—she could feel it all.

"Landon," she whispered to herself. Landon's heartbeat was not far away. Naomi concentrated and homed in on his soul. She channeled the magic toward him, and Katia tumbled out gently to the ground near where he stood.

With magical eyes, she saw several things at once: Reynolds, the lost souls, the Underdemon Harrow, and the monstrous fight on the ground. At the head of it all was Shon, a man with long dark hair much like Pera's, his eyes now fixed on her, staring with peculiar greed.

"I'm what you're waiting for." Naomi knew her words reached him.

Shon lifted his hands to the air, and the dragon-creature cried with delight.

"Magix," he said with his forked tongue. "I have wanted you for a long time." He moved quick as lightning toward her.

Naomi pushed her energy upward, dodging his long claws. She wasn't flying, but weightless, using the elements near her—the smooth, polished stone and loose earth below—for balance.

"I will drain you," she heard the voice of Shon echo in her mind. "I will suck the marrow from your bones."

Naomi felt the heat of her magic swell. Could she have done this her whole life? The Vivatera thumped so hard that it felt like it would burst, the power taking over all her action.

The monster soared at her again, his hands outstretched. "Snatch. Crush. You are mine." Shon's voice filled her ears over and over.

Naomi held out her hands. A wall of energy appeared, protective. "You cannot touch me, son of death." Her voice echoed around her own head. The voice was not hers. She and Pera were one.

Naomi stretched out her hands and pushed. A slow cry came from the dragon-creature's mouth, turning into a scream. The deep red scales around its body began to peel away one by one, revealing red raw flesh underneath. As soon as the tender skin hit the air, it began to crisp and burn like embers.

A bolt of lightning came toward her. Naomi deflected it with her hands, directing it upward where it cracked the roof of the great palace, sending tremendous amounts of debris raining down into the pit.

Naomi pushed harder on the creature. It roared in pain, its giant mouth lifting upward until its sharp teeth began to break apart, the bone disintegrating. The sight took her away from herself. The power was too much. She pulled back, but the creature continued to disintegrate.

"What have I done?" Naomi looked at her hands. They looked so small, too small to make such terrible destruction.

"This needs to be done." The voice came out of her mouth, Pera's voice.

She was going mad. Her heartbeat quickened. She couldn't do this. She wasn't made to kill but to heal. She could have healed the creature, changed him, soothed the monster inside. She was not a destroyer. She couldn't do it. She wouldn't.

Naomi's heart began to thump hard and loud. A light source within her body brightened until it surrounded her, evolving everything. Too late she realized what was happening. Heat from the Vivatera began burning her skin, choking her breath. Then, with a flare, it finally burst within her. She screamed. The magic rushed out in a furious push of energy so intense everything went white, consumed by the magic.

She couldn't move, couldn't think. Her body was being taken over.

In a blinding flash, the Naomi that valiantly carried the burden of the world . . .

Vanished.

Watching, Taren fought for breath. The magic pushed against his chest, holding him back.

"I'm sorry," were her last words to him.

Then her magic flared out, as beautiful as it had ever been. It radiated from her body in perfect streams of light, like it had when she'd come to him and spoken to his magic.

The entire room went silent at the sight, as awestruck as he himself.

"Naomi!" he yelled, but she never turned. The magic had her, controlled her.

Taren stood but was forced back again. Her magic was too strong. There was nothing he could do.

Quickly, he looked around. Down on the ground floor was a fight which no one could win. Prince Bryant fought hand to hand with some of the guards, while Reynolds ran toward Sharrod, but, again, Taren's magic told him something was wrong. He scanned again and found another Reynolds fighting Taren's worst enemy, his own father.

That was his answer.

Landon wiped the blood from his brow. He was better at magic than sword fighting. However, the man who joined him in his fight was seasoned and strong. Without him, Landon would be in much worse shape.

"How's your head?" the man asked, steadying himself.

"I've had worse." But the dizziness had settled in, and his legs wobbled. "Who are you?"

"Mahoney. An ally." He caught Landon by the arm. "Sit," he ordered. "You're in no shape to fight."

"I can't." Landon caught his breath. "I have to save her."

Mahoney didn't wait for an answer, just set Landon on the edge of a boulder and sprinted over a pile of rock.

Landon sat there feeling weak, but his will was strong. He tried to push himself up but changed his mind once his head again began to swim.

A scream demanded his attention. He knew that scream. It was just like in the Echoes when the glass bridge had fallen. Katia was falling, and this time he couldn't save her.

"Kat!" he yelled, his head pounding but his vision clear. For him, time had stopped and every moment, every memory of her flashed through his mind. His heart hammered in his chest. He thought quickly of his magic— any stones, debris, anything—but he could do nothing to help her. "Katia, no," he wept. His tears mixed with the blood on his cheeks.

Then he heard another cry, someone from across the pit, and suddenly everything brightened like a flash of lightning.

And he saw her, bright as a star—Naomi. She had come, just as she had promised. Her magic flowed out so quickly, he thought it would swallow everything in sight. Landon toppled backward over the rock as a long twisting strand came straight at him. He shielded his eyes from the brightness.

Something thumped in front of him, and he looked through his fingers.

Landon stood slowly. He rubbed at his eyes, making doubly sure he was not seeing things.

Katia tumbled to the ground, gasping for air, shaking, not knowing he was there.

She looked so different to him all of a sudden. The thin, tall, outspoken pain in the neck that she had always been now looked so small, so frail. He thought she had left him forever, but here she was alive—shaken, broken, but alive.

"Ka-Kat," he choked out, voice filled with disbelief. He ran to her and took in her condition: scratches, bruises, possible broken bones. Landon feared if he touched her he might hurt her more.

Katia slowly turned her head and winced in pain. Her tear-stained eyes landed upon him, and something lit within her, like she had never seen anything so wonderful in her whole life.

Landon dropped to his knees, uncertain, apprehensive, but she reached for him, and he gathered her in his arms, all doubt erased.

"She saved me," Katia sobbed into his shoulder. "I don't know how. She saved me."

"Hush." Landon stroked her ginger hair. He looked again to the magic filling the room. Naomi shone as bright as the sun. "I know."

"Oh, my dear heavens." Wenlock pointed for Zander to look at the strange dragon-creature. "It's got Katia."

Zander stood up, his heart desperate with worry. He looked with his new magic-revealing eyes and saw the strange man with the dragon aura twisting Katia in the air.

Then it threw her into the air. Zander opened his mouth to yell, but the sound came from someone else.

A flash of light burst from the other side of the pit above everything. A star illuminated the entire expanse.

And just as she had appeared in his dream, Naomi came forward and grabbed the falling girl from the air and set her gracefully on the ground.

Zander rubbed his eyes. It wasn't a dream; she was there. "Naomi!" he yelled at the top of his lungs, but the energy coming from her absorbed the sound. He stumbled back, not believing she was there, ready to save the world.

Reynolds slammed backward into the wall, the powerful magic still pressing against his chest. His sight of the physical room faded, but his other senses were still there. Someone was close, but he couldn't tell where.

He stumbled to his feet, again desperate for sight. Someone came near, no magic to him, only a very faint black aura. Reynolds swung out and missed. He felt a blow to his side, and he went down again.

"Lost your fight, Fairborne?" The voice sounded familiar, but he still couldn't see him. He choked as a knee came to his chest.

Reynolds shook his head. He had to focus and quickly. The magic could help him if he could concentrate.

And then the face came to his mind. He lifted his body and caught the fist mid-swing. "Not today, Lockwood."

The army captain and long-time servant to Sharrod stood with his fist caught midflight as Reynolds tried to push him back. Their strength equally matched, Reynolds deflected the advance, and Lockwood fell forward into the rock.

Something rushed past his head and hit Lockwood again. He could see the dark velvet aura of Browneyes, but it was cloaked in the spirit of someone he recognized. He smiled. She had done as he asked.

"Nice to see you, Reynolds." It alarmed him to hear her voice coming from what looked like his own body. "Like the new me?"

"I'm impressed, as always." Reynolds dusted himself off.

Browneyes stood now before him, dressed like a mirror of himself. "Do me a favor. Miss me this time." She turned and ran directly at Sharrod.

"Wait!" he yelled, but she had already gone, launching herself at the man in black. A push of magic kicked her back, and she fell to the ground.

At the side of him, Reynolds felt others and stretched his senses to see the battle on the ground. He felt helpless again, the angst of the blind. He closed his eyes to what he could see and focused on the energy he could feel.

"You won't win," Lockwood's voice came from behind. He felt the cool blade cutting the air and jumped back. He swung his own blade to meet it.

Enraged, Lockwood came at Reynolds with all the energy he had. Reynolds reacted with instinct, but without sight, he had no idea of the obstacles around him. He stumbled backward into a pile of rubble. Lockwood slashed, but Reynolds rolled away, guarding his body with the sword.

Lockwood came at him again and again while Reynolds was on the ground. Reynolds could feel the direction of each hit and could predict the power behind it. He pushed away the sword hard as he scrambled back to his feet.

Reynolds felt a wall behind him.

Lockwood snarled, "Trapped."

A flash of light burst before him. Flames shot out and hit Lockwood in the chest. The heat of the fire burned green with magic. Lockwood slapped at the flames, dropping his weapon, ready to flee. A figure dropped down from above. Lockwood made an exhale of air before dropping to the ground, a knife through his heart.

Taren raced down toward Reynolds, desperation fueling his actions. Few guards got in his way: some took fright and were fleeing, others watched the spectacle of Naomi's magic, but he didn't have time to do the same.

He made it to the floor and readied his magic. The heat felt good in his hands. He watched as Reynolds fell backward into a pile of rubble. Taren quickly shot off a fireball.

It hit his target and gave him time to race down. Quickly, Taren grabbed his knife.

Lockwood raised his sword, preparing it for Reynolds' head. Taren jumped and landed between the two. The knife came down with such force, such precision, Lockwood had no reaction. He grabbed at his chest before looking into his son's eyes, shocked.

Taren said nothing, just watched his father fall to the ground, the horrible memories dying with him.

He turned to see Reynolds staring. "Are you okay?"

Reynolds nodded. "What's happened?"

Taren pushed him behind a rock, away from any magic thrown their way. "Naomi's about to die," he spat out. "I don't think we can save her. She's ready, and the magic told me."

Reynolds waved his hands. "Taren, I don't know how to save—"

Taren shook him. "No, listen. The ancient spirit of Pera is within her. She's going to take over Naomi."

Reynolds' eyes grew big. "How do you know this?"

"We don't have time!" Taren shook his shoulders in frustration.

"Pera?" Reynolds' eyes grew wider as the gears clicked into place. "Pera, the first death. So that's how this is going to play out."

"Are you listening to me?" Taren felt heat rise in his cheeks as the magic lit within him.

Reynolds turned sharply. "Of course I'm listening. I've heard every word."

Taren crouched closer. "Reyn, if we don't act now, we'll both lose her."

A large rock shattered close to them. They were running out of time.

Reynolds sat up. "Okay. I have a solution, but you may not like it."

"Anything. I'll do anything."

"All the magic needs to be emptied from the stones."

Taren looked at the streams coming out of the pedestals. "It's nearly complete."

"Good. And then," Reynolds hesitated, "Pera needs to take over Naomi."

Taren's chest heaved hard. "N-no," he stammered. "No!"

Reynolds looked around, searching for something. "We need to wait for the right time."

"We have no time." Taren pushed him, but Reynolds shrugged him off. "We may not get her back."

"I understand the risk, but it's the only way. Trust me."

Taren's eyes narrowed with anger. "I can't. I've never trusted you."

Reynolds straightened. "Wrong. You've always trusted me." He pointed his finger straight at him. "I was the older one, the wiser one you always looked up to, that you came to for all the answers. I may not have known all of them when I was younger, but I searched for them. I've blamed myself for years, Taren. Years. And I know the answer. You ran to me for help just now as you did when we were kids. You know I can fix this. And you're right, I can. I can save her. But dammit, Taren, you have to trust me."

Taren couldn't stand looking at Reynolds, his eyes blazing with truth. "Fine. Explain to me how we save her."

Reynolds pointed to the man standing near the edge of the pit. "Do you see Sharrod?"

Taren nodded.

"That is a disguise. The man you see is actually Shon, god of the Underworld. Do you see Harrow?"

Taren looked at the ghostly figure fighting the other Reynolds—or the Louving disguised as Reynolds. "Yes."

"Harrow's banishment ends tonight when Shon is filled with the magic. Do you see any souls coming for us?"

Taren looked closer. He remembered the fiery hell and the river of souls, but he didn't see any now. "No."

"Well, I can," Reynolds told him. "They're clawing to the surface to poison the world so demons can come above ground."

"But what about Sharrod?"

"He was a man but is now a dragon, a transformation to give Shon a body of flesh and blood." He pointed upward to the angry beast flying about. "But Sharrod and Harrow are both puppets. We need to take care of Shon.

Pera is the only one who can take this fight. With Naomi's magic, she can resolve it."

A giant roar erupted from above where they were hiding. Both Taren and Reynolds stood to see what was happening. The creature Naomi was fighting began shedding like a snake, scales dropping away from its body.

Taren's eyes widened with shock. He turned toward where Shon stood. Something horrible was about to happen.

Naomi glowed like a mythical phoenix, with magic encircling her, creating wings. Light appeared near her chest.

It burst like an exploding star, sparks flowing around her, enveloping the magic with color. A white light began growing and growing, more bright and brilliant. It grew until it hurt his eyes. He shielded them from the glare but couldn't look away.

Naomi's golden hair slowly changed to black, the shade of midnight. Her body grew lean and tall, her eyes sparkling like stars.

Taren clenched his fists, dropping to his knees. Naomi was disappearing, just as the magic had told him. The despair crippled him. He couldn't watch any more.

CHAPTER THIRTY

The room fell silent. Naomi captivated everyone's attention as she changed into Pera, the guardian of the world. But Reynolds could see what the others could not. The physical world had disappeared to his magical eyes, yet he couldn't comprehend what those eyes told him.

Reynolds looked at the faces of those near. All stood still, watching the magnificence, transfixed by what they were truly seeing. Then he turned to Taren, whose face was pale with horror. "What do you see?" he demanded.

Taren didn't answer, just collapsed to his knees.

Reynolds shook Taren's shoulders. "Help me see."

"She's gone," he whispered. "Naomi disappeared. You said you could save her, but you couldn't. She's gone."

Reynolds strained his eyes to see what others saw. Naomi. Where was Naomi?

Ribbons of magic stretched out with tremendous energy around her, blanketing the truth from him. An aura of gold surrounded her, pushing out rays like the sun. In the center of everything shone a star that lifted and left her body.

Reynolds watched this little star travel away from the battle. In the middle of the grand ceiling, it stopped and grew brighter. It wasn't just the star that lit the room, but a heavenly aura traveling downward. In the strange plane of magic, Reynolds could see a texture liked crumpled paper line the sides of his vision. As the lines became clearer, he saw they weren't wrinkles but cracks, a breaking between the world of sight and the world of magic.

A great tearing ripped the ceiling open and light poured in along with thousands of tiny fluttering forms. Were they butterflies or angels? They filled the roof until there was nothing but light.

Reynolds nudged Taren and pointed. "Do you see this? Look."

Taren shrugged off Reynolds' touch.

"Something's happening," Reynolds tried again, but it was evident he was the only one to witness it. He felt as if the heavens were opening up and descending on this place. The light spilled into every corner of what was left of the palace, touching each rock or marble.

As it did so, it revealed many other things. The dragon-creature, the once powerful Sharrod, curled up near one of the piles of rubble, whimpering like a limp dog. In a tight spiral, the white butterflies surrounded Sharrod and lifted him up. They flew 'round and 'round until they suddenly burst out in different directions, and Sharrod was gone.

The desperate souls stopped in their path, also mesmerized by the magic and light. Reynolds was positive they could see the angels above. A beautiful sound arose, like tiny bells chiming at the same time, all in harmonious tones.

Everything froze in time as Pera descended to the floor.

Shon's disguise had also washed away. He thrust his hand upward toward her. Bolts of energy struck one after another.

The magical protection surrounding Pera gently deflected it away.

Again Shon tried, and again it rebounded.

Pera's voice rang like a bell. "It is I, it is Pera. I've come to take you home."

Shon stood still near the edge of the pit. "I have no home. I have claimed the surface. You have no right to take me anywhere."

Pera's feet barely touched the ground. "The fight is over. Your suffering is over."

"I suffer in my sins for eternity," Shon yelled. "You cannot take this from me. My sins are of greed and hate. I have placed myself in chains, awaiting release. My servant has found me a way to see the glorious sun. You cannot destroy me."

Shon again tried everything he could to harm Pera, but her barrier would not break.

Pera began to float down closer to Shon. Reynolds was just as mesmerized as everyone, but then something else started happening. The star in the center of the room held his attention, like it was speaking to him, protecting him. A familiar feeling came over him. And even though he couldn't see Naomi, he knew she was there. She was still around.

Taren stood up, knocking Reynolds out of his trance.

"Taren." Reynolds grabbed his arms. "Don't do anything stupid. There's still time to save her."

Taren's magic was hot in his hands. "I don't believe you."

"You don't want to mess with the ancient gods of the world. You can't do anything here."

Taren turned to him. "I can't stand and watch this."

"You're not listening. Naomi's safe. I can feel her. This isn't about her anymore. This isn't her fight, this is their fight."

Taren looked completely lost in his head. "Nothing I did saved her. I didn't matter."

The star burst into streams of light that connected to each pedestal, protecting the stones.

. . . and Reynolds knew what he had to do. "Of course it does. The magic isn't whole. It isn't complete. I can see what has to be done. Do you see the streams?" Reynolds pointed to the stones.

Taren shook his head. "Reyn. You can't fix this. Stop being the hero. You were never the hero."

"It's not about that." Reynolds straightened his shoulders. "It's about doing what is right."

A spark of light captured their attention. Pera now stood on the stone right in front of the fire which surrounded Shon, the magic wrapped around her like a robe. She raised her hand to brush his cheek. "Dearest brother," the voice was so smooth, so lulling, Reynolds was immediately drawn back to her. "We are surrounded by the children of Yulin, brother and ruler of the sky, forever cursed to the heavens. All this for a crime that is forgiven."

Shon looked stung by the words. "I have stirred in these echoes, beneath the world which I also helped create, doomed to misery. The souls of those forbidden to die haunt the living world. They feast on the flesh of life. It is unjust to live in either world."

"That is why I am here." Pera again gestured with her hands. "I am the guardian and still protect it, as I am now protecting it. This world needs balance."

Shon raised his arms, a surge of energy built around his hands. "I will not return to the hell I have been in before." A terrible thundering shook the walls. "I have suffered long enough."

"As you wish, my brother. Come with me."

Reynolds felt the shift of balance as Shon considered her gift, her sacrifice. Something was about to happen. Shon's power was growing. The fire pit below began to glow.

Then a flash of fire moved past him. Taren had shot toward Shon.

"What are you doing?" Reynolds grabbed at him, but Taren shoved him back.

"Stay out of this!" Taren ran toward Shon with all the magic he could conjure.

Shon was caught off guard at first but raised his hands to deflect any attack that came at him.

Reynolds heard a gasp from somewhere near, a sharp intake that he immediately recognized and which caused his insides to compress.

It was Naomi. Reynolds looked up toward the star. He knew she wasn't far, that she could see and feel what was happening.

"Save him," her voice spoke to him.

Reynolds started after him, so quickly his feet lagged behind. "Taren!"

Taren was nearly upon Shon when the man angrily pushed out a magical field of energy, the force so strong it knocked down everything in its path, clearing out the radius around him. Taren tried again to stand but couldn't.

"My dear brother," Pera's voice came again. "Soften your anger. I am here to save you."

The pressure lessened. Shon's hands lowered. "I am not worth saving."

Reynolds felt Naomi's hurt. He understood it, like he had in the apothecary so many years ago. Taren was so young. He was like a brother to him. Once again, he felt that kind of love toward him and knew what the younger boy was about to do.

"Taren!" he yelled, but couldn't stop him.

Taren hit Shon with all the force he could. The impact knocked both off the side of the rim and into the pit.

"No!" Reynolds rushed after them but stopped near the edge. Naomi's despair ran through his body.

Fire engulfed both figures as they fell.

Pera's eyes landed on Reynolds. "Young Fairborne." Her voice sounded as if she had watched over him for years, a mother figure in his life. "Save the world."

Reynolds' heart thumped within his chest. He reached deep in his pocket and pulled out the Everstone, the magic rippling inside with waves of excitement.

He closed his eyes, wishing one last time that he had never created the stone, the magic, the chaos of everything, and knew what to do.

Reynolds opened his eyes, his vision clear, and his heart full. He looked up at the star surrounded by the hosts of heaven. With all of his strength Reynolds pulled back his arm and threw the Everstone as hard as he could at the center of the ceiling.

It shot up and connected with the star. Light burst out, showering everything with sparks raining down from above.

A shattering sound erupted through the hall. The cracks around the walls began to widen, letting the light show through. Tremors rippled through the ground.

The star disappeared, creating a deep tear in space. The blazing angels were drawn into it, a swirling spiral of gold siphoning through. The stone pillars shook, popping each stone out until they, too, flew up into the vortex.

The ghostly souls also lost their hold on the world. A strong wind pulled them away, a fury of mist funneling all the struggle out. The fire had extinguished and left this world.

Then Reynolds felt it: the pull inside him. His magic also needed to go. He felt the ripping inside his body, the stretch on every fiber he had, every connection to the world of magic. It lifted him up, away from the ground. He did not struggle. Reynolds kept his eyes wide open as he ascended toward the deep vortex, accepting his fate.

Closer and closer he came to the opening, the wind whipping his clothes and face. He smiled, a small laugh escaping his mouth.

A light brighter than anything took his vision as the vortex swallowed him up, sealing behind him.

Zander wanted to run forward, but Wenlock grabbed his arm, keeping him close as a wind came up from the underbelly of the world. He shielded his face but could see a strange orange glow growing from the pit.

Near the top of the palace rotunda light split the ceiling and the brightness of angels swirled about as the steady stream of bound souls lifted from their chains of prison and followed upward. An inhuman sound of joy began to swell until it was so strong Zander could feel the vibration within his heart.

Then with a sharp crack, light spread around touching everything, everyone, and *flash*—it was gone as fast as it came.

The light faded and something else took its place. In a crack at the top of the ceiling, a ray of sunshine came through, illuminating a spot near the pit where no one stood. More sunlight came from the side.

Zander couldn't stop. He ran forward, freeing himself from Wenlock and raced toward the spot of sun.

Landon stood awestruck at what he had witnessed. Katia clung to his side wincing through the pain. As the light began to fade, Landon looked at Katia, his heart pumping. "She's gone." His voice was barely audible.

"No." Katia exhaled. "No, she's not."

"And Reynolds." Landon's hand grabbed his head in disbelief. "They did it, Kat. They're gone. Both."

Katia's face filled with pain. "No. Stop it. They are not gone."

Landon tried to help her, but she pushed away. "Look around you. Look what's happening."

The cracks around the rotunda revealed a rare sight—blue sky. Light filtered in anywhere it could. The sky outside was clearing away the gray clouds that had shadowed the world for so long. Even the sounds were becoming clearer.

"Birds." Katia stifled a sob.

Landon grabbed her close. She pounded his chest until she couldn't fight any more and gave in. Landon's head rested on hers, and he let the tears roll down his cheeks.

Zander ran as fast as he could. No one stopped him now. Everyone left standing was in awe of what they just witnessed. He saw Bryant walk near the spot of sun and place his hand in it as if nothing were real about it. Zander watched his hand circle and circle in the new, fresh sunlight.

"Bryant!" he yelled as he grew closer.

Bryant dropped his weapon and embraced the boy. Zander couldn't hold back the tears.

"You're still here." Bryant brushed back Zander's hair with his hands. "I'm proud of you. Where is Silexa? Where is she?"

Zander shook his head.

"Find Silexa!" he shouted to anyone around. "I command you as your king to find her."

All the guards left—those who had surrendered under the fight bowed and began searching for the princess.

Zander couldn't help it and turned close to Bryant. "Naomi's—" he broke off. He couldn't say the word. He had seen everything. She was gone. He had believed in her always, knew she would come and rescue him, save the world. He would never get the chance to see her again.

Bryant wept with him.

Others started to come closer to the patch of sun as it grew brighter and brighter. All the guards remaining dropped to one knee and bowed. Noticing the change in the world, civilians had filtered into the palace, saw the prince once again, and honored him the same.

"My lord." It was one of the guards. The prince stood. Zander stayed attached to his side. The guard didn't speak but stepped aside to allow two men to walk forward. Both carried limp forms. Zander gulped. He knew Mahoney carried Ferra cradled in his arms; the other guard looked a great deal like Reynolds and similarly carried another sister in a strong hold.

Softly, one by one, they lay the bodies in the ever-growing sunlight. Both men stayed close.

"Silexa." Bryant grew panicked.

"She didn't make it," a girl said and came forward, her long braids tucked behind her pointed ears. "There's no way any sister made it out alive."

"How would you know, Louving?" Bryant nearly spat.

"Browneyes," she corrected. "And don't think I didn't lose something in this fight too. The only man I have ever loved just vanished, sacrificing his life for this." She passed her hand in the sunlight.

"Vespa?" Zander looked up at Bryant.

Bryant breathed in and shook his head. "What of Fontine?"

"I was there," a voice came from the other side. It was Landon, holding the hand of a girl with almond eyes. "Fontine, she . . ." His breath caught. "She saved me, but she . . . she didn't make it either."

The girl next to him stood away. "I know where Silexa is. I was with her. Vanya and I."

"Vanya?" Bryant asked, remembering the boy his father used as an advisor.

"Yes. I'm Katia. Vanya's my brother."

"Please, go," Bryant begged.

Katia pushed away from Landon and straightened up as best she could. "I need to do this." She navigated through the rock to a tunnel near the edge.

No one spoke, but everyone felt the atmosphere change. Such a loss: all the daughters, everyone Zander loved, and Naomi—his greatest sorrow, he would never get the chance to be with her again.

Zander held tighter to Bryant and feared the worst.

The moments of silence hummed with an unusual peace, a remembrance of the lives fought and lost, the world changing by every ray of sunlight.

Someone emerged from the tunnel. It was Katia holding the hand of a boy younger than Zander. Tears were in her eyes. She didn't need to say anything.

Bryant fell to his knees, his strong shoulders now weak. He clung to Zander as if his life depended on it. Zander held fast and stood brave as the sun surrounded them, blessing them with a new world, unknown to everyone.

Until he broke in half and cried until his eyes could no longer make tears.

CHAPTER THIRTY-ONE

The brilliant light of magic which had surrounded Reynolds began to fade. The outline of tall stone pillars revealed intricate detail. They were set like guardians amid a thick forest of trees. The monoliths rose high and carried the vines of wisteria flowers with them. The sun rested near the horizon, casting a glow of orange light between the pillars. Ahead of him, stairs led up to a platform in the center, several thrones perched on it, each decorated with jewels of all kinds and carved with craftsmanship unknown in Parbraven.

Around the pillars stood several people, and beyond them were more, and down the cascading hill even more—hundreds, thousands—all silent, watching Reynolds walk forward past the gate under the canopy of wisteria.

He stepped on the first stair and looked around. He didn't know where he was. This place felt familiar, like a dream he couldn't quite remember. He glanced at all the people. Though no one spoke, he got the impression they were waiting for him to ascend. Looking up, he saw several stairs without seeing the landing. He took the next step and the next, each one feeling more majestic, more powerful than the last.

Up on the last few stairs, he heard a tremendous noise. It was cheering.

Reynolds took his last step to a thunderous applause from those around him. Standing before him were each of the daughters of King Prolius wearing robes like their stones. Near more steps stood a king and queen—Prolius and his wife, Andriana.

Then a man stepped out from behind them. It was his father, accompanied by a woman with soft brown hair and gray eyes. Reynolds nearly lost his step. It was his mother, a woman he'd never known, had only ever dreamt about.

Then the applause quieted as each person took their place at their specifically crafted throne, his father and mother doing the same. Two people emerged from each side of the pillars. Pera entered first with her dark train of crimson, a gold band curling around her head. Trailing behind her, with her own crown of glory, was Naomi.

Reynolds was so overcome, he quietly wiped his face with his sleeve.

He glanced toward Naomi—her head was bowed, but she looked as if she smiled the whole way toward him, her golden gown reflecting sunlight.

Pera stopped before a gem-laden shape. The Everstar glimmered with jewels of every color on the ground. "Reynolds Fairborne, kneel before me."

Reynolds did as she asked, not questioning for a moment, just feeling the honor ride through him.

"Reynolds Fairborne," she spoke in a quiet, yet commanding tone. "The people of Parbraven are no longer trapped between the world of men and the world of magic. You have freed all the souls trapped within that world. You have opened again the gate that was sealed for so long." Pera walked forward and placed a wreath upon his head. "I crown thee, dearest Fairborne, with the highest honor."

Pera motioned to each of the sisters. They all walked forward, each in order from oldest to youngest. He raised his head and greeted them. He knew them all, some better than others.

Sera approached first, giving him a wink before placing a kiss on each cheek. Then Silexa, Ymber, Vespa, Fontine, and Ferra, each bowing and placing a kiss. Lastly Naomi walked forward, her eyes on the floor.

Reynolds tensed. He knew it was her duty as a sister, but she meant more than the others.

Naomi slowly curtsied before him. Reynolds thought she looked more stunning than he had ever seen her. The color in her cheeks had returned, and her neck and chest bore no scar. Her hair was long and golden as it had been in the bright light of day. He blinked, forgetting himself.

Naomi lifted her eyes to him. She held them only a second before she placed her kiss on his cheek. He closed his eyes at the touch, feeling it burn in his skin forever, then opened them again in time to see her steal one more glance his way. He had no idea what she was thinking.

"Sisters," Pera addressed them in a line. "You, as stone-bearers, have a choice. For the curse upon you, you have each earned a place within the stars. Your choice is mortality or immortality. The unfairness of your life gives you a chance to live it to the fullest, so you can enjoy the joys and sorrows of a mortal existence, if that is what you choose."

Holding hands with one another, the sisters smiled, bowed, and thanked Pera before returning to their parents.

However, Naomi stayed near Reynolds.

He turned to her, wanting to speak before Pera continued. He failed.

"Reynolds Fairborne, you may arise."

A loud applause came again from all the people, even those below.

Reynolds looked around, still confused. Rising to his feet, he turned toward Pera. "I don't understand. Why applaud me?"

"You have broken the curse."

"But this should go to Naomi, not me. Naomi saved the world."

Naomi kept smiling but looked to Pera for an explanation.

Pera walked closer until she stood in the middle of the star. "Naomi has her place as well, but it was you of whom the prophecy spoke, you who understood the magic and had the faith that it could be restored. It was your own guilt that drove you to resolution. And it was the decisions you made in efforts to correct your mistakes that led to the triumph of the world being whole."

"Me?" He could hardly believe it, consumed with his own insignificance. "I only did what I thought was right."

"Your virtue is rewarded."

Reynolds looked again at Naomi, seeing her clear, unharmed skin. He turned his gaze to the others who were in attendance. "But what of Taren and the Vivatera?"

Pera's mouth turned down. "The Vivatera and the Everstone have the same origin, as you remember. Although Taren Lockwood had valiant ideas of saving the magic and freeing the world of its curse, the outcome would be the same, in whatever design it chose. The magic needed to be one, all that is true. The magic spoke truth to him, and he obeyed. It may have been more difficult for Naomi if he had not chosen to act. The Vivatera chose Naomi and wished to remain with her. That solidified two pieces. You and the Everstone were the last pieces it needed to be whole."

"So what will become of Taren?" Reynolds demanded. "He deserves this crown as much as I do."

It was Naomi who spoke, a small hitch in her voice. "Taren . . . Taren can't . . ."

Pera put a hand on her shoulder. "Taren is needed as well, but not here."

"Why not?" Reynolds asked. "I think Taren deserves this honor more than I do. He suffered much more than me. He—" He cleared his voice before continuing. "He would have done anything to save Naomi. Anything. And I told him to not do anything foolish, and he—" He stopped himself, afraid of the emotion that might come out.

Pera held up her hand to quiet him. "The world may have healed and the gate reopened, but the demands of balance will always remain."

She stretched out her long arm behind her, pointing to the highest pillar. Two men sat atop, one in a white robe with gold lining, and the other in a dark blue cloak. "My brothers, Yulin and Shon."

"Shon?" Reynolds reflexively stood taller. "How?"

"Together, the three of us have earned passage to a higher kingdom, one where our father lives."

"But Shon was pushed off the edge."

Pera's mouth thinned. "Parbraven is passing to other hands. I came to collect my brother, not to destroy him. Our time to keep balance in the world is over. As we are ascending, we need others to take our places."

Reynolds at last understood. "And Taren is—"

"Taren received a fatal wound," Shon spoke up, his deep voice echoing through the entire valley. "His heart was damaged in the fall. I understand now that he acted with great courage to save the princess of light. He will heal slowly over time but cannot return to the surface. He will take my place in the Underworld."

Reynolds felt the shock throughout his body. "And he agreed to this?"

Shon's cloak rippled majestically in the wind. "In time, he will ascend like us and take an honorable place among the stars. He has understanding which I did not. He understands love and hate, jealousy and virtue. He will reign far more justly than I."

Reynolds ached as the reality of Taren's choice settled in. "What about the others?"

Pera turned back to him. "Yes. We are in need of a Guardian and a Starkeeper."

Reynolds had no intention of being either. He spotted Naomi out of the corner of his eye and fear crept in. "She will not be your guardian," he blurted out, pointing right to her. "No. I forbid it."

Naomi looked slightly shocked.

Pera looked up.

"No." Reynolds held up his finger. "Not Naomi. She has been through enough. She needs a normal life, one that isn't plagued with misfortune or danger or always being hunted. Parentless. Abandoned. Hopeless. No. Not anymore. She needs a life where she is free to choose what she wants and experience everything she loves about the world."

Naomi turned toward him.

Pera's lips turned up to a half smile. She started to speak, but Reynolds waved his hands.

"No. You can't have her. Do you know that the flowers and trees love her? And animals and butterflies, and she's never had the opportunity to love them back. She's .. ." He finally looked at her, finally let her see his emotions, everything he'd hid for so long. "She's the loveliest thing that was ever created. And I can't . . ." He gave up trying to explain.

"Reynolds Fairborne," Pera addressed him, drawing his attention back. "Like the other sisters, Naomi has a choice to return or to ascend. She will have a seat beside me when she returns. But for now she has a choice."

Reynolds watched Naomi bow her head to Pera in respect. "I'm not fit for a royal life. I'm a farmer at heart, like Reynolds said. I wouldn't be much good as a guardian."

Pera inclined her head in acknowledgement.

Reynolds' heart nearly leapt from his chest, though he kept a calm exterior.

Naomi glanced toward him before raising her head again to the others.

Pera raised her arms. "Who among us will step forward to take their place as the Guardian?"

The response came quickly. "I will," a small voice replied. A dark purple cloak stepped out from her parents' side and carefully walked before Pera.

"Sweet Vespa, daughter of Prolius." Pera touched her forehead with the other girl's in loving acknowledgement of her choice. "The fairies will be so pleased to have you there."

Vespa bowed and walked to the side of the staircase.

"And what of my Starkeeper?"

It remained quiet for a long time before a man stepped forward from the crowd.

"Lytte," Reynolds whispered his name.

"I will honor the name, my lady."

Lytte strode forward, took Pera's hand, and kissed it.

Pera bent low and also placed a kiss on his magnificent white head.

Lytte went to take a place on the other side of the stairs when Naomi ran to him and hugged him freely, not caring about any silly ceremony. Reynolds loved her more for it.

"It is settled." Pera raised her hands. The sun was now setting, and the first stars of night began appearing. As they did, the people from below disappeared, each twinkling before a swirl of magic whisked them away to the stars.

Naomi moved to stand next to Reynolds. She looked at him with her bright green eyes. She was so small. He had forgotten. She seemed so much bigger and stronger than any human could be.

Reynolds reached out his hand to her. What a simple gesture to show the enormous importance she held for him.

She didn't take it but instead rushed into his arms, burying her head in his chest. Reynolds' head fell forward as he embraced her with everything he had.

"Don't lose me," Naomi sobbed quietly into his tunic. "Never again."

Zander lay in a large, empty room near the top tower—Bryant's room. He had not been brave enough to sleep alone.

Not tonight.

He didn't dare leave the prince alone.

Not tonight.

Bryant had not returned. He had been setting the affairs of the kingdom back in order. There was so much to rebuild, to bring forth. All Zander did was remind him that he no longer had the love of his life.

Zander glanced at the crumpled papers of the journal lying on the table. Its pages burned, torn, ripped from use, but he still treasured it—his only connection to the life he had with Naomi and the wonder it had been, if only for a little while.

The sun was gone and the sky filled with stars. He hadn't seen so many before. The heavens couldn't hold back the amazement of what had happened that day. Zander couldn't help but feel tired, drained, achy, but the stars kept him awake, dreamy in their own way.

He felt as if he knew the stars personally, like they were speaking to him.

Close your eyes, sweet prince.

We are watching you.

Zander hadn't noticed he had closed his eyes.

Tunneling . . .

The pull . . .

Bright white

Ethereal beauty

She is there

She is smiling.

"Zander . . ."

Hold a hand out to him.

Zander runs.

> *Grabs.*

> > *Holds*

She is real.

"You are real."

> *Soft hands brush through his hair.*

> *Soft lips touch his head.*

"I am real."

Lifts up and takes in her eyes.

"Take my hand, Zander.

Touch.

Warm skin, energy pulsing around her.

"Pull me through."

His heart tugs . . .

And holds tight to the brightest love he has known.

Bright light surrounds . . .

> *. . . Tunneling*

> > > *. . . the Pull*

> > > > *. . . Thousands of stars*

look past the most brilliant,

> *forever brightest,*

> > *the Everstar. . .*

EPILOGUE

Katia's arm rested against the sun-warmed iron rail. She casually looked down at her own reflection in the glassy water below. It was her, she knew, but the slow ripple made her already awkward frame seem unnatural. The circlet of flowers slumped forward on her head, jabbing the side of her temple. She pulled it off and looked at the delicate white flowers interlaced with pale blue eyelet blossoms. The arrangement was pretty but not what she would pick for her own wedding: too delicate, too perfect.

Katia picked a few of the petals off and tossed them down in the water, completely absorbed in her thoughts.

"There you are," a voice interrupted the quiet.

Katia jerked, previously unaware of his presence. She turned with a petal still in hand. "Don't creep up on me like that."

Landon smiled his toothy grin, his scarred face still handsome despite the burns he received. His right cheek was still red and marred from the injury. "And what fun would that be?"

Katia didn't answer and turned back to the water. A soft lap of waves hit against the rock as it traveled down toward the Southwick Sea.

Landon came next to her, obnoxiously close, touching right to her elbow. She should be mad but didn't move her arm away.

"Seriously," he said. "Are you okay? I told you, Ferra is just a friend."

Katia sighed. "You say that—"

"Of course I do," Landon huffed. "It's true. And I don't think you noticed, because you were busy being jealous, but I think if she were interested in anyone it would be Mahoney."

Katia fingered through her circlet again. "I'm not worried about that."

"All right, then what?" Landon's hands grabbed the rail, trying to get her attention.

Katia was never one to keep quiet. She turned toward Landon, taking in his dark brown eyes and impish grin. "What did you think of all this?"

Landon laughed. "You mean the wedding?"

Katia felt color in her cheeks. "Yes." She felt dumb the moment the words left her mouth.

Landon ruffled his hair uncomfortably. "Honestly? Not my taste."

"Really?"

"Yeah." Landon looked out at the water. "I mean, Silexa was stunning and everything, and she'll make a great queen. And they will have interesting babies and all, with Bryant's fairy blood."

Katia snorted a laugh.

"I don't know." He knocked her arm with his elbow. "What did you think?"

"I think I'm ready to go home." Katia threw the flower in her hand on the water. It floated for a moment before churning with the current.

Landon tilted his head toward her. "Kat, where is home? We don't belong anywhere."

Katia slumped her shoulders. "I don't know. I want to take my father's ashes back to Tapoof. And Vanya's never seen my mother's grave. I've been in Southwick too long. It's too boring."

Landon laughed. "Boring? A few months ago you wouldn't have said boring. You've already forgotten that both of us nearly died here."

Katia's insides twisted at the memory.

"A lot has happened, Kat." Landon's voice quieted. "We're different people than we were before."

"What do you mean?" Katia whipped around to face him.

"Whoa, nothing. Really." His hands waved away the offense. "But we've been through a lot. There's no camp to return to, no home you abandoned, and just look at this world." Landon spread his arms wide. "Look at the sun, Kat. There's never been a sun like this." He put his arm around her shoulders and turned her toward the west. "See those mountains? I have no idea what's beyond them. We could take Blizzard up there and—"

"Blizzard." Katia laughed at Landon's unusual fondness for the brilliant white horse they'd stolen from the king's army near the Durundin. A few days previously, Landon found him in the court stables.

"Truth is," Landon came back and grabbed her hand. "We aren't the city type. We're adventurers. I mean, you wouldn't want a fancy wedding like this?"

Katia flushed. "Wedding?" A slow course of magic stirred within her. Not everything had left. She still had a reserve to act on if she needed it.

Landon stumbled over his words. "Well, you know what I mean." He looked slightly embarrassed but didn't drop her hand. "Let's go back to the celebration. Wenlock wanted to dance with you."

"With his new engineered legs? No. I'm not dancing." Katia took her circlet and placed it on Landon's head. It sat awkwardly, too small for his head. "I don't dance."

Landon grabbed around her waist and started swaying. "What are you doing?"

"Not dancing." Landon slid his hand down her arm until he grasped it tightly and flipped her around. "You have to dance with Wenlock. He's a genius making those mechanical legs. I think he's happier than he's ever been."

Katia giggled but slugged him. "Fine. I'll go back. It's just not the same without—"

"Naomi," Landon answered. He quietly rested his head on hers. "I know. Come on."

Zander ran down the stairs of the palace. The new polished marble treads wrapped around now, instead of going straight down like they did before. It meant he had to travel farther than before. If the flowers and decorations hadn't had been placed all around the railing, he would have slid all the way down.

He looked down at the Grand Hall. The reconstruction was still going on. The large hole couldn't be sealed, so instead, it had been covered with patterns of thick glass, with several bridges across. It was very pretty, but Zander still didn't have the nerve to get near the center. The dwarves from UnderElm began building several bridges beneath the glass, sharing the space together. Different colored lights illuminated parts of the floor. He liked those the best.

Zander glanced at the ledge where the cage had fallen. It was still under construction. Someday it would hold an aviary. Bryant had liked his idea and incorporated it into the design.

Zander hit the landing with a bound and turned toward the garden. The small pouch bounced in his hand, but he held it carefully. He couldn't believe that he forgot to get it before the ceremony.

He flew past the stone columns until he saw the celebration feast. He slowed and began walking again with dignity, placing the pouch near his chest.

Several of the wedding party noticed his entrance. Zander ignored the attention and continued to the head table.

Silexa's smile radiated as she saw him approach, a look of gentle surprise. Maybe she didn't know what Bryant had prepared for her. Zander put his head down, trying to hide his excitement.

Zander walked up the stairs to the dais for the honored guests. Sera had interrupted her conversation with Colonel Rasmussen as Zander walked behind her.

"You got it?" Sera whispered to him.

Zander held up the pouch as he continued on.

Ferra looked over from the other side and waved. Captain Mahoney raised his glass to him.

Zander made it to where King Bryant sat at the head of the table. "Sorry," came out of his mouth.

Bryant patted him on the back and smiled. "Thank you, Zander."

Zander went back to his seat on the right side of the king. He let out a big sigh. Others in the room had noticed him enter: the Shadowers were near the back with Mother and her sons. Lottie sat near Vanya, showing him how to balance a spoon on his nose. Zander wished he could sit with them instead of in front of everyone. Then toward the back, Katia and Landon snuck in, trying to be unnoticed for arriving late to the dinner. Landon gave him a wink before sitting down next to Wenlock and his wife, Mae.

Bryant clinked his glass for attention. The room silenced as he stood up.

"I am not a fit king," he stated in his best kingly voice. "I have a queen who far surpasses me in every sense of the word. I am humble and grateful."

Zander watched as Silexa looked upon her new husband. An ornate tiara stood out from her black hair. Her eyes expressed her love and adoration. Zander saw in that moment the secret girl locked away in the palace, Bryant's treasure. She'd always seen good in him from the very beginning.

The beginning . . . Zander thought back to the day he first saw Silexa in the town square of Sharlot, the day that started his adventure and changed his life. Naomi's lovely face came into his mind, and he smiled at the thought of her. He glanced at the empty seats near the newly crowned king, still reserved for her and Reynolds.

Naomi only had one chance, and Zander understood, but he wished that it wasn't the same day as the prince's wedding. But the gate only opened once a year, and she had to try.

"I'll be back." Naomi had winked at him before she left on the fire-eater. "I won't leave you again."

A clinking of goblets returned his thoughts to the wedding.

Bryant continued. "My dear friends. Thank you all for coming. We are entering a new world, and it is left to us to keep the balance. Tonight is our solstice, the night when the stars are closest to us. Several are missing from this table, ones who chose a different path. But they will be close to us tonight, smiling down from the heavens."

Bryant held up the pouch he had asked Zander to fetch. He slowly unwrapped the strings from the top and revealed a delicate light. From inside, out stepped a tiny fairy, one Zander hadn't seen. Since the shift of magic in the world, fairies had disappeared. Bryant assured him it wouldn't be forever, but they took time to grow.

As the fairy stepped forward, she unfolded her lacey wings, which sparkled with their own light. The wings fluttered slightly, and traces of white wisps faded away in faint clouds.

"Today is the beginning of a new era in Parbraven," Bryant's voice echoed through the room. "Tonight we mark the dawn of a new age, one harmonious with the elements."

The fairy lifted her wings and took flight. A light within the tiny thing began to glow. With each flutter it grew and grew. Streams of flowing magic filtered down on the attendees and spread out until the whole room was lit from that one point.

Zander stared in amazement.

The fairy soared around the room, captivating everyone before returning to Bryant's outstretched hand. Then, the light began to fade and returned to that of candles and the setting sun.

Bryant set the fairy down on the table and grabbed the goblet near him. "Please raise your glass to all those we hold within us: at long last they have rest. And to the new day that is upon us."

Everyone held their glasses up.

Zander raised his too but didn't feel like drinking. He watched the smiling faces of the Prolius sisters, but there was still a noticeable absence. Ymber and Fontine had chosen to move on and not return to this world. Vespa was now the Guardian, protector of the balance of life. His thoughts turned to Naomi and where she was that night, Reynolds with her. However, seeing the brilliant fairy helped Zander's heart.

A warm feeling came over him, and he bashfully smiled as he took a sip from his cup.

Naomi reached the top of the tree near sunset, just as Spotswood had told her to do. The climb felt incredible. She looked out at the world around her. Tiny tinkling chimes played music in the air, a sweet call of the charm this tree had for her. Last time, Taren stood at the bottom of the tree, the memory so clear it felt as if he still waited for her below, though she knew he was not.

Below her, Linnonbury sparkled as the firelights lit in the homes. She smiled inside at knowing the beautiful village and the people who lived there. All the snow had melted, but the wind still carried a chill. It refreshed and calmed her nerves.

She steadied her back against the trunk and pulled out the little instrument Wenlock had given her. The Meridian spun around in different directions. It was nearly time.

Connecting with her magic used to be easy; it was instant. But the most powerful, commanding elements had left her, leaving only the scar of the Vivatera and traces of what once lived within her: the ghost of the feeling of power surging inside. She had never expected the magic to be so strong in her, but having lived with it her whole life, she was used to it. Now she only had fragments left, sensations, feelings, intuition, phantoms of what once was. Here on the top of everything, looking over Parbraven and the world of elemental balance, Naomi closed her eyes and gathered all her strength to ignite the instrument.

Wenlock assured her the Meridian would work, but she had to be in the right plane at the right moment in time. The solstice gave her the opportunity she sought.

The wedding was also today, but Bryant and Silexa insisted she do what her heart needed to do and come when she could. This conversation ate at her daily. She felt she needed to make things right.

She opened her eyes. "Okay, I'm ready."

The sunlight hit the crest of the western mountains and flared different rays, casting a warm glow across the span of the land. The Meridian spun to life, all the energy she had fueling the spindles. A bright blue line shot out before her. A nervous knot formed in her stomach.

The light surrounded her, and she felt the gateway open.

Taren appeared before her. He wore a long, black robe and stood near a slick ledge, like the lava rock of Mount Ignis.

Naomi approached close enough to touch him.

Taren froze, his hands clenched tightly before him. He didn't speak for a minute. He only stared at her. "How . . ." he started but lost speech again. "I watched you disappear."

"Taren," Naomi spoke quickly.

"Naomi, this is impossible. How did you find me—?"

"I don't have much time and have so much tell you," Naomi interrupted.

Taren's eyes spoke of unimaginable sadness. She faltered in her speech, unclear of what to say. "Taren, I . . . I never got a chance to thank you."

"Me?" he questioned, still searching her face.

"Thank you for protecting me and saving me."

Taren's head turned down. "Naomi, please don't." He held out his hand to stop anything she was about to tell him. "The one thing I didn't do was save you. If I would have listened to Reynolds, I wouldn't be here."

"But Shon said you had a choice."

"Yes, I did." Taren looked back at her, his dark eyes filled with sadness. "Naomi. You are the choice. You are an unreal creature. You're like the sun, something that should never be touched. I knew it was dangerous getting close to you, and I did it anyway, because I would be lying if I said it wasn't worth it. It was. Every moment."

Naomi's heart ached. "I know what you did. I could see it. I watched from something like a window. I watched you leap toward Shon. He was ready to kill Pera, and if that would have happened, the world would have seen no more light. It gave Reynolds enough time to finish. Your sacrifice made the combining possible."

Taren's hands came near his face, wiping away any emotion. "I'm glad I did something of worth to you." He looked at her again and shook his head. "You need to go. You shouldn't be here."

Naomi didn't want to go. Not yet. "I made you a promise."

Taren looked back. "There is no promise."

"Yes," Naomi insisted. "You asked me to tell you why the trees obey me."

Taren's face looked perplexed.

"It's very simple magic." She came close and held out her palm. Inside was a tiny seed. "You can plant it. It doesn't need sunlight. And it will connect you to the outside world."

She dropped it into his hand.

"No. I don't want it."

"Trees live in all three worlds, knowing the soil, surface, and sky." Naomi stretched her hand to touch him but stopped short, afraid. She looked up at him. "I am all three, Taren. Just as a tree. We share the same blood."

"What are you telling me?"

"I still have magic, Taren. Pera changed me. The poison is gone, but the magic has grown inside me. Not as powerful as it once was, but it still flows in my veins. Plant this and I will be with you."

Taren stared at his palm. "I will treasure it."

Naomi could feel the pull in the Meridian. She only had a moment left.

She slipped off her scarf, the one she had worn nearly her whole life, the gift from Malindra from so long ago. She no longer needed it.

Taren stood still as Naomi placed the scarf sweetly around his neck. She turned and kissed him on his cheek before the Meridian pulled her back.

"Naomi?" the sound of his voice rang in her ears, through time and space. She didn't get to say goodbye. But in the kiss she placed every word, every thought in one action.

The wind stung her wet eyes as she found herself back in the tree, the half-light of sunset still dancing around the horizon.

"Naomi?" she heard from near the bottom of the tree. The sound came like a memory, as if Taren were there as he had been before, waiting for her to climb down. The thought startled her heart, but it couldn't be true. She peered down through the branches.

Reynolds stood near the base of the cliff. Her heart began to race.

"Don't move!" she yelled, looking for a way down. "The light is fading. I'll be right there."

Naomi quickly maneuvered her way through the twisted branches, the tree helping her when it could. She hopped to the base of the trunk. Her hand delicately grazed the loveliness of the tree, and it thanked her for visiting.

"Reynolds, I'm here. Right behind you."

Reynolds turned slowly, and Naomi noticed the strange blue spectacles on his face.

"Reynolds. You can't be up here. It's too dangerous."

"I thought I'd try these out. What do you think?"

Naomi immediately thought, *how ridiculous*, but then changed her mind. He was trying to see the world of the living again, and any effort he made would be applauded. "Do they help?"

"A bit," he said, looking around. "Now with the light fading they're not great, but climbing up I could see nearly everything."

Naomi slipped her arm around his waist. "Let me help you down."

"Now wait a second," Reynolds resisted. "Did it work?"

Naomi lifted her head. "Yes, but not for long. I don't know where he is. The Meridian just took me to him."

Reynolds stroked her arm. "Are you okay? Your aura is orange."

Naomi lifted her hand to her bare neck. "Yes. I think so."

Reynolds watched her silently and then brushed his fingers against her neck. A thrill raced down her back, just as it did any time he touched her. He leaned down and examined it. "Your mark is still here."

Naomi tensed with him so close. "Yes," she exhaled.

Reynolds bent down and kissed it. Naomi closed her eyes for a fraction of a second and forgot to breathe.

"Easy," he whispered in her ear. "Am I making you nervous?"

Naomi made a tiny laugh, not hiding her smile. "Very."

Reynolds pulled back. "Good." He leaned toward her.

Naomi fell under his spell and let herself get lost in his kiss, the warmth of his lips and arms around her. For this brief moment, she forgot all the hurt still felt in the healing of the world, the deep scars that would never heal, and the troubling ache in her heart that would never go away. Just then, at that moment, she was home. His kisses were better than magic.

He pulled away. "Where did you put your scarf?"

Naomi looked at the brilliant sunset. "I left a trinket." The wind picked up, and the small chimes in the ancient tree began to tinkle with all the different wishes left by those sending messages to their loved ones. "It still has magic that I think someone can use."

"I'm sure it does."

"We should go." Naomi pulled at his arm. "It will be dark soon."

Reynolds gazed upward. "I can see better in the dark."

Naomi looked again at the wondrous sky and all those souls watching them from above. The Starkeeper smiled on them, she was sure of it. She glanced back at Reynolds, still gazing upward. "You finished?"

Reynolds wrapped his arms around her and turned to kiss her as the stars came out one by one. "Never."

THE END

READER'S EDITION

BONUS

MATERIAL

INTERVIEW WITH THE AUTHOR

I was both thrilled and intimidated to be asked to interview Candace for her reader's edition of the Vivatera series. It's a dangerous and brave thing to ask a fellow author to do this and Candace is certainly one of the bravest women I know. Since the day we met back in 2015, we've been fast friends and each other's personal cheerleaders as we continue to explore the everchanging world of publishing. It was my goal to make Candace dig deeply into her books and characters and share all the gems she found there. I hope you, dear reader, enjoy this discussion as much as I enjoyed interviewing my dear friend.

What are the biggest motivating forces for your main character Naomi as she progresses through the series?
Wow. Good question. Naomi's journey is first motivated by fear, as fear is a large motivator for a lot of our actions. When others were in danger, Naomi's instinct is a maternal one, to protect. This is what her guardian Malindra taught Naomi in her young life, before Malindra's murder. Losing someone at this young age makes a huge impact on her. She is afraid of losing others. The first thing that she considers when Reynolds kidnaps her is not her safety, but Zander's, then it is the safety of Reynolds after leaving her in the Willows. Her fear of losing people drives her decisions. Later I think it is her resignation to her fate, no longer afraid but understanding of a bigger picture, the greater good. Without understanding her own fear, which she faces with the Trolls, she may not have had the understanding she needs to make that final decision.

Of all the characters you've created within Vivatera, which one surprised you the most?

There are a few. Browneyes for sure. She was a villain I wanted to root for. Her jaded history with Reynolds came very easily and I really enjoyed getting into her psyche. (SIDENOTE: That story is currently in the works . . . squee!.) Little Lovely came so easy. That beautiful little fairy popped into existence very naturally and she was a joy to write. The one that truly surprised me the most was Wenlock Brighton, Landon's eccentric uncle. Wenlock's magic with numbers knocked my writer's cap clean off. It's astounding how it just poured out of my brain and into my fingers like that. I wrote it fast in a deep, creative moment where I let my brain loose to do whatever it wanted. It makes sense in my scientific mind, so much so that I had to immediately share it with my mother after I wrote it. His magic might be my favorite of all.

What was the lesson Naomi most needed to learn in each book?

In the first book, Vivatera, I think it's all about self-worth, everything – finding strength that you never knew you had until you are faced with impossible things and push through them. Conjectrix was fun and complex, I had a ball writing this one, because I got to explore the realm of the dead. I called this one "Naomi goes to Hell," and basically that's what she did. She had to understand the impact of the separation of magic and how to saves these souls trapped here. This type of magic fascinates me and I really enjoyed exploring it. Everstar was hard for me to write with the understanding that everything needed to end, Naomi included. Accepting the burden and becoming the vessel for Para was her purpose. When it came down to writing those last scenes, I struggled, knowing the outcome. I think all the sacrifice and planning was worth it in the end.

After Naomi, Reynolds is the next most important character. How does her influence help him become the man he needs to be by the end of the series?

Reynolds' journey was one of guilt and obligation. He made promises to Jeanus and Malindra and hid from the truth of his actions as long as he could. His actions served himself at first. What surprised him was the result of his actions introducing Naomi to magic and it living and growing with her. She had power that overwhelmed him, and it really did scare him. Those first moments with Naomi impacted him deeply. He called it her 'charm' but it was untrained, untethered power. Reynolds knew after their experience in the Blackwoods that he had created the most powerful being alive. His efforts to rescue her had bonded them together, much like other traumatic experiences might. Both have the same magic, though that wasn't brought up in the first book, and the likeness brought them closer, like this unspoken understanding. Unknowingly to him, Naomi needed that experience to use as a compass to find him. Reynolds fought the connection in Conjectrix, but once he lost his sight in the human world, he needed that bond to make the decision in the end.

Did you allow any of your characters to believe something that wasn't true to create a powerful moment?

Reynolds always thought the prophecy in the Histories was about Naomi, but really it could apply to him as well. There is very clever wording in that poem. He was the one that created the Everstone and he was the last piece to the puzzle. He thinks Naomi's dead for most of Everstar, so when she fought Aline at the end of Conjectrix, her sacrifice really affected him. I'd like to think that was instrumental in his sacrificial determination in the last book. Small story — Did any of you watch He-Man? I can't say I loved it or hated it, but being from a poor family who lived in the middle of nowhere and having only three stations to pick from limits your options. There was this episode of He-Man where Skeletor discovers a specific species that lives on Eternia that has a really low heart rate.. Then, Skeletor builds a ridiculously tall tower and He-Man has to chase him around it and can't seem to get to him. So, being He-Man, he decides to punch through the tower and it falls and crushes the creature with the low heart-rate, killing him (wink!) No one knows that he's still alive but Skeletor. He-Man was so distraught, he decided never to be He-Man again, once again letting Skeletor win his battle to rule Castle Greyskull. How He-Man got back the castle wasn't important to me; why I remember this episode so clearly was the emotion that came from He-Man specifically thinking someone innocent had died by his hands. That to me at that age was powerful storytelling because that was the first time I had experienced the torturous pain that comes when you know you're responsible. I couldn't get over. The concept has fascinated me. I needed Reynolds to hit that low, just like He-Man. It was a critical turning point for Reynolds and how he viewed his role in the end. He needed to understand that type of sorrow to comprehend joy at Naomi being alive. When he could see her and her light, the most brilliant light he could see with his dimmed eyes, it's like my favorite part of the whole thing. It's meant to burst your heart wide-open.

Every good story needs a driving force and Taren makes a compelling and misunderstood antagonist. In your opinion, what was absolutely the hardest thing he had to do?

Convincing the audience that he was the bad guy. Taren was driven by the magic inside him, the dark magic forced on him when he was young. The magic drove him to act in ways he wouldn't have if give the right chance. In the beginning prologue, you can tell that Taren never liked to go along with Reynolds' schemes, but yet, trying to be cool and not left behind, he followed Reynolds and helped him mix the magic. His action against Naomi in the first book was to rescue her, to have the Vivatera make the decision to save her and make it whole. It wasn't until Naomi released him from that darkness that you get to see that side of him again. His feelings were real and genuine for Naomi, and if given the choice, he would have continued after her. Taking the position as the Protector of the UnderRealm is something he volunteered to do. He understands the magic better than anyone and it qualifies him nicely. This also gives me an opportunity to bring him back in other Vivatera stories, and that should be a lot of fun.

What setting was your favorite to create and what real life locations inspired you?

Awesome question. I watched a documentary of underwater caves and this was really important to me when creating the Echoes. Herculaneum, with its pyroclastic cloud that basically turned people instantly into stone was clearly my inspiration for my Netherfields. And Tapoof was a thinly layered Tattooine. I have an inspiration board on my Pinterest that also helped me imagine places. I love trees and nature and secrets and history of places. To me, a place has magic when it tells stories, and I love hearing what they have to say.

There is a unique magic system at work within Parbraven. What did it look like when you first imagined it and how did it change over the course of writing the books?

Honestly, when I thought of this story, I was very far from magic systems. I had never read any books with a hard-magic system. LOTR and Sword of Shannara were not clear on their magic at all. I was, ironically, more involved with radiation, because of my medical job in a hospital. Radiation was what I used as a base for my magic. Gamma, Beta, Alpha, Rads… I was required to be trained on this yearly, what could shield with lead versus what could shield with paper.

This subconscious knowledge brimmed a bit when thinking about how the magic worked and who was exposed to it. That's the basic magic system. What was important for this magic was how it worked within males versus females. The boys in the camp had to work with instruction, telling the magic what to do. But with girls, it didn't work that way. They had to befriend it and like it in order for it to cooperate. I really liked that touch.

Last of all, how did writing this series change you as an author?

I've thought of a lot of different ways to answer this question, delving into my childhood and personal battles, put what I would honestly say is I'm just as surprised at it as anyone else. This series has giving me opportunities that I never believed possible. It has given me a chance to meet like-minded creatives, grow in stories and ideas, and prove to myself that I can do hard things. I've matured as a person and enjoy the process more. I love creativity more than about everything. I appreciate it and value it and never take it for granted. It's the best job.

Jodi L. Milner is an award-winning author of YA fantasy and speculative short fiction. Her YA noble dark fantasy Stonebearer's Betrayal earned a Recommended Read at the 2019 Quills Conference. She loves pretty fountain pens, solving Rubik's cubes, and crocheting tiny sidekicks. Find out more at her website: jodilmilner.com

Acknowledgments

I knew this book would be a difficult one for me to write. From its earliest inception during a restless night of insomnia, I knew Naomi's final hours would be a test of strength for me as the author. I struggled with the best way to handle such delicacy. In the end, it came down to you, my adoring reader. I included you as a character, active in participating. You were with me during every decision, every sorrow, every triumph. This book was made, with love and sacrifice, for you. Thank you for helping me through it.

My heartfelt appreciation goes out to Elizabeth Gilliland, the first one to believe in me. You taught me how to edit, encouraged me to create, and came with me through all three books. May fortune smile on us again someday.

To all my lovely family for words of encouragement, especially my husband Kevin, thank you and loves. Hugs to my dearest friends who have been with me through the entire journey and are my biggest cheerleaders—our friendship is golden.

My creative community of authors speak the language of art, you inspire me daily. Special acknowledgements go out to Alyson, Jen, Christine, Ben, Michael, Jodi, and Lauri for understanding the struggles of being creative, reminding me I'm not alone, and sharing the joy of having the best job in the world.

And finally, Julia and Mia, thank you for choosing me as your mother. You are my best friends. I hope this inspires you to make the best out of your young lives. Reach stars. Soar with eagles. Dance in rainbows. Inspire others.

ABOUT THE AUTHOR

Photo courtesy of Virginia Benincosa

CANDACE J. THOMAS is author of the VIVATERA SERIES, winner of the Diamond Award for Novel of the Year and Silver Quill. She has also penned VAMPIRE-ISH: A HYPOCHONDRIAC'S TALE, THE HAWKEED, and WANDERING BEAUTIFUL: Poetry for Dark Days, acclaimed 2019 Recommended Read by the League of Utah Writers.

Candace is an advocate for imagination and the emotionally healing it can provide to those who dare to dream in daylight. Her bumpersticker reads, "Baby Yoda is my co-pilot."

Candace lives in Salt Lake City, Utah with her husband, two daughters, and her Siamese Snowshoe.

Follow Candace J. Thomas on:

candacejthomas.com

Facebook.com/candacejthomas.author

Twitter: @cjtwrites

Instagram: @candacejthomas

Other Books by
Candace J. Thomas

Young Adult Fantasy
The Vivatera Series
Vivatera
Conjectrix
Everstar

Paranormal Satire
Vampire-ish: A Hypochondriac's Tale

Short Stories
The Hawkweed
Of Snow and Moonlight

Non-Fiction
Six Simple Steps: Build A World

Poetry
Wandering Beautiful: Poetry for Dark Days

9 781733 501163